Nora Roberts

The MacGregors

Alan & Grant

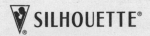

Silhouette and Colophon are registered trademarks of
Harlequin Books S.A., used under licence.
Silhouette Books, Eton House, 18-24 Paradise Road,
Richmond, Surrey TW9 1SR

First published 2000. This edition 2008.

THE MacGREGORS: ALAN & GRANT
© Nora Roberts 1999

The publisher acknowledges the copyright holder of the
individual works as follows:

All the Possibilities © Nora Roberts 1985
One Man's Art © Nora Roberts 1985

ISBN: 978 0 263 86590 5

025-0308

Printed and bound in Spain
by Litografia Rosés S.A., Barcelona

CONTENTS

All the Possibilities

Chapter One

Shelby knew Washington was a crazy town. That's why she loved it. She could have elegance and history, if that's what she wanted, or dingy clubs and burlesque. On a trip from one side of town to the other, she could go from grace and style to mean streets—there was always a choice: gleaming white monuments, dignified state buildings, old brick row houses, steel and glass boxes; statues that had oxidized too long ago to remember what they'd oxidized from; cobblestoned streets or Watergate.

But the city hadn't been built around one particular structure for nothing. The Capitol was the core, and politics was always the name of the game. Washington bustled frantically—not with the careless ongoing rush of New York, but with a wary, look-over-your-shoulder sort of frenzy. For the bulk of the men and women who worked there, their jobs were on the line

from election to election. One thing Washington was
not, was a blanket of security. That's why Shelby
loved it. Security equaled complacency and complacency equaled boredom. She'd always made it her
first order of business never to be bored.

Georgetown suited her because it was yet it wasn't
D.C. It had the energy of youth: the University, bou-
tiques, coffee houses, half-price beer on Wednesday
nights. It had the dignity of age: residential streets,
ivied red brick walls, painted shutters, neat women
walking neat dogs. Because it couldn't be strictly labeled as part of something else, she was comfortable
there. Her shop faced out on one of the narrow cobblestoned streets with her living quarters on the second floor. She had a balcony, so she could sit out on
warm summer nights and listen to the city move. She
had bamboo slats at the windows so she could have
privacy if she chose. She rarely did.

Shelby Campbell had been made for people, for
conversations and crowds. Strangers were just as fascinating to talk to as old friends, and noise was more
appealing than silence. Still, she liked to live at her
own pace, so her roommates weren't of the human
sort. Moshe Dayan was a one-eyed tomcat, and
Auntie Em was a parrot who refused to converse with
anyone. They lived together in relative peace in the
cluttered disorder Shelby called home.

She was a potter by trade and a merchant by whim.
The little shop she had called Calliope had become a
popular success in the three years since she'd opened
the doors. She'd found she enjoyed dealing with customers almost as much as she enjoyed sitting at her
potter's wheel with a lump of clay and her imagina-

tion. The paperwork was a matter of constant annoyance. But then, to Shelby, annoyances gave life its bite. So, to her family's amusement and the surprise of many friends, she'd gone into trade and made an undeniable success of it.

At six, she locked the shop. From the outset, Shelby had made a firm policy not to give her evenings to her business. She might work with clay or glazes until the early hours of the morning, or go out and mix with the streetlife, but the merchant in her didn't believe in overtime. Tonight, however, she faced something she avoided whenever possible and took completely seriously when she couldn't: an obligation. Switching off lights as she went, Shelby climbed the stairs to the second floor.

The cat leapt nimbly from his perch on the windowsill, stretched and padded toward her. When Shelby came in, dinner wasn't far behind. The bird fluffed her wings and began to gnaw on her cuttle-bone.

"How's it going?" She gave Moshe an absent scratch behind the ears where he liked it best. With a sound of approval, he looked up at her with his one eye, tilting his head so that the patch he wore looked raffish and right. "Yeah, I'll feed you." Shelby pressed a hand to her own stomach. She was starving, and the best she could hope for that evening would be liver wrapped in bacon and crackers.

"Oh, well," she murmured as she went into the kitchen to feed the cat. She'd promised her mother she'd make an appearance at Congressman Write's cocktail party, so she was stuck. Deborah Campbell was probably the only one capable of making Shelby feel stuck.

Shelby was fond of her mother, over and above the basic love of a child for her parent. There were times they were taken for sisters, despite the twenty-five-year difference in their ages. The coloring was the same—bright red hair too fiery for chestnut, too dark for titian. While her mother wore hers short and sleek, Shelby let hers curl naturally with a frizz of bangs that always seemed just a tad too long. Shelby had inherited her mother's porcelain complexion and smoky eyes, but whereas the combination made Deborah look delicately elegant, Shelby somehow came across looking more like a waif who'd sell flowers on a streetcorner. Her face was narrow, with a hint of bone and hollow. She often exploited her image with a clever hand at makeup and an affection for antique clothes.

She might have inherited her looks from her mother, but her personality was hers alone. Shelby never thought about being freewheeling or eccentric, she simply was. Her background and upbringing were lodged in Washington, and overtones of politics had dominated her childhood. Election-year pressure, the campaign trail that had taken her father away from home for weeks at a time, lobbying, bills to pass or block—they were all part of her past.

There'd been careful children's parties that had been as much a part of the game as a press conference. The children of Senator Robert Campbell were important to his image—an image that had been carefully projected as suitable for the Oval Office. And a great deal of the image, as Shelby remembered, had been simple fact. He'd been a good man, fair-minded, affectionate, dedicated, with a keen sense of the ridiculous. That hadn't saved him from a madman's bullet fifteen years before.

She'd made up her mind then that politics had killed her father. Death came to everyone—even at eleven, she'd understood that. But it had come too soon for Robert Campbell. And if it could strike him, who she'd imagined was invulnerable, it could strike anyone, anytime. Shelby had decided with all the fervor of a young child to enjoy every moment of her life and to squeeze it for everything there was to have. Since then, nothing had changed her analysis. So, she'd go to Write's cocktail party at his spacious home across the river and find something there to amuse or interest her. Shelby never doubted she'd succeed.

Shelby was late, but then, she always was. It wasn't from any conscious carelessness or need to make an entrance. She was always late because she never finished anything as quickly as she thought she would. Besides, the white brick Colonial was crowded, filled with enough people that a latecomer wasn't noticed.

The room was as wide as Shelby's entire apartment and twice as long. It was done in whites and ivories and creams, which added to the sense of uncluttered space. A few excellent French landscapes hung on the walls in ornate frames. Shelby approved the ambience, though she couldn't have lived with it herself. She liked the scent of the place—tobaccos, mixed perfumes and colognes, the faintest trace of light sweat. It was the aroma of people and parties.

Conversations were typical of most cocktail parties—clothes, other parties, golf scores—but running through it were murmurs on the price index, the current NATO talks, and the Secretary of the Treasury's recent interview on "Face to Face."

Shelby knew most of the people there, dressed in thin silks or in tailored dark suits. She evaded capture by any of them with quick smiles and greetings as she worked her way with practiced skill to the buffet. Food was one thing she took very seriously. When she spotted finger-sized quiches, she decided her evening wasn't going to be a total loss after all.

"Why, Shelby, I didn't even know you were here. How nice to see you." Carol Write, looking quietly elegant in mauve linen, had slipped through the crowd without spilling a drop of her sherry.

"I was late," Shelby told her, returning the brief hug with her mouth full. "You have a beautiful home, Mrs. Write."

"Why, thank you, Shelby. I'd love to give you a tour a little later if I can slip away." She gave a quick, satisfied glance around at the crowd—the banner of a Washington hostess. "How are things at your shop?"

"Fine. I hope the congressman's well."

"Oh, yes. He'll want to see you—I can't tell you how much he loves that urn you made for his office." Though she had a soft Georgian drawl, Carol could talk as quickly as a New York shopkeeper making a pitch. "He still says it was the best birthday present I ever bought him. Now, you must mingle." Carol had Shelby's elbow before she could grab another quiche. "No one's better at keeping conversations moving than you are. Too much shop talk can simply murder a party. There are several people here you know of course, but—ah, here's Deborah. I'll just leave you to her a moment and play hostess.''

Released, Shelby eased back toward the buffet. ''Hello, Mama.''

''I was beginning to think you'd backed out.'' Deborah skimmed a glance over her daughter, marveling that the rainbow-colored skirt, peasant blouse, and bolero looked so right on her when it would have been a costume on anyone else.

''Um-um, I promised.'' Shelby cast a connoisseur's eye over the buffet before she made her next choice. ''Food's better than I expected.''

''Shelby, get your mind off your stomach.'' With a half sigh, Deborah hooked arms with her daughter. ''In case you haven't noticed, there are several nice young men here.''

''Still trying to marry me off?'' Shelby kissed her lightly on the cheek. ''I'd almost forgiven you for the pediatrician you tried to foist on me.''

''He was a very personable young man.''

''Hmmm.'' Shelby decided not to mention that the personable young man had had six pairs of hands— all very active.

''Besides, I'm not trying to marry you off; I just want you to be happy.''

''Are you happy?'' Shelby countered with a quick gleam in her eye.

''Why, yes,'' Absently Deborah tightened the diamond stud in her left ear. ''Of course I am.''

''When are you going to get married?''

''I've *been* married,'' Deborah reminded her with a little huff. ''I've had two children, and—''

"Who adore you. I've got two tickets for the ballet at the Kennedy Center next week. Want to come with me?"

The faint frown of annoyance vanished from Deborah's brow. How many women, she thought, had a daughter who could exasperate and please so fully at the same time? "A clever way to change the subject, and I'd love to."

"Can I come to dinner first?" she asked, then beamed a smile to her left. "Hi, Steve." She tested a solid upper arm. "You've been working out."

Deborah watched her offspring spill charm over the Assistant Press Secretary, then dole out more to the newly appointed head of the EPA without missing a beat. Effortless, genuine, Deborah mused. No one enjoyed, or was enjoyed by a crowd, so much as Shelby. Then, why did she so scrupulously avoid the one-on-one entanglements? If it had been simply marriage that Shelby avoided, Deborah would have accepted it, but for a long time, she'd suspected it was something else Shelby blocked off.

Deborah would never have wished her daughter unhappiness, but even that would have relieved her mind. She'd watched Shelby avoid emotional pain one way or another for fifteen years. Without pain, Deborah knew, there was never true fulfillment. Yet…she sighed when Shelby laughed that smoky careless laugh as she drew out various members of the group she'd joined. Yet Shelby was so vital, so bright. Perhaps she was worrying over nothing. Happiness was a very personal thing.

Alan watched the woman with flaming hair who was dressed like a wealthy Gypsy. He could hear her laugh float across the room, at once sensuous and innocent. An interesting face, he mused, more unique than beautiful. What was she? he wondered. Eighteen? Thirty? She didn't seem to belong to a Washington party—God knows he'd been at enough of them to know who did. There was nothing sleek or cautious about her. That dress hadn't come from one of the accepted shops the political wives patronized, and her hair certainly hadn't been styled in any sophisticated salon. But she fit in. Despite the touch of L.A. flair and New York savvy, she fit right in. But who the hell—

"Well, Senator." Write gave Alan a firm slap on the back. "It's good to see you outside the arena. We don't lure you out often enough."

"Good Scotch, Charlie." Alan lifted his glass again. "It always does the trick."

"It usually takes more than that," Write corrected. "You burn a lot of midnight oil, Alan."

Alan smiled easily. No one's moves were secret in Washington. "There seems to be a lot to burn at the moment."

With a nod for agreement, Write sipped his drink. "I'm interested in your views on Breiderman's bill coming up next week."

Alan met the congressman's eyes calmly, knowing Write was one of Breiderman's leading supporters. "I'm against it," he said simply. "We can't afford any more cuts in education."

"Well, Alan, you and I know things aren't so black and white."

"Sometimes the gray area gets too large—then it's

best to go back to basics.'' He didn't want a debate, and he discovered he didn't want shop talk. It was a poor mood to be in for a senator at a political party. But Alan MacGregor was enough politician to evade questions when it suited him. ''You know, I thought I knew everyone here.'' Alan glanced idly around the room. ''The woman who seems to be a cross between Esmeralda and Heidi—who is she?''

''Who?'' Write repeated, intrigued enough by the description to forget his planned retort and follow Alan's gaze. ''Oh, don't tell me you haven't met Shelby.'' He grinned, enjoying the description more now that he knew whom it referred to. ''Want an introduction?''

''I think I'll handle it myself,'' Alan murmured. ''Thanks.''

Alan wandered away, moving easily through the groups of people, stopping when pressed to. Like Shelby, he was made for crowds. Handshakes, smiles, the right word at the right time, a good memory for faces. It was stock-in-trade for a man whose career hinged on public whim as much as on his own skill. And he was skilled.

Alan knew the law; was familiar with all its shades and angles, though unlike his brother, Caine, also a lawyer, Alan had been drawn to the theory of law more than the individual cases. It had been the overview that had fascinated him—how the law, or the basis for it, the Constitution, worked for the people. Politics had caught his imagination in college, and even now at thirty-five; with a term in Congress behind him and his first term in the Senate under way, he enjoyed exploring its endless possibilities.

"Alone, Alan?" Myra Ditmeyer, a Supreme Court Justice's wife, plucked at his arm as he edged away from a group.

Alan grinned and with the privilege of an old friend, kissed her cheek. "Is that an offer?"

She gave one of her booming laughs, shaking so that the ruby drops at her ears danced. "Oh, you devil, if it only could be. Twenty years, you Scottish heartbreaker; all I'd need would be twenty years—a drop in the bucket." Her smile was genuine, her eyes shrewd as she studied him. "Why don't you have one of those polished cosmopolitan types of yours on your arm tonight?"

"I was hoping to talk you into a weekend in Puerto Vallarta."

This time Myra poked a long scarlet nail into his chest as she laughed. "It would serve you right if I took you up on it. You think I'm safe." She sighed, her round, finely lined face falling into wistful lines. "Unfortunately true. We need to find you someone dangerous, Alan MacGregor. A man your age still single." She clucked her tongue. "Americans like their presidents tidily married, my dear."

Alan's grin only widened. "Now you sound like my father."

"That old pirate." Myra sniffed, but a gleam of amusement shone in her eyes. "Still, you'd be wise to take his advice on a thing or two. A successful politician is a couple."

"I should get married to advance my career?"

"Don't try to outsmart me," Myra ordered, then saw his eyes shift in the direction of a low, familiar laugh.

Well, well, she thought, wouldn't that be an interesting match? The fox and the butterfly.

"I'm having a dinner party next week," she decided on the spot. "Just a few friends. My secretary will call your office with the details." Patting his cheek with a many-ringed hand, she moved away to find a strategic spot to watch.

Seeing Shelby drift away from the trio she was talking with, Alan moved in her direction. When he was near, the first thing he noticed was her scent—not floral, not spicy or musk, but a teasing merging of all three. It was more an aura than a perfume, and unforgettable. Shelby had crouched down in front of a curio cabinet, her nose pressed close.

"Eighteenth-century china," she murmured, sensing someone behind her. "'Tea-dust' glaze. Spectacular, isn't it?"

Alan glanced down at the bowl that seemed to fascinate her, then at the crown of vivid red hair. "It certainly draws attention."

She looked up over her shoulder and smiled—as stunning and unique an allure as her scent. "Hello."

"Hello." He took the hand she held up—strong and hard, a paradox with her looks—and helped her to her feet. He didn't relinquish it as he normally would have done without thinking, but continued to hold it as she smiled up at him.

"I got distracted on my way to my objective. Would you do me a favor?"

His brow lifted. There was a ring of both finishing school and the streets in her speech. "What?"

"Just stand here." In a swift move, she steered around him, slipped a plate off the buffet, and began to fill it. "Every time I start to do this, someone sees me and hauls me off. I missed my dinner. There." Satisfied, she nudged Alan's arm. "Let's go out on the terrace." Shelby slipped around the table and through the French doors.

Warm air and the scent of early lilacs. Moonlight fell over grass that had been freshly mowed and tidily raked. There was an old willow with tender new branches that dipped onto the flagstone. With a sigh of pure sensual greed, Shelby popped a chilled shrimp into her mouth. "I don't know what this is," she murmured, giving a tiny hors d'oeuvre a close study. "Have a taste and tell me."

Intrigued, Alan bit into the finger food she held to his mouth. "Pâté wrapped in pastry with…a touch of chestnut."

"*Hmm.* Okay." Shelby devoured the rest of it. "I'm Shelby," she told him, setting the plate on a glass table and sitting behind it.

"I'm Alan." A smile lingered on his mouth as he sat beside her. Where did this street waif come from? he wondered. He decided he could spend the time to find out, and the spring air was a welcome relief from the tobacco smoke and hothouse flowers inside. "Are you going to share any of that?"

Shelby studied him as she considered. She'd noticed him across the room, perhaps because he was tall with a naturally athletic build you didn't often see at a Washington party. You saw carefully maintained builds, the kind that spoke of workouts three times a week and racquetball, but his was more like a swimmer's—a channel swimmer's—long and lean. He'd cut through currents with little resistance.

His face wasn't smooth; there were a few lines of care in it that complemented the aristocratic cast of his face and his long, thin mouth. His nose was slightly out of alignment, which appealed to her. The dark hair and dark eyes made her think of a Brontë hero—Heathcliff or Rochester, she wasn't sure. But he had a thoughtful, brooding quality about him that was both restful and distracting. Shelby's lips curved again.

"Sure. I guess you earned it. What are you drinking?"

Alan reached toward the plate. "Scotch, straight up."

"I knew you could be trusted." Shelby took the glass from him and sipped. Her eyes laughed over the rim; the faint breeze played with her hair. Moonlight, starlight, suited her. She looked, for a moment, like an elf who might vanish with a puff at will.

"What are you doing here?" he asked her.

"Maternal pressure," she told him easily. "Have you ever experienced it?"

His smile was wry and appealing. "Paternal pressure is my specialty."

"I don't imagine there's much difference," Shelby decided over a full mouth. Swallowing, she rested the side of her face on her palm. "Do you live in Alexandria?"

"No, Georgetown."

"Really? Where?"

The moonlight glimmered in her eyes, showing him they were as pure a gray as he'd ever seen. "P Street."

"Funny we haven't run into each other in the local market. My shop's only a few blocks from there."

"You run a shop?" Funky dresses, velvet jackets, he imagined. Perhaps jewelry.

"I'm a potter." Shelby pushed his glass back across the table.

"A potter." On impulse, Alan took her hand, turning it over to examine it. Small and narrow, her fingers were long, with the nails clipped short and unpainted. He liked the feel of her hand, and the look of her wrist under a heavy gold bracelet. "Are you any good?"

"I'm terrific." For the first time that she could remember, she had to suppress the urge to break contact. It ran through her mind that if she didn't, he was going to hold her there until she forgot she had other places to go. "You're not a Washington native," she continued, experimenting by letting her hand stay in his. "What is it...New England?"

"Massachusetts. Very good." Sensing the slight resistance in her hand, Alan kept it in his as he picked up another hors d'oeuvre and offered it.

"Ah, the trace of Harvard lingers." So did a slight disdain in her voice. His eyes narrowed fractionally at it. "Not medicine," she speculated as she allowed her fingers to lace with his. It was already becoming a very comfortable sensation. "Your palms aren't smooth enough for medicine."

Perhaps one of the arts? she wondered, again noticing that romantically brooding expression in his eyes. A dreamer, she suspected—a man who tended to think things through layer by layer before he acted.

"Law." Alan accepted the careful study as well as the faint surprise on her face. "Disappointed?"

"Surprised." Although his voice suited the law, she decided—smooth and clean with undercurrents that might have been drama or humor. "But then I suppose my conception of lawyers is at fault. Mine has jowls and wears tortoiseshell glasses. Don't you think the law tends to get in the way of a lot of ordinary things?"

His brow lifted in direct harmony with the corner of his mouth. "Such as murder and mayhem?"

"Those aren't ordinary things—well, maybe mayhem," Shelby corrected as she took another sip from his glass. "I suppose I mean the endless red tape of bureaucracy. Do you know all the forms I have to fill out just to sell my pieces? Then someone has to read those forms, someone else has to file them, and someone else has to send out more when the time comes. Wouldn't it be simpler just to let me sell a vase and make my living?"

"Difficult when you're dealing with millions." Alan forgot that he hadn't wanted to debate as he idly toyed with the ring she wore on her pinky. "Not everyone would adhere to a fair profit balance, no one would pay taxes, and the small businessman would have no more protection than the consumer would."

"It's hard to believe filling out my social security number in triplicate accomplishes all that." His touch moving in a half-friendly, half-seductive manner over her skin was distracting enough, but when he smiled—when he really smiled—Shelby decided he was the most irresistible male she'd ever encountered.

Perhaps it was that touch of sobriety lurking around the edges of humor.

"There's always a large overlap between bureaucracy and necessity." He wondered—only for a moment—what in hell he was doing having this conversation with a woman who looked like a nineteenth-century waif and smelled like every man's dream.

"The best thing about rules is the infinite variety of ways to break them." Shelby gave a trickle of the laughter that had first attracted him. "I suppose that's what keeps you in business."

A voice drifted through the open window, brisk, cool, and authoritative. "Nadonley might have his finger on the pulse of American-Israeli relations, but he isn't making many friends with his current policy."

"And his frumpy, tourist-class travel look is wearing a bit thin."

"Typical," Shelby murmured, with the shadow of a frown in her eyes. "Clothes are as political as beliefs—probably more. Dark suits, white shirt, you're a conservative. Loafers and a cashmere sweater, a liberal."

He'd heard that slick arrogance toward his profession before—quiet or noisy depending on the occasion. Normally Alan ignored it. This time it irked him. "You tend to simplify, don't you?"

"Only what I don't have any patience with," she acknowledged carelessly. "Politics've been an annoying byproduct of society since before Moses debated with Ramses."

The smile began to play around his mouth again.

Shelby didn't know him well enough yet to realize it was a challenging one. To think he'd nearly given in to the urge to stay home and spend a quiet evening with a book. "You don't care for politicians."

"It's one of the few generalizations I'm prone to. They come in several flavors—stuffy, zealot, hungry, shaky. I've always found it frightening that a handful of men run this strange world. So…" With a shrug, she pushed aside her plate. "I make it a habit to pretend I really do have control over my own destiny." She leaned closer again, enjoying the way the shadows of the willow played over his face. It was tempting to test the shape and feel of it with her fingers. "Would you like to go back in?"

"No." Alan let his thumb trace lightly over her wrist. He felt the quick, almost surprised increase of her pulse. "I had no idea how bored I was in there until I came out here."

Shelby's smile was instant and brilliant. "The highest of compliments, glibly stated. You're not Irish, are you?"

He shook his head, wondering just how that mobile, pixielike mouth was going to taste. "Scottish."

"Good God, so am I." The shadow crossed her eyes again as a trickle of anticipation ran along her skin. "I'm beginning to think it's fate. I've never been comfortable with fate."

"Controlling your own destiny?" Giving in to a rare impulse, he lifted her fingers to his lips.

"I prefer the driver's seat," she agreed, but she let her hand linger there, pleasing them both. "The Campbell practicality."

This time it was Alan's turn to laugh, long and with

unbridled amusement. "To old feuds," he said, lifting his glass to her. "Undoubtedly our ancestors slaughtered one another to the wailing of bagpipes. I'm of the clan MacGregor."

Shelby grinned. "My grandfather would put me on bread and water for giving you the right time. A damn mad MacGregor." Alan's grin widened while hers slowly faded. "Alan MacGregor," she said quietly. "Senator from Massachusetts."

"Guilty."

Shelby sighed as she rose. "A pity."

Alan didn't relinquish her hand, but stood so that their bodies were close enough to brush, close enough to transmit the instant, complicated attraction. "Why is that?"

"I might have risked my grandfather's fury..." Shelby gave his face another quick study, intrigued by the unsteady rate of her own heart. "Yes, I believe I would have—but I don't date politicians."

"Really?" Alan's gaze lowered to her mouth then came back to hers. He hadn't asked her for one. He understood, and didn't entirely approve, that she was the kind of woman who'd do her own asking when it suited her. "Is that one of Shelby's rules?"

"Yes, one of the few."

Her mouth was tempting—small, unpainted, and faintly curved as if she considered the entire thing a joke on both of them. Yes, her mouth was tempting, but the amusement in her eyes was a challenge. Instead of doing the obvious, Alan brought her hand up and pressed his lips to her wrist, watching her. He felt the quick jerk and scramble of her pulse, saw the wariness touched with heat flicker in her eyes. "The best thing about rules,'' Alan quoted softly, ''is the infinite variety of ways to break them.''

''Hoist with my own petard,'' she murmured as she drew her hand away. It was ridiculous, Shelby told herself, to be unsteady over an old-fashioned romantic gesture. But there was a look in those dark brown eyes that told her he'd done it as much for that purpose as to please himself.

''Well, Senator,'' she began with a firmer voice, ''it's been nice. It's time I put in another appearance inside.''

Alan let her get almost to the doors before he spoke. ''I'll see you again, Shelby.''

She stopped to glance over her shoulder. ''It's a possibility.''

''A certainty,'' he corrected.

She narrowed her eyes a moment. He stood near the glass table with the moon at his back—tall, dark, and built for action. His face was very calm, his stance relaxed, yet she had the feeling if she thumbed her nose at him, he could be on her before she'd drawn a breath. That alone nearly tempted her to try it. Shelby gave her head a little toss to send the bangs shifting on her forehead. The half-smile he was giving her was infuriating, especially since it made her want to return it. Without a word, she opened the doors and slipped inside.

That, she told herself, would be the end of that. She very nearly believed it.

Chapter Two

Shelby had hired a part-time shop assistant almost two years before so she'd be free to take an hour or a day off when it suited her mood, or to spend several days at a time if it struck her, with her craft. She'd found her answer in Kyle, a struggling poet whose hours were flexible and whose temperament suited hers. He worked for Shelby regularly on Wednesdays and Saturdays, and for sporadic hours whenever she called him. In return, Shelby paid him well and listened to his poetry. The first nourished his body, the second his soul.

Shelby invariably set aside Saturdays to toss or to turn clay, though she would have been amused if anyone had termed her disciplined: she still thought she worked then because she chose to, not because she'd fallen into a routine. Nor did she fully realize just how much those quiet Saturdays at her wheel centered her life.

Her workroom was at the rear of the shop. There were sturdy shelves lining two walls, crowded with projects that had been fired to biscuit or were waiting for their turn in the kiln. There were rows and rows of glazes—her palette of color—no less important to her than to any artist. There were tools: long wooden-handled needles, varied-shaped brushes, firing cones. Dominating the back wall was a large walk-in kiln, closed now, with its shelves stacked with glazed and decorated pottery in their final firing.

Because the vents were open and the room itself wasn't large, the high temperature of the kiln kept the room sultry. Shelby worked at her wheel in a T-shirt and cutoffs with a white-bibbed apron designed to protect her from most of the splatters.

There were two windows, both opening out on the alley, so she heard little of the weekend street noises. She used the radio for company, and with her hair pulled back by a leather thong, bent over the wheel with the last clay ball she intended to throw that day.

Perhaps she liked this part of her craft the best—taking a lump of clay and forming it into whatever her skill and imagination produced. It might be a vase or a bowl, squat or slender, ridged or smooth. It might be an urn that would have to wait for her to add the handles, or a pot that would one day hold jasmine tea or spiced coffee. Possibilities. Shelby never ceased to be fascinated by them.

The glazing, the adding of color and design, appealed to a different part of her nature. That was finishing work—creative certainly, and taxing. She could be lavish or frugal with color as she chose, using careful detail or bold splashes. Working the clay was more primitive, and therefore more challenging.

With bare hands she would mold and nudge and coax a formless ball of clay to her own will. Shelby realized people often did that to one another, and to their children in particular. She didn't like the idea and focused that aspect of her ego on the clay: she would mold, flatten, and remold until it suited her. She preferred people to be less malleable; molds were for the inanimate. Anyone who fit into one too neatly was already half dead.

She'd worked the air bubbles out of the clay. It was damp and fresh, carefully mixed to give her the right consistency. She added the grog, coarsely ground bits of broken pottery, to increase the stiffness and was ready to begin. The moistened bat was waiting. Using both hands, Shelby pressed the clay down as the wheel began to turn. She held the soft, cool earth firmly in cupped hands until it ran true on the wheel, allowing herself to feel the shape she wanted to create.

Absorbed, she worked with the radio murmuring unheard behind her. The wheel hummed. The clay spun, succumbing to the pressure of her hands, yielding to the unrelenting demands of her imagination. She formed a thick-walled ring, pressing her thumb in the center of the ball, then slowly, very slowly, pulled it upward between her thumb and fingers to form a cylinder. She could flatten it into a plate now, open it into a bowl, perhaps close it into a sphere, according to her own pleasure.

She was both in control and driven. Her hands dominated the clay as surely as her creativity dominated her. She felt the need for something symmetrical, poised. In the back of her mind was a strong image of masculinity—something with clean, polished lines and understated elegance. She began to open the clay, her hands deft and sure, slick now with the reddish-brown material. A bowl became her objective, deep with a wide ridge, along the lines of a Roman krater, handleless. The rotation and the pressure of her hands forced the clay wall up. The shape was no longer only in her mind as she molded the clay inside and out.

With skilled hands and an experienced eye, she molded the shape into proportion, tapering it out for the stem of the base, then flattening. The time and patience she applied here she took for granted, and spared for few other aspects of her life. Only the energy touched all of her.

Shelby could already envision it finished in a dark jade green with hints, but only hints, of something softer beneath the surface of the glaze. No decoration, no fluting or scrolled edges—the bowl would be judged on its shape and strength alone.

When the shape was complete, she resisted the urge to fuss. Too much care was as dangerous as too little. Turning off the wheel, Shelby gave the bowl one long critical study before taking it to the shelf she reserved for drying. The next day, when it was leather-hard, she'd put it back on the wheel and use her tools to refine it, shaving off any unwanted clay. Yes, jade green, she decided. And with careful inglazing, she could produce those hints of softness under the rich, bold tone.

Absently she arched her back, working out the tiny,

nagging kinks she hadn't noticed while the wheel was on. A hot bath, Shelby decided, before she went out to join some friends in that new little club on M Street. With a sigh that was as much from satisfaction as weariness, she turned. Then gasped.

"That was quite an education." Alan slipped his hands out of his pockets and crossed to her. "Do you know what shape you're after when you start, or does it come as you're working?"

Shelby blew her bangs out of her eyes before she answered. She wouldn't do the expected and ask him what he was doing there, or how he'd gotten in. "It depends."

She lifted a brow, vaguely surprised to see him in jeans and a sweatshirt. The man she had met the night before had seemed too polished for such casual clothes, especially for denim white at the stress points from wear. The tennis shoes were expensive, but they weren't new. Neither was the gold watch at the end of a subtly muscled arm. Wealth suited him, and yet he didn't seem the sort of man who'd be careless with it. He'd know his own bank balance—something Shelby couldn't claim to—what stocks he owned and their market value.

Alan didn't fidget during the survey. He'd grown too used to being in the public eye to be concerned with any sort of dissection. And, he thought she was entitled to her turn as he'd done little else but stare at her for the last thirty minutes.

"I suppose I should say I'm surprised to see you here, Senator, since I am." A hint of amusement touched her mouth. "And since I imagine you intended for me to be."

In acknowledgement, he inclined his head. "You work hard," he commented, glancing down at her clay-coated hands. "I've always thought artists must burn up as much energy as athletes when the adrenaline's flowing. I like your shop."

"Thanks." Because the compliment had been simple and genuine, Shelby smiled fully. "Did you come in to browse?"

"In a manner of speaking." Alan resisted the urge to skim a glance over her legs again. They were much, much longer than he had imagined. "It seems I hit closing time. Your assistant said to tell you he'd lock up."

"Oh." Shelby looked over at the windows as if to gauge the time. She never wore a watch when she worked. Using her shoulder, she rubbed at an itch on her cheek. The T-shirt shifted over small, firm breasts. "Well, one of the benefits of owning the place is to open or close when I choose. You can go out and take a look around while I wash up if you'd like."

"Actually…" He gathered the short, tumbling ponytail into his hand as if testing its weight. "I was thinking more of dinner together. You haven't eaten."

"No, I haven't," Shelby answered, though it hadn't been a question. "But I'm not going out to dinner with you, Senator. Can I interest you in an Oriental-style crock or a bud vase?"

Alan took a step closer, enjoying her absolute confidence and the idea that he'd be able to shake it. After all, that's why he'd come, wasn't it? he reminded himself. To toss back a few of those clever little potshots she'd taken at his profession, and therefore at him. "We could eat in," he suggested, letting his hand slip from her hair to the back or her neck. "I'm not picky."

"Alan." Shelby gave an exaggerated sigh and pretended there weren't any pulses of pleasure shooting down her spine from the point where his fingers rubbed. "In your profession, you understand policies. Foreign policies, budget policies, defense policies." Unable to resist, she stretched a little under his hand. All the twinges in her muscles had vanished. "I told you mine last night."

"Mmm-hmm." How slender her neck was, he thought. And the skin there was soft enough to give him a hint how she would feel under that apron and T-shirt.

"Well then, there shouldn't be a problem." He must do something physical with his hands, she thought fleetingly. His weren't the palms of a paper-pusher. The edge in her voice was calculated to combat the attraction and the vulnerability that went with it. "You strike me as too intelligent a man to require repetition."

With the slightest pressure, he inched Shelby toward him. "It's standard procedure to review policies from time to time."

"When I do, I'll—" To stop her own forward progress, Shelby pushed a hand against his chest. Both of them remembered the state of her hands at the same time and looked down. Her gurgle of laughter had his eyes lifting back to hers. "You had it coming," she told him, smiling. Her eyes lightened as humor replaced the prickles of tension. His shirt had a fairly clear imprint of her hand, dead center.

"This," she said, studying the stain, "might just be the next rage. We should patent it quick. Got any connections?"

"A few." He looked down at his shirt, then back into her face. He didn't mind a bit of dirt when the job called for it. "It'd be an awful lot of paperwork."

"You're right. And since I refuse to fill out any more forms than I already have to, we'd better forget it." Turning away, she began to scrub her hands and arms in a large double sink. "Here, strip that off," she told him as she let the water continue to run. "You'd better get the clay out." Without waiting for an answer, Shelby grabbed a towel and, drying her hands, went to check her kiln.

He wondered, because of the ease of her order, if she made a habit of entertaining half-naked men in her shop. "Did you make everything in the shop?" Alan scanned the shelves after he tugged the shirt over his head. "Everything in here?"

"Mmm-hmm."

"How did you get started?"

"Probably with the modeling clay my governess gave me to keep me out of trouble. I still got into trouble," she added as she checked the vents. "But I really liked poking at the clay. I never had the same feeling for wood or stone." She bent to make an adjustment. Alan turned his head in time to see the denim strain dangerously across her hips. Desire thudded with unexpected force in the pit of his stomach. "How's the shirt?"

Distracted, Alan looked back to where water pounded against cotton. It surprised him that his heartbeat wasn't quite steady. He was going to have to do something about this, he decided. Quite a bit of thinking and reassessing—tomorrow. "It's fine." After switching off the tap, he squeezed the excess water out of the material. "Walking home's going to be...interesting half-dressed," Alan mused as he dropped the shirt over the lip of the sink.

Shelby shot a look over her shoulder, but the retort she had in mind slipped away from her. He was lean enough so she could have counted his ribs, but there was a sense of power and endurance in the breadth of his chest and shoulders, the streamlined waist. His body made her forget any other man she'd ever seen.

It had been he, she realized all at once, whom she'd been thinking of when she'd thrown the clay into that clean-lined bowl.

Shelby let the first flow of arousal rush through her because it was as sweet as it was sharp. Then she tensed against it, rendering it a distant throb she could control.

"You're in excellent shape," she commented lightly. "You should be able to make it to P Street in under three minutes at a steady jog."

"Shelby, that's downright unfriendly."

"I thought is was more rude," she corrected as she struggled against a grin. "I suppose I could be a nice guy and throw it in the dryer for you."

"It was your clay."

"It was *your* move," she reminded him, but snatched up the damp shirt. "Okay, come on upstairs." With one hand, she tugged off her work apron, tossing it aside as she breezed through the doorway. "I suppose you're entitled to one drink on the house."

"You're all heart," Alan murmured as he followed her up the stairs.

"My reputation for generosity precedes me." Shelby pushed open the door. "If you want Scotch, it's over there." Motioning in a vague gesture, she headed in the opposite direction. "If you'd rather have coffee, the kitchen's straight ahead—there's a percolator on the counter and a half-pound in the cabinet next to the window." With this, she disappeared with his shirt into an adjoining room.

Alan glanced around. The interest he'd felt for the woman was only increased now by her living quarters. It was a hodgepodge of colors that should have clashed but didn't. Bold greens, vivid blues, and the occasional slash of scarlet. Bohemian. Perhaps flamboyant was a better description. Either adjective fit, just as either fit the woman who lived there. Just as neither fit his life-style or his taste.

There were chunky striped pillows crowded on a long armless sofa. A huge standing urn, deep blue with wild oversize poppies splashed over the surface, held a leafy Roosevelt fern. The rug was a zigzag of color over bare wood.

A wall hanging dominated one side of the room, of a geometric design that gave Alan the impression of a forest fire. A pair of impossibly high Italian heels lay drunkenly next to an ornately carved chair. A mint green ceramic hippopotamus of about three feet in length sat on the other side.

It wasn't a room for quiet contemplation and lazy evenings, but a room of action, energy, and demand.

Alan turned toward the direction Shelby had indicated, then stopped short when he saw the cat. Moshe lay stretched on the arm of a chair, watching him suspiciously out of his good eye. The cat didn't move a whisker, so for a moment Alan took him to be as inanimate as the hippo. The patch should have looked ridiculous, but like the colors in the room, it simply suited.

Above the cat hung an octagon cage. Inside it was a rather drab-looking parrot. Like Moshe, the bird watched Alan with what seemed to be a mixture of suspicion and curiosity. With a shake of his head for his own fantasies, Alan walked up to them.

"Fix you a drink?" he murmured to the cat, then with an expert's touch he scratched under Moshe's chin. The cat's eyes narrowed with pleasure.

"Well, that shouldn't take more than ten or fifteen minutes," Shelby announced as she came back in. She could hear her cat purring from ten feet away. "So, you've met my roommates."

"Apparently. Why the patch?"

"Moshe Dayan lost his eye in the war. Doesn't like to talk about it." Because her tone seemed too careless for deliberate humor, Alan sent her a searching look she didn't notice as she crossed to the liquor cabinet. "I don't smell any coffee—did you decide on Scotch?"

"I suppose. Does the bird talk?"

"Hasn't said a word in two years." Shelby splashed liquor into glasses. "That's when Moshe came to live with us. Auntie Em's an expert on holding grudges—he only knocked over her cage once."

"Auntie Em?"

"You remember—there's no place like home. Follow the yellow brick road. I've always thought Dorothy's Aunt Em was the quintessential comfortable aunt. Here you go.'' Walking to him, Shelby offered the glass.

''Thanks.'' Her choice of names for her pets reminded him that Shelby wasn't altogether the type of woman he thought he'd always understood. ''How long have you lived here?''

''*Mmm,* about three years.'' Shelby dropped onto the couch, drew up her legs, and sat like an Indian. On the coffee table in front of her were a pair of orange-handled scissors, a copy of *The Washington Post* opened to the comic section, a single earring winking with sapphires, what must have been several days worth of unopened mail, and a well-thumbed copy of *Macbeth.*

''I didn't put it together last night,'' he said as he moved to join her. ''Robert Campbell was your father?''

''Yes, did you know him?''

''Of him. I was still in college when he was killed. I've met your mother, of course. She's a lovely woman.''

''Yes, she is.'' Shelby sipped. The Scotch was dark and smooth. ''I've often wondered why she never ran for office herself. She's always loved the life.''

He caught it—the very, very faint edge of resentment. That was something to explore later, Alan decided. Timing was often the ultimate reason for success or failure in any campaign. ''You have a brother, don't you?''

''Grant?'' For a moment, her gaze touched on the newspaper. ''Yes, he steers clear of Washington for the most part.'' A siren screamed outside the window, echoing then fading. "He prefers the relative peace of Maine." A flicker of amusement crossed her face—a secret that intrigued Alan. Instinct told him he wouldn't learn it yet. Then logic reminded him he had no real interest in her secrets. "In any case, neither of us seem to have inherited the public servant syndrome."

"Is that what you call it?" Alan shifted. The pillow against his back was cool and satin. He imagined her skin would feel like that against his.

"Doesn't it fit?" she countered. "A dedication to the masses, a fetish for paperwork. A taste for power."

It was there again, that light arrogance touched with disdain. "You haven't a taste for power?"

"Just over my own life. I don't like to interfere with other people's."

Alan toyed with the leather thong in her hair until he'd loosened it. Perhaps he had come to debate with her after all. She seemed to urge him to defend what he'd always believed in. "Do you think any of us go through the cycle without touching off ripples in other lives?"

Shelby said nothing as her hair fell free. It tickled her neck, reminding her of the feel of his fingers on almost the same spot. She discovered it was as simple as she had thought it would be to sit beside him with those lean muscles naked and within easy reach.

"It's up to everyone to ward off or work with the ripples in their own way," she said at length. "Well, that does in my philosophy for the day; I'll see if your shirt's dry."

Alan tightened his grip on her hair as she started

to rise. Shelby turned her head to find those brooding, considering eyes on her face. "The ripples haven't even started between us," he said quietly. "Perhaps you'd better start working with them."

"Alan…" Shelby kept her voice mild and patient as excitement ripped through her. "I've already told you, *nothing's* going to get started between us. Don't take it personally," she added with a half-smile. "You're very attractive. I'm just not interested."

"No?" With his free hand, he circled her wrist. "Your pulse is racing."

Her annoyance was quick, mirrored in the sudden flare in her eyes, the sudden jerk of her chin. "I'm always happy to boost an ego," she said evenly. "Now, I'll get your shirt."

"Boost it a little higher," he suggested and drew her closer. One kiss, he thought, and he'd be satisfied. Flamboyant, overly aggressive women held no appeal for him. Shelby was certainly that. One kiss, he thought again, and he'd be satisfied on all counts.

She hadn't expected him to be stubborn, any more than she'd expected that fierce tug of longing when his breath fluttered over her lips. She let out a quick sigh of annoyance that she hoped would infuriate him. So, the Senator from Massachusetts wants to try his luck with a free-thinking artist, just for variety. Relaxing, she tilted up her chin. All right, then, she decided. She'd give him a kiss that would knock him flat—right before she bundled him up and hauled him out the door.

But he didn't touch his lips to hers yet, only looked at her. Why wasn't she handling him? she wondered as his mouth slowly lowered. Why wasn't she…?

Then his tongue traced a lazy line over her lips and she wasn't capable of wondering. There was nothing more she could do other than close her eyes and experience.

She'd never known anyone to take such care with a kiss—and his lips had yet to touch hers. The tip of his tongue outlined and tested the fullness of her mouth so softly, so slowly. All sensation, all arousal, was centered there. How could she have known a mouth could feel so much? How could she have known a kiss that wasn't a kiss would make her incapable of moving?

Then he captured her bottom lip between his teeth and her breath started to shudder. He nibbled, then drew it inside his mouth to suck until she felt the answering, unrelenting tug deep inside her. There was a rhythm, he was guiding her to it, and Shelby had forgotten to resist. His thumb was running up then down over the vein in her wrist; his fingertips skimmed the base of her neck. The points of pleasure spread out until her whole body hummed with them. Still his lips hadn't pressed onto her.

She moaned, a low, throaty sound that was as much of demand as surrender. Then they were mouth to mouth, spinning from arousal to passion at the instant of contact.

He'd known her mouth would taste like this—hot and eager. He'd known her body would be like this against his—soft and strong. Had that been why he'd woken thinking of her? Had that been why he'd found himself standing outside her shop as afternoon was waning into evening? For the first time in his life,

Alan found that the reasons didn't matter. They were pressed close, and that was enough for him.

Her hair carried that undefinable scent he remembered. He dove his hands into it as if he would have the fragrance seep into his pores. It drove him deeper. Her tongue met his, seeking, searching, until her taste was all the tastes he'd ever coveted. The pillows rustled with soft whispers as he pressed her between them and himself.

She hadn't expected this kind of raw, consuming passion from him. Style—she would have expected style and a seduction with all the traditional trimmings. Those she could have resisted or evaded. But there was no resisting a need that had so quickly found and tapped her own. There was no evading a passion that had already captured her. She ran her hands up his naked back and moaned as the feel of him lit new fires.

This was something too firm to be molded, too hard to be changed. The man had styled himself as he had chosen. Shelby knew it instinctively and felt desire rise for this reason alone. But with desire came the knowledge that she was growing too soft, too pliant; came the fear that he might have already changed her shape with a kiss.

"Alan." She gathered her forces for resistance when every pore, every cell, was crying out for her to submit. "Enough," she managed against his mouth.

"Not nearly," he corrected, trapping her close when she would have struggled away.

He was taking her deep again, where she had no control over the moment, or the outcome of it.

"Alan." She drew back far enough to see his face. "I want you to stop." Her breathing wasn't steady, her eyes were dark as smoke, but the resistance in her body was very real. Alan felt a hot flash of anger, which he expertly controlled, and a sharp stab of desire, which he had more trouble with.

"All right." He loosened his hold. "Why?"

It was rare for her to have to order herself to do something as natural as relax. Even after she had, there was a light band of tension at the base of her neck. "You kiss very well," she said with forced casualness.

"For a politician?"

Shelby let out a little hiss of breath and rose. Damn him for knowing just what rib to punch—and for his skill in punching without raising a sweat. Pompous, Shelby told herself. Pompous, smug, and self-absorbed.

The apartment was nearly dark. She flicked on a light, surprised that so much time had passed when everything had seemed to happen so quickly. "Alan..." Shelby linked her hands together as she did when she'd decided to be patient.

"You didn't answer my question," he pointed out and made himself relax against the pillows that brought back memories of her skin.

"Perhaps I haven't made myself clear enough." She fought the urge to say something that would erase that mildly interested look in his eyes. Damn, he was clever, she thought grudgingly—with words, with expressions. She'd like to come up against him again when her heart wasn't thudding. "I meant everything I said last night."

"So did I." He tilted his head as if to study her from a new angle. "But maybe like your bird, you're quite an expert on holding grudges too."

When she stiffened, the hands that were linked fell apart. "Don't press."

"I generally don't on old wounds." The hurt was there; he saw it, and an anger that was well rooted. It was difficult for him to remember he'd known her for less than a day and had no right to pry, or to expect. "I'm sorry," he added as he rose.

Her rigidness vanished with the apology. He had a way of saying simple things with simple genuineness, Shelby thought, and found she liked him for it—if for nothing else. "It's all right." She crossed the room and came back moments later with his shirt. "Good as new," she promised as she tossed it to him. "Well, it's been nice; don't let me keep you."

He had to grin. "Am I being helped out the door?"

Not bothering to disguise a smile, she gave a mock sigh. "I've always been too obvious. Good night, Senator. Look both ways when you cross the street." She went to open the side door that led to the outside stairs.

Alan pulled the shirt over his head before he crossed to her. He'd always thought it had been his brother, Caine, who'd never been able to take a simple no with a polite bow. Perhaps he'd been wrong, Alan mused, and it was a basic MacGregor trait. "The Scotch can be stubborn," he commented as he paused beside her.

"You'll remember I'm a Campbell. Who'd know better?" Shelby opened the door a bit wider.

"Then, we both know where we stand." He

cupped her chin in his hand to hold her face still as he gave her a last hard kiss that seemed suspiciously like a threat. "Till next time."

Shelby closed the door behind him and stood leaning against it a moment. He was going to be trouble, she decided. Alan MacGregor was going to be very serious trouble.

Chapter Three

It turned out to be busy for a Monday morning. By eleven, Shelby had sold several pieces, including three that she had taken out of the kiln only the evening before. Between customers, she sat behind the counter wiring a lamp she had made in the shape of a Greek amphora. To have simply sat during the idle time would have been impossible for her. To have dusted or fiddled with the displays would have bored her to distraction. She left such things to Kyle, to their mutual satisfaction.

Because it was warm, she kept the door of the shop open. It was, Shelby knew, more tempting to stroll through an open door than to open a closed one. Spring came in, along with the unique sound of cars riding over cobblestone. She had a steady stream of browsers who bought nothing. Shelby didn't mind. They were company as much as potential buyers. The woman carrying the manicured poodle in a hand-knit sweater was an interesting diversion. The restless teenager who came in to poke around gave her a chance to touch on the problems of youth and unemployment. Shelby hired him to wash the windows. While she wired, the boy stood on the street side running a squeegee over the glass while a portable radio bounced out tunes at his feet. She enjoyed the sound as it mixed with the occasional snatches of conversations from passersby.

Did you see the price of that dress?
If he doesn't call me tonight, I'm going to...
...notes on her lecture on pre-Hitler Germany.

Idly she finished the conversations in her head as she worked. Shelby was threading the wire up the inside of the lamp when Myra Ditmeyer sauntered in. She wore a breezy vermilion suit that matched the shade of her lipstick. The powerful punch of her scent filled the little shop.

"Well, Shelby, always keeping those clever hands busy."

With a smile of pure pleasure, Shelby leaned over the counter to kiss Myra's powdered cheek. If you want some acerbic gossip or just plain fun, there was no one, in Shelby's opinion, better than Myra. "I thought you'd be home planning all the wonderful things you're going to feed me tonight."

"Oh, my dear, that's all seen to." Myra set down her alligator bag. "The cook's in a creative spin even as we speak."

"I've always loved eating at your house." Shelby

pulled the wire through the top of the lamp. "None of those stingy little meals or inedible sauces disguised as exotic." Absently she tapped her foot to the beat of the radio. "You did say Mama was coming."

"Yes, with Ambassador Dilleneau."

"Oh, yeah—the Frenchman with the big ears."

"Is that any way to talk about a diplomat?"

"She's been seeing him quite a bit," Shelby said casually. "I've wondered if I'm going to have a Gallic steppapa."

"You could do worse," Myra pointed out.

"*Mmm.* So, tell me, Myra…" Shelby attached the light fixture to the cord with a few deft turns. "Who've you set up for me tonight?"

"Set up," Myra repeated, wrinkling her nose. "What an unromantic phrase."

"Sorry. How about—who are you planning to loose Cupid's arrows on?"

"It's still unromantic when you're smirking." Myra watched Shelby screw in a light bulb. "In any case, I think you should be surprised. You've always been fond of surprises."

"I like giving better than getting."

"How well I know. How old were you? Eight, as I recall, when you and Grant…surprised a small, rather influential gathering in your mother's parlor with uncomfortably accurate caricatures of the Cabinet."

"It was Grant's idea," Shelby said, with a lingering twinge of regret that she hadn't thought of it first. "Papa laughed about it for days."

"He had a unique sense of humor."

"As *I* recall you offered Grant two thousand for the one of the Secretary of State."

"And the scoundrel wouldn't sell it to me. Good God," she mused. "What it would be worth now?"

"It would depend what name he signed to it, wouldn't it?"

"How is Grant? I haven't seen him since Christmas."

"The same—brilliant, grumpy." A laugh stole through the words. "Guarding his lighthouse fortress and his anonymity. I think I might sneak up there and bother him for a couple of weeks this summer."

"Such a gorgeous young man," Myra mused. "What a waste for him to seclude himself on that little bit of coast."

"It's what he wants," Shelby said simply. "For now."

"Excuse me?"

Both women looked toward the door where a young man stood in a crisp messenger's uniform. Shelby glanced at the basket over his arm. "Can I help you?"

"Miss Shelby Campbell?"

"Yes, I'm Shelby."

He shifted the basket he carried from his arm to his hand as he walked to her. "Delivery for you, Miss Campbell."

"Thanks." Automatically, she reached into the cash drawer for a dollar. "Who's it from?"

"Card's inside," he told her, pocketing the bill. "Enjoy."

She played the game. Shelby had been known to study and poke at a package on Christmas morning for twenty minutes before ripping off the paper. There were such possibilities in the unknown. She tilted the package from side to side, peered at it, then cupped her chin on both hands and stared at it.

"Oh, come on, Shelby!" Myra shifted her weight from foot to foot with impatience. "Lift off the cover; I'm dying to see."

"In a minute," Shelby murmured. "It might be— a picnic. Who'd send me a picnic? Or a puppy." She bent her ear close and listened. "Too quiet for a puppy. And it smells like…" Closing her eyes she drew in a deep breath and held it. "That's funny, who'd send me—" She opened the lid. "Strawberries."

The basket was rich with them—plump and moistly red. Their scent drifted up with memories of the sun-warmed field they'd been plucked from. Shelby lifted one and held it under her nose, savoring.

"Wonderful," she decided. "Really, really wonderful.

Myra plucked one out and bit it neatly in half. *"Mmm."* She popped the rest into her mouth. "Aren't you going to read the card?"

Still holding the berry, Shelby lifted out the plain white envelope, balancing it in her palm as if testing the weight. She turned it over, held it up to the light then turned it back to the front.

"Shelby!"

"Oh, all right." She ripped open the seal and drew out the card.

Shelby,
They made me think of you.

Alan

Watching her carefully, Myra saw the surprise, the pleasure, and something that wasn't regret or wariness but had aspects of both.

"Anyone I know?" she said dryly when Shelby didn't speak.

"What?" She looked up blankly, then shook her head. "Yes, I suppose you do." But she slipped the card back into the envelope without saying. "Myra." The name was on a long drawn-out sigh. "I think I'm in trouble."

"Good." She gave Shelby a smug smile and a nod. "It's about time you were. Would you like me to drive my cook crazy and add another name to my list for dinner tonight?"

Oh, it was tempting. Shelby nearly agreed before she stopped herself. "No. No, I don't think it would be wise."

"Only the young think they know anything about wisdom," Myra stated with a sniff. "Very well, then; I'll see you at seven." She chose another berry before she picked up her purse. "Oh, and Shelby, pack up that lamp and bring it along. Just put it on my account."

She'd have to call him, Shelby told herself when she was alone. Dammit, she'd have to call and thank him. She bit into a berry so that the juice and sweetness exploded inside her mouth—a sensual taste, part sun, part earth. And she remembered how Alan's taste had exploded inside her mouth.

Why hadn't he sent her something ordinary like flowers? Flowers she could have passed off and forgotten. She looked down into the basket, filled with berries brilliantly red and begging to be tasted. How did you deal with a man who sent you a basket of strawberries on a spring morning?

He'd known it, of course, she decided abruptly. A man like him would be a quick and clever judge of people. She felt simultaneous twinges of annoyance and admiration. She didn't like to be read so easily but...she couldn't help respecting someone who could.

Leaving the lid open, Shelby reached for the phone.

Alan calculated he had between fifteen and twenty minutes before the Senate was called back to the floor. He'd use the time to review the proposed budget cuts. A deficit that edged uncomfortably close to two-hundred billion had to be trimmed, but Alan viewed the proposed cuts in education as unacceptable. Congress had already partially rejected the sought-after domestic spending cuts, and he felt he had enough support to influence a modification on the education snipping.

There was more on his mind than deficits and budgets, however. Though it was the spring following an election year, Alan had been approached by the Senate Majority Leader. He'd been carefully felt out by an expert at saying nothing while hardly pausing for breath. It didn't take magic for Alan to conclude that he was being considered as the party's hope for the next decade. But did he want the top rung?

He'd thought about it—he wasn't a fool or without ambition. Still, he had believed if he ever decided to take a grab at the presidential brass ring, it would be in another fifteen, perhaps twenty years. The possibility of making his move sooner, at his party's urging, was something he would have to weigh carefully.

Nevertheless, as far as Alan's father was concerned, there had never been any question that his eldest son would run for president—and win. Daniel MacGregor liked to think he still held the strings guiding his offsprings' lives. Sometimes they gave him the gift of his illusions. Alan could still remember his sister's announcement of her pregnancy that past winter. Daniel's attention was centered on that and the marriage of their brother, Caine, so that the pressure had lifted from Alan. For now, he thought wryly. It shouldn't be long before he got one of his father's famous phone calls.

Your mother misses you. She worries about you. When are you going to take the time to come visit? Why aren't you married yet? Your sister can't carry on the line by herself, you know.

That might be simplifying it, Alan thought with a grin. But that would be the essence of the call. Strange, he'd always been able to shrug off his father's views on marriage and children. But now…

Why was it a woman he'd met only a few days before made him think of marriage? People didn't bind themselves willingly to someone they didn't know. She wasn't even the type of woman who'd appealed to him in the past. She wasn't sleek and cool. She wouldn't be undemanding, or make a comfortable hostess for elegant state dinners. She wouldn't be gracious, and she'd be anything but tactful. And, Alan added with a glimmer of a smile, she wouldn't even have dinner with him.

A challenge. She would be a challenge and he'd always enjoyed working his way through one. But that wasn't why. A mystery. She was a mystery and he'd always liked solving them, step by step. But that wasn't why. She had the verve of the very young, the skill of an artist and the flash of a rebel. She had passion that boiled rather than simmered and eyes as quiet as a foggy evening. She had a child's mouth and a woman's allure and a mind that would never adhere to the logical one-step-at-a-time structure of his own. The chemistry between them was almost absurdly wrong. And yet...

And yet, at thirty-five, Alan suddenly believed there was such a phenomenon as love at first sight. So, he would wage his patience and tenacity against her flash and energy and see who won in the end. If indeed there could ever be a winner between oil and water.

The phone rang beside him. Alan let it go until he remembered his secretary wasn't in the outer office. Mildly annoyed, he pushed the blinking button and answered. "Senator MacGregor."

"Thanks."

His lips curved as he leaned back in his chair. "You're welcome. How do they taste?"

Shelby brought a berry to her mouth for a nibble. "Fantastic. My shop smells like a strawberry patch. Dammit, Alan," she said with an exasperated sigh. "Strawberries are an unfair tactic. You're supposed to fight with orchids or diamonds. I could have coped very nicely with a big tacky diamond or five-dozen African orchids.''

He tapped the pen he'd been using on the stack of papers on his desk. ''I'll be certain not to give you either. When are you going to see me, Shelby?''

She was silent for a moment, torn, tempted. Ridiculous, she thought, shaking her head. Just because he had a bit of whimsy under the political protocol was no reason to toss aside a lifelong belief. ''Alan, it simply wouldn't work. I'm saving us both a lot of trouble by saying no.''

''You don't strike me as the type to avoid trouble.''

''Maybe not—I'm making an exception in your case. Years from now, when you have ten grandchildren and bursitis, you'll thank me.''

''Do I have to wait that long for you to have dinner with me?''

She laughed, cursing him at the same time. ''I really like you.'' He heard another quick sound of frustration. ''Dammit, Alan, don't be charming anymore. We'll both end up on thin ice. I just can't take it breaking under me again.''

He started to speak, then heard the signal—the buzzers and lights that warned of a quorum call. ''Shelby, I have to go. We're going to talk about this some more.''

''No.'' Her voice was firm now as she cursed herself for saying more than she had intended. ''I hate repeating myself. It's boring. Just consider that I've done you a favor. Good-bye, Alan.''

She hung up, then slammed the lid closed on the strawberries. Oh, God, she asked herself, how had he managed to get to her so quickly?

While she dressed for Myra's dinner party, Shelby listened to an old Bogart film. She listened only because the television had lost its shaky grip on the horizontal hold two weeks before. Currently she was amused by the situation. It was like having a large, rather ostentatious radio that took a great deal more imagination than a full-color twenty-inch screen.

While Bogey spoke in his weary, tough-guy voice, she slipped her narrow beaded vest over her frilled lace shirt.

Shelby had shoved aside her uncertain mood of the afternoon. She had always believed if you simply refused to admit you were upset or to acknowledge depression, you wouldn't be upset or depressed. In any case, she was sure that now that she had made herself crystal-clear and had refused Alan MacGregor for the third time, he would get the picture.

If she regretted the fact that there would be no more baskets of strawberries or surprises, she told herself she didn't. No one could make Shelby believe that something that she said was untrue was really more true than Shelby would admit to herself.

She stepped into a pair of foolish evening shoes that had more heel than leather as she dropped a few essentials into her bag—keys, a well-used lipstick and a half-roll of Life Savers.

"Are you staying in tonight, Moshe?" she asked as she passed by the cat who lounged on her bed. When he only opened his eye in acknowledgment, she breezed out of the room. "Okay, don't wait up." Shelby dropped her purse on top of the box that held Myra's lamp and prepared to lift both when someone knocked on the door. "You expecting someone?" she asked Auntie Em. The bird merely fluttered her wings, unconcerned. Hefting the box, Shelby went to answer.

Pleasure. She had to acknowledge it as well as annoyance when she saw Alan. "Another neighborly visit?" she asked, planting herself in the doorway. She skimmed a glance down the silk tie and trim, dark suit. "You don't look dressed for strolling."

The sarcasm didn't concern him—he'd seen that quick flash of unguarded pleasure. "As a public servant, I feel an obligation to conserve our natural resources and protect the environment." Reaching over, he clipped a tiny sprig of sweet pea into her hair. "I'm going to give you a lift to the Ditmeyers'. You might say we're carpooling."

Shelby could smell the fragrance that drifted from just above her right ear. She had an urge to put her hand up and feel the small blossoms. Since when, she demanded of herself, had she been so vulnerable to charm? "You're going to Myra's little...get-together?"

"Yes. Are you ready?"

Shelby narrowed her eyes, trying to figure out how Myra could have learned the name of the strawberry sender. "When did she ask you?"

"Hmm?" He was distracted by the way the thin lace rose at her neck. "Last week—at the Writes'."

Some of her suspicions eased. Perhaps it was just coincidence after all. "Well, I appreciate the offer, Senator, but I'll drive myself. See you over the canapés."

"Then, I'll ride with you," he said amiably. "We don't want to put any more carbon monoxide in the air than necessary. Shall I put that in the car for you?''

Shelby took a firmer grip on the box as her hold in other areas started to slip. It was that damn serious smile and those thoughtful eyes, she decided. They made a woman feel as though she were the only one he'd ever looked at in quite that way.

''Alan,'' she began, a bit amused by his persistence. ''What is this?''

''This...'' He leaned over and captured her mouth with his, lingering until her fingers threatened to dig holes in the stiff cardboard she held. ''Is what our ancestors would have called a siege,'' he finished softly. ''And MacGregors are notoriously successful at laying siege.''

Her breath shuddered out to merge with his. ''You don't do badly at hand-to-hand combat either.'' He chuckled and would have kissed her again if she hadn't managed to step back. ''All right.'' Shelby thrust the box into his arms, considering it a strategic move. ''We'll carpool. I don't want to be condemned as an air-polluter. You drive,'' she decided with a sudden mood-switching grin. ''Then, I can have an extra glass of wine at dinner.''

''You left your TV on,'' Alan commended as he stepped aside to let her pass.

''That's all right. It's broken anyway.'' Shelby clattered down the steps, heedless of her fragile heels and the steep drop. The sun had nearly set, sending wild streaks of red into a darkening, sober sky. Shelby laughed, turning back to Alan when she reached the narrow alleyway. ''Carpool, my foot. But it's still not a date, MacGregor. What we'll call this is a...a civilized transit agreement. That sounds bureaucratic enough. I like your car,'' she added, patting the hood of his Mercedes. ''Very sedate.''

Alan opened the trunk and set the box inside. He glanced back up at Shelby as he closed it. ''You have an interesting way of insulting someone.''

She laughed, that free smoke-edged laugh as she went to him. ''Dammit, Alan, I like you.'' Throwing her arms around his neck, she gave him a friendly hug that sent jolts of need careening through him. ''I really like you,'' she added, tilting back her head with a smile that lit her whole face with a sense of fun. ''I could probably have said that to a dozen other men who'd never have realized I was insulting them.''

''So.'' His hands settled at her hips. ''I get points for perception.''

''And a few other things.'' When her gaze slipped to his mouth, she felt the strength of longing weaken all the memories and all the vows. ''I'm going to hate myself for this,'' she murmured. ''But I want to kiss you again. Here, while the light's fading.'' Her eyes came back to his, still smiling, but darkened with an anticipation he knew had nothing to do with surrender. ''I've always thought you could do mad things at dusk without any consequences.''

Tightening her arms around his neck, Shelby pressed her mouth to his.

He was careful, very careful not to give in to the urgent desire to drag her closer. This time he'd let her lead him, and in doing so, lead herself where he wanted them both to go.

The light was softly dying. There was an impatient honking from the street on the other side of the shop.

Through the window of the apartment across the alley came the rich tang of spaghetti sauce and the bluesy sounds of an old Gershwin record. Straining closer, Shelby felt the fast, even beat of Alan's heart against her own.

His taste was the same quietly debilitating flavor as she remembered. Shelby could hardly believe she'd lived for so long without knowing that one particular taste. It seemed less possible she'd be able to live without it now. Or the feel of those strong steady arms around her—the firm body that transmitted safety and danger to her at the same time.

He'd know how to protect her if something threatened. He knew how to take her to the brink of an abyss she'd so cleverly avoided. And Shelby was too aware that he could take her over the edge.

But his mouth was so tempting, his taste so enticing. And dusk was still holding back the night sky. She gave herself to it longer than she should have—and not as long as she wanted to.

"Alan..." He felt his name form against his lips before she drew away. Their gaze held a moment while his arms and hers kept their bodies pressed close. There was strength in his face—a face she could trust. But there was so much between them. "We'd better go," Shelby murmured. "It's nearly dark."

The Ditmeyers' home was lit though there was still color in the western sky. Shelby could just see the riot of phlox in the rock garden as she stepped from the car. Her mother was already there, Shelby discovered when she caught a glimpse of the diplomatic plates on the Lincoln in the drive.

"You know Ambassador Dilleneau?" Shelby offered her hand to Alan as they stepped onto the walk.

"Slightly."

"He's in love with my mother." She brushed her bangs out of her eyes as she turned to him. "Men are, typically, but I think she has a soft spot for him."

"That amuses you?" Watching her, Alan pressed the doorbell.

"A little," she admitted. "It's rather sweet. She blushes," Shelby added with a quick laugh. "It's a very odd feeling for a daughter to see her mother blush over a man."

"You wouldn't?" Alan skimmed a thumb over her cheekbone. Shelby forgot her mother altogether.

"Wouldn't what?"

"Blush," he said softly, tracing her jawline. "Over a man."

"Once—I was twelve and he was thirty-two." She had to talk—just keep talking to remember who she was. "He, uh, came to fix the water heater."

"How'd he make you blush?"

"He grinned at me. He had a chipped tooth I thought was really sexy."

On a quick ripple of laughter, Alan kissed her just as Myra opened the door.

"Well, well." She didn't bother to disguise a self-satisfied smile. "Good evening. I see you two have met."

"What makes you think that?" Shelby countered breezily as she stepped inside.

Myra glanced from one to the other. "Do I smell strawberries?" she asked sweetly.

"Your lamp." Shelby gave her a bland look and indicated the box Alan carried. "Where would you like it?"

"Oh, just set it down there, Alan. It's so nice to have just a few friends in," Myra continued as she tucked an arm through each of theirs. "Gossip is so much more intimate that way. Herbert, pour two more of those marvelous aperitifs—you must try it," she added to both Shelby and Alan. "I've just discovered this marvelous little blackberry liqueur."

"Herbert." Shelby walked over to the Justice and gave him a smacking kiss. "You've been out sailing again." She grinned at his sunburned nose. "When are we going to the beach to wind-surf?"

"The child almost makes me believe I could do it," he commented as he gave her a squeeze. "Good to see you, Alan." His face folded into comfortable grandfatherly lines that made people forget he was one of the top judiciary figures in the country. "I think you know everyone. I'll just get those drinks."

"Hello, Mama." Shelby bent to kiss her mother's cheek when the emerald clusters on Deborah's ears caught her eye. "I haven't seen these before—I'd have borrowed them immediately."

"Anton gave them to me." A delicate color seeped into her cheeks. "In—appreciation for that party I hostessed for him."

"I see." Shelby's gaze shifted to the trim Frenchman beside her mother. "You have exquisite taste, Ambassador," she told him as she offered her hand.

His eyes twinkled as he brought it to his lips—a

trait that made up for the ears as far as Shelby was concerned. "You look lovely as always, Shelby. Senator, a pleasure to see you in such a relaxed atmosphere."

"Senator MacGregor." Deborah smiled up at him. "I didn't realize you and Shelby were acquainted."

"We're working on disrupting an old family tradition." He accepted the glass the Justice offered.

"He means feud," Shelby explained at her mother's blank look. She sipped the liqueur, approved it, then sat on the arm of Myra's chair.

"Oh… *Oh*," Deborah repeated as she remembered. "The Campbells and the MacGregors were blood enemies in Scotland—though I can't quite remember why."

"They stole our land," Alan put in mildly.

"That's what you say." Shelby shot him a look as she sipped again. "We *acquired* MacGregor land through a royal decree. They weren't good sports about it."

Alan gave her a thoughtful smile. "I'd be interested to hear you debate that issue with my father."

"What a match," Myra said, brightening at the thought. "Herbert, can you just see our Shelby nose-to-nose with Daniel? All that red hair and stubbornness. You really should arrange it, Alan."

"I've been giving it some thought."

"Have you?" Shelby's brows lifted to disappear completely under her frizz of bangs.

"Quite a bit of thought," he said in the same even tone.

"I've been to that wonderful anachronism in Hyannis Port." Myra gave Shelby a brief pat on the thigh.

"It's right up your alley, dear. She's so fond of the—well, let's say unique, shall we?"

"Yes." Deborah sent Shelby a fond smile. "I could never figure out why. But then, both of my children have always been a mystery. Perhaps it's because they're so bright and clever and restless. I'm always hoping they'll settle down." This time she beamed the smile at Alan. "You're not married either, are you, Senator?"

"If you'd like," Shelby said as she studied the color of her liqueur through the crystal, "I could just step out while you discuss the terms of the dowry."

"Shelby, really," Deborah murmured over the sound of the Justice's chuckle.

"It's so difficult for parents to see their children as capable adults," the Ambassador commented in his light, soothing voice. "For myself, I have two daughters with children of their own. Still, I worry. How are your children, Myra? You have a new grandson, don't you?"

Nothing could have been better calculated to change the subject. Shelby sent him a faint admiring nod and watched his eyes twinkle as Myra began an enthusiastic description of her grandson's first tooth.

He'd suit her, Shelby decided, watching her mother from under her lashes. She was the type of woman who never felt quite whole without a man. And she'd been shaped and polished into a political wife years before. The gloss was still there. Elegant manners, elegant style, elegant patience. Shelby gave a little sigh she didn't even hear. How could she and her mother look so much alike and be so very different? Elegance had always seemed a silk-lined cage to

Shelby—and a cage equaled restrictions no matter how it was formed. She still remembered too many of them.

The bodyguards—discreet, but always there. The carefully screened parties, the sophisticated alarm systems, the intrusion of the press. The security hadn't saved her father, though a photographer had gotten an award-winning picture of the gunman—seconds too late to do any good.

Shelby knew what was behind the elegance; the state dinners, the speeches, the galas. There were a hundred tiny fears, a millennium of doubts. The memory of too many political assassinations and assassination attempts in hardly more than twenty years.

No, her mother was made for the life. Patient, with a rod of steel beneath the fragile skin. Shelby wouldn't choose it, nor would she let it choose her. She'd love no one who could leave her again so horribly.

Letting the conversation flow around her, Shelby tilted back her glass. Her eyes met Alan's. It was there—that quietly brooding patience that promised to last a lifetime. She could almost feel him calmly peeling off layer after layer of whatever bits and pieces made up her personality to get to the tiny core she kept private.

You bastard. She nearly said it out loud. Certainly it reflected in her eyes for he smiled at her in simple acknowledgment. The siege was definitely under way. She only hoped she had enough provisions to outlast him.

Chapter Four

Shelby put in a very full week, dominated by the creative overload she experienced every few months. Kyle managed the shop for three days running while she closeted herself in her workroom, to sit for hours at the wheel or with her glazes. If she started at 7:00 A.M., Shelby still had enough juice to toss clay until late into the night. She knew herself well enough to understand and to accept that this sort of mood struck her when she was having trouble blocking out something that worried her.

When she worked, she would focus both mind and emotion on the project in her hands, and in that way, whatever problem she had simply ceased to be a problem for that amount of time. Normally when she'd run out of steam, she'd come up with a solution. Not this time.

The impetus that had driven her most of the week

dried up late Friday night. Alan was still lodged in
her mind. He shouldn't have been. Shelby could tell
herself that as impatiently as she liked, but it didn't
change the fact that he was as firmly in her thoughts
as he had been when they'd last been together.

It hadn't mattered that she'd managed to keep the
rest of the evening at the Ditmeyers' casual. Alan had
still stopped her in her tracks with one of those slow,
devastating kisses at her side door. He hadn't insisted
on coming in. Shelby might have been grateful for
that if she hadn't suspected it was just part of his
planned siege. Confuse the enemy, assail her with
doubts, leave her with her nerve ends tingling. Very
clever strategy.

He'd been in Boston for several days—Shelby
knew because he'd called to tell her he was going,
though she'd given him no encouragement. She told
herself it was a respite. If he was a few hundred miles
away, he couldn't be popping up on her doorstep unexpectedly. She told herself when and if he popped
up again, she'd keep the door locked. She wanted
badly to believe she could.

Then halfway through the week the pig had
come—a big lavender stuffed pig with a foolish grin
and velvet ears. Shelby had tried to toss it into a closet
and forget it. He seemed to know that the way to get
to her was through her sense of the ridiculous. She
hadn't thought he had one—he shouldn't have, but
there it was. What was a man who had such stuffy,
straight-line views on rules and order doing buying
stuffed animals anyway? She'd nearly softened. It
was nice to know he was capable of such a gesture,
particularly since it was so out of character. It was

nice to know that she was the one who brought out that side of him. But… There was no way Alan was going to weaken her resolve with a silly toy that was meant for children or softheaded women.

She called it MacGregor and kept it on her bed—a joke on both of them, she thought. The pig was the only MacGregor she was going to sleep with.

But she dreamed of him. At night, in her big brass bed, no matter how hard she had worked, no matter how many friends she had been with, it always came back to Alan. Once she imagined there were a dozen of him, surrounding her town house. She couldn't go out without being captured; she couldn't stay in without going mad. She woke cursing him and his sieges and her own fertile imagination.

By the end of the week, Shelby promised herself she wouldn't accept any more deliveries and would simply hang up when she heard Alan's voice on the phone. If reason and patience hadn't gotten through to him, downright rudeness would. Even a Mac-Gregor had to have some common sense.

Because of the schedule she'd put herself on the week before, Shelby had given Kyle the keys to the shop with instructions that he open up at ten on Saturday. She was sleeping in. There wasn't any need to go into her workroom, even if some of the creative juices had still been flowing. In the past few days, she had accumulated enough inventory to last for weeks. Now she would put as much thought and energy into being lazy as she had put into slaving.

Shelby heard the knock on the door, and shifting under the sheets, considered ignoring it. Still half-asleep, she tumbled out of bed. It simply wasn't in her makeup to let a ringing phone or a knock go unanswered. Because she tripped over the robe she'd thrown on the floor the night before, Shelby remembered to tug it on as she walked from the room. With her eyes narrowed protectively against the sunlight, she opened the door.

"'Morning, Miss Campbell. Another delivery."

The boy who had brought her both the strawberries and the pig stood in the doorway and grinned.

"Thanks." Too disoriented to remember her vow, Shelby reached out. He handed her the bound-together strings of two-dozen pink and yellow balloons. He was gone and Shelby was back inside before she woke up enough to realize what had happened. "Oh, no." Looking up, she watched the balloons dance at the tops of their strings. Hanging by a ribbon at the end was a little white card.

She wouldn't even open it, she told herself. She knew who they were from anyway. Who else? No, she wasn't going to open it. In fact, she was going to find a pin and pop every last balloon. What were they but a bunch of hot air? It was ridiculous. To prove a point, Shelby let the strings go so the balloons drifted up to the ceiling. If he thought he was going to win her over with silly presents and clever little notes...he was absolutely right, dammit.

Shelby jumped up, swearing when she missed the strings by inches. Hauling over a chair, she climbed into it and grabbed the card.

The yellow's for sunshine, the pink's for spring. Share them with me.

Alan

"You drive me crazy," she muttered, standing in the chair with the balloons in one hand and the card in the other. How did he know, how *could* he know just the sort of thing that would get to her? Strawberries and pigs and balloons—it was hopeless. Shelby stared up at them, wishing she didn't need to smile.

It was time to be firm—very, very firm, she told herself as she stepped down. If she ignored it, he'd just send her something else. So, she'd call him and tell him—no, she'd *demand* that he stop. She'd say he was annoying—no, *boring* her. Boring was unforgivably insulting. Shelby twisted the balloon strings around her wrist as she reached for the phone. He'd given her his home number, which she'd refused to write down. Of course, she remembered every digit. As she pushed buttons Shelby worked herself into her haughtiest mood.

"Hello."

Her mood deflated as if she'd been pricked with a pin. "Alan."

"Shelby."

She struggled not to be moved by the quiet, serious tone that should never have moved her. She liked men with a laugh in their voice. "Alan, this has to stop."

"Does is? It hasn't even started."

"Alan—" She tried to remember her decision to be firm. "I mean it. You have to stop sending me things; you're only wasting your time."

"I have a bit to spare," he said mildly. "How was your week?"

"Busy. Listen, I—"

"I missed you."

The simple statement threw the rest of her lecture into oblivion. "Alan, don't—"

"Every day," he continued. "Every night. Have you been to Boston, Shelby?"

"Uh…yes," she managed, busy fighting off the weakness creeping into her. Helplessly she stared up at the balloons. How could she fight something so insubstantial it floated?

"I'd like to take you there in the fall, when it smells of damp leaves and smoke."

Shelby told herself her heart was not fluttering. "Alan, I didn't call to talk about Boston. Now, to put it in very simple terms, I want you to stop calling me, I want you to stop dropping by, and—" Her voice began to rise in frustration as she pictured him listening with that patient, serious smile and calm eyes. "I want you to stop sending me balloons and pigs and everything! Is that clear?"

"Perfectly. Spend the day with me."

Did the man never stop being patient? She couldn't abide patient men. "For God's sake, Alan!"

"We'll call it an experimental outing," he suggested in the same even tone. "Not a date."

"No!" she said, barely choking back a laugh. Couldn't abide it, she tried to remember. She preferred the flashy, the freewheeling. "No, no, no!"

"Not bureaucratic enough." His voice was so calm, so…so *senatorial*, she decided, she wanted to scream. But the scream bubbled perilously close to another laugh. "All right, let me think—a standard daytime expedition for furthering amiable relations between opposing clans."

"You're trying to be charming again," Shelby muttered.

"Am I succeeding?"

Some questions were best ignored. "I really don't know how to be more succinct, Alan."

Was that part of the appeal? he wondered. The fact that the free-spirited Gypsy could turn into the regal duchess in the blink of an eye. He doubted she had any notion she was as much one as the other. "You have a wonderful speaking voice. What time will you be ready?"

Shelby huffed and frowned and considered. "*If* I agree to spend some time with you today, will you stop sending me things?"

Alan was silent for a long moment. "Are you going to take a politician's word?"

Now she had to laugh. "All right, you've boxed me in on that one."

"It's a beautiful day, Shelby. I haven't had a free Saturday in over a month. Come out with me."

She twined the phone cord around her finger. A refusal seemed so petty, so bad-natured. He was really asking her for very little, and—dammit—she wanted to see him. "All right, Alan, every rule needs to be bent a bit now and again to prove it's really a rule after all."

"If you say so. Where would you like to go? There's an exhibition of Flemish art at the National Gallery."

Shelby's lips curved. "The zoo," she said and waited for his reaction.

"Fine," Alan agreed without missing a beat. "I'll be there in ten minutes."

With a sigh, Shelby decided he just wasn't an easy man to shake. "Alan, I'm not dressed."

"I'll be there in five."

On a burst of laughter, she slammed down the phone.

"I like the snakes. They're so slimily arrogant."

While Alan watched, Shelby pressed close to the glass to study a boa who looked more bored than disdainful. When she had suggested the zoo, he hadn't been certain if she had done so because she wanted to go or had wanted to see how he would react. It didn't take a great deal of thought to discern it had been a combination of both.

A visit to the National Zoo on a sunny spring Saturday promised crowds and hordes of children. The Snake House was packed, echoing with squeals. Shelby didn't seem to mind the elbow-to-elbow proposition as she maneuvered her way to a fat python.

"Looks like our representative from Nebraska."

A giggle bubbled up in Shelby's throat as she pictured the thick-necked, squinty-eyed congressman. Pleased with Alan's observation, she twisted her head to grin at him. Another inch and their lips would have made contact. She could have backed away, even though it meant stepping on a few toes. She could have simply turned her head back to the python. Instead Shelby tilted her chin so that their eyes stayed in a direct line.

What was there about him that made her want to tempt fate? she wondered. For surely that's what she would be doing if she allowed the afternoon to amount to any more than a friendly outing. He wasn't a man a woman could disentangle herself from easily, after she'd taken that last step. A man like him could quietly dominate and methodically absorb the people around him before they had any idea what was happening. For that reason alone she would have been wary of him, treating him with more caution than her other male companions. But she couldn't forget who he was—an up-and-coming young senator whose future all but demanded a bid for the top office.

No, to prevent pain on both sides, she'd keep it light. No matter how much she wanted him.

"It's crowded," she murmured as her eyes laughed into his.

"The longer we're in here…" His thighs brushed against hers as a toddler wiggled up to the glass. "The fonder I am of snakes."

"Yeah, they get to me too. It's the basic aura of evil that's so appealing." Her breasts pressed into his chest as people crowded in on all sides.

"The original sin," Alan murmured, easily catching her scent over the mingling aroma of humanity. "The serpent tempted Eve, and Eve tempted Adam."

"I've always thought Adam got off too lightly in that business," Shelby commented. Her heartbeat was fast, and not altogether steady against his, but she didn't back away. She was going to have to experience this before she understood how to prevent it. "Snakes and women took the real heat, and man came off as an innocent bystander."

"Or a creature who could rarely resist temptation in the form of a woman."

His voice had become entirely too soft. Considering it a strategic retreat, Shelby grabbed his hand and drew him away. "Let's go outside and look at the elephants."

Shelby wound her way through the people, skirting around babies in strollers as she pulled Alan outside. He would've strolled. She would always race. In the sunshine, she pushed a pair of oversize tinted glasses on her nose without slacking pace.

The aroma of animal drifted everywhere, pungent and primitive, on the breeze. You could hear them—the occasional roar, screech, or bellow. She darted along the paths, stopping at a cage, leaning against a retaining wall, taking it all in as though it were her first time. Around them were families, couples old and young, and children with dripping ice cream cones. A babble of languages flowed from both in front and behind the cages.

"There, he reminds me of you." Shelby indicated a black panther stretched in a path of sunlight, calmly watching the river of people who passed by.

"Is that so?" Alan studied the cat. "Indolent? Subdued?"

Shelby let out her smoke-edged laugh. "Oh, no, Senator. Patient, brooding. And arrogant enough to believe this confinement is nothing he can't work with." Turning, she leaned back against the barrier to consider Alan as she had considered the panther. "He's taken stock of the situation, and decided he can pretty much have his own way as things are. I wonder..." Her brows drew together in concentration. "I wonder just what he'd do if he were really crossed. He doesn't appear to have a temper. Cats usually don't until they're pushed too far just that one time, and then—they're deadly."

Alan gave her an odd smile before he took her hand to draw her toward the path again. "He normally sees that he's not often crossed."

Shelby tossed her head and met the smile with a bland look. "Let's go look at the monkeys. It always makes me think I'm sitting in the Senate Gallery."

"Nasty," he commented and tugged on her hair.

"I know. I couldn't help it." Briefly she rested her head on his shoulder as they walked. "I'm often not a nice person. Grant and I both seem to have inherited a streak of sarcasm—or maybe it's cynicism. Probably from my grandfather on my father's side. *He's* like one of those grizzlies we looked at. Prowling, pacing, bad-tempered."

"And you're crazy about him."

"Yeah. I'll buy you some popcorn." In a swift change of mood, she motioned toward a vendor. "You can't wander around the zoo all day without popcorn. That's second only to sitting through a double feature without some. The big one," she told the vendor as she dug a bill from the back pocket of her jeans. Shelby cradled the bucket in one arm as she stuffed the change back in her pocket. "Alan..." Changing her mind, Shelby shook her head and began to walk again.

"What?" Casually Alan reached across her for some popcorn.

"I was going to make a confession. Then I remembered I don't make them very well. We still need to see the monkeys."

"You don't really think I'm going to let a provocative statement like that slip by, do you?"

"Well...I thought the best way to discourage you

was to agree to go out with you—to some place like this, which I thought would bore you to distraction—then be as obnoxious as possible.''

''Have you been obnoxious?'' His tone was mild and entirely too serious. ''I thought you've been behaving very naturally.''

''Ouch.'' Shelby rubbed at the figurative wound under her heart. ''In any case, I get the distinct impression that I haven't discouraged you at all.''

''Really?'' Reaching for more popcorn, he leaned close and spoke gently in her ear. ''How did you come by that?''

''Oh—'' She cleared her throat. ''Just a hunch.''

He found that tiny show of nerves very rewarding. Yes, the puzzle was coming together, piece by careful piece. It was the way he'd always structured his life. ''Odd. And not once since we've been here have I mentioned that I'd like to find a small, dim room and make love to you, over and over.''

Warily Shelby slid her eyes to his. ''I'd just as soon you didn't.''

''All right.'' Alan slipped an arm around her waist. ''I won't mention it while we're here.''

A smile tugged at her mouth, but she shook her head. ''It's not going to come to that, Alan. It can't.''

''We have a fundamental disagreement.'' He paused on a bridge. Beneath them, swans floated haughtily. ''Because to my way of thinking it has to.''

''You don't understand me.'' Shelby turned away to watch the birds on the water because his eyes were tripping some tiny little release she hadn't even been aware was inside her. ''Once I've made up my mind, I'm rock hard.''

"We've more than ancestry in common." He watched the sunlight add more heat to the flames of her hair. Touching it, lightly, fingertips only, Alan wondered how it would look after they'd made love. Wild strands of fire. "I wanted you from the minute I saw you, Shelby. I want you more with every minute that passes."

She turned her head at that, surprised and unwillingly excited. It hadn't been an empty phrase or cliché. Alan MacGregor said precisely what he meant.

"And when I want something that immediately and that badly," he murmured while his fingertips strayed to her jawline, "I don't walk away from it."

Her lips parted as his thumb brushed over them. She couldn't prevent it, or the lightning-flash thrill of desire. "So—" Striving to be casual, Shelby dug out some more popcorn before she set the bucket on a bench. "You put your energies into convincing me that I want you."

He smiled. Slowly, irresistibly, he circled her neck with his fingers. "I don't have to convince you of that. What I have to convince you of," he began as he drew her closer, "is that the stand you're taking is unproductive, self-defeating, and hopeless."

She found herself weakening, wanting to be convinced. His lips hovered just above hers. Yet he was careful; even focused on her own vulnerabilities. She understood that. He'd always been circumspect in public. She'd always be careless. It annoyed her. It intrigued her too.

His eyes, so serious, so calm, seemed to cut through every logical defense she could—or would—have thrown between them. Before she could make a move toward or away, something tugged impatiently at her T-shirt.

Confused, Shelby glanced down and saw a small Oriental boy of around eight staring up at her. He began a rapid, musical spiel, complete with gestures and eye-rolling. Shelby understood the frustration if not the content.

"Slow down," she ordered, grinning as she slipped from Alan's hold to crouch in front of him. Her first thought was that he'd lost his parents. His eyes were dark and beautiful, but they were annoyed rather than frightened. Again he went off into a peal of what she suspected was Korean, then with a very adult sigh, he held up two nickels, indicating the bird feed dispenser behind him.

Ten cents, Shelby realized on a chuckle. He had the right amount but didn't understand the coinage. Before she could reach in her pocket, Alan held out a dime. Solemnly he went through a few simple gestures, showing that the two nickels put together made one dime. He saw the boy's eyes brighten with understanding before he plucked the dime out of Alan's hand and offered the two nickels. Alan's initial inclination to refuse the money altered quickly with a scan of the boy's face. Instead he accepted them, giving a slight bow. The boy gave another quick burst of Korean, returned Alan's bow, then dashed back to the dispenser.

Another man, Shelby thought as she watched the child hurl the feed to the swans, would have insisted on being magnanimous—if for no other reason than to impress the woman he was with. But Alan had understood that children have pride. He'd made the exchange of two nickels for a dime into a man-to-man business transaction instead of an adult-to-child bit of whimsy. And all without a word.

Leaning on the rail, she watched the swans race after feed, bending those slender necks, then gobbling greedily. Now and again one would honk and peck at another who edged into its territory. Alan's hands rested on the rail on either side of her. Forgetting everything but the moment, Shelby leaned back against him, letting her head find that comfortably intimate spot between his jaw and shoulder.

"It's a beautiful afternoon," she murmured.

Alan laid his hands over hers where they rested lightly. "The last time I was at the zoo, I was around twelve. My father had made one of his rare business trips to New York and insisted we go en masse." He brushed his cheek against her hair, enjoying the soft, intimate feel of it. "I felt obliged to pretend I was too old to enjoy looking at lions and tigers, yet my father had the best time of all. It's strange, that little patch of adulthood we go through when we're very young."

"Mine lasted about six months," Shelby remembered. His, she knew, would never have completely dissipated. "That's about how long I called my mother by her first name."

"How old were you?"

"Thirteen. 'Deborah,' I would say in the cultured tones I was affecting at the time, 'I believe I'm quite old enough to have blonde streaks in my hair.' She'd say something about our discussing it very soon. Then she'd go on about how proud she was that I was mature enough to make adult decisions—how relieved she was that I wasn't spoiled or frivolous like so many girls my age."

"And naturally you basked in that and forgot the streaks."

"Naturally." With a laugh, Shelby hooked her arm through his and began to walk again. "I don't think I appreciated just how clever she was until I was over twenty. Grant and I weren't easy children."

"Is he like you?"

"Grant? Like me?" Shelby pondered it a moment. "In some ways, but he's a loner. I've never been. When Grant's with people, he observes—absorbs, really. He tucks them all away and takes them out again as he chooses. He can do without them for weeks or months at a time. I can't."

"No, but you still take them out again as you choose. And I don't think you've ever let anyone— any man at any rate," he corrected, tilting his head to study her profile, "get too close."

Shelby flirted with an angry retort and decided on a subtler one. "That sounds like your ego talking," she said mildly. "Just because I turned you down."

"Put me off," Alan countered as he brought her hand to his lips. "One might point out that you are here, and so am I."

"Mmm." Shelby glanced around at the flood of people as a wailing baby was carried past by a frustrated parent. "And in such intimate surroundings too."

"We're both used to crowds."

On an impulse of mischief, she stopped in the center of the path to twine her arms around his neck. "In a manner of speaking, Senator."

She expected him to laugh and pull her along again or perhaps to give an exasperated shake of his head before he disentangled himself. What she didn't expect was for him to hold her there, his lips close, hinting of promise. His eyes were level with hers, telling her very clearly where the promise would lead. There was a threat of passion, a promise of intimacy. No, she hadn't expected him to turn her own ploy against her so successfully. Perhaps for a moment Shelby had forgotten he was a man of fundamental strategies.

Against his, her heart began to thud lightly. Though the moment was brief, it touched her in every way— heart and mind and body. She couldn't hold back the regret for what she felt could never be—but she hadn't known it would be so sharp. When she drew away, it echoed in her voice and mirrored in her eyes.

"I think we'd better head back."

He ached and nearly swore from the frustration of it. "It's too damn late for that," he muttered as he steered her in the direction of the parking lot.

Shelby lifted a brow at the tone. Annoyance—it was the first time she'd heard it from him. She thought she'd caught a flicker or two in his eyes before, but it had been so quickly banked she couldn't be sure. Well then, she mused, perhaps that was the key. She would annoy him enough that he would go away.

Her skin was still warm—too warm and too tender. At the rate she was weakening, she would find herself involved with him whether she wanted it or not. Perhaps the real problem was she already was involved. The fact that they weren't lovers didn't stop him from drawing on her thoughts and her feelings. A successful break was going to hurt, but it would hurt less if it was quick and soon.

So, she would have to get under his skin. Shelby gave a smile that was more of a grimace as she stepped into his car. If there was one thing she could do well when she put her mind to it, it was to get under someone's skin.

"Well, that was fun," she said lightly as he maneuvered out of the lot. "I'm really glad you talked me into going out. My day was a blank page until seven."

That long, quiet moment lingered in his mind even as it lingered in Shelby's. Alan shifted, hoping to ease the thudding in the pit of his stomach. "Always happy to help someone fill in a few empty spaces." Alan controlled the speed of the car through force of will. Holding her hadn't soothed him but rather had only served to remind him how much time had passed since he had last held her.

"Actually you're an easy man to be with, Alan, for a politician." *Easy?* Shelby repeated to herself as she pressed the button to lower her window. Her blood was still throbbing from a meeting of eyes that had lasted less than ten seconds. If he was any *easier,* she'd be head over heels in love with him and headed for disaster. "I mean, you're not really pompous."

He shot her a look, long and cool, that boosted her confidence. "No?" he murmured after a humming silence.

"Hardly at all." Shelby sent him a smile. "Why, I'd probably vote for you myself."

Alan paused at a red light, studying it thoughtfully

before he turned to her. "Your insults aren't as subtle today, Shelby."

"Insults?" She gave him a bland stare. "Odd, I thought it was more flattery. Isn't a vote what it all comes down to? Votes, and that all-encompassing need to win."

The light stayed green for five full seconds before he cruised through it. "Be careful."

A nerve, she thought, hating herself more than a little. "You're a little touchy. That's all right." She brushed at the thigh of her jeans. "I don't mind a little oversensitivity."

"The subject of my sensitivity isn't the issue, but you're succeeding in being obnoxious."

"My, my, aren't we all Capitol Hill all of a sudden." Deliberately she looked at her watch as he pulled into the alleyway next to her building. "That was good timing. I'll have a chance to take a bath and a change before I go out." Shelby leaned over to give him a careless kiss on the cheek before she slipped from the car. "Thanks, Alan. *Ciao.*"

Despising herself, Shelby made it all the way to the top landing before he caught her arm. She fixed a mildly surprised expression on her face before she turned her head.

"What the hell is this all about?" he demanded. There was enough pressure on her arm to make her turn fully around.

"What the hell is all what about?"

"Don't play games, Shelby."

She sighed sharply, as if bored. "It was a nice afternoon, a...change of pace for both of us, I imagine." She unlocked her apartment door.

Alan tightened his grip fractionally to prevent her from slipping inside. Temper—he never, or rarely, gave in to it. It was a by-product of his heritage, the stock-in-trade of his family, but he'd always been the controlled one. The clearheaded one. He fought to remember it. "And?"

"And?" Shelby repeated, lifting both brows. "There is no *and,* Alan. We spent a couple of hours at the zoo, had a few laughs. That certainly doesn't mean I'm required to sleep with you."

She saw the anger, volatile and fierce, sweep into his eyes. A bit stunned at the strength of it, Shelby took an automatic step back. Her throat went dry instantly. Had that been sleeping in there the whole time? she wondered.

"Do you think that's all I want?" he asked in a deadly voice as he backed her into the door. "If I only wanted you in bed, you'd have been there." His hand came up to circle her throat as she stared at the livid fury on his face.

"There's the matter of what I want," she managed, surprised that her voice was thready and breathless. Was it fear? she asked herself swiftly. Or was it excitement?

"The hell with what you want."

When he took a step closer, Shelby pressed back so the door gave way. She would have stumbled if he hadn't been quick enough to grab her. Then they were just inside, with her body crushed close against his, her hands on his shoulders, for once indecisive.

She tossed back her head, furious that her knees had liquefied with fear while her blood pumped hard and fast with pure desire. "Alan, you can't—"

"Can't?" His hand was in her hair, dragging her head back further. It poured into him fluidly—anger, resentment, passion. He'd never felt all at once. "I can. We both know I can now, and could have before." And I should have, he told himself as fury and frustration took over. "You want me right now; I can see it."

She shook her head but couldn't dislodge his hand. How could she have forgotten the panther so soon? "No, I don't."

"Do you think you can take shots at what I do, at what I am, with impunity, Shelby?" The arm around her waist tightened so that she struggled not to gasp. "Do you think you can push me so far and not pay any price?"

She swallowed, but her throat stayed dry. "You're acting as though I've encouraged you when I've done precisely the opposite," she told him in what almost succeeded in being a mildly annoyed tone. "Let me go, Alan."

"When I'm ready."

His mouth came down toward hers. Shelby sucked in her breath—whether in protest or anticipation, she wasn't sure. But he stopped, just short of contact so she was trembling. All she could see in his eyes was fury, and her own reflection. Yes, she'd forgotten the panther, and that wicked, seething temper of the Brontë heroes he'd first reminded her of.

"Do you think you're what I want? What I can rationally, easily, say I want? You're everything but what suits me. You flout everything that's vital to my life."

That hurt. Though it was precisely what she'd set

out to do, it hurt that he could say it. "I'm exactly what I am," she tossed back. "Exactly what I want to be. Why don't you leave me alone and go find one of those cool blondes who look so perfect in an Oscar de la Renta? They're tailor-made for a senator's companion. I don't want any part of it."

"Maybe not." The anger was building. He'd never felt anything build so quickly. "Maybe not. But tell me—" His grip tightened. "Tell me you don't want me."

Her breath came quickly; short pants that couldn't seem to fill her lungs. She wasn't even aware that her fingers had dug into his shoulders or that her tongue, in a swift, nervous movement, darted out to moisten her lips. Shelby had always known there was a time and a place for lies.

"I don't want you."

But the denial ended on a moan of shivering excitement as his mouth captured hers. This wasn't the patient, endless seduction of a kiss he'd first treated her to, but its antithesis. Hard, ruthless, his lips dominated hers as no one's had ever done. As no man had ever dared. Then she was spinning, and groping for the guideposts that were no longer there.

She could taste his anger and met it with a helpless passion that built too quickly to be controlled. She could feel his fury and met it with a fire that flamed too high to be banked. There was no sharp stab of regret. She was where she wanted to be. The fingers that gripped his shoulders urged him to demand more, and as he demanded, she took.

Alan twisted her closer, forgetting the gentleness that had always been an innate part of his lovemaking.

Her mouth was wild under his, greedy for possession. But this time he wasn't content with it. His hand snaked under her shirt to find her.

So slim, so soft, yet her heart pounded under his roaming palm with the strength of a marathon runner's. She strained against him, moaning what might have been his name. Her taste was as wild and free as her scent, inciting the urgency to drum in him until it was a pounding. He could take her—on the floor or where they stood—in seconds or in an hour. Just knowing it sent an agony of desire rocketing through him. This was no yielding, but rather passion to passion, fire to fire. He'd never subdue her, but he could have her.

And if he took her now, though she was willing, he risked having nothing when it was done. He risked making that careless, cutting remark of hers no less than the truth.

On an oath uncharacteristically savage, Alan yanked her away. His eyes, when they met hers, were no less angry than they had been, and no less hard. The look held in silence but for the sound of unsteady breathing. Without a word, he turned and strode through the open door.

Chapter Five

She tried not to think about it. Shelby flipped through the magazine section of the Sunday paper with her feet propped up and her second cup of coffee still steaming and really tried not to think about it. Moshe sprawled across the back of the sofa as if he were reading over her shoulder, his nose occasionally twitching from the scent of her coffee. Shelby sipped and skimmed an article on French cooking on a budget.

She couldn't help but think about it.

It had been entirely her fault; she couldn't deny it. Being rude and nasty wasn't something she set out to do often, but she'd done a good job of it. Hurting someone else was something she usually did only in the blind heat of rage. But she couldn't deny there'd been hurt as well as anger in Alan's eyes. Even though her purpose had been self-preservation, Shelby was having a difficult time forgiving herself.

Do you think you're what I want?

No. Shelby sat back, cupping her mug in both hands. No, she'd known right from the start that she hadn't suited him, his image, any more than he'd suited hers. Yet she'd sensed something about him, and herself, that first evening on the Writes' terrace. They'd seen too much in each other too quickly. Something had been nudging at the back of her mind even then. *He could be the one.* Silly fancies for a woman who'd never considered she'd wanted anyone to be *the one,* but she hadn't been able to shake it off.

She wondered if she'd shaken Alan off. Certainly she'd deserved his fury and the icy temper in his eyes when he'd walked back through her doorway. She had the power to bring that out in him. It was frightening and somehow…yes, somehow seducing. But she could turn vicious with it; that was something else. The viciousness came again from self-preservation when she sensed his power over her was too strong. So, perhaps she'd also deserved, though it was no easier to live with today, the aching and the wanting he'd left her with.

She circled her tongue over her lips, remembering. There were two sides of Alan MacGregor, she mused. The even-tempered and reasonable, and the hard and the ruthless. It only made him more appealing. More dangerous, she added grimly.

Setting aside the mug, Shelby snapped the paper into place and tried to concentrate. After all, she'd pushed him away, just as she'd set out to do. There was no use feeling miserable about it. In almost the same breath, she tossed the paper aside and leapt up to pace. She wasn't going to call and apologize. It would only complicate things.

Still, if she made it clear it was a formal apology and nothing more… No, that wasn't smart, she reminded herself with a shake of the head. Worse, it was weak and wishy-washy. She'd made her decision. Shelby had always prided herself on knowing her own mind and sticking to it.

Her gaze alighted on the balloons jumbled on her kitchen table. They'd lost the power to hang high in the air, and lay comfortably now, like a reminder of a happy celebration. Her breath came out in a sigh. She should have popped them and tossed out the corpses. Shelby ran a finger down a squishy yellow sphere. It was too late now.

If she called and absolutely refused to get involved in a conversation—just an apology and nothing more. Three minutes. Shelby gnawed on her lip and wondered if she could find her egg timer. Her conscience would be clear in a few polite sentences. What could happen in three minutes over the phone? She glanced down at the balloons again. A lot, she remembered. It had been a phone call that had started the whole mess the day before.

Even as she stood, irresolute, someone knocked at the door. She glanced over quickly, anticipation shimmering. Before the knock could sound twice, she was jerking the door open.

"I was just— Oh, hello, Mama."

"I'm sorry I'm not who you were hoping for." Deborah gave Shelby a quick peck on the cheek before she strolled inside.

"It's better that you weren't," Shelby murmured

as she closed the door. "Well, I'll get you some coffee," she said with a flash of a smile. "It's not often you drop in on a Sunday morning."

"You can make it a half a cup if you're expecting someone."

"I'm not." Shelby's tone was flat and final.

Deborah pondered her daughter's back a moment, speculating. With a rueful shake of her head, she wondered why she bothered. She hadn't been able to outguess Shelby in over ten years. "If you're not doing anything this afternoon, perhaps you'd like to go with me to see that new exhibit of Flemish art at the National Gallery."

Shelby swore ripely, then stuck her thumb knuckle into her mouth.

"Oh, did you burn yourself. Let me—"

"It's nothing," Shelby said too sharply and swore again. "I'm sorry," she managed in a calmer voice. "I just spilled a little on me, that's all. Sit down, Mama." In an almost violent gesture, she swept the balloons off the table and onto the floor.

"Well, that hasn't changed," Deborah observed mildly. "You still have your own way of tidying up." She waited until Shelby sat across from her. "Is something wrong?"

"Wrong?" Shelby nursed her thumb a moment longer. "No, why?"

"You're rarely jumpy." Stirring her coffee, Deborah leveled one of her long, steady stares. "Have you seen the paper this morning?"

"Of course." Shelby folded her legs under her. "I wouldn't miss Grant's Sunday edition."

"No, I didn't mean that."

Vaguely interested, Shelby lifted her brows. "I glanced at the front page and didn't see anything I wanted to dip into too deeply first thing in the morning. Did I miss something?"

"Apparently." Without another word, Deborah rose and went over to the sofa. She ruffled through the disorder of Shelby's paper until she found the section she wanted. There was a half-smile on her lips as she walked over to drop the paper, faceup, in front of her daughter. Shelby looked down and said nothing.

There was a well-framed, very clear picture of her and Alan as they stood on the bridge overlooking the swans. Shelby remembered the moment: she had leaned back against him, resting her head between his shoulder and jaw. The photograph had captured that instant and a look of quiet contentment on her face that she wasn't certain had ever been there before.

The column beneath it was brief, giving her name and age, a mention of her father, and a quick plug for her shop. It also touched on Alan's campaign on housing for the homeless before it drifted into speculation on their relationship. There was nothing offensive in the short, chatty little slice of Washington gossip. She was surprised by a sharp stab of resentment as she scanned the story.

She'd been right, Shelby told herself as her gaze skimmed back to the picture. The eighth of a page proved that she'd been right from the beginning. Politics, in all its aspects, would always be between them. They'd had their afternoon as ordinary people, but it hadn't lasted. It never would.

Deliberately Shelby pushed the paper aside before

she picked up her coffee. ''Well, I wouldn't be surprised if I had quite a crowd on Monday morning thanks to this. I had a woman drive down from Baltimore last winter after she'd seen a picture of me with Myra's nephew.'' She made herself sip, aware that she was dangerously close to rambling. ''It's a good thing I went on a binge last week and stocked the back room. Do you want a doughnut to go with that coffee? I think I might have one somewhere.''

''Shelby.'' Deborah laid both her hands on her daughter's before Shelby could rise. The half-smile had been replaced by a look of concern. ''I've never known you to mind this kind of publicity. That's Grant's phobia, not yours.''

''Why should I mind?'' Shelby countered, struggling to keep her fingers from curling into fists. ''If anything, it should bring me a few sales. Some enterprising tourist recognized Alan and cashed in, that's all. It's harmless.''

''Yes.'' With a slow nod, Deborah soothed the agitated hands beneath hers. ''It is.''

''No, it's not!'' Shelby retorted with sudden passion. ''It's not harmless, none of it.'' She sprang up from the table to whirl around the room as Deborah had seen her do countless times before. ''I can't cope with it. I *won't* cope with it.'' She kicked at a sneaker that got in her way. ''Why the hell couldn't he be a nuclear physicist or own bowling alleys? Why does he have to look at me as if he's known me all my life and doesn't mind all the flaws? I don't want him to pull at me this way. I won't have it!'' On a final burst of rage, she swooped the scattered sections of the paper from the sofa to the floor.

"It doesn't matter." Shelby stopped, dragging a hand through her hair as she leveled her breathing. "It doesn't matter," she repeated. "I've made up my mind in any case, so..." Shaking her head, she walked back to the stove to fetch the coffeepot. "Shall I heat that up for you?"

Too used to Shelby to be confused by the outburst, Deborah nodded. "Just a touch. What have you made up your mind about, Shelby?"

"That I'm not going to get involved with him." After replacing the pot, Shelby came back to sit down. "Why don't we have lunch in the Gallery cafeteria?"

"All right." Deborah sipped her coffee. "Did you have a good time at the zoo?"

Shelby shrugged and stared into her mug. "It was a nice day." She brought the mug to her lips, then set it aside without drinking.

Deborah glanced down at the picture again. When was the last time she'd seen Shelby look serene? Had she ever? Oh, perhaps, she mused with a quick, almost forgotten pang, when a little girl had sat with her father sharing some private thought. Deborah held back a sigh and feigned an interest in her coffee.

"I suppose you've made your position clear to Senator MacGregor."

"I told Alan right from the start that I wouldn't even date him."

"You came with him to the Ditmeyers' last week."

"That was different." She toyed restlessly with the edges of the paper. "And yesterday was just a lapse."

"He's not your father, Shelby."

Gray eyes lifted, so unexpectedly tormented that

Deborah reached for her hand again. "He's so much like him," Shelby whispered. "It's frightening. The tranquillity, the dedication, that spark that tells you he's going to reach for the top and probably get it, unless..." She broke off and shut her eyes. Unless some maniac with an obscure cause and a gun stopped him. "Oh, God, I think I'm falling in love with him, and I want to run."

Deborah tightened her grip. "Where?"

"Anywhere." Taking a long, steadying breath, Shelby opened her eyes. "I don't want to fall in love with him for dozens of reasons. We're nothing alike, he and I."

For the first time since she had handed Shelby the paper, Deborah smiled. "Should you be?"

"Don't confuse me when I'm trying to be logical." Settling a bit, Shelby smiled back. "Mama, I'd drive the man crazy in a week. I could never ask him to acclimate to my sort of life. I'd never be able to acclimate to his. You only need to talk with him for a few minutes to see that he has an ordered mind, the kind that works like a superior chess game. He'd be accustomed to having his meals at certain times, knowing precisely what shirts he'd sent to be laundered."

"Darling, even you must realize how foolish that sounds."

"By itself, maybe it would." Her gaze drifted to the balloons that lay on the floor. "But when you add in everything else."

"By everything else, you meant the fact that he's a politician. Shelby..." Deborah waited until her daughter's eyes met hers. "You can't special-order the kind of man you fall in love with."

"I'm not going to fall in love with him." Her face settled into stubborn lines. "I like my life just as it is. No one's going to make me change it before I'm ready. Come on." She was up and moving again. "We'll go look at your Flemish art, then I'll treat you to lunch."

Deborah watched as Shelby dashed around the apartment looking for shoes. No, she didn't wish her daughter pain, Deborah thought again, but she knew it was coming. Shelby would have to deal with it.

Alan sat behind the huge antique desk in his study with the window open at his back. He could just smell the lilacs blooming on the bush in the little patch of yard outside. He remembered there had been the scent of lilacs the first evening he'd met Shelby. But he wouldn't think of her now.

Spread out on his desk were responses and information on the volunteer shelters he was campaigning for. He had a meeting with the mayor of Washington the following day and could only hope it went as well as his discussion with the mayor of Boston had. He had the facts—his staff had been working on compiling the information he needed for weeks. He had the pictures in front of him. Alan lifted one of two men sharing the tatters of a blanket in a doorway near 14th and Belmont. It wasn't just sad, it was inexcusable. Shelter was the first basic need.

It was one thing to concentrate on the causes—unemployment, recession, the bugs in the welfare system—and another to watch people live without the most elemental needs met while the wheels of social reform slowly turned. His idea was to provide the needs—shelter, food, clothing—in return for labor and time. No free rides, no sting of charity.

But he needed funds—and just as important—he needed volunteers. He'd put things in motion in Boston after a long, at times frustrating, battle, but it was too soon to show substantial results. He was going to have to depend on the information compiled by his staff and his own powers of persuasion. If he could add the mayor's influence, Alan thought he might just be able to wrangle the federal funds he wanted. Eventually.

Stacking the papers, Alan slipped them inside his briefcase. There was nothing more he could do until the following day. And he was expecting a visitor—he checked his watch—in ten minutes. Alan leaned back in the comfortably worn leather chair and allowed his mind to empty.

He'd always been able to relax in this room. The paneling was dark and gleaming, the ceiling high. In the winter, he kept a low fire going in the rosy marble fireplace. Lining the mantel were pictures in the odd-shaped antique frames he collected. His family—from tintypes of his great-grandparents who'd never stepped off Scottish soil, to snapshots of his brother and sister. He'd be adding one of his niece or nephew when his sister, Rena, had the baby.

Alan glanced up at the picture of an elegant fair-haired woman with laughing eyes and a stubborn mouth. Strange how many shades hair came in, he mused. Rena's hair was nothing like Shelby's. Shelby's was all undisciplined curls of fire and flame.

Undisciplined. The word suited her—and attracted him despite his better judgment. Handling her would be a lifelong challenge. Having her would be a constant surprise. Strange that a man who'd always preferred the well-ordered and logical would now know his life wouldn't be complete without disruption.

He glanced around the room—walls of books, meticulously filed and stacked, a pale-gray carpet that showed signs of wear but no dirt, the prim Victorian sofa in deep burgundy. The room was organized and neat—like his life. He was asking for a whirlwind. Alan had no interest in subduing it, just in experiencing it.

When the doorbell rang, he glanced at his watch again. Myra was right on time.

"Good morning, McGee." Myra breezed in with a smile for Alan's sturdy Scottish butler.

"Good morning, Mrs. Ditmeyer." McGee was sixtwo, solid as a brick wall, and closing in on seventy. He'd been Alan's family butler for thirty years before leaving Hyannis Port for Georgetown at his own insistence. Mister Alan would need him, he'd said in his gravel-edged burr. That, as far as McGee was concerned, had been that.

"I don't suppose you made any of those marvelous scones?"

"With clotted cream," McGee told her, coming as close as he ever did to cracking a smile.

"Ah, McGee, I adore you. Alan…" Myra held out her hand as he came down the hall. "So sweet of you to let me bother you on a Sunday."

"It's never a bother, Myra." He kissed her cheek before leading her into the parlor.

This room was done in quiet, masculine colors—ecrus and creams with an occasional touch of deep green. The furniture was mostly Chippendale, the carpet a faded Oriental. It was a calm, comfortable room with the surprise of a large oil painting depicting a storm-tossed landscape—all jagged mountains, boiling clouds, and threatening lightning—on the south wall. Myra had always considered it an interesting, and telling, addition.

With a sigh, she sat in a high-back chair and slipped out of her shoes—skinny heels in the same shocking pink as her bag. "What a relief," she murmured. "I simply can't convince myself to buy the right size. What a price we pay for vanity." Her toes wriggled comfortably. "I got the sweetest note from Rena," she continued, rubbing one foot over the other to restore circulation as she smiled at Alan. "She wanted to know when Herbert and I are coming up to Atlantic City to lose money in her casino."

"I dropped a bit myself the last time I was up there." Alan sat back knowing Myra would get to the point of her visit in her own time.

"How's Caine? What a naughty boy he always was," she went on before Alan could answer. "Whoever thought he'd turn out to be a brilliant attorney?"

"Life's full of surprises," Alan murmured. Caine had been the naughty boy and he the disciplined one. Why should he think of that now?

"Oh, how true. Ah, here goes my diet. Thank God," she announced as McGee entered with a tray. "I'll pour, McGee, bless you." Myra lifted the Meissen teapot, busying herself while Alan watched her with amusement. Whatever she was up to, she was going to enjoy her scones and tea first. "How I envy you your butler," she told Alan as she handed him a cup. "Did you know I tried to steal him away from your parents twenty years ago?"

"No, I didn't." Alan grinned. "But then McGee's much too discreet to have mentioned it."

"And too loyal to succumb to my clever bribes. It was the first time I tasted one of these." Myra bit into a scone and rolled her eyes. "Naturally I thought it was the cook's doing and considered snatching her, but when I found out the scones were McGee's...ah, well, my consolation is that if I'd succeeded, I'd be as big as an elephant. Which reminds me." She dusted her fingers on a napkin. "I noticed you've taken an interest in elephants."

Alan lifted a brow as he sipped. So this was it. "I'm always interested in the opposing party," he said mildly.

"I'm not talking about political symbols," Myra retorted archly. "Did you have a good time at the zoo?"

"You've seen the paper."

"Of course. I must say the two of you looked very good together. I thought you would." She took a self-satisfied sip of tea. "Was Shelby annoyed by the picture?"

"I don't know." Alan's brows lowered in puzzlement. He'd lived his life in the public eye too long to give it any more than a passing thought. "Should she be?"

"Normally no; but then, Shelby's prone to feel and do the unexpected. I'm not prying, Alan—yes, I am," she corrected with an irresistible grin. "But only because I've known you both since you were children. I'm very fond of both you and Shelby.'' Giving in to temptation with only a token struggle, she helped herself to another scone. ''I was quite pleased when I saw the picture this morning.''

Enjoying her healthy appetite as well as her irrepressible meddling, Alan smiled back at her. ''Why?''

''Actually...'' Myra helped herself to a generous spoonful of cream. ''I shouldn't be. I was planning to get you two together myself. It's really put my nose out of joint that you handled matters without me, even though I approve of the end result.''

Knowing the way her mind worked, Alan leaned back against the sofa, resting one arm over the back. ''An afternoon at the zoo doesn't equal matrimony.''

''Spoken like a true politician.'' With a sigh of pure gastronomic pleasure, Myra sat back. ''If I could only wrangle the recipe for these scones out of McGee...''

Alan gave her a smile that was more amused than apologetic. ''I don't think so.''

''Ah, well. I happened to be in Shelby's shop when a basket of strawberries was delivered,'' she added casually. ''You wouldn't happen to know anything about that, would you, dear?''

''Strawberries?'' Alan gave another noncommital smile. ''I'm quite fond of them myself.''

''I'm much too clever to be conned,'' Myra told him, shaking her finger. ''And I know you entirely too well. A man like you doesn't send baskets of strawberries or spend afternoons at the zoo unless he's infatuated.''

"I'm not infatuated with Shelby," Alan corrected mildly as he sipped his tea. "I'm in love with her."

Myra's planned retort came out as a huff of breath. "Well then," she managed. "That was quicker than even I expected."

"It was instant," Alan murmured, not quite as easy now that he'd made the statement.

"Lovely." Myra leaned forward to pat his knee. "I can't think of anyone who deserves the shock of love at first sight more."

He had to laugh, though his mood was no longer light. "Shelby's not having it."

"What do you mean she's not?" Myra demanded with a frown.

"Just that." It still hurt, Alan discovered as he set down his tea. The memory of her words, that careless tone, still slashed him. "She isn't even interested in seeing me."

"Poppycock." Myra sniffed and set aside a half-eaten scone. "I was with her when she got those strawberries. And I know Shelby nearly as well as I know you." She punctuated the statement with a quick jab at his knee. "It was the first time in my life I'd seen her look quite that way."

Alan stared into middle distance a moment, considering. "She's a very stubborn woman," he said thoughtfully. "She's determined to avoid any sort of personal entanglement with me because of my profession."

"Ah, I see." Myra nodded slowly as she began to tap a long red nail against the arm of the chair. "I should have known."

"She's not indifferent," Alan murmured, thinking

aloud as he remembered the way her mouth had heated beneath his. "Just obstinate."

"Not obstinate," Myra corrected, bringing him back. "Frightened. She was very close to her father."

"I gathered that, Myra, and I understand it must have been hard, very hard, to lose him the way she did, but I can't see what it has to do with us." His impatience was edging through, and his frustration. Alan rose, no longer able to sit still, and paced the room. "If her father had been an architect, would it make sense for her to write architects off?" He dragged a hand through his hair in a rare gesture of exasperation. "Dammit, Myra, it's bloody ridiculous for her to shut me out because her father was a senator."

"You're being logical, Alan," Myra said patiently. "Shelby rarely is—unless you consider that she uses her own brand of logic. She adored Robert Campbell, and I don't use the word lightly." She paused again, her sympathies aroused for both of them. "She was only eleven years old when he was shot and killed not twenty feet away from her."

Alan stopped pacing to slowly turn around. "She was there?"

"Both her and Grant." Myra set aside her cup, wishing her memory weren't quite so clear. "It was a miracle that Deborah managed to keep the press from exploiting that angle. She used every contact she had."

He felt a flash of empathy, so stunning and sharp it left him dazed. "Oh, God, I can't even imagine how horrible it must have been for her."

"She didn't speak—not a word—for days. I spent

a lot of time with her as Deborah was trying to cope with her own grief, the children's, the press.'' She shook her head, remembering Deborah's quietly desperate attempts to reach her daughter, and Shelby's mute withdrawal. ''It was a dreadful time, Alan. Political assassinations add public scope to our private grief.''

A long, weary sigh escaped—a sound she rarely gave in to. ''Shelby didn't break down until the day after the funeral. She mourned like—like an animal,'' Myra said. ''Raw, wild grief that lasted as long as her silence had. Then she snapped out of it, maybe too well.''

He wasn't certain he wanted to hear more, picturing the child that was the woman he loved shattered, lost, and groping. He'd have been in his second year at Harvard then, secure in his world, within easy reach of his family. Even at thirty-five, he'd never suffered any devastating loss. His father—Alan tried to imagine the sudden violent loss of the robust and vital Daniel MacGregor. It was too searing a pain to be felt. He stared out the window at spring-green leaves and fresh blossoms.

''What did she do?''

''She lived—using every drop of that surplus of energy she's always had. Once when she was sixteen,'' Myra remembered, ''Shelby told me that life was a game called Who Knows? and that she was going to give everything a try before it played a trick on her.''

''That sounds like her,'' Alan murmured.

''Yes, and all in all she's the most well-adjusted creature I know. Content with her own flaws—perhaps proud of a few of them. But Shelby's a vortex of emotion. The more she uses, the more she has. Perhaps she's never really stopped grieving.''

"She can't dictate her emotions," Alan said with fresh frustration as Myra's words ate at him. "No matter how much her father's death affected her.''

"No, but Shelby would think she could.''

"She thinks too damn much," he muttered.

"No, she *feels* too damn much. She won't be an easy woman to love, or to live with.''

Alan forced himself to sit again. "I stopped wanting an easy woman when I met Shelby." Things were a bit clearer now and therefore more easily solved. Specific, tangible problems were his specialty. He began to play back Shelby's words to him of the afternoon before—the biting carelessness. He remembered, as he forced himself to be calm, that quick flicker of regret he'd seen in her eyes. "She gave me my walking papers yesterday," he said softly.

Myra set down her tea with a snap. "What nonsense. The girl needs—" She interrupted herself with another huff. "If you're that easily discouraged, I don't know why I bother. Young people expect everything to be handed to them on a platter, I suppose. The first stumbling block, and it's all over. Your father," she continued, heating up, "could find a way to bulldoze through anything. And your mother, whom I've always thought you took after, simply eased her way through any problem without creating a ripple. A fine president you'll make," she finished grumpily. "I'm going to reconsider voting for you.''

"I'm not running for president," Alan said as soberly as his grin would allow.

"Yet."

"Yet," he agreed. "And I'm going to marry Shelby."

"Oh." Deflated, Myra sat back again. "Perhaps I'll vote for you after all. When?"

Staring at the ceiling, Alan considered, calculating, turning over angles. "I've always liked Hyannis Port in the fall," he mused. Shifting his gaze, he gave Myra his slow, serious smile. "Shelby should enjoy getting married in a drafty castle, don't you think?"

Chapter Six

A week was only seven days. Shelby made it through almost six of them by pretending she wasn't going crazy. By midafternoon on Friday, she was running low on excuses for her bad temper and absent-mindedness.

She wasn't sleeping well; that's why she was listless. She wasn't sleeping well because she'd been so busy—at the shop and with a round of social engagements. Shelby hadn't turned down any invitation that had come her way all week. Because she was listless, or overtired or whatever, she was forgetting things—like eating. Because she had thrown her system off schedule, she was cranky. And because she was cranky, she didn't have any appetite.

Shelby had managed this circular sort of justification for days without once bringing the reason back to Alan. Several times she told herself she hadn't

thought of him at all. Not once. As it happened,
Shelby began to tell herself several times a day that
she hadn't thought of him. Once she was so pleased
with herself for not giving him a thought, she
smashed a delft-blue flowerpot against her workroom
wall.

This was so blatantly out of character that Shelby
was forced to resort to her circular route of rationale
all over again.

She worked when she could—late at night when
she couldn't bear to lie awake in bed, early in the
morning for the same reason. When she went out, she
was almost desperately bright and cheerful so that a
few of her closer friends began to watch her with
some concern. Filling her time became of paramount
importance. Then she would forget that she'd made
arrangements to meet friends for dinner and bury herself in her workroom.

It could be the weather, Shelby mused as she sat
behind the counter with her chin on her hand. The
radio gave her music and welcome noise, with regular
announcements that the rain would end by Sunday.
To Shelby, Sunday was light-years away.

Rain depressed a lot of people, and just because it
had never depressed her before didn't mean it wasn't
doing so this time. Two solid days of streaming, soaking rain could make anyone grumpy. Brooding,
Shelby watched through the shop window as it continued to fall.

Rain wasn't good for business, she decided. She'd
had a little more than a trickle of customers that day
and the day before. Normally she would have closed
up shop with a philosophical shrug and found some-

thing else to do. But she stayed, frowning, as gloomy as the rain.

Maybe she'd just go away for the weekend, she thought. Hop on a plane and shoot up to Maine and surprise Grant. Oh, he'd be furious, Shelby thought with the first real smile she'd managed in days. He'd give her hell for dropping in unannounced. Then they'd have such a good time badgering each other. No one made bickering as much fun as Grant.

Grant saw too much, Shelby remembered with a sigh. He'd know something was wrong, and though he was fierce about his own privacy, he'd pick at her until she told him everything. She could tell her mother—at least part of it—but she couldn't tell Grant. Maybe because he understood too well.

So…Shelby gave another long sigh and considered her options. She could stay in Georgetown and be miserable over the weekend or she could leave. It might be fun to just toss a few things in the car and drive until she left the rain behind. Skyline Drive in Virginia or the beach at Nags Head. A change of scene, she decided abruptly. Any scene at all.

Impulsively Shelby jumped up and prepared to turn over the *Closed* sign. The door opened, letting in a *whoosh* of chilled air and a scattering of rain. A woman in a yellow slicker and boots closed the door with a slam.

"Miserable weather," she said cheerfully.

"The worst," Shelby pushed the impatience back. Ten minutes before she'd considered standing on one foot and juggling to attract a customer. "Is there something in particular I can show you?"

"I'll just poke around."

Oh, sure, Shelby thought, pinning on an amiable smile. I could be halfway to sunshine by the time she finishes poking. Shelby considered telling the woman she had ten minutes. "Take your time," she said instead.

"I found out about your shop from a neighbor." The woman stopped to study a fat speckled pot suitable for a patio or terrace. "She'd bought a coffee set I admired. A very pale blue with pansies dashed over it."

"Yes, I remember it." Shelby managed to keep the friendly smile in place as she watched the woman's back. "I don't do duplicates, but if you're interested in coffee sets, I have one along similar lines." Scanning the shop, she tried to remember where she'd set it.

"Actually it wasn't the specific set as much as the workmanship that caught my eye. She told me you make all your stock yourself."

"That's right." Shelby forced herself not to fidget and concentrated on the woman. Attractive, mid-thirties, friendly. The sleek brunette hair had a subtle and sophisticated frosting of wheat-toned blond. Shelby wished the woman would go back to wherever she came from, then was immediately furious with herself. "I have my wheel in the back room," she went on, making more of an effort. "I do all the firing and glazing there as well."

The customer crouched down beside a standing urn, studying it meticulously. "Do you ever use molds?"

"Once in a while, for something like that bull there, or the gnome, but I prefer the wheel."

"You know, you have a marvelous talent—and quite a supply of energy." Rising, the woman ran a fingertip down the spout of a coffeepot. "I can imagine how much time and patience it takes to produce all this, over and above the skill."

"Thank you. I suppose when you enjoy something, you don't think about the time it takes."

"*Mmm,* I know. I'm a decorator." Walking over, she handed Shelby a business card. *Maureen Francis, Interior Design.* "I'm doing my own apartment at the moment, and I have to have that pot, that urn, and that vase." She pointed to each of her choices before turning back to Shelby. "Can I give you a deposit and have you hold them for me until Monday? I don't want to cart them around in the rain."

"Of course. I'll have them packed up for you when you're ready for them."

"Terrific." Maureen pulled a checkbook out of the leather hobo bag she carried. "You know, I have a feeling we're going to be doing quite a bit of business. I've only been in D.C. about a month, but I do have a couple of interesting jobs coming up." She glanced up with another smile before she continued to write out the check. "I like to use handcrafted pieces in my work. There's nothing worse than a room that shrieks of professional decorator."

The statement, from someone who made her living at it, intrigued Shelby. She forgot her inclination to rush Maureen out the door. "Where are you from?"

"Chicago. I worked for a large firm there—ten years." She ripped off the check and handed it to Shelby. "I got the itch to strike out on my own."

Nodding, Shelby finished making out her receipt. "Are you any good?"

Maureen blinked at the blunt question, then grinned. "I'm very good."

Shelby studied her face a moment—candid eyes, a touch of humor. Going, as always, on impulse, she scrawled a name and address on the back of the receipt. "Myra Ditmeyer," Shelby told her. "If anyone who's anyone in the area is toying with redecorating, she'll know. Tell her I gave you her name."

A bit stunned, Maureen stared down at the receipt. She'd been in D.C. long enough to know of Myra Ditmeyer. "Thanks."

"Myra'll expect your life history in lieu of a percentage, but—" Shelby broke off as the door to the shop opened again. She had the unexpected, and for her, unique experience of going completely blank.

Alan closed the door, then calmly stripped out of his wet coat before he crossed to her. Giving Maureen a friendly nod, he cupped Shelby's chin, leaned over the counter, and kissed her. "I brought you a present."

"No!" The quick panic in her voice infuriated her. After shoving at his hand, she stepped back. "Go away."

Alan leaned on the counter as he turned to Maureen. "Is that any way to act when someone brings you a present?"

"Well, I…" Maureen looked from Shelby to Alan before she gave a noncommittal shrug.

"Of course it isn't," he went on as if she'd agreed. He drew a box out of his coat pocket and set it on the counter.

"I'm not going to open it." Shelby looked down at the box only because it prevented her from looking at Alan. She wouldn't risk having her mind swept clean again so soon. "And I'm closed."

"Not for fifteen minutes. Shelby's often rude," he told Maureen. "Would you like to see what I brought her?"

Torn between a desire to run for cover and creeping curiosity, Maureen hesitated a moment too long. Alan plucked off the cover of the box and pulled out a small piece of colored glass in the shape of a rainbow. Shelby's hand was halfway to it before she stopped herself.

"Dammit, Alan," How could he have known how badly she'd needed to see a rainbow?

"That's her traditional response," he told Maureen. "It means she likes it."

"I told you to stop sending me things."

"I didn't send it," he pointed out as he dropped the rainbow in her hand. "I brought it."

"I don't want it," she said heatedly, but her fingers curled around it. "If you weren't a thick-skinned, boneheaded MacGregor, you'd leave me alone."

"Fortunately for both of us, we share some of the same traits." He had her hand in his before she could prevent it. "Your pulse is racing again, Shelby."

Maureen cleared her throat. "Well, I think I'll just be running along." She stuffed the receipt in her bag as Shelby stared helplessly at Alan. "I'll be back Monday," she added, though neither of them acknowledged her departure. "If someone gave me a rainbow on a day like today," she commented as she headed for the door. "I'd be sunk."

Sunk, Shelby repeated silently. It wasn't until the
door closed that she snapped back. "Stop it," she
ordered and snatched her hand away. When she
flicked off the radio, the room fell into silence, ac-
centuated by the drumming rain. Too late, she realized she'd made her first mistake. Now it was all too
apparent that her breathing wasn't as steady as it
should be. "Alan, I'm closing shop."

"Good idea." He strode over to the door, flipped
around the sign, then shot the bolt.

"Now, just a minute," she began furiously. "You
can't—" She broke off as he began to come toward
her. The calmly determined look in his eyes had her
taking a step back and swallowing. "This is my shop,
and you—" Her back hit the wall as he skirted around
the counter.

"And *we,*" he began when he stopped directly in
front of her, "are going out to dinner."

"I'm not going anywhere."

"You are," he corrected.

Shelby stared up at him, confused and pulsing. His
voice hadn't been fierce or impatient. There wasn't
any anger in his eyes. She'd have preferred anger to
that simple, unarguable confidence. Temper made it
so easy to defend with temper. If he was going to be
calm, she told herself, she'd be calm too. "Alan, you
can't tell me what to do. After all—"

"I am telling you," he countered easily. "I've
come to the conclusion you've been asked too often
in your life and not told often enough."

"Your conclusions don't interest me in the least,"
she shot back. "Who the hell are you to tell me anything?" For an answer, he pulled her closer. "I'm not

going," Shelby began, experiencing what she realized must be desperation. "I have plans for the weekend. I'm—I'm leaving for the beach."

"Where's your coat?"

"Alan, I said—"

Spotting the light jacket hanging on the coatrack behind the counter, Alan slipped it off and handed it to her. "Do you want your purse?"

"Will you get it through your head that I am *not* going with you?"

He ignored her and plucked the shoulder bag from behind the counter. Taking the keys that lay beside it, he gripped Shelby's arm and pulled her through the rear of the shop.

"Dammit, Alan, I said I'm not going." Shelby found herself presumptuously shoved into the rain while Alan locked her back door. "I don't want to go anywhere with you."

"Too bad." He pocketed her keys, then slipped into his own coat while Shelby stood stubbornly in the downpour.

She swiped the dripping hair out of her eyes and planted her feet. "You can't make me."

He lifted a brow, taking a long, thoughtful study of her. She was livid and drenched and beautiful in her own fashion. And he noted, with satisfaction, just a little unsure of herself. It was about time. "We're going to have to start to keep count of how many times you tell me I can't," he commented before he grabbed her arm and dragged her to his car.

"If you think—" Shelby broke off as she was shoved, unceremoniously, inside. "If you think," she began again, "that I'm impressed by the caveman routine, you couldn't be more mistaken.'' It wasn't often that she was haughtily dignified, but when she put her mind to it, no one did it better than Shelby. Even soaking wet. ''Give me back my keys.'' Imperiously she held out her hand, palm up.

Alan took it, pressed a lingering kiss to the center, then started the car.

Shelby curled her hand into a fist as if to subdue the warmth that started in her palm and shot out everywhere. ''Alan, I don't know what's gotten into you, but it has to stop. Now, I want my keys so I can get back inside.''

''After dinner,'' he said pleasantly and backed out of the alley. ''How was your week?''

Shelby sat back and folded her arms. It wasn't until then that she realized she still had Alan's rainbow in her hand. She stuffed it in the pocket of the jacket that lay in a heap beside her, then flopped back again. ''I'm not having dinner with you.''

''I thought someplace quiet would be best.'' He turned right, keeping pace with the heavy, sluggish traffic. ''You look a bit tired, love; haven't you been sleeping well?''

''I've been sleeping just fine,'' she lied. ''I was out late last night.'' Deliberately she turned to him. ''On a date.''

Alan controlled the swift surge of jealousy. Her ability to push the right buttons to get under his skin was no longer a surprise. He met the simmering gray eyes briefly. ''Have a good time?''

''I had a *marvelous* time. David's a musician, very sensitive. Very passionate,'' she added with relish. ''I'm crazy about him.'' David might have been surprised, as he was engaged to one of Shelby's closest friends, but she doubted the subject would come up again. "As a matter of fact," she continued with sudden inspiration, "he's coming by to pick me up at seven. So, I'd appreciate it if you'd just turn around and take me home."

Instead of obliging as she hoped or raging as she expected, Alan glanced at his watch. "That's too bad. I doubt we'll be back by then." While Shelby sat in stony silence he pulled up to the curb. "Better put on your jacket; we'll have to walk half a block." When she neither moved nor spoke, he leaned across her as if to open the door. His mouth brushed over her ear. "Unless you'd like to stay in the car and neck."

Shelby turned her head, ready with a furious retort. She found her lips against his, lightly, devastatingly. In a quick move, she pushed out of her side of the car, whipping the jacket over her shoulders.

They'd play the scenario out, she told herself as she worked on leveling her breathing. And when she got back her keys, she was going to make him suffer for every minute of it. Alan joined her on the sidewalk, took her hands, and just looked at her. He felt her initial resistance melt before the time could be measured.

"You tasted of the rain," he murmured, before he gave in to the temptation to finish the promise of that brief meeting of lips, the press of bodies. The week of staying away from her had nearly driven him mad.

Rain pelted them, and Shelby thought of waterfalls. Her jacket slipped off her shoulders, and she thought of rainbows. All needs, all wishes, sped through her: sweet pangs of longing, half-formed dreams. How had she gone all her life without him when she could no longer keep sane for a week without being touched like this?

Reluctantly Alan drew her away. A moment longer, he knew, and he'd forget they were on a public street. Her face was pale ivory dashed with sweet spring rain. Drops clung to the lashes surrounding those pure gray eyes. They should be alone, he thought, in some gloomy evening forest or rain-splattered field. Then there'd be no drawing away. He slipped the jacket back over her shoulders.

"I like your hair wet." In a slow possessive move, he ran a hand through it. Without another word, he draped an arm around her and led her down the street.

Shelby knew the restaurant. All dim corners and smoky music. By ten o'clock that night, it would be noisy and jammed with people. A man like Alan would avoid it then, while she would seek it out. Now it was subdued—pale wooden floors, flickering candles, muted conversations.

"Good evening, Senator." The maître d' beamed over Alan before his gaze shifted to Shelby. He beamed again. "Nice to see you again, Ms. Campbell."

"Good evening, Mario," Shelby returned, searching for her hauteur.

"Your table's waiting." He guided them through to a back corner table where the candle was burned halfway down. There was enough Latin in Mario that he scented romance and appreciated it. "A bottle of wine?" he asked as he held Shelby's chair.

"Pouilly Fuisse, Bichot," Alan told him without consulting Shelby.

"1979," Mario said with a nod of approval. "Your waiter will be with you shortly.

Shelby flipped her damp hair out of her eyes. "Maybe I want a beer."

"Next time," Alan agreed amiably.

"There isn't going to be a next time. I mean it, Alan," she said jerkily as he traced a line down the back of her hand with his fingertip. "I wouldn't be here if you hadn't locked me out of my house. Don't touch me that way," she added in a furious undertone.

"How would you like me to touch you? You have very sensitive hands," he murmured before she could answer. He grazed a thumb over her knuckle and felt the quick tremor. Tonight, he promised himself, he was going to feel that tremor again—at every pulse point. "How many times did you think of me this week?"

"I didn't think of you," Shelby tossed back, then felt a flash of guilt at the new lie. "All right, what if I did?" She attempted to snatch her hand away, but Alan merely slipped his fingers through hers and held it still. It was a simple, conventional gesture, one a civilized man could use in a public place without drawing eyes. Though she knew it, tried to scorn it, Shelby felt the pleasure ripple down to her toes. "I felt badly because I'd been nasty. After your behavior tonight, I only wish I'd been nastier. I can be," she added on a threat.

Alan only smiled as Mario brought the wine to the table. Watching Shelby, Alan tasted it, then nodded. "Very good. It's the sort of flavor that stays with you for hours. Later, when I kiss you, the taste will still be there.''

The blood began to hum in her ears. "I'm only here because you dragged me."

To his credit, Mario didn't spill a drop of the wine he poured as he listened.

Her eyes heated as Alan continued to smile. "And since you refuse to give me my keys, I'll simply walk to the nearest phone and call a locksmith. *You'll* get the bill."

"After dinner," Alan suggested. "How do you like the wine?"

Scowling, Shelby lifted the glass and drained half the contents. "It's fine." Her eyes, insolent now, stayed level with his. "This isn't a date, you know."

"It's becoming more of a filibuster, isn't it? More wine?"

The patience was back. She wanted to pound her fists on the table in the teeth of it. That would set the tongues wagging, she thought, tempted. And serve him right. Then she thought of the chatty little article in the paper and ground her teeth instead. Shelby shrugged as he topped off her glass. "Wine and candlelight won't do you any good."

"No?" He decided against pointing out that she was holding his hand now as much as he was holding hers. "Well, I thought it was time for something more traditional."

"Really?" She had to smile. "Then, I should've gotten a box of chocolates or a bouquet of roses. *That's* traditional."

"I knew you'd rather have a rainbow."

"You know too damn much." She plucked up the

menu the waiter set at her elbow and buried her face
behind it. Since he'd dragged her out in the rain, she
might as well eat. Stuff herself, Shelby corrected. Her
appetite had returned in full force. So had her energy,
she reluctantly admitted. The moment she'd seen him
again, the listlessness had vanished.

"Are you ready to order, Ms. Campbell?"

Shelby glanced up at the waiter and aimed a smile.
"Yes, I am. I'll have the seafood salad with avocado,
the consommé, the loin of lamb with bearnaise sauce,
a baked potato, and the artichoke hearts. I'll look at
the pastry cart later."

The waiter scribbled, without flicking an eyebrow
at the length of her order. "Senator?"

"The house salad," he said, grinning at Shelby's
bland expression. "And the scampi. The walk in the
rain gave you an appetite, I see."

"Since I'm here, I might as well choke down a few
bites. Well…" In one of her lightning changes of
moods, she rested her folded arms on the table and
leaned over them. "We have to pass the time, don't
we? What shall we talk about, Senator? How are
things on the Hill?"

"Busy."

"Ah, the classic understatement. You've been
working overtime to block Breiderman's bill. Well
done, I'm forced to say. Then there's your current pet
project. Any progress in squeezing out the Federal
funds you need."

"There've been a few steps forward." He eyed her
thoughtfully a moment. For a woman who had such
an aversion to politics, she was well informed. "The
mayor's enthusiastic about setting up the same kind

of shelters here that we started in Boston. For now, we'll have to rely mostly on contributions and volunteers. We'll need a lot more before we can count on the support to set them up nationwide.''

"You've got a long fight on your hands with the current financial picture and the budget cuts.''

"I know. I'll win eventually.'' A smile touched his lips lightly. "I can be very patient up to a point, and then I can be very...insistent.''

Not quite trusting the gleam in his eyes, Shelby remained silent as their salads were served. "You stepped on a few toes in Breiderman's case; they'll step back.''

"That's the name of the game. Nothing worthwhile's ever without complications. I—'' He filled her glass again. "Have a penchant for solving them as they come.''

Not bothering to pretend she misunderstood him this time, Shelby speared a forkful of salad and ate it thoughtfully. "You can't organize a romance like a campaign, Senator. Particularly with someone who knows a great many of the moves.''

"It is an interesting concept.'' Humor was in his eyes and around the edges of his slow, serious smile. Shelby found that her fingers were itching to touch his face. "You'll admit my statements have been clear. I haven't made any promises I won't keep, Shelby.''

"I'm not one of your constituents.''

"That doesn't change my platform.''

Shelby shook her head, half-exasperated, half-amused. "I'm not going to argue with you on your turf.'' Toying with the remains of her salad, she glanced back up at him. "I suppose you saw the picture in the paper."

"Yes." It had bothered her, he realized, though she spoke lightly and with a trace of a smile. "I enjoyed being reminded of that particular moment. I'm sorry it upset you."

"It didn't," she said too quickly. On a faint sound of annoyance, she shook her head. "Not really." The waiter removed her salad and replaced it with consommé. Shelby began to stir it absently. "I suppose it just reminded me how much you're in the public eye. Does it ever bother you?"

"Off and on. Publicity's an intricate part of my profession. It can be a means to an end, or a basic nuisance." He wanted to see her smile. "Of course, I'm interested to get my father's reaction when he gets wind I was at the zoo with a Campbell."

The faint tension in her shoulders relaxed when she laughed. "Do you fear for your inheritance, Alan?"

"My skin more," he countered. "My hearing at the least. I expect to pick up the phone any day and be bellowed at."

She grinned as she picked up her wine. "Do you let him think he intimidates you?"

"From time to time. It keeps him happy."

Shelby picked up a roll, broke it in two, and offered half to Alan "If you were smart, you'd give me a very wide berth. You really shouldn't risk a broken eardrum: it makes it difficult to hear what the opposition's plotting in the next room."

"I can deal with my father—when the time comes."

Nibbling on the roll, she gave him a steady look. "Meaning after you've dealt with me."

He lifted his glass in a small toast. "Precisely."

"Alan." She smiled again, more confident after food and wine. "You're not going to deal with me."

"We'll have to see, won't we?" he said easily. "Here's your lamb."

Chapter Seven

Shelby might have wished she hadn't enjoyed herself quite so much. She might have wished Alan hadn't been able to make her laugh quite so easily. Or that he hadn't been able to charm her into walking down M Street in the rain to window-shop and people-watch—and to have one last glass of wine at a crowded little café.

Shelby might have wished it, but she didn't. For the first time in a week, she could laugh and relax and enjoy without effort. There'd be consequences—there were always consequences. She'd think about them tomorrow.

More than once someone breezed by their table with a greeting for Shelby and a speculative look at Alan. It reminded her that smoky little clubs were her territory. Ballet openings were his. That was something else she'd think about tomorrow.

"Hello, gorgeous."

Shelby glanced up and around as hands dropped onto her shoulders. "Hello, David. Hi, Wendy."

"Hey, you were supposed to give us a call tonight," David reminded her. The piano player switched to something hot and pulsing. David glanced over automatically. "We caught the new play at Ford's without you."

Wendy, soft and graceful with hair rippling past her waist, grinned as she slipped an arm around David's waist. "You didn't miss anything."

"I got..." Shelby cast a glance at Alan. "Sidetracked. Alan, David and Wendy."

"Nice to meet you." Alan gave the gangly man with the wisp of beard a slow smile. "Would you like to join us?"

"Thanks, but we're just heading out." David ruffled Shelby's hair before he snitched her wine for a quick sip. "Got to play at a wedding tomorrow."

"David's still trying to figure out how he can play at ours next month. Hey, I've got to call you later about that Greek caterer you told me about." Wendy sent Alan a friendly grin. "Shelby says ouzo livens up a reception. Listen, we'll see you later," she added as she tugged on David's arm.

Alan watched them skirt around tables on their way to the door. "He works fast," Alan commented as he lifted his wine.

"David?" Shelby sent him a puzzled look. "Actually his fastest speed is crawl unless he's got a guitar in his hands."

"Really?" Alan's eyes met hers as he sipped, but she didn't understand the amusement in them. "You only stood him up tonight, and already he's planning his wedding to someone else.''

"Stood him—'' she began on a laugh, then remembered. ''Oh.'' Torn between annoyance and her own sense of the ridiculous, Shelby toyed with the stem of her glass. ''Men are fickle creatures,'' she decided.

''Apparently.'' Reaching over, he lifted her chin with a fingertip. ''You're holding up well.''

''I don't like to wear my heart on my sleeve.'' Exasperated, amused, she muffled a laugh. ''Dammit, he would have to pick tonight to show up here.''

''Of all the gin joints in all the towns…''

This time the laugh escaped fully. ''Well done,'' Shelby told him. ''I should've thought of that line myself; I heard the movie not long ago.''

''Heard it?''

''*Mmm-hmm.* Well…'' She lifted her glass in a toast. ''To broken hearts?''

''Or foolish lies?'' Alan countered.

Shelby wrinkled her nose as she tapped her glass against his. ''I usually tell very good ones. Besides, I *did* date David. Once. Three years ago.'' She finished off her wine. ''Maybe four. You can stop grinning in that smug, masculine way any time, Senator.''

''Was I?'' Rising, he offered Shelby her damp jacket. ''How rude of me.''

''It would've been more polite not to acknowledge that you'd caught me in a lie,'' she commented as they worked their way through the crowd and back into the rain. ''Which you wouldn't have done if you hadn't made me so mad that I couldn't think of a handier name to give you in the first place.''

''If I work my way through the morass of that sentence it seems to be my fault." Alan slipped an arm around her shoulders in so casually friendly a manner she didn't protest. "Suppose I apologize for not giving you time to think of a lie that would hold up?"

"It seems fair." Shelby lifted her face to the rain, forgetting how she had cursed it only hours before. It was soft and cool and clean on her skin. She could have walked in it for hours. "But I'm not going to thank you for dinner," she added with a flash of laughter in her eyes. She turned, leaning back against the door of his car when they reached it. "Or the wine and the candlelight."

Alan looked into the insolent, rain-washed face and wanted her, desperately. She'd bring touches of that insolence to her passion, and touches of the freshness. He dipped his hands into his pockets before he could give in to the urge to pull her to him then and there. "How about the rainbow?"

A smile tilted the corners of her mouth. "Maybe I'll thank you for that. I haven't decided." Quickly she slipped into the car. Her knees had gone weak, she'd discovered, with that one long look he'd given her before he'd spoken. It would be wise to keep the mood as light as it had been in the café—at least until she was safely inside her apartment and he was safely out. "You know," she went on as Alan slid behind the wheel, "I was planning to drive to the beach tonight. You mucked up my plans."

"Do you like the beach in the rain?"

"It might not have been raining there," Shelby pointed out while the engine purred. "And anyway I do."

"I like it best in a storm." Alan steered the Mercedes around a corner. "At dusk—when there's just enough light to watch the sky and the water churn."

"Really?" Intrigued, she studied his profile. "I would have thought you'd prefer quiet winter beaches where you could take long walks and think deep thoughts."

"Everything in its time," Alan murmured.

She could see it—the lightning, the thunder, the breath of windy excitement. Something more than wine warmed her blood. Undercurrents. She'd known there were undercurrents in him from the first moment she'd seen him, but now they seemed closer to the surface. There'd be a time, if she wasn't careful, when they'd simply sweep her away.

"My sister lives in Atlantic City," Alan said casually. "I like to shoot up there at odd times during the off-season to spend a couple of days at the beach and lose money in her casino."

"Your sister owns a casino?" Shelby turned back to him again.

"She's partners with her husband in a couple of them." Amused by the surprise in Shelby's voice, he sent her a quick grin. "Rena used to deal blackjack. Still does occasionally. Did you consider that my family would be very staid, very proper, and very dull, Shelby?"

"Not precisely," she answered, though she had for the most part. "At least not from what I've heard about your father. Myra seems very fond of him."

"They like to argue with each other. He's every bit as opinionated as she is."

He parked beside her building, then got out before Shelby could tell him not to bother to see her to the door. "You've gotten your share of dunkings tonight, Senator." As they climbed the stairs she automatically reached into her purse for her keys.

"I still have them," Alan reminded her as he drew them out of his pocket. Watching her, he jiggled them in his palm. "They should be worth a cup of coffee."

Shelby frowned at him. "I think that's bribery."

"Bribery?" His stare was mild and reasonable. "No, it was a supposition."

Shelby hesitated, then sighed. She understood him well enough by now to know that they could end up debating his supposition for an hour on the landing. And he'd still end up with his cup of coffee. Stepping aside, she gestured for him to unlock the door. "Coffee," she said as though stating the boundary lines. After she stripped out of her jacket, Shelby tossed it carelessly over a kitchen chair. The cat struggled out from under it, leapt to the floor, and glared out of his good eye. "Oh, sorry." Shelby poked into a cabinet and came out with an envelope of cat food. "It's his fault," she told Moshe. As the cat attacked his meal Shelby looked back at Alan. "He doesn't appreciate it when I'm late with his dinner. He's very regimented."

Alan gave the plump, greedy cat a cursory glance. "He doesn't appear deprived."

"No." Tossing her bangs out of her eyes, Shelby turned to the sink to fill the percolator. "But he's easily annoyed. If I—" She lost her train of thought when Alan's hands descended to her shoulders. "If I forget to feed him, he—" The percolator clattered into the sink as Alan's mouth grazed her ear. "Sulks," she finished, switching off the tap with a jerk. "Roommates who sulk," she managed in an abruptly thready voice as she set the percolator on the counter, "make things difficult."

"I imagine," Alan murmured. Brushing the hair away from the nape of her neck, he nibbled on the sensitive skin. Shelby felt the fire start and fought to get the plug into the wall socket. "Shelby…" His hands skimmed down her sides to rest at her waist.

She was going to ignore it, she told herself. Absolutely ignore what he was doing to her. "What?"

"Mmm." Alan trailed his lips around the side of her neck. Her scent was more vibrant there, he discovered, just there above the collarbone. He skimmed his tongue over it and listened to her quick, unsteady inhalation of breath. "You didn't put any coffee in the pot."

She shivered, then gripped the counter with both hands to keep it from happening again. "What?"

Alan reached around her to pull the plug out. "You didn't," he began and turned her to face him, "put any coffee in." He brushed a kiss at one corner of her mouth, then just as lightly, at the other.

For a moment, she weakened, closing her eyes. "In where?"

His lips curved against her cheekbone. "In the percolator."

"It'll perk in a minute," she murmured when his lips skimmed over her eyelids. She heard him laugh softly and wondered why it sounded triumphant. It took all her effort to fight off the brushfire that was already getting out of control. "Alan…" Featherlight kisses trailed over her face, adding fuel to the blaze. "You're trying to seduce me."

"No, I'm not." He nipped gently at her lips, then left them unsatisfied as he journeyed to her throat. He wanted to feel that desperately pounding pulse. "I *am* seducing you."

"No." Shelby lifted her hands to his chest to push him away. Somehow they crept up around his neck. "We're not going to make love."

Alan barely controlled the urgent flare of need as his fingers wound their way into her hair. "No?" He teased her lips again. "Why?"

"Because…" She fought to remember who she was. Where she was. "Because it's…the road to perdition?"

He gave a muffled laugh against her mouth before his tongue slipped in to tempt her. "Try again."

"Because…" It was building too quickly, beyond what she understood. Needs weren't supposed to be so painful. Hunger wasn't supposed to come in waves that enervated you. She knew that because she'd felt both before. This had to be something different, and yet it seemed to have no name at all. There was weakness, such weakness, and a driving, burning force that threatened to consume everything she thought she knew. "No." Panic, sharp and real, broke through. "No, I want you too much. I can't let this happen, don't you see?"

"Too late." Still roaming her face with kisses, he guided her through the apartment. "Much too late, Shelby." He slipped the blouse from her shoulders and let it float to the floor. This time, the first time, he thought, it would be a seduction. One that both of them would remember in all the years to come. "Soft," he murmured, "much too soft to resist."

Taking his time, he trailed his hands up her arms, over her shoulders. "Do you know how often I've thought of being with you like this? How often I've thought of touching you—" his fingers brushed over the thin camisole to stroke her breast "—like this." Without a sound, her skirt dropped to the floor at the doorway to the bedroom. "Do you hear the rain, Shelby?"

She felt the bedspread brush her shoulders as they eased onto the bed. "Yes."

"I'm going to make love with you." His lips were at her ear again, destroying even the pretense of refusal. "And every time you hear the rain, you'll remember."

She wouldn't need the rain to remember, Shelby thought. Had her heart ever beat so fast? Had her skin ever seemed so soft? Yes, she could hear the rain, drumming and drumming on the roof, against the windowpane. But she wouldn't need to hear the sound of it again to remember the way his mouth fit so perfectly against hers, the way her body seemed to mold itself to the lines of his. She would only have to think of him to remember the way the rain-dampened freshness clung to his hair or the way the sound of her name came in a whisper through his lips.

She'd never given the gift of her pliancy to a man before, though she wasn't aware of it. Now, she yielded, letting him guide her where she'd been so reluctant—or so afraid—to go. To mindlessness.

He seemed to want to touch, to taste, all of her, but so slowly, so thoroughly, she could float, insubstantial as a mist, on feelings alone. With only fingertips, with only lips, he aroused her to a plane of contentment that was irresistible.

Shelby hadn't understood true languor until she reached for the buttons of his shirt. Her arms were so heavy. Her hands, always so clever, her fingers always so deft, fumbled, drawing out the process and unwittingly driving him to desperation.

His mouth grew suddenly greedy on hers, his body pressing down to trap her hands between them. Perhaps it was that unconscious show of dominance, or perhaps it was the overload of suppressed needs, but she ceased to yield against him and began to take.

Her hunger matched his, and when it threatened to surpass him, his built to balance it again. Shelby found those strong, subtle muscles, freed of the shirt, but her hands no longer fumbled. It seemed like a race, who could drive whom further, and faster. His mouth sped down her, lingering at points of pleasure she hadn't known existed until he found them, exploited them, then moved on. He drew the bare swathe of silk down, and further down, though his caresses had ceased to be gentle. Neither of them looked for gentleness. What was between them had ignited at the first meeting and had simmered too long.

Alan felt her tremble wherever he touched, wherever his tongue flicked over her skin. He knew she'd left fear far behind. This was the passion, the pure, undiluted passion he'd known she would give to him if he waited for her. It was the whirlwind he'd needed, and the whirlwind she brought.

Aggressive, all fire, all flash, she moved with him, against him, for him, until his control was ripped apart—shredded and forgotten. He could taste her with each breath he drew into his lungs—everything wild and sweet and tempting.

Neither was leading now, but both were led. Shelby took him into her on a cry that was muffled against his mouth and had nothing to do with surrender. Thunder and lightning, they fed each other.

The rain still fell. The sound was no softer, no louder. They might have lain together for hours or for moments. Neither had any thought of time, only of place. Here.

Shelby curled into Alan, eyes closed, breathing steady at last, her mind and body so peaceful the storm might never have taken place. But it had been the storm, her part in it, her yielding to it, that had given her the serenity she hadn't even known she craved. Alan—Alan was her peace, her heart, her home.

Steady, solid, whimsical, persistent. There were too many labels for him—perhaps that was why she was drawn to him again and again, and why she'd continued to step away.

Alan shifted, drawing her closer. He could still feel the ripples: excitement, passion, emotions too vibrant to name. Shelby continued to pour through him like a heady, breathtaking wind that blew in all directions at once. Brisk or sultry, she was a breeze that whisked away the harshness of the world he knew too much about. He needed that kind of magic from her, the same way he needed to give her whatever it was in him she was drawn to.

Lazily…possessively he ran a hand down her back.

"*Mmm,* again," Shelby murmured.

With a quiet laugh, Alan stroked up and down until

she was ready to purr. "Shelby..." She gave another sigh as an answer and snuggled closer. "Shelby, there's something warm and fluffy under my feet."

"Mm-hmm."

"If it's your cat, he's not breathing."

"MacGregor."

He kissed the top of her head. "What?"

She gave a muffled laugh against his shoulder. "MacGregor," she repeated. "My pig."

There was silence for a moment while he tried to digest this. "I beg your pardon?"

The dry serious tone had more laughter bubbling up. Would she ever be able to face a day without hearing it? "Oh, say that again. I love it." Because she had to see his face, Shelby found the energy to lean across him and grope for the matches on the nightstand. Skin rubbed distractingly against skin while she struck one and lit a candle. "MacGregor," she said, giving Alan a quick kiss before she gestured to the foot of the bed.

Alan studied the smiling porcine face. "You named a stuffed purple pig after me?"

"Alan, is that any way to talk about our child?" His eyes shifted to hers in an expression so masculine and ironic, she collapsed on his chest in a fit of giggles. "I put him there because he was supposed to be the only MacGregor who charmed his way into my bed."

"Really." Alan tugged on her hair until she lifted her face, full of amusement and fun, to his. "Is that what I did?"

"You knew damn well I wouldn't be able to resist balloons and rainbows forever." The candlelight flickered over his face. Shelby traced the shifting light with a fingertip. "I meant to resist your charms; I really did. I wasn't going to do this."

Alan took her wrist, guiding her hand over so that he could press a kiss to the palm. "Make love with me?"

"No." Shelby's gaze traveled from his mouth to his eyes. "Be in love with you."

She felt his fingers tighten on her wrist, then loosen slowly as his eyes stayed dark and fixed on hers. Beneath her, she felt the change in his heartbeat. "And are you?"

"Yes." The word, hardly audible, thundered in his head.

Alan brought her to him, cradling her head against his chest, feeling her low slow expulsion of air as his arm came around her. He hadn't expected her to give him so much so soon. "When?"

"When?" Shelby repeated, enjoying the solid feel of his chest under her cheek. "Sometime between when we first stepped out on the Writes' terrace and when I opened a basket of strawberries."

"It took you that long? All I had to do was look at you."

Shelby brought her head up and found her eyes locked with his. He wouldn't exaggerate, she knew. It wasn't his style. Simple words with simple truth. Overwhelmed, she framed his face in her hands. "If you had told me that a week ago, a day ago, I would have thought you were mad." On a flow of laughter, she pressed her mouth to his. "Maybe you are—it doesn't seem to matter." With a sigh, she melted against him. "It doesn't seem to matter at all."

She knew she had tenderness in her—for children and small animals. She'd never felt real tenderness for a man. But when she kissed him now, with words of love still echoing in her head, Shelby was swamped with it. Her hands came back to his face, her artist's fingers tracing, molding the shape until she thought she knew it well enough to conjure it out of air if someone asked her to.

Then she trailed them down, over the column of his throat, along the shoulders firm with muscle. Shoulders to depend on—strong enough to hold your problems if you needed them to. But she wouldn't ask; it was enough to know they were there. With her mouth still tasting, still lingering on his, she ran her fingers down his arms as if in the first storm of love-making she'd been too frantic to really see the whole man. She realized as she nuzzled into his neck that she could smell herself on him, and thought it was wonderful. His arms came around her and they stayed just so for a moment naked, entwined, content.

"Can I tell you something without it going to your head?" Shelby murmured as she ran her fingers down his chest, over his ribs.

"Probably not." His voice had thickened from the pleasure of being touched. "I'm easily flattered."

"In my workroom..." Shelby pressed her lips to his chest and felt his heartbeat thud faster against them. "When I messed up your shirt and you took it off to rinse it? I turned around and saw you—I wanted to get my hands on you like this." She ran her palms up, then down again to where his waist narrowed. "Just like this, I nearly did."

Alan felt his blood start to pound—in his head, his

heart, his loins. "I wouldn't have put up much of a fight."

"If I'd decided to have you, Senator," she murmured on a sultry laugh, "you wouldn't have had a chance."

"Is that so?"

Shelby ran her tongue down his rib cage. *"Mmm,"* she said when she heard the small, quick intake of breath. "Just so. A MacGregor will always buckle under to a Campbell."

Alan started to form a retort, then her fingers skimmed his thigh. As a politician, he knew the value of a debate—but sometimes they didn't require words. She could have the floor first.

He could float under the strong, skilled touch of her hands. As the need built in power, so did the pleasure of the prolonging. She seemed absorbed with the shape of his body, the texture of his skin. The candlelight flickered, pale red, against the back of his eyelids as he lay steeped in what she brought him. The rain continued its monotonous song, but he began to hear only Shelby's quiet sighs and murmurs.

She moved slowly, loitering here, nibbling there. A touch could weaken or excite. A kiss could soothe or madden. His pulse beat faster, then faster still, until he knew it was time to present his side. In a swift move, he rolled her beneath him.

Her face was flushed with heat, her breathing unsteady with the edges of passion just begun. Alan looked at her, wanting this memory for cold nights and listless afternoons.

The wild splash of red that was her hair tumbled over the vivid green of the bedspread. Shadows from the candle shifted over her face, reminding him of the impression he'd first had of her—the gypsy—open fires, weeping violins. Her eyes were dark, pure gray, and waiting.

"We MacGregors," he murmured, "have ways of...dealing with Campbells."

His mouth lowered but paused a whisper from hers. He saw that her lids had fluttered down yet hadn't closed. She watched him through her lashes while her breath came quickly. Slowly he shifted his head to nibble along her jawline.

Shelby closed her eyes on a moan that was as much in protest as appreciation. Her lips were aching for his, but the feel of that clever mouth teasing over her skin brought such quick, such vibrant, thrills. His hands were already on her, moving with a thoroughness she knew he would always bring to her.

Lazy, lengthy, devastating circles were traced around her breasts with tongue and teeth and lips; however, he didn't allow her to concentrate on only the sensation there. His fingers skimmed low over her stomach, taunting, promising, until she arched against him, desperate for that blinding flash of heat. But he was in no hurry now and so drew out her pleasure; built her needs layer by layer with that intense patience that left her helpless.

His mouth inched lower, his tongue flicking fires, his hand fanning them. Neither knew the moment when the world ceased to exist. It might have been winked out in an instant; it might have spun slowly to a stop. But there was nothing but them, flesh against flesh, sigh for sigh, need for need.

His mouth came back to hers, drawing out that last

moment before oblivion would claim them. She was trembling when he slipped inside her, harnessing the power rushing through him. He would pleasure her until they were both mad from it. He took her slowly, listening to the deep, shuddering breaths that mixed with his as their lips clung, drinking in the hot, moist tastes of her mouth.

Time seemed to hold for them, then it came spinning back until it was all speed, all whirling urgency. Alan buried his face at her throat and went with the madness.

Chapter Eight

Dingy gloomy mornings tended to make Shelby pull the covers over her head and tune out for an extra hour after her mental alarm rang. This morning, feeling the warmth of Alan beside her, she snuggled closer and prepared to do the same thing. It was obvious, after his hand slid down her back and intimately over her bottom, that he had other plans.

"Are you awake?" he murmured next to her ear. "Or should I wake you?"

She gave him an *mmm* for an answer.

"I take that to mean you're undecided." Alan moved his lips down to her throat where her pulse beat slow and steady. How long, he wondered idly, would it take him to change that? "Maybe I can influence you to take a firmer stand."

Slowly, enjoying her drowsy response, he began to kiss and fondle. It seemed impossible, he knew, that he could have steeped himself in her the night before and still want her so feverishly this morning. But her skin was so warm and soft—so was her mouth. Her movements beneath him remained lazy but not sluggish. He felt, as he wanted to, the gradual increase of her pulse.

Passion slept in her so that she seemed content to let him touch and explore as he chose while she aroused him with her sighs alone. The morning grew late—but they had forever.

Their lovemaking had a misty, dreamy aura that lasted from the first casual touch to the last breathless kiss.

"I think," Shelby said as Alan nuzzled lazily between her breasts, "that we should stay in bed until it stops raining."

"Too soon," he murmured. "You should have thought of that days ago." With his eyes closed, he could see her lying sleepily beneath him, her skin still heated from his. "Are you going to open the shop today?"

She yawned, running her hands along the ridge of muscles in his upper back. "Kyle takes care of it on Saturdays. We can stay right here and sleep."

He kissed the curve of her breasts, then slowly worked up to her throat. "I've a luncheon meeting this afternoon and some paperwork that has to be taken care of before Monday."

Of course, she thought, biting back a sigh. To a man like Alan, Saturday was just another day of the week. A glance at the clock showed her it was barely seven. In reflex, she curled into him. Time was already slipping away. "That gives us a few hours to stay right here."

"What about breakfast?"

Shelby considered for a minute, then decided she was lazier than she was hungry. "Can you cook?"

"No."

Drawing her brows together, she grabbed both of his ears and drew his head up. "Not at all? That's remarkably chauvinistic for a man whose policies primarily reflect the feminist viewpoint."

Alan lifted a brow. "I don't expect you to be able to cook either." Amusement shot into his eyes. "Can you?"

Shelby struggled with a grin. "Barely."

"I find that odd for someone with your appetite."

"I eat out a lot. What about you?"

"McGee sees to it."

"McGee?"

"He's what you might term a family retainer." Alan twined a tumbled curl around his finger. "He was our butler when I was a boy, and when I moved to D.C., he insisted, in his stoic, unmovable way, on coming with me." He gave her the quick flash of grin that came rarely to him. "I've always been his favorite."

"Is that so?" Lazily Shelby folded her arms behind her head. She could picture him as a boy, seeing beyond what other boys saw and storing it. "Why?"

"If I weren't modest, I'd confess that I was always a well-mannered, even-tempered child who never gave my parents a moment's trouble."

"Liar," she said easily. "How'd you get the broken nose?"

The grin became rueful. "Rena punched me."

"Your sister broke your nose?" Shelby burst out with delighted and unsympathetic laughter. "The blackjack dealer, right? Oh, I love it!"

Alan caught Shelby's nose between two fingers and gave it a quick twist. "It was rather painful at the time."

"I imagine." She kept right on laughing as he shifted to her side. "Did she make a habit of beating you up?"

"She didn't beat me up," he corrected with some dignity. "She was trying to beat Caine up because he'd teased her about making calf's eyes at one of his friends."

"Typical brotherly intimidation."

"In any event," Alan put in mildly, "I went to drag her off him, she took another swing, missed him, and hit me. A full-power roundhouse, as I remember. That's when," he continued as Shelby gave another peal of laughter, "I decided against being a diplomat. It's always the neutral party that gets punched in the face."

"I'm sure..." Shelby dropped her head on his shoulder. "I'm sure she was sorry."

"Initially. But as I recall, after I'd stopped bleeding and threatening to kill both her and Caine, her reaction was a great deal like yours."

"Insensitive." Shelby ran apologetic kisses over his face. "Poor baby. Tell you what, I'll do penance and see about fixing you breakfast." With a quick burst of energy, she gave him a last kiss and bounded from the bed. "Come on, let's see what's in the kitchen." Finding a robe that had been tossed over a chair, Shelby waited until Alan slipped into his slacks. "You can make the coffee," she told him, "while I see if there's anything edible in the fridge."

"Sounds promising," Alan murmured.

"Now, don't get snotty before you know what might turn up," she advised. They passed through the living room where the cat simply rolled over on the sofa and ignored them. "He's still sulking," Shelby stated with a sigh. "Now I'll have to buy him chicken livers or something." She stopped to pull the water dish out of Auntie Em's cage. "He's a moody creature, isn't he?" she said to the bird. Auntie Em gave one impatient squawk, the extent of her vocabulary.

"Sounds like she got up on the wrong side of the perch," Alan commented.

"Oh, no. She's in a good mood if she says anything."

He gave Shelby an interested glance. "Did she?"

For an answer, she handed him the water bowl. "Here, you can take care of this before you start the coffee." Without waiting for an assent, she went through the kitchen to the side door to bring in the paper. Alan looked down at the container like a man who'd been handed a small damp-bottomed child. "It seems the President's Mideast tour is still the top story," she noted before she tossed the paper onto the counter. "Do you like to travel?"

Recognizing the meaning behind the query, Alan switched off the water before he answered. "At times I enjoy it. At times it's simply a necessity. It isn't always possible to choose when and where I go."

Deliberately she shook off the mood. "I suppose not." Shelby opened the refrigerator and stared inside until she heard him move away to see to the bird. *Don't think about it,* she ordered herself fiercely. *You're not to think about it today.*

"Well," she began brightly when Alan came back into the room. "What we have here is a quart of milk, a couple of leftover cartons of Chinese, a very small slice of goat cheese, half a pack of Fig Newtons, and an egg."

Alan came up to look over her shoulder. "One egg?"

"All right, just wait a minute," Shelby told him while she nibbled on her lower lip. "You have to consider the possibilities."

"We could consider the restaurant around the corner."

"The man has no vision," Shelby muttered as she concentrated. "Let me see…" Moving aside, she rummaged through a cupboard. "Okay, I have… three, four, five slices of bread, if you count the heels. French toast." She smiled triumphantly. "That's two and a half pieces for each of us."

Alan nodded. "All right, you take the heels."

"Picky." Clucking her tongue, Shelby went back for the milk and the egg.

"Discriminating," he corrected, and left her to her creation while he made coffee.

For a few moments, they worked in companionable silence: Alan measured out coffee and water; Shelby dumped what she thought might be the right amount of milk into a bowl. Alan watched her rummage through a cupboard, pushing aside an empty jar, a large plastic container without a lid, and a loose-leaf notebook. "So there's where that is," she was muttering until she came up with a frying pan. As she rose Shelby caught his eye and the gleam of amusement.

"I don't do a great deal of this." Shelby put the pan on a burner and flicked on the flame.

"I'd remind you of that restaurant around the corner except..." His gaze flicked over the robe that dipped deep at her breasts and skimmed her thighs. "You'd have to get dressed."

Shelby smiled, a slow invitation, but when he took a step toward her, she dunked bread into the batter. "Get a plate."

He reached into the cupboard she indicated, then drew two plates out before he came to stand behind her. Leaning over, he brushed his lips below her ear, pleased with the quick tremor of response.

"The ones I burn," Shelby warned, "are all yours."

He chuckled and set the plates beside the stove. "Got any powdered sugar?"

"For what?" Catching her tongue between her teeth, Shelby flipped the bread over.

"For that." Alan opened three likely drawers before he located the flatware.

Rubbing her nose with the back of her hand, she glanced over as the last piece began to simmer in the pan. "Don't you use syrup?"

"No."

With a careless shrug, she slipped the last slice of toast onto a plate. "Well, you do today. I probably have some in...the second cabinet to the left," she decided. While he looked she meticulously divided one piece in half. Shelby had poured the coffee and brought the plates and cups to the table before he managed to locate the bottle.

"It looks like we have about a tablespoon," Alan decided as he tilted the bottle to its side.

"That's one and a half spoonfuls apiece." Sitting, Shelby held out her hand for the bottle. After pouring carefully, she passed the syrup back to him. "I have a hard time remembering what I'm nearly out of," she told him as she began to eat.

He fought to squeeze out the last drops from the bottle. "You must have six boxes of cat food in that cupboard."

"Moshe gets cranky if I don't keep a variety."

After tasting his breakfast, Alan found it better than he had expected. "I have a hard time understanding anyone as strong-willed as you being intimidated by a temperamental cat."

Shelby lifted her shoulders and continued to eat. "We all have our weaknesses. Besides, as roommates go, he's perfect. He doesn't listen in on my phone calls or borrow my clothes."

"Are those your prerequisites?"

"They're certainly in the top ten."

Watching her, Alan nodded. She'd plowed her way through the toast in record time. "If I promised to restrain myself from doing either of those things, would you marry me?"

The cup she had lifted froze halfway to her lips. For the first time since he'd met her, Alan saw Shelby totally and completely stunned. She put the coffee down untasted, then stared at it while hundreds of thoughts raced through her head. Dominating them all was the simple and basic emotion of fear.

"Shelby?"

Quickly she shook her head. She rose, clattering the flatware onto her plate and scooping it up to take it to the sink. She didn't speak—didn't dare speak yet. What threatened to come out was *yes,* and she feared that most of all. There was a pressure in her chest, a weight, a pain. It reminded her to let out the breath she'd been holding. As she did Shelby leaned heavily against the sink and stared into the rain. When Alan's hands came to her shoulders, she closed her eyes.

Why hadn't she been prepared? She knew that for a man like Alan love would lead to marriage. And marriage to children, she told herself as she tried to calm her nerves. If it wasn't what she wanted as well, she wouldn't feel this frenzied urge to say yes, and to say yes quickly. But it wasn't as simple as love to marriage to children, not with Alan. There was the Senator in front of his name, and that wouldn't be the highest title he'd attempt.

"Shelby." His voice was still gentle, though she thought she could feel tiny pulses of impatience and frustration in the fingers that moved on her shoulders. "I love you. You're the only woman I've ever wanted to spend my life with. I need mornings like this— waking with you."

"So do I."

He turned her to face him. The intensity was back in his eyes, that dark seriousness that had first attracted her to him. He scanned her face, slowly, thoroughly. "Then, marry me."

"You make it sound so simple—"

"No," he interrupted. "Not simple. Necessary, vital, but not simple."

"Don't ask me now." Shelby wrapped her arms around him and held him close. "Please don't. We're together, and I love you. Let that be enough for now."

He wanted to press. Instinct told him he had only to demand an answer to hear the one he needed. And yet... He'd seen vulnerability when he'd looked into her face. He'd seen a plea in her eyes—two things rare in Shelby Campbell. Two things that made it impossible for him to demand anything.

"I'll want you just as much tomorrow," he murmured, stroking her hair. "And a year from tomorrow. I can promise to wait to ask you again, Shelby, but I can't promise to wait until you're ready to answer."

"You don't have to promise." Tilting back her head, she put a hand on either side of his face. "You don't have to give me any promises. For now, let's just enjoy what we have—a rainy weekend with each other. We don't need to think about tomorrows, Alan, when we have so much today. Questions are for later." When she pressed her mouth to his, Shelby felt a wave of love so intense, it brought shivers of fear to her skin. "Come back to bed. Make love with me again. When you do, there's nothing and no one but you and me."

He felt her desperation, though he didn't fully understand it. Without a word, Alan picked her up and carried her back to bed.

"I can still send my regrets," Alan stated as he pulled the car up in front of his house.

"Alan, I don't mind going, really." Shelby leaned over to give him a quick kiss before she slid out of the car. The rain had slowed to a drizzling evening mist that dampened the shoulders of her short velvet jacket. "Besides, these dinner dances can be fun— even when they're disguised political functions."

Alan joined her on the sidewalk to tilt her chin for another kiss. "I believe you'd go anywhere as long as food was on the bill."

"It is an incentive all its own." Hooking an arm through his, Shelby started up the walk. "And I also get the opportunity of poking around your house while you're changing."

"You might find it a bit...sedate for your tastes."

With a smoky laugh, Shelby bit his ear. "You're not."

"I think," Alan considered as he opened the front door, "we'd have a more stimulating evening at home."

"I could be persuaded." After stepping inside, Shelby turned to wind her arms around his neck. "If you'd like to make the effort."

Before Alan could oblige, he heard a stiff little cough. McGee stood near the parlor doors, sturdy as a tree. His long lined face was expressionless. Over the distance of six feet, Alan felt the waves of disapproval. He nearly sighed. McGee could still stand like the perfectly mannered servant and throw off vibrations like a stern uncle. Since he'd been sixteen, Alan had had to deal with that dignified disapproval whenever he'd come home late or not in the most sober of conditions.

"You had several calls, Senator."

Alan's mouth nearly twitched before he controlled it. The *senator* was reserved for use in the presence of company. "Anything urgent, McGee?"

"Nothing urgent, Senator," he replied, rolling the *r* for emphasis and delighting Shelby.

"I'll see to them later, then. Shelby, this is McGee. He's been with my family since I was a boy."

"Hello, McGee." With no self-consciousness, Shelby released Alan to walk to his servant and offer her hand. "Are you a Highlander?"

"Ma'am. From Perthshire."

Her smile would have charmed the bark off any tree, even such a gnarled one. "My grandfather came from Dalmally. Do you know it?"

"Aye." Alan watched the faded eyes warm. "It's country worth seeing twice."

"I thought so myself, though I haven't been since I was seven. It's the mountains I remember most. Do you go back often?"

"Every spring to see the heather blooming. There's nothing like walking in the heather in June."

It was the longest, and Alan mused, the most romantic statement he had ever heard McGee make in the presence of anyone who wasn't family. Yet it didn't surprise him. "McGee, if you'll make some tea, I'll go up and change. Perhaps you could serve Ms. Campbell in the parlor."

"Campbell?" McGee's habitual stone face cracked with surprise as he stared from Alan to Shelby. "Campbell..." Briefly, very briefly, Shelby thought she caught a look of unholy glee in his eyes. "There's going t'be a ruckus," he murmured before turning on his heel to stride toward the kitchen.

"Not everyone would have gotten that much out of him," Alan commented as he steered Shelby into the parlor.

"Was that a lot?"

"My love, for McGee, that was an oratory."

"*Hmm,* well, I liked him," Shelby decided as she wandered through the room. "Especially the way he scolded you, without saying a word, for staying out all night."

Slipping her hands into the deep pockets of her slim skirt, she studied the seascape on the wall. The room was ordered, calm, with subtle touches of turbulence. It suited the man, she mused. Shelby remembered the jade krater she'd made the day after she'd met him. He'd have to have it for this room, she reflected. Strange that she should have made something then that fit so perfectly into his world. Why couldn't she?

Forcing the thought back, she turned around to smile at him. "I like how you live."

The simple statement surprised him. Simple statements weren't the norm for Shelby. He'd expected some lighthearted comment with a slick double edge. Going to her, Alan ran his hands up the arms of her jacket, still damp from the drizzle. "I like seeing you here."

She wanted to cling to him then, right then, desperately. If only he could tell her everything would always be as it was at that moment—that nothing would change or interfere... Instead she touched a palm to his cheek and kept her voice light. "You'd better go up and change, Senator. The sooner we get there—" now she grinned "—the sooner we can get away."

He pressed her palm to his lips. "I like your thought process. I won't be long."

Alone, Shelby closed her eyes and gave in to the panic. What was she going to do? How could she love him, need him, like this when her head was screaming with warnings. *Don't. Be careful. Remember.*

There were a dozen solid, viable reasons why they didn't belong together. She could list them all...when he wasn't looking at her. She didn't even need that shivery misty fear that she kept trapped in the back of her mind.

She looked at the room again, closely. There was a basic order here, a style she admired, the understated wealth she understood. Fastidiousness without fussiness. But it wasn't *her* style. Shelby lived in chaos not because she was too lazy or too indifferent to order her life, but because she *chose* chaos.

There was an innate goodness in Alan she wasn't sure she had. A tolerance she was sure she didn't. Alan ran on facts or theories that had been well thought-out. She ran on imagination and possibilities. It was crazy, Shelby told herself as she dragged a hand through her hair. How could two people with so little common ground love each other so much?

She should have run, she told herself. She should have run fast and far the first minute she set eyes on him. With a half laugh, Shelby paced to the other end of the room. It would have done her no good. She could have fled like a crazed rabbit. Alan would have tracked her, calmly, unhurriedly. When she had collapsed, out of breath, he would just simply have been there waiting for her.

"Your tea, Miss Campbell."

Shelby turned to see McGee enter with a porcelain tea service she simply had to touch. "Oh, Meissen—red stoneware." She lifted the delicately painted, marbleized cup. "Johann Böttger, early 1700s... Wonderful." Shelby studied the cup as any art student studies the work of a master. She'd always felt museums had the right to preserve some irreplaceables behind glass while the rest should be handled, touched, and used. "He never reached his lifelong aim," she murmured, "to achieve that Oriental perfection of color decoration—but what marvelous things he produced trying."

Catching the butler's eye, Shelby realized she was being weighed as a possible gold digger. Amused, she set the cup back on the tray. "Sorry, McGee, I get carried away. I've an affection for clay."

"Clay, miss?"

She tapped a finger against the cup. "It all starts out that way. Just a lump of different sorts of dirt."

"Yes, miss." He decided it would be undignified to pursue the matter. "Perhaps you'd care to sit on the sofa."

Shelby obliged him, then watched as he carefully arranged the service on the table in front of her. "McGee...has Alan always been so quietly unbeatable?"

"Yes, miss," he answered without thinking. The phrase had been so perfectly apt.

"I was afraid so," Shelby murmured.

"I beg your pardon, miss?"

"What?" Distracted, Shelby glanced up, then shook her head. "Nothing, nothing at all. Thank you, McGee."

Shelby sipped, wondering why she had bothered to ask when she had known the answer. Alan would always win in whatever aspect of his life he concentrated on. For a moment, she stared into the pale gold tea. That was exactly what she most feared.

"What's the current price for a thought in these days of inflation?" Alan wondered aloud as he paused in the doorway. She'd looked so beautiful, he reflected. So distant. Then she glanced up with a smile that enhanced the first and erased the second.

"That was quick," Shelby complimented him and avoided the question with equal ease. "I'm afraid I admired your tea set a bit too strongly and made your butler nervous. He might be wondering if I'll slip the saucer into my bag." Setting down the cup, she rose. "Are you ready to go be charming and distinguished? You look as though you would be."

Alan lifted a brow. "I have a feeling *distinguished* comes perilously close to *sedate* in your book."

"No, you've lots of room yet," she told him as she breezed into the hall. "I'll give you a jab of you start teetering toward *sedate*."

Alan stopped her in the hall by slipping his arms around her waist. "I haven't done this in one hour and twenty-three minutes." His mouth covered hers, slowly, confidently. As her lips parted and offered he took, taking the kiss just to the border, but no further, of madness. "I love you." He caught her bottom lip between his teeth, then released her mouth only to change the angle and deepen the kiss. He felt her heartbeat sprint against his, felt that long, lazy melting of her bones he knew happened just before she went from pliant to avid. "Tonight, no matter who you dance with, think of me."

Breathless, she looked up. In his eyes, she saw that banked brooding passion she could never resist. He'd overwhelm her if she let him; absorb her. He had the power. Shelby tilted her head so her lips stayed within a whisper of his. "Tonight," she said huskily, "no matter who you dance with, you'll want me." Her arms stayed around him when she rested her head on his shoulder. "And I'll know."

Just then she caught a glimpse of them in the long beveled mirror framed on the wall. Alan, sleek and sophisticated, was as conventional in black tie as she was unorthodox in the snug velvet jacket and narrow rose-hued skirt she'd found in a shop that specialized in cast-off heirlooms "Alan," Shelby nudged him around until he faced the mirror with her. "What do you see?"

With his arm around her waist, he studied their reflections. The top of her head came to the base of his jaw. He wondered what other redhead could have not only worn that shade of rose, but looked so stunning in it. She might have stepped out of that antique looking glass in the century in which it had been fashioned. But there was no cameo at her neck. Instead there was a thick twisted gold chain that probably came from a narrow little Georgetown shop. Her hair curled riotously, untamedly, around her pale angled face. The faint shadow of trouble in her eyes made her look more like the waif he'd first compared her to.

"I see two people in love," he said with his gaze fixed on hers in the glass. "Two very different people who look extraordinarily well together."

Shelby leaned her head on his shoulder again, unsure if she was glad or annoyed that he read her so perfectly. "He would look very good, and much more suitable, with a cool blonde in a very classic black dress."

Alan seemed to consider for a moment. "Do you know," he said mildly. "That's the first time I've heard you sound like a complete ass."

She stared back at his image, at the faintly interested, fully reasonable expression on his face. She laughed. There seemed to be nothing else for her to do. "All right, just for that, I'm going to be every bit as dignified as you are."

"God forbid," Alan muttered before he pulled her out the front door.

Elegant lighting and the sparkle of crystal. White linen tablecloths and the gleam of silver. Shelby sat at one of the more than two-dozen large round tables with Alan on one hand and the head of the Ways and Means Committee on the other. She spooned at her lobster bisque and kept up a flowing conversation.

"If you weren't so stubborn, Leo, and tried an aluminum racket, you might just see an improvement in your game."

"My game *has* improved." The balding bull-shouldered statesman shook his spoon at her. "We haven't had a match in six months. You wouldn't beat me in straight sets now.''

Shelby smiled, sipping from her water glass as one course was cleared and replaced by the next. ''We'll see if I can't squeeze out a couple of hours and get to the club.''

''You do that. Damned if I wouldn't enjoy whipping you.''

''You're going to have to watch those foot faults, Leo,'' she reminded him with the grin still in her eyes.

She thanked fate for seating her next to Leo. With him, she could be easy, natural. There were dozens of people in the huge high-ceilinged room she knew, and a handful she'd have been genuinely pleased to spend an hour with.

Ambition. It wafted through the room like expensive perfume. She didn't mind that, but the stiff, unbending rules and traditions that went hand in hand with it. Hand in hand with Alan, she remembered, then pushed the thought aside. She'd promised him she'd be on her best behavior. God knows she was trying.

''Then there's your weak backhand...''

''Just leave my backhand alone,'' he told her with a sniff. Leaning forward a bit, he frowned at Alan. ''You ever played tennis with this hustler, MacGregor?''

''No, I haven't—'' his eyes skimmed over to Shelby's ''—yet.''

''Well, I'll warn you, this little girl takes a vicious delight in winning. No respect for age either,'' he added as he picked up his fork.

"I'm still not going to spot you points for years, Leo," Shelby stated easily. "You have a habit of adding them indiscriminately when you're behind in sets."

A smile twitched at his mouth. "Devil," he accused. "You wait until the rematch."

With a laugh, Shelby turned back to Alan. "Do you play tennis, Senator?"

"Now and then," he said with the ghost of a smile. He didn't add he'd lettered in the sport at Harvard.

"I'd imagine chess would be your game—plotting, long-term strategy."

His smile remained enigmatic as he reached for his wine. "We'll have to have a game."

Shelby's low laugh drifted over him. "I believe we already have."

His hand brushed lightly over hers. "Want a rematch?"

Shelby gave him a look that made his blood spring hotly. "No. You might not outmaneuver me a second time."

God, but he wished the interminable meal would end. He wanted her alone—alone where he could peel off those clothes layer by layer and feel her skin warm. He could watch those laughing gray eyes cloud until he knew she thought of nothing but him. It was her scent that was hammering at his senses, not the arrangement of baby roses in the center of the table, not the aroma of food as yet another course was served. It was her voice he heard—low and just a little throaty—not the tones and textures of the voices all around him. He could talk with the congresswoman on his right, talk as if he were vitally interested in everything she told him. But he thought about holding Shelby and hearing her murmur his name when she touched him.

This sharpness of need would ease, Alan told himself. It had to. A man could go mad wanting a woman this intensely. In time it would become a more comfortable sensation—a touch in the middle of the night, a smile across the room. He glanced at her profile as she continued to tease Leo. Those sharp pixie features, that tousled flame of hair—she'd never be comfortable. The need would never ease. And she was his destiny as much as he was hers. Neither of them could stop it.

The conversations ebbed and flowed over the muted dinner music. A curtain of smoke rose up toward the ceiling from cigarettes and pipes and after-dinner cigars. Talk centered around politics, edgy at times, pragmatic at others. Whatever other topic that came up was invariably linked to the core of the world they revolved in. Alan heard Shelby give a concise and unflattering opinion of a controversial bill slated to come before Congress the following week. It infuriated the man she spoke with, though he maintained a tight-lipped control Shelby seemed implacably trying to break. Though he agreed with her stand, her tactics were…rebellious? he decided after a moment. A diplomat she would never be.

Did she know how complex she was? he wondered. Here was a woman dead set against politicians as a group, yet she could meet them on their own terms, talk to them in their own voice without revealing the slightest discomfort. If indeed she felt any, Alan added. No, if there was discomfort, it was on the opposing side. His gaze skimmed over the other people at their table as he continued his conversation with the congresswoman. Shelby didn't have their polish, their gloss. And Alan knew it was through her own choosing. More than that, she was dedicatedly opposed to possessing it. She didn't exploit the unique, she simply *was* the unique.

The sleek brunette across from him might be more beautiful, the blonde more regal—but it was Shelby you would remember when the evening was over. The representative from Ohio might have a wicked wit, the Assistant Secretary of State might be erudite—but it was Shelby you wanted to talk to. Why? The reason was there was no reason you could name. It was simply so.

He felt her shift before her lips brushed close to his ear. "Are you going to dance with me, Senator? It's the only dignified way I can get my hands on you at the moment."

Alan let the first wave of desire take him—a rush that blanked everyone else from his sight and hearing for one heady instant. Carefully he banked it before he rose and took her hand. "Strange how closely our minds work." After leading her to the dance floor he gathered her to him. "And how well," he murmured as their bodies melded together, "we fit."

Shelby tilted her head back. "We shouldn't." Her eyes promised hot, private secrets. Her lips tempted—just parted, just curved. The hand on his shoulder moved nearer to his neck so she could brush his skin with her fingertips. "We shouldn't fit. We shouldn't understand each other. I can't quite figure out why we do."

"You defy logic, Shelby. And therefore, logically, there's no reasonable answer."

She laughed, pleased with the structured workings of his mind. "Oh, Alan, you're much too sensible to be argued with."

"Which means you'll constantly do so."

"Exactly." Still smiling, she rested her head on his shoulder. "You know me too well for my own good, Alan…and perhaps for yours. I'm in danger of adoring you."

He remembered Myra had used that word to describe Shelby's feelings for her father. "I'll take the risk. Will you?"

With her eyes closed, she made a slight movement with her head. Neither of them knew if it was assent or denial.

As the evening wore on they danced again, each thinking of the other as they moved to the music with someone else. From time to time if they saw each other across the room a message would pass, too strong and too direct not to be observed by people whose livelihoods depended on the interpretation of a look or gesture. Undercurrents of all kinds were an intimate part of the game in Washington. Some flowed with them, others against them, but all acknowledged them.

"Well, Alan." Leo clamped a hand on Alan's shoulder as Shelby was led onto the dance floor again. "You're making some progress on your personal windmill."

Alan settled back with his wine, half-smiling. He didn't mind the allusion to Don Quixote when it came to his housing project. That sort of tag would have certain advantages in the long run. It was human nature to at least root for the underdog even if doing nothing tangible to help. "A bit. I'm beginning to get some positive feedback from Boston on the progress of the shelters there."

"It would be to your benefit if you could get and keep the ball rolling during this administration." He flipped out a lighter and flicked it at the end of a long fragrant cigar. "It should bring a lot of support your way if you decide to toss your hat in the ring."

Alan tasted the wine and watched Shelby. "It's early days yet for that, Leo."

"You know better." Leo puffed smoke toward the ceiling. "I never wanted that…particular race for myself. But you…a lot of people are willing to swing your way when the time comes, if you give the nod."

Alan turned to give his colleague a long look. "So I've been told," he said cautiously. "I appreciate it. It isn't a decision I'll make lightly, one way or the other."

"Let me give you a few pros because, bluntly, I'm not enthusiastic about what we have in the bull pen at the moment." He leaned a bit closer. "Your record's impressive—even though it leans a bit to the left for some tastes. You had a solid run in Congress and your term as senator's running smoothly. I won't get into a point by point of your policies or your individual bills—let's stick with image." He puffed on the cigar again as he considered.

"Your youth is to your advantage. It gives us time. Your education was slick and impressive—and the fact that you did well in sports never hurts. People like to think that their leader can handle himself on any playing field. Your family background's clean and solid. The fact that your mother is a highly successful professional works strongly in your favor.''

"She'll be glad to hear it,'' Alan said dryly.

"You're too smart to think it doesn't matter,'' Leo reminded him, gesturing with his cigar. ''It shows that you can relate and understand professional women— a healthy chunk of the voting power. Your father has a reputation for going his own way, but going honestly. There's no hornet's nest to keep locked in the attic.''

"Leo…'' Alan swirled his wine before he shot Leo a direct look. "Who asked you to speak to me?''

"And you're perceptive,'' Leo returned without missing a beat. "Let's just say I was asked to approach you and touch on some generalities.''

"All right. Generally speaking, I haven't ruled out the possibility of entering the primaries when the time comes.''

"Fair enough.'' Leo nodded toward Shelby. "I'm personally fond of the girl. But will she be an asset to you? I never would have seen the two of you as a couple.''

"Oh?'' The word was mild, but Alan's eyes narrowed ever so slightly.

"Campbell's daughter—she knows the ropes, being on the campaign trail as a child.'' Leo pursed his lips, cautiously weighing the pros and cons. "Shelby grew up with politics, so she wouldn't have to be tutored on protocol or diplomacy. Of course, she's a bit of a maverick.'' He tapped his cigar thoughtfully. "More than a bit when it comes to it. She's put her considerable energy into flouting the Washington social scene for years. There are those that rather like her for it, myself for one, but she's put a few noses out of joint in her day.''

Leo popped the cigar back into his mouth and chewed on it while Alan remained flatly silent. ''But then, it's possible to polish off a few rough edges. She's young; the flamboyance could be toned down. Her education and family background are above reproach. There's enough glamour attached to her to attract, not enough to alienate. She runs her own business successfully and knows how to handle a crowd. An excellent choice, all in all,'' he decided. ''If you can whip her into shape.''

Alan set down his glass to prevent himself from throwing it. ''Shelby isn't required to be an asset,'' he said in a deadly controlled voice. ''She isn't required to be anything but what she chooses. Our relationship isn't grist for the political mill, Leo.''

Leo frowned at the tip of his cigar. He'd touched a nerve, he realized, but was rather pleased with the manner in which Alan controlled rage. It wasn't wise to have a hothead commanding the armed forces. ''I realize you feel entitled to a certain amount of privacy, Alan. But once you toss your hat in the ring, you toss your lady's in too. We're a culture of couples. One reflects the other.''

Knowing it was true only infuriated him more. This was what Shelby backed away from, what she feared. How could he protect her from it and remain what he was? ''Whatever I decide to do, Shelby remains free to be exactly what Shelby is.'' Alan rose. ''That's the bottom line.''

Chapter Nine

With sunshine and the best of spirits, Shelby opened the doors of Calliope Monday morning. If there had been a monsoon outside the windows, it wouldn't have jarred her mood. She had spent a long lazy Sunday with Alan, never once venturing outside her apartment. Never once wanting to.

Now Shelby sat behind the counter and decided to allow a little of the outside world into her sphere. Taking the morning paper, she opened it first, as always, to the comics. What characters would appear in Macintosh and what would they have to say for themselves? With her elbows propped, her hands supporting her chin, Shelby gave a snort of laughter. As usual Macintosh hit things on the head, but at a tilted angle that couldn't be resisted. She hoped the Vice President kept his sense of humor after he'd read his little part in this morning's column. From her experience, people in the limelight rarely objected to being caricaturized—to a point. Exposure, satirical or not, was exposure.

Shelby glanced at the signature line, the simple G.C. identifying the cartoonist. Perhaps when one hit so often and so truly at the ego, it was best to opt for anonymity. She couldn't do it, she realized. It simply wasn't in her nature to be clever anonymously.

Reaching absently for her half-cup of cooling coffee, Shelby continued down the page. Humor always eased her into the day and affirmed her view that whatever oddities there were in the world, there was a place for them. Still sipping, she glanced up as the door to the shop opened.

"Hi." With a smile for Maureen Francis, she pushed the paper aside. The brunette didn't look like a woman who'd even own a slicker, much less wear one. This morning it was silk, robin's egg blue cut into a slim spring suit. "Hey, you look great," Shelby told her, admiring the suit without imagining herself in it.

"Thanks." Maureen set a trim leather briefcase on the counter. "I came by to pick up my pottery and to thank you."

"I'll get the boxes." She slipped into the back room where she'd instructed Kyle to store them. "What do I get thanked for?" she called out.

"The contact." Unable to contain her curiosity, Maureen slipped around the counter to poke her head into Shelby's workroom. "This is wonderful," she decided, staring with layman's perplexity at the wheel before she scanned the shelves. "I'd love to watch you work sometime."

"Catch me in the right mood on a Wednesday or Saturday, and I'll give you a quick lesson if you'd like."

"Can I ask you a stupid question?"

"Sure." Shelby glanced back over her shoulder. "Everyone's entitled to three a week."

Maureen gestured to encompass the workroom and the shop. "How do you manage all this by yourself? I mean, I *know* what it's like to start your own business. It's difficult and complicated enough, but when you add this kind of creativity, the hours it takes you to produce something—then to switch gears and go into merchandising."

"That's not a stupid question," Shelby decided after a moment. "I suppose I like dipping my hands into both elements. In here, I'm normally very isolated. Out there—" she gestured toward the shop "—I'm not. And I like calling my own tune." With a grin, she began shuffling cartons. "I imagine you do, too, or you'd still be with that firm in Chicago."

"Yes, but I still have moments when I'm tempted to race back to safety." She studied Shelby's back. "I don't imagine you do."

"There's a certain amount of fun in instability, isn't there?" Shelby countered. "Especially if you believe there's bound to be a net somewhere to catch you if you slip off the edge."

With a laugh, Maureen shook her head. "That's one way of looking at it. Enjoy, and take the rest on faith."

"In a nutshell." Shelby handed Maureen the first box, then hefted the other two herself. "By the contact you mentioned, I suppose you mean Myra."

"*Mmm,* yes. I called her Saturday afternoon. All I had to do was say Shelby, and she invited me for brunch this morning."

"Myra doesn't believe in wasting time." Shelby blew her bangs out of her eyes as she set the boxes on the counter. "Will you let me know how it goes?"

"You'll be the first," Maureen promised. "You know, not everyone's so willing to hand out favors— to close friends, let alone strangers. I really appreciate it."

"You said you were good," Shelby reminded her with a grin as she started to make out a final receipt. "I thought you might be. In any event, you might not consider it so much a favor by this afternoon. Myra's a tough lady."

"So'm I." Maureen drew out her checkbook. "And an insatiably curious one. You can tell me to mind my own business," she began, glancing back up at Shelby. "But I have to ask you how things worked out with Senator MacGregor. I'm afraid I didn't recognize him at the time. I took him for your average lovesick maniac."

Shelby considered the phrase and found it to her liking. "He's a stubborn man," she told Maureen and ripped off her copy of the receipt. "Thank God."

"Good. I like a man who thinks in rainbows. Well, I'd better get these boxes into the car if I don't want to be late."

"I'll give you a hand." Holding boxes, Shelby propped the door open so Maureen could pass.

"The car's right here." She popped open the rear door of a trim little hatchback. "I might just drop in on you on one of those Wednesdays or Saturdays."

"Fine. If I snarl, just back off until the mood passes. Good luck."

"Thanks." Maureen shut the hatch and moved around to the driver's side. "Give the Senator my regards, will you?"

Laughing, Shelby waved her away before she went back into the shop. She'd box up that green krater, she decided. This time she'd give Alan a surprise.

He was about to get one in any case—though it shouldn't have been a surprise to him.

Alan didn't often feel harassed, but this morning had been one continual stream of meetings. He didn't often feel pressured by the press, but the reporter who had been lying in wait for him outside the new Senate office building had been both tenacious and irritating. Perhaps he still carried a layer of annoyance from his conversation with Leo, or perhaps he had simply been working too hard, but by the time Alan stepped off the elevator onto his own floor of the building, his patience was strained to the breaking point.

"Senator." His assistant sprang up from her chair, looking nearly as frazzled as he felt. "The phones hardly stopped all morning." She carried a leather ledger with her and was already thumbing through it. "A Ned Brewster with the AFL-CIO; Congresswoman Platt; Shiver at the mayor's office in Boston in reference to the Back Bay Shelter; Smith, the Media Adviser; a Rita Cardova, a social worker in northeast who insists on speaking to you personally about your housing project; and—"

"Later." Alan strode through to his office and closed the door. Ten minutes—he promised himself ten minutes as he dropped his briefcase on his desk.

He'd been answering a merry-go-round of demands since eight-thirty that morning. Damn if he wouldn't steal ten minutes before he hopped back on again.

It wasn't like him to need them, he thought with a sound of frustration as he frowned out the window. He could see the east side of the Capitol, the white dome symbolizing democracy, freedom of thought, justice—everything Alan had always believed in. He could see Capitol Plaza with its huge round pots filled with flowers. They'd been put in after the bombing—an aesthetic barricade. They represented what Alan knew was part of the human web. Some sought to build; some sought to destroy. Terrorism was frighteningly logical. If he, as Leo had put it, threw his hat into the ring, it was something he would have to deal with every day.

His decision couldn't be put off much longer. Oh, normally, he could bide his time, test the waters. And in essence he would do so—publicly. But privately his decision had to come soon. There'd be no asking Shelby to marry him again until he could first tell her what he was considering. He would be asking her to share more than name, home, and family if he eventually sought the presidency. He would be asking her to elect to give a section of her life to him, to their country, to the wheels of protocol and politics. Alan no longer considered the decision to be his alone. Shelby was already his wife in all but the legal sense—he had only to convince her of that.

When the buzzer on his desk sounded, he eyed it with displeasure. He'd only had five of his ten minutes. Annoyed, he picked up the phone. "Yes?"

"I'm sorry to disturb you, Senator, but your father's on line one."

He dragged a hand through his hair as he sat. "All right, I'll take it. Arlene—*I'm* sorry, it's been a rough morning."

Her tone underwent a quick and total change. "It's okay. Your father sounds...characteristically exuberant, Senator."

"Arlene, you should have opted for the diplomatic corps." He heard her light chuckle before he switched lines. "Hello, Dad."

"Well, well, well, so you're still alive." The booming, full-bodied voice was not so subtly laced with sarcasm. "Your mother and I thought you'd met with some fatal accident."

Alan managed to keep the grin out of his voice. "I nicked myself shaving last week. How are you?"

"He asks how I am!" Daniel heaved a sigh that should have been patented for long-suffering fathers everywhere. "I wonder you even remember *who* I am. But that's all right—it doesn't matter about me. Your mother, now, she's been expecting her son to call. Her firstborn."

Alan leaned back. How often had he cursed fate for making him the eldest and giving his father that neat little phrase to needle him with? Of course, he remembered philosophically, Daniel had phrases for Rena and Caine as well—the only daughter, the youngest son. It was all relative. "Things've been a little hectic. Is Mom there?"

"Had an emergency at the hospital." Wild horses wouldn't have made Daniel admit that his wife, Anna, would have lectured him for an hour if she'd known what he was up to. Daniel considered it basic strategy not to tell her until it was done. "Since she's been moping and sighing around here," he lied without qualm, "I thought I'd bury my pride and call you myself. It's time you took a weekend and came to see your mother."

Alan lifted a wry brow, knowing his father all too well. "I'd think *she'd* be all wrapped up in her first prospective grandchild. How is Rena?"

"You can see for yourself this weekend," Daniel informed him. "I—that is, Rena and Justin have decided they want to spend a weekend with the family. Caine and Diana are coming too."

"You've been busy," Alan murmured.

"What was that? Don't mumble, boy."

"I said you'll be busy," Alan amended prudently.

"For your mother's sake, I can sacrifice my peace and quiet. She worries about all of you—you especially since you're still without wife and family. The firstborn," he added, working himself up, "and both your brother and sister settled before you. The eldest son, my own father's namesake, and too busy flitting around to do his duty to the MacGregor line."

Alan thought about his grueling morning and nearly smiled. "The MacGregor line seems to be moving along nicely. Maybe Rena'll have twins."

"Hah!" But Daniel considered the idea for a moment. He thought he recalled twins a couple of generations back on his mother's side. He made a mental note to check the family tree after he hung up. "We'll expect you Friday night. Now..." Daniel leaned across his massive desk and puffed on one of his forbidden cigars. "What the hell is all this I read in the papers?"

"Narrow it down for me," Alan suggested.

"I suppose it might have been a misprint," Daniel considered, frowning at the tip of his cigar before he tapped it in the ashtray he kept secreted in the bottom drawer of his desk. "I think I know my own flesh and blood well enough."

"Narrow it just a bit further," Alan requested, though he'd already gotten the drift. It was simply too good to end it too soon.

"When I read that my own son—my heir, as things are—is spending time fraternizing with a Campbell, I know it's a simple matter of a misspelling. What's the girl's name?"

Along with a surge of affection, Alan felt a tug of pure and simple mischief. "Which girl is that?"

"Dammit, boy! The girl you're seeing who looks like a pixie. Fetching young thing from the picture I saw. Good bones; holds herself well."

"Shelby," Alan said, then waited a beat. "Shelby Campbell."

Dead silence. Leaning back in his chair, Alan wondered how long it would be before his father remembered to take a breath. It was a pity, he mused, a real pity that he couldn't see the old pirate's face.

"*Campbell!*" The word erupted. "A thieving, murdering Campbell!"

"Yes, she's fond of MacGregors as well."

"No son of mine gives the time of day to one of the clan Campbell!" Daniel bellowed. "I'll take a strap to you, Alan Duncan MacGregor!" The threat was as empty now as it had been when Alan had been eight, but delivered in the same full-pitched roar. "I'll wear the hide off you."

"You'll have the chance to try this weekend when you meet Shelby."

"A Campbell in *my* house! Hah!"

"A Campbell in your house," Alan repeated mildly. "And a Campbell in your family before the end of the year if I have my way."

"You—" Emotions warred in him. A Campbell versus his firmest aspiration: to see each of his children married and settled, and himself laden with grandchildren. "You're thinking of marriage to a Campbell?"

"I've already asked her. She won't have me... yet," he added.

"Won't have you!" Paternal pride dominated all else. "What kind of a nitwit is she? Typical Campbell," he muttered. "Mindless pagans." Daniel suspected they'd had some sorcerers sprinkled among them. "Probably bewitched the boy," he mumbled, scowling into space. "Always had good sense before this. Aye, you bring your Campbell to me," he ordered roundly. "I'll get to the bottom of it."

Alan smothered a laugh, forgetting the poor mood that had plagued him only minutes earlier. "I'll ask her."

"*Ask?* Hah! You bring the girl, that daughter of a Campbell, here."

Picturing Shelby, Alan decided he wouldn't miss the meeting for two-thirds of the popular vote. "I'll see you Friday, Dad. Give Mom my love."

"Friday," Daniel murmured, puffing avidly on his cigar. "Aye, aye, Friday."

As he hung up Alan could all but see his father rubbing his huge hands together in anticipation. It should be an interesting weekend.

When he pulled up in the alleyway beside Shelby's town house, Alan forgot his fatigue. The ten-hour day was behind him, with all its reams of paperwork, facts, and figures.

But when Shelby opened the door to him, she saw the weariness and the dregs of annoyance still in his eyes. "Bad day for democracy?" With a smile, she took his face in her hands and kissed him lightly.

"Long," he corrected and pulled her closer for a more satisfactory embrace. And he knew he could face a hundred more like it if he just had her when it was over. "Sorry I'm late."

"You're not. You're here. Want a drink?"

"I wouldn't turn one down."

"Come on, I'll pretend I'm domestic for a few minutes." Shelby led him in to the couch. After nudging him down, she loosened his tie herself, drew it off, then undid the top two buttons of his shirt. Alan watched with a half-grin as she pulled off his shoes. "I could get used to this."

"Well, don't," she advised on her way to the bar. "You never know when you'll come in and find me collapsed on the couch and refusing to budge."

"Then I'll pamper you," he offered as she handed him a Scotch. Shelby sat down to curl beside him. "I needed this."

"The drink?"

"You." When she tilted back her head, he gave her a long lingering kiss. "Just you."

"You want to tell me about all the nasty officials or lobbyists or whatever that messed up your day."

He laughed and let the Scotch linger on his tongue. "I had a rather lengthy go-round with Congresswoman Platt."

"Martha Platt." Shelby let out a knowing sigh. "She was a hard-line, opinionated, penny-pinching bureaucrat when I was a girl."

The description suited to a tee. "Still is."

"My father always said she'd have made an excellent CPA. She thinks in fiscal dollars and cents."

Laughing, he set down his glass. Who needed Scotch when he had Shelby? "What about you? How are things in the business world?"

"Slow this morning, hectic this afternoon. I had a flood of college students. It seems pottery is in. Speaking of which, I have something for you." She sprang up and dashed away while Alan stretched out his legs and realized he wasn't tired at all—just more relaxed than he would have believed possible even twenty minutes before.

"A present," Shelby told him as she set a box in his lap. "It might not be as romantic as your style, but it is unique." She dropped back down beside him as Alan flipped the lid from the box.

In silence, he lifted out the krater, cupping the bowl in both hands. Somehow she'd pictured him holding it that way, as one of the Roman leaders might have done. Seeing it in his hands gave her pleasure.

Alan studied it without speaking. It was smooth and deeply green with faint hints of something lighter just beneath the surface. The lines were clean and simple, exquisite in the very lack of decoration. He could think of nothing he'd been given that had seemed more important.

"Shelby, it's beautiful. Really, really beautiful." Shifting it to one hand, he took hers with the other. "It's fascinated me, right from the start, that such small hands hold such large talent." He kissed her fingers before his eyes lifted to hers. "Thank you. You were making this the day I came into your workroom."

"You don't miss much, do you?" Pleased, she ran a finger down the side of the bowl. "I was making it...and thinking of you. It seemed only right that you should have it when it was finished. Then when I saw your house, I knew it was right for you."

"It's right for me," he agreed before he settled the krater back in its box. Setting it carefully on the floor, he drew her close again. "So are you."

She rested her head on his shoulder. It seemed true when he said it. "Let's send out for Chinese."

"*Hmm.* I thought you wanted to see that movie down the street."

"That was this morning. Tonight I'd rather eat sweet and sour pork and neck with you on the couch. In fact," she considered as she began to nibble on his neck, "I could probably make do with a few stale crackers and some cheese."

Alan turned so his lips could toy with hers. "How about we neck first and eat later?"

"You have such a well-ordered mind," Shelby commented as she eased back against the jumble of pillows, drawing him with her. "I just love the way it works. Kiss me, Alan, the way you did when we first sat here. It drove me mad."

Her eyes were half-closed, her lips just parted. Alan tangled his fingers in the hair that tumbled wildly over the bold odd-shaped pillows. He didn't feel the patience now he had forced himself to feel that first time. With Shelby, imagining what it would be like wasn't nearly as arousing as knowing what it was like. She was more titillating than the most pagan fantasy, more desirable than any fevered dream. And she was here, for him.

Alan tasted her lips slowly, as she had wanted him to. The need to devour could be controlled when he knew there would be a time for it. She sighed, then trembled. The combination nearly pushed him over the edge before he'd realized he'd been that close to it. He hadn't even touched her but for that light, teasing play of mouth on mouth.

He hadn't known torture could be so exquisite. But he knew the sweet allure of agony now, with his mouth fastened on Shelby's, with her fingers opening his shirt to explore him.

She loved the feel of him. Each time she could touch him freely, Shelby knew she'd never tire of doing so. It always brought such pure pleasure, such sharp greed. Always when she saw something she admired, she wanted to test the feel of it, the weight, the texture. It was no different with Alan. Yet each time she did, it might have been the first.

The scent of his soap—no, her soap, she remembered—lingered on him, but with the faint musky fragrance the day had worked on him. His heart beat quickly, though his mouth still made love to hers with slow, enervating thoroughness. Her fingers slid up to his shoulders to push the shirt away, to explore with more liberty. His kiss lost its patience with an abruptness that left her breathless.

Now she was spinning through the storm he could conjure like a magician. Boiling black clouds, bold lightning. She could have sworn she heard thunder, but it was only the thud of her own pulse. His hands were quick, undressing her in something like a rage, then molding her with hard, sure strokes that had her passing from one convulsive shudder to another. She crested rapidly, mindlessly, without the control to do any more than spin with the tempest.

He heard her call to him, but he was too tangled in his own web to answer. The lazy, satiating love of the day before hadn't done this to him. There was something wild in him, something fierce that had never been given full freedom. It came now, like the panther would come if it finally tore free of its cage. He was ravaging her, and even knowing it, couldn't stop. Her body was eager and trembling beneath his. Everywhere his mouth touched he tasted passion and promise.

She arched, moaning. With his tongue, he drove her ruthlessly to another peak. Her body was on fire, her mind wiped clean of thought, to be ruled only by sensations. She didn't know what he asked her, though she heard the urgent huskiness of his voice. She didn't know what she answered, only that nothing he could have demanded would have been too much. Dimly through the curtain of passion, she saw his face above hers. His eyes weren't brooding, that was all that was clear. They were dark, almost savage.

"I can't live without you," he said in a whisper that seemed to echo endlessly in her head. "I won't."

Then his mouth crushed down on hers, and everything was lost in the delirium.

"Sure you don't want any more?"

Two hours later Shelby sat cross-legged on the bed in a skimpy Japanese-print silk robe that left her legs bare. She stuck her fork into a little white cardboard carton and scooped out some cooling sweet and sour pork. Behind her the television played on low volume with no picture at all. Alan stayed comfortably stretched out, his head propped on her pillows.

"No." He watched her dig for more. "Shelby, why don't you get that set fixed?"

"*Mmm,* sooner or later," she said vaguely before she set the carton aside. Pushing a hand against her stomach she sighed lustily. "I'm stuffed." With a considering smile on her face, she let her gaze wander down from his face over his leanly muscled body. "I wonder how many people in the Washington metropolitan area know just how terrific Senator Mac-Gregor looks in his underwear."

"A select few."

"You must have thought about image projection, Senator." She ran a fingertip down the top of his foot. "You should consider doing some of those ads, you know, like the ball players…I never meet with foreign dignitaries without my B.V.D.'s."

"One can only be grateful you're not the Media Adviser."

"Stuffy, that's the whole problem." She dropped, full-length, on top of him. "Just think of the possibilities."

Alan slipped a hand under her robe. "I am."

"Discreetly placed ads in national magazines, thirty-minute spots in prime time." Shelby propped her elbows on his shoulders. "I'd definitely get my set fixed."

"Think of the trend it might start. Federal official everywhere stripped down to their respective shorts."

Shelby's brows drew together as she pictured it. "Good God, it could precipitate a national calamity."

"Worldwide," Alan corrected. "Once the ball got rolling, there'd be no stopping it."

"All right, you've convinced me." She gave him a smacking kiss. "It's your patriotic duty to keep your clothes on. Except in here," she added with a gleam in her eye as she toyed with his waistband.

Laughing, he drew her mouth back to his. "Shelby..." Her tongue skimmed over his while he cupped the back of her neck more firmly. "Shelby," he repeated a moment later, "there was something I wanted to talk to you about earlier, and I'm in danger of becoming as distracted now as I was then."

"Promise?" She moved her lips to his throat.

"I have a command performance this weekend."

"Oh?" She switched to his ear.

In self-defense, Alan rolled over and pinned her beneath him. "I got a call from my father this afternoon."

"Ah." Humor danced in her eyes. "The laird."

"The title would appeal to him." Alan grasped her wrists to prevent her from clouding his mind as she seemed bent on doing. "It seems he's planned one of his famous family weekends. Come with me."

One brow lifted. "To the MacGregor fortress in Hyannis Port? Unarmed?"

"We'll hoist the white flag."

She wanted to go. She wanted to say no. A visit to his family home came perilously close to that final commitment she was so carefully sidestepping. Questions, speculation—there'd be no avoiding them. Alan heard her thought as clearly as if it had been spoken. Pushing back frustration, he changed tactics.

"I have orders to bring that girl—" he watched her eyes narrow "—that daughter of the thieving, murdering Campbells, with me."

"Oh, is that so?"

"Just so," Alan returned mildly.

Shelby lifted her chin. "When do we leave?"

Chapter Ten

Shelby's first thought when she saw the house on the cliff was that she couldn't have done better herself. It was glorious. Rough, unpampered, it sat high with towers rising and turrets jutting. It was made of stone and hinted of the sea—gloomy and mysterious in the lowering light. A fortress, a castle, an anachronism—she wouldn't label it, only appreciate.

When she turned to Alan, Shelby saw that his brow was lifted as he waited for her verdict. There was that touch of humor in his eyes she'd learned to detect, and the irony that went with it. On a laugh, she leaned on the dash again to look her fill.

"You knew I'd love it."

Because he couldn't resist, Alan reached forward just to touch his fingertips to her hair. "I thought it might…appeal to you."

Shelby chuckled at the dry tone and continued to

look at the house while Alan drove the rented car up the sloping road. "If I'd grown up here, I'd have had headless ghosts for playmates and kept my room in a tower."

Alan maneuvered around one of the winding curves that only added to the atmosphere. The sea was close enough so its scent and sound drifted in the open windows. "There aren't any ghosts, though my father periodically threatened to import a few bloodthirsty ones from Scotland." With his lips just curved, he sent Shelby a quick sidelong look. "He keeps his office in a tower room."

She turned, lifted a brow, then leaned on the dash again. *"Hmm."* Brows still arched, she studied the slit windows of the tower. Daniel MacGregor. Yes, she was looking forward to meeting him, she decided. Even if it was on his home turf. But before she did, Shelby was going to enjoy the view.

The flowers were a nice touch, she reflected—rivers of them flowing out from the base of the house in a wild concoction of spring fancy. Did The MacGregor have the last say on the landscaping as well, Shelby wondered, or was this his wife's province? Perhaps the thoracic surgeon relaxed by planting petunias. Shelby considered and decided it made sense. Clever hands and a clever mind would need just that sort of creative outlet.

If the house had been Daniel's design and the gardens Anna's, Shelby concluded they must suit each other very well. Both aspects were unique, strong, and unapologetic. Meeting them, she mused, might prove very interesting.

No sooner had Alan stopped the car than Shelby

was climbing out to dash to the edge of a flower bed where she could stand and take in the whole structure at once. She was laughing again, her head thrown back, the unmanageable curls tossing in the wind. In the gloaming, she thought the house would be at its best.

Alan leaned against the hood of the car and watched her. With Shelby, sometimes watching was enough.

He liked the look of her against the backdrop of wildly colored flowers and the dull stone of the house, with her hands in the pockets of loosely fitting trousers, the thin material of her blouse rippling in the wind. The tiny tulips decorating the neckline had been painstakingly stitched more than fifty years before. She wore a slim digital watch on her wrist.

"I'd definitely have had ghosts," she decided, then held out her hand to him. "Fierce, clanking ghosts, none of those moony, ethereal types." Her fingers linked with Alan's, and for a moment, they looked up at the house together. "Kiss me, MacGregor," she demanded as she tossed windblown hair out of her eyes. "Hard. I've never seen a more perfect spot for it."

Even as she spoke her body was pressing against his, her free hand running firmly up his back to bring him close. When their mouths met, she thought she could smell a storm at sea—no matter that the skies were clear. She could touch him and feel the shivering jolt of lightning. If he whispered her name as their lips moved together, she could hear thunder.

Then they were straining against each other, lost, oblivious of the world that had simply come to a halt around them. There might have been seabirds coming to nest as night approached; the moon might have started its slow, slow rise even as the sun descended. It didn't matter. Their world had its center in each other.

Her hands brushed over his cheeks and remained lightly on his skin as they drew apart. Regret washed over her for what she couldn't yet give him, for what she might never be able to give him. A commitment that could transcend all fear, all doubt, and a promise she had made to herself.

"I love you, Alan," she murmured. "Believe it."

In her eyes, he could see the clouds of passion, and the struggle. Yes, she loved him, but... Not yet, Alan ordered himself. He could wait just a bit longer before he pressed her for more. "I believe it," he said as he took her wrists. Gently he kissed both her hands before slipping an arm around her waist. "Come inside."

Shelby tilted her head just enough to rest it briefly on his shoulder as they walked to the door. "I'm relying on your word that I'll walk out again in one piece at the end of the weekend."

He only grinned. "I told you my stand on playing the mediator."

"Thanks a lot." She glanced up at the door, noting the heavy brass crest that served as a door knocker. The MacGregor lion stared coolly at her with its Gaelic motto over its crowned head. "Your father isn't one to hide his light under a bushel, is he?"

"Let's just say he has a strong sense of family pride." Alan lifted the knocker, then let it fall heavily against the thick door. Shelby imagined the sound would vibrate into every nook and cranny in the house. "The Clan MacGregor," Alan began in a low rolling burr, "is one of the few permitted to use the crown in their crest. Good blood. Strong stock."

"Hah!" Shelby's disdainful look turned to one of mild curiosity as Alan burst out with a roar of laughter. "Something funny?"

Before he could answer, the door swung open. Shelby saw a tall man, blond with arresting blue eyes that hinted toward violet. He had a lean face that spoke of intelligence and cunning. Leaning against the door, he gave Alan a quick grin. "You can laugh," he said. "Dad's been ranting and muttering for an hour. Something about—" his gaze shifted and lingered on Shelby "—traitors and infidels. Hello, you must be the infidel."

The friendly irony in his voice had Shelby's lips curving. "I must be."

"Shelby Campbell, my brother, Caine."

"The first Campbell ever to step into the Mac Gregor keep. Enter at your own risk." Caine offered his hand as Shelby crossed the threshold. His first thought was that she had the face of a mermaid—not quite beautiful, but alluring and not easily forgotten.

Shelby glanced around the wide hall, approving the faded tapestries and heavy old furniture. She caught the scent of spring flowers, a wisp of dust and old polish. No, she couldn't have done it better herself. "Well, the roof didn't cave in," she commented as she studied a crested shield on the wall. "So far so good."

"Alan!" Serena came down the stairs quickly despite the encumbrance of pregnancy. Shelby saw an elegant violet-eyed woman with hair somehow both delicate and richly blonde. She saw, too, pleasure, love, humor, before Serena threw her arms around Alan's neck. "I've missed you."

"You look beautiful, Rena." Gently he laid a hand on the mound of her belly. His sister, he thought as wonder and pride mixed together. His baby sister. "I can't get used to it," he murmured.

Serena put her hand on his. "You don't have a great deal more time to get used to it." She felt the baby move under their joined hands and grinned as Alan's gaze dropped to them. "He or she is impatient to begin." Tilting her head, she studied Alan's face. "Dad's suddenly gotten it into his head there might be two…I wonder who might have planted that seed?"

His eyes smiled as he lifted them to his sister's. "It was purely a defensive maneuver."

"Mmm-hmm." Turning, she held out both hands. "You must be Shelby. I'm glad you could come."

Shelby felt the warmth, more carefree than Alan's, the welcome, less curious than Caine's. "So am I. I've been wanting to meet the woman who broke Alan's nose."

With a muffled chuckle, Serena jerked her head toward Caine. "It was supposed to be his." She narrowed her eyes a moment as Caine dipped his hands into his pockets and grinned. "It *should* have been his. Come on in and meet the rest of the family," she continued as she tucked her arm through Shelby's. "God, I hope Alan prepared you."

"In his own way."

"If you start to feel overwhelmed, just shoot me a

look. These days all I have to do is sigh to distract Dad's attention for an hour and a half.''

Alan looked after the two women as they walked down the hall. ''Looks like Rena's taking it from here,'' he murmured.

Caine gave a crooked grin as he draped an arm over his brother's shoulder. ''The truth is we've all been dying to see your Campbell since Dad made his, uh, announcement.'' He didn't ask Alan if it was serious—he didn't have to. He cast another speculative look at Shelby as they, too, started down the hall. ''I hope you told her that Dad's all bark and no bite.''

''Now, why would I do that?''

Shelby had a moment to take in the scene in the drawing room as she paused in the doorway. There was a dark man, smoking calmly, in an old bulky chair. Shelby had the impression that while he hardly seemed to move at all, he could move quickly when necessary. On the arm of his chair, sat a woman with the same coloring. Her hands were folded neatly on the lap of her vivid green skirt. A striking couple, Shelby mused. Then, it seemed the MacGregors were a striking crowd.

Across from them was a woman working serenely with embroidery hoop and needle. Shelby could see not only where Alan got his features but that appealing, serious smile. In the center of the group, was a wide high-back chair, ornately carved. It suited the man who sat in it.

Shelby noted that Daniel MacGregor was massive. A dramatic-looking man with flaming red hair, shoulders like a tank and a lined, florid face. She saw, with a twinge of amusement, that he wore the MacGregor plaid sashed across his suit jacket. He was, indisputably, holding court.

"Rena should be getting more rest," he stated, shoving a wide blunt-edged finger at the man in the chair. "A woman in her condition's got no business being in a casino till all hours."

Justin blew out a long lazy stream of smoke. "The casino *is* Serena's business."

"When a woman's with child..." Daniel paused long enough to shoot Diana an inquiring look. Shelby watched the dark woman struggle with a grin before she shook her head. Daniel sighed, then turned back to Justin. "When a woman's with child—"

"She can function like any other healthy woman," Serena finished for him.

Before Daniel could bluster out with whatever retort he had in mind, he spotted Shelby. His broad shoulders lifted, his wide chin tilted to a stubborn angle. "Well," he said briefly and left it at that.

"Shelby Campbell," Serena began smoothly as she swept into the room with Shelby at her side. "The rest of our family. My husband, Justin Blade." Shelby found herself fixed with a pair of very calm, very shrewd green eyes. He took his time about smiling, but when he did, it was worth it. "My sister-in-law, Diana."

"You're related." Shelby cut into the introductions as she studied both Justin and Diana. "Brother and sister?"

Diana nodded, liking the candor in Shelby's eyes. "That's right."

"What tribe?" she asked.

Justin smiled again as he blew out another stream of smoke. "Comanche."

"Good stock," Daniel stated with a thump of his hand on the arm of his chair. Shelby sent him a silent look.

"My mother," Serena continued, swallowing a chuckle.

"We're so pleased you could come, Shelby." Anna's voice was quiet, soothing. Her hand, when it took Shelby's was firm and strong.

"Thank you. I was admiring your garden, Dr. MacGregor. It's spectacular."

Anna smiled, giving Shelby's hand a quick squeeze. "Thank you. It's one of my vanities." When Daniel cleared his throat, loudly, a flicker of amusement crossed Anna's face. "Did you have a good flight?" she asked easily.

"Yes." With her back to Daniel, Shelby grinned. "Very smooth."

"Let me get a look at the girl!" Daniel demanded with another thump on the arm of his chair.

Shelby heard Serena muffle another chuckle. Slowly she turned to face Daniel. Her chin was lifted at the same arrogant angle as his own. "Shelby Campbell," Alan said, enjoying the moment, "my father, Daniel MacGregor."

"Campbell," Daniel repeated, tapping both wide hands on the arms of his chair.

Shelby moved to him but didn't offer her hand. "Aye," she said because her blood seemed to demand it. "Campbell."

Daniel turned the corners of his mouth down and drew his brows together in what he considered his most formidable look. Shelby didn't blink. "My kin would sooner have a badger in their house than a Campbell."

Alan saw his mother open her mouth and shook his head to silence her. He not only knew Shelby could hold her own but wanted to see her do it.

"Most MacGregors were comfortable enough with badgers in the parlor."

"Barbarians!" Daniel sucked in his breath. "The Campbells were barbarians, each and every one of them."

Shelby tilted her head as if to study him from a new angle. "The MacGregors have a reputation for being sore losers."

Instantly Daniel's face went nearly as red as his hair. "Losers? Hah! There's never been a Campbell born who could stand up to a MacGregor in a fair fight. Back-stabbers."

"We'll have Rob Roy's biography again in a minute," Shelby heard Caine mutter. "You don't have a drink, Dad," he said, hoping to distract him. "Shelby?"

"Yes." She shifted her gaze to him, noting he was doing his best to maintain sobriety. "Scotch," she told him, with a quick irrepressible wink. "Straight up. If the MacGregors had been wiser," she continued without missing a beat, "perhaps they wouldn't have lost their land and their kilts and the name. Kings," she want on mildly as Daniel began to huff and puff, "have a habit of getting testy when someone's trying to overthrow them."

"*Kings!*" Daniel exploded. "An English king, by

God! No true Scotsman needed an English king to tell him how to live on his land.''

Shelby's lips curved as Caine handed her a glass. ''That's a truth I can drink to.''

''Hah!'' Daniel lifted his glass and drained it in one swallow before he thumped it onto the table at his side. Cocking a brow, Shelby eyed the Scotch in her glass, then proceeded to follow Daniel's example.

For a moment, he frowned at the empty glass beside his. Slowly, with the room deadly silent, he shifted his gaze back to Shelby. His eyes were fierce, hers insolent. Heaving himself out of his chair, he towered over her, a great bear of a man with fiery hair. She put both hands on her hips, a willow-slim woman with curls equally dramatic. Alan wished fleetingly he could paint.

Daniel's laugh, when he threw back his head and let it loose, was rich and loud and long. ''Aye, by God, here's a lass!''

Shelby found herself swept off her feet in a crushing hug that held welcome.

It didn't take long for Shelby to sketch a mental outline of the MacGregor family. Daniel was bold, dramatic, and demanding—and an absolute marshmallow when it came to his children. Anna had eyes and a temperament like her eldest son. She could, Shelby concluded, quietly dominate anyone, including her husband. Watching her throughout the evening, Shelby realized she would have to stay on her toes with Alan. He had his mother's patience and her insight. A formidable combination.

She liked Alan's family—the similarities and the

contrasts. Individually she would have found them interesting. As a group, she found them fascinating. The house itself was something Shelby could never have resisted. Vaulted ceilings, gargoyles, odd suits of armor, and endless passages. They ate dinner in a dining hall as big as the average house. Spears were crossed over an enormous fireplace now filled with greenery rather than blazing logs. Windows were high and leaded, but light came from an enormous Waterford chandelier. Wealth, its eccentricities and ostentations, suited Daniel MacGregor.

Shelby sat on Daniel's left and ran her finger around the rim of her dinner plate. "This is a beautiful setting," she commented. "Wedgwood's jasperware, late eighteenth century. The yellow's very rare."

"My grandmother's," Anna told her. "Her one and only prize. I'm afraid I didn't realize the color was rare."

"Blues, lavenders, greens, and blacks are produced more commonly by oxide staining. I've never seen this tone outside of a museum."

"Never understood all the fuss over a plate," Daniel put in.

"Because you're more interested in what goes on it," Serena commented.

"Shelby's a potter," Alan said mildly before his father could retort.

"A potter?" Daniel's brows drew together as he studied her. "You make pots?"

"Among other things," Shelby said dryly.

"Our mother made pottery," Diana murmured. "I remember her working at a little manual wheel when

I was a girl. It's fascinating to see what can be made out of a little ball of clay. Do you remember, Justin?''

"Yes. She sometimes sold her pieces to the little store in town. Do you sell your work?" he asked Shelby. "Or is it a hobby?"

"I have a shop in Georgetown." She sensed a strong bond between brother and sister.

"A shopkeeper." Daniel nodded in approval. Commerce was something he appreciated. "You sell your own wares, then. Are you clever at it?"

Shelby lifted her wine. "I like to think so." Tossing her bangs out of her eyes, she turned to Alan. "Would you say I was clever at it, Senator?"

"Amazingly so," he returned. "For someone without any sense of organization, you manage to work at your craft, run a shop, and live precisely as you choose."

"I like odd compliments," Shelby decided after a moment. "Alan's accustomed to a more structured routine. He'd never run out of gas on the freeway."

"I like odd insults," Alan murmured into his wine.

"Makes a good balance." Daniel gestured at both of them with his fork. "Know your own mind, don't you, girl?"

"As much as anyone."

"You'll make a good First Lady, Shelby Campbell."

Shelby's fingers tightened on her wineglass, an involuntary gesture noticed only by Alan and his mother. "Perhaps," she returned calmly, "if it were one of my ambitions."

"Ambition or not, it's fate when you're paired with this one." Daniel stabbed his fork toward Alan.

"You're a little premature." Alan cut cleanly through his meat, swearing fluidly in his mind only. "I haven't decided to run for president, and Shelby hasn't agreed to marry me."

"Haven't decided? Hah!" Daniel swilled down wine. "Hasn't agreed?" He set down the glass with a bang. "The girl doesn't look like a fool to me, Campbell or no," he continued. "She's good Scottish stock, no matter what her clan. This one'll breed true MacGregors."

"He'd still like me to change my name," Justin commented, deliberately trying to shift the attention onto himself.

"It's been done to ensure the line before," Daniel told him. "but Rena's babe'll be as much MacGregor as not. As will Caine's when he's a mind to remember his duty and start making one." He sent his younger son a lowered-brow look that was met with an insolent grin. "But Alan's the firstborn, duty-bound to marry and produce and sire..."

Alan turned, intending on putting an end to the topic, when he caught Shelby's grin. She'd folded her arms on the table, forgetting her dinner in the pure enjoyment of watching Daniel MacGregor on a roll. "Having fun?" Alan muttered near her ear.

"Wouldn't miss it. Is he always like this?"

Alan glanced over, watching his father gesture with his lecture. "Yes."

Shelby sighed. "I think I'm in love. Daniel..." She interrupted his flow of words by tugging sharply on his sleeve. "No offense to Alan, or to your wife, but I think if I were going to marry a MacGregor, he'd have to be you."

Still caught up in his own diatribe, Daniel stared at her. Abruptly his features shifted and his laugh rang out. "You're a pistol, you are, Shelby Campbell. Here…" He lifted a bottle of wine. "Your glass is empty."

"That was well-done," Alan told her later as he gave Shelby a limited tour of the house.

"Was it?" Laughing, she linked her hand with his. "He's a difficult man to resist." She rose on her toes to nibble his earlobe. "So's his firstborn."

"That term's to be used reverently," Alan warned her. "Personally I've always found it a pain in the—"

"Oh, this is fabulous!" Shelby lifted a glassy porcelain vase from a high table. "French Chantilly. Alan, I swear this house is better than a sunken galleon. I'd never get tired of wandering from one corridor to another." After setting the vase down, she turned to grin at him. "Did you ever climb into one of those suits of armor?"

"Caine did once—it took me over an hour to pry him out."

Shelby gave a murmur of sympathy as she framed his face with her hands. "You were such a good boy." Her laugh was muffled against his lips in a sudden searing kiss. All heat, all fire, without a moment's warning.

"He climbed in," Alan continued as he tugged her hair back to deepen the kiss, "because I suggested it might be an interesting experience."

Breathless, Shelby stared up at him. When would she be prepared for those sudden dangerous turns of his nature? "An instigator," she managed.

"An objective leader," he corrected before he released her. "And I did manage to get him out...after he'd scared the wits out of Rena."

For a moment she leaned against the wall watching him, while the throbbing in her body slowly, very slowly, lessened. "I don't believe you were nearly as well-mannered as you once told me. You probably deserved that broken nose."

"Caine deserved it more."

Shelby laughed again as they moved down another corridor. "I like your family."

"So do I."

"And you enjoyed watching me go nose-to-nose with your father."

"I've always been fond of drawing-room comedies."

"Drawing room? It's more like a throne room." She leaned her head against his shoulder. "It's wonderful. Alan...where did your father get the idea we were going to be married?"

He flicked on a switch that brought a rather gloomy light into the hallway. "I told him I'd asked you," he said easily. "My father has a difficult time understanding that anyone could refuse his firstborn." Alan turned, effectively trapping Shelby between the wall and himself.

The dim light deepened the hollows in his face, casting his eyes into shadow. She could feel the strength from him though their bodies were barely touching. He could be fierce, she knew, just as easily as he could be gentle. "Alan..."

"How long are you going to ask me to wait?" He hadn't intended to press; had promised himself he wouldn't. But seeing her in his childhood home, with his family, with his memories, had only intensified his need for her. For all of her. "I love you, Shelby."

"I know." Her arms went around him, her cheek pressed against his. "I love you. Give me a little more time, Alan, just a little more time. It's too much to ask, I know." She held on tightly a moment before she drew away far enough to see his face. "You're more fair than I, kinder, more patient. I have to take advantage of that."

He didn't feel fair or kind or patient. He wanted to back her into a corner and demand, insist—beg. There was too much MacGregor in him to allow for the last, and the look in her eyes wouldn't permit him to resort to the first two. "All right. But, Shelby, there are things we have to talk about when we're back in Washington. Once I make my decision, I'll have to ask you to make yours."

She moistened her lips, afraid she knew what his decision related to. Not now, she told herself. She wouldn't think about it now. In Washington, she would make herself deal with it, but here, now, she wanted Alan to herself with no cloud of politics, no hints of the future. "We'll talk in Washington," she agreed. "And I promise you an answer."

Nodding, Alan circled her throat with his hand. "Make it the one I want," he murmured, then kissed her with no patience at all. "It's late," he added, knowing she was both surprised and vulnerable as he continued to take greedy possession of her mouth. "I imagine everyone's gone to bed."

"We should go too."

He laughed, capturing her earlobe between his teeth. "How about a midnight swim?"

"Swim?" On a sigh, Shelby closed her eyes and let the sensations take her. "I didn't bring a suit."

"Good." Alan led her down the hall to two large double doors. After pulling them open, he nudged Shelby inside, then closed and locked the doors behind them.

"Well." With her hands on her hips, she surveyed the room.

It was large, as was typical of everything in the house. One wall was entirely glassed with huge lush plants hung at staggered levels. Shelby could see the moonlight ripple through. The floor was made of tiny mosaic tiles in an intricate pattern of blues and greens. Centered in the room was an enormous blue-tinted pool.

"Daniel MacGregor doesn't piddle around, does he?" Her voice echoed hollowly off the water from the high ceiling. With a grin, Shelby turned back to Alan. "I bet you swam every day of your life. The first time I saw you I had this flash of a channel swimmer, marathon. It's the way you're built." She gave his shoulder a quick squeeze. "Maybe I wasn't so far off."

Alan only smiled and drew her away from the pool. "We'll have a sauna first."

"Oh, will we?"

"Yeah." He hooked a hand in the waistband of her trousers and drew her closer. "Open the pores a bit." In a quick move, he unhooked them, then drew them over her hips.

"Since you insist." Shelby began undoing his tie.

"Have you noticed, Senator, that most of the time you wear a great many more clothes than I?"

"As a matter of fact..." He slipped his hands under her blouse and found her. "I have."

Her fingers fumbled on his buttons. "Unless you want to take your sauna fully dressed, you'll have to stop." Letting out a long breath, Shelby tugged off his shirt. "We'll need towels," she added, then ran her hands in one long stroke down his chest to his belt.

Slowly Alan slid the blouse from her shoulders, allowing himself a lengthy look at her before he reached to the shelf behind him for towels. She was pale, slender—alluring and challenging—and his. Keeping her eyes on his, Shelby draped the towel saronglike around her.

Dry heat rushed over her when Alan opened the door to the small room. Shelby stood still a moment, absorbing it, before she moved to a bench. "I haven't done this in months," she murmured, then shut her eyes and leaned back. "It's wonderful."

"I'm told my father cemented a number of profitable deals in this room." Alan eased down beside her.

Shelby opened her eyes to slits. "I imagine he did. By the time he was through, he could've reduced most normally built men to puddles." Idly she trailed a fingertip down Alan's thigh. "Do you ever use saunas for vital government intrigue, Senator?"

"I'm inclined to think of other things in small hot rooms." Bending, he brushed his lips over her bare shoulder—the touch of a tongue, the quick pressure of teeth. "Vital, certainly, but more personal."

"Mmm." Shelby tilted her head as he trailed his lips closer to her throat. "How personal?"

"Highly confidential." Alan drew her into his lap and began those slow nibbling kisses that always drugged her. Her mouth moved against his with lazy heat-soaked passion. "Your body fascinates me, Shelby. Slender, smooth, agile." His lips trailed down further, to linger just above the loose knot in the towel. "And your mind—that's agile, too, and as clever as your hands. I've never been clear which attracted me first. Perhaps it was both at once."

She was content to lie back and let him make love to her with words and with the gentle brush of lips. Her muscles were lax from the heat, her skin soft and damp. When his lips came back to hers, she found she hardly had the strength to lift her arm around his neck and bring him closer. But her mouth could move, to slant against his, to open, to invite, to entice. She concentrated all her power there as her body seemed to melt from the heat and the longing.

While he kissed her, slowly, deeply, his fingertip nudged the knot of the towel until it loosened, leaving her vulnerable to him.

He felt her moan once against his mouth, tasted the trembling breath as it merged with his own. Her scent, always exciting, seemed to fill the tiny room until there was nothing else. So he touched her, first with lazy possession, seeing each sensitive curve in his mind's eye as his fingertips glided.

With his arm hooked around her back, he drew her closer. Skin, slick from the heat, seemed to fuse together. Their lips, still hungry, drew more and more in a kiss that hinted of forever. There was response wherever he touched, response that became more frantic as his hands sought less patiently. When she began to shudder, he felt a fresh thrill rip through him. Now, it demanded. Take her now, here and now. On an unsteady breath, he forced the need aside and pleasured himself by shattering her sanity.

He found her hot and moist. When she arched against his hand, he felt her passion build then explode. Mindlessly she moaned his name, and only his name. It was all he wanted to hear. Then she was pliant again, limp and soft. He could have held her just so for hours. Gathering her closer, he stood.

"It's dangerous to stay in here too long." Briefly he rubbed his mouth against hers. "We'll cool off."

"Impossible," Shelby murmured and lay back against his shoulder. "Absolutely impossible." They left the towels behind.

"The water's cool…almost as soft as your skin."

With a half-sigh, she turned to glance at the still surface of the pool. "I can take it if you can." She hooked her arms more securely around his neck. "But I don't think I even have the strength to tread water."

"We'll use the buddy system," Alan suggested, then shifting her weight slightly, jumped in with her.

Shelby gave a quick gasp at the shock of cold, then surfaced, drawing in air and tangling with Alan. "It's freezing!"

"No, actually it's kept at around seventy-six degrees. It's just the abrupt change in temperature."

Shelby narrowed her eyes and splashed water into his face before she broke away to skim along the bottom of the pool. Her muscles felt limber, ready to flex and stretch. When she reached the other end of the pool, Alan was waiting for her.

"Show-off," she accused, tossing wet hair out of her eyes. Then, with her tongue caught between her teeth, she let her gaze roam slowly down him from where the water dripped from his hair to where it lapped gently just below his waist. It didn't matter how many times she saw him, how often she touched, his body would always excite her.

"You look great, Senator. I think I could get used to seeing you wet and naked." Lazily she dipped back to float. "If you ever decide to ditch politics, I imagine you could have a successful career as a lifeguard at a nude beach."

"It's always good to have something to fall back on." He watched her a moment, her body white and smooth against the darker water. Moonlight poured through the windows and shivered on the surface. The desire he'd felt only moments before came back in full force. In one stroke, he was beside her, an arm hooked around her waist. Shelby gripped his shoulders for balance while her head tilted back, her hair streaming into the water. He saw it in her eyes, the excitement, the mutual need. Then her mouth rushed to meet his, and he saw nothing.

She knew there'd be no lazy, patient loving now. His mouth crushed hers, and she tasted the hints of savagery and desperation. The hand at her hip molded her to him. Shelby hadn't known her passion could rise again so swiftly, but it sprang up in her as ripe and hot as before. Desire came in waves, fast, each higher than the one before until she was submerged in it and struggling for air. Their bodies pressed together, wet and urgent. She dove her fingers into his hair, murmuring a thousand promises, a thousand demands.

The water slowed their movements, seeming to tease them when they both would have hurried. Neither had the patience for the dreamlike or the languid now when hunger was so sharp and consuming. She felt the water lap over her shoulders, cool and sensual, while Alan's mouth heated and became more firm, more greedy, on hers. She could smell it on his skin, taste it as her lips trailed over him—that faint trace of chlorine vying with the scent and flavor she had grown so used to. It alone reminded her that they were in a pool and not some sheltered lagoon a thousand miles away.

But when he took her in a frenzy of passion, they might have been anywhere at all.

Chapter Eleven

Hi.''

Shelby stifled a yawn as she rounded the last bend in the stairs and caught sight of Serena. "Hi."

"It looks like you and I are the only ones not already involved with some disgustingly productive activity this morning. Had breakfast?"

"Uh-uh." Shelby dropped her hand to her stomach. "I'm starving."

"Good. We usually eat breakfast in a room off the kitchen, as all of us have different hours. Caine," Serena continued as they started down the hall, "is always up at the crack of dawn—a habit I always wanted to strangle him for as a child. Alan and my parents are hardly better. Diana considers 8:00 A.M. late enough for anyone, and Justin runs on a clock I've yet to understand. Anyway, I've got this for an excuse now." She patted her well-rounded stomach.

Shelby grinned. "I don't use any."

"More power to you."

Serena swept into a sun-filled breakfast room that would have been considered large and formal by anything but Daniel MacGregor's standards. Rich royal-blue drapes were tied back from high windows with thick tassels. The carpet was Aubusson in faded blues and golds.

"I can't get over this place." Shelby wandered to a Chippendale server to study a collection of New England pewter.

"Neither can I," Serena said with a laugh. "How do you feel about waffles?"

Shelby grinned over her shoulders. "I have very warm, friendly feelings about waffles."

"I knew I liked you," Serena said with a nod. "Be right back." She disappeared through a side door.

Alone, Shelby wandered, studying a muted French landscape, sniffing fresh flowers in a crystal basket. It would take her all weekend to see every room, she decided. And a lifetime to really appreciate everything in them. Yet she felt at home here, she realized while she stared out the window overlooking the south lawn. She was as comfortable with Alan's family as she was with her own. It should all be so simple for them to love, to marry, to have children.... With a sigh, she rested her forehead against the glass. If it were only so simple for them.

"Shelby?"

Straightening, she turned to see Serena quietly studying her. "I've brought in some coffee," she said after a brief hesitation. She hadn't expected to see those candid gray eyes troubled. "The waffles'll be along in a minute."

"Thanks." Shelby took a seat at the table while Serena poured. "Alan tells me you run a casino in Atlantic City."

"Yes. Justin and I are partners there, and in several other hotels. The rest," she added as she lifted her cup, "he owns alone...for now."

Shelby grinned, liking her. "You'll convince him he needs a partner in the others as well."

"One at a time. I've learned how to handle him rather well the last year or so—especially since he lost the bet and had to marry me."

"You're going to have to clear that one up."

"He's a gambler. So am I. We settled on a flip of a coin." She smiled, remembering. "Heads I win, tails you lose."

Laughing, Shelby set down her cup. "Your coin, I take it."

"You bet your life. Of course he knew, but in all this time, I've never let him see that quarter." In an unconscious gesture, she rested a hand on her stomach. "Keeps him on his toes."

"He's crazy about you," Shelby murmured. "You can see it in the way he looks at you when you walk into a room."

"We've been through a lot, Justin and I." She lapsed into silence a moment, thinking back over the first stormy months after they met, the love that grew despite them, and the fear of making that final commitment. "Caine and Diana too," she went on. "Justin and Diana had a difficult childhood. That made it hard for them to give themselves to a relationship.

Strange, I think I loved Justin almost from the start, though I didn't realize it. It was the same for Caine with Diana.'' She paused, with her warm, candid eyes on Shelby's.

"You MacGregors know your minds quickly.''

"I wondered if Alan would ever love anyone, until I saw him with you.'' She reached across the table to touch Shelby's hand. "I was so glad when I saw you weren't the kind of woman I'd been afraid he'd fall for.''

"What kind was that?'' Shelby asked with a half-smile.

"Cool, smooth, a sleek blonde perhaps with soft hands and impeccably boring manners.'' Her eyes lit with humor. "Someone I couldn't bear to have coffee with in the morning.''

Though Shelby laughed, she shook her head as she sipped again. "She sounds like someone very suited for Senator Alan MacGregor to me.''

"Suited to the title,'' Serena countered, "not the man. And the man's my brother. He tends to be too serious at times, to work too hard—to care too much. He needs someone to help him remember to relax and to laugh.''

"I wish that were all he needed,'' Shelby said quietly.

Seeing the trouble shadow Shelby's eyes again, Serena felt an instant flood of sympathy. With difficulty, she harnessed it, knowing sympathy too often led to interference. "Shelby, I'm not prying—well, maybe just a bit. I really just wanted you to know how I felt. I love Alan very much.''

Shelby stared into her empty cup before lifting her gaze to Serena's. "So do I."

Serena sat back, wishing she could say something wise. "It's never just that easy, is it?"

Shelby shook her head again. "No, no, it's not."

"So, you decided to get up after all." Alan broke the silence as he came through the doorway. Though he noticed something pass between Shelby and his sister, he didn't comment.

"It's barely ten," Shelby stated, tilting back her head for the kiss. "Have you eaten?"

"Hours ago. Any more coffee?"

"Plenty," Serena told him. "Just get a cup from the buffet. Have you seen Justin?"

"Upstairs with Dad."

"Ah, plotting some new brilliant financial scheme."

"Stud poker," Alan corrected as he poured coffee. "Dad's down about five hundred."

"Caine?"

"Down about three."

Serena tried to look disapproving and failed. "I don't know what to do about Justin continuing to fleece my family. How much did you lose?"

Alan shrugged and sipped. "About one seventy-five." Catching Shelby's eye, he grinned. "I only play with Justin for diplomatic reasons." As she continued to stare he leaned back against the buffet. "And, dammit, one day I'm going to beat him."

"I don't believe gambling's legal in this state," Shelby mused, glancing over as the waffles were brought in. "I imagine the fine's rather hefty."

Ignoring her, Alan eyed her plate. "Are you going to eat all those?"

"Yes." Shelby picked up the syrup and used it generously. "Since men's-only clubs are archaic, chauvinistic, and unconstitutional, I suppose I could sit in on a game."

Alan watched the waffles disappear. "None of us has ever considered money has a gender." He twirled one of her curls around his finger. "Are you prepared to lose?"

Shelby smiled as she slipped the fork between her lips. "I don't make a habit of it."

"I believe I'll watch for a bit," Serena considered. "Where are Mom and Diana?"

"In the gardens," Alan told her. "Diana wanted a few tips for the house she and Caine just bought."

"That should give us an hour or two," Serena said with a nod as she rose.

"Doesn't your mother approve of cards?"

"My father's cigars," Serena corrected as they left the room. "He hides them from her—or she lets him think he does."

Remembering Anna's calmly observant eyes, Shelby decided it was probably the latter. Anna, like Alan, would miss little.

As they started up the tower steps Daniel's voice boomed down to them. "Damn your eyes, Justin Blade; you've the luck of the devil."

"Sore losers, those MacGregors," Shelby sighed, sliding her gaze to Alan's.

"We'll see if the Campbells can do any better. New blood," Alan announced from the doorway.

Smoke hung in the air, the rich, fragrant sting of

expensive tobacco. They were using Daniel's huge old desk as a table, with chairs pulled up to it. The three men looked over as Shelby and Serena walked in.

"I don't like taking my wife's money," Justin commented, sending her a grin as he clamped a cigar between his teeth.

"You won't have the opportunity of trying." Serena lowered herself to the arm of his chair with a quiet sigh. "Shelby'd like a game or two."

"A Campbell!" Daniel rubbed his hands together. "Aye then, we'll see how the wind blows now. Have a chair, lass. Three raise, ten-dollar limit, jacks or better to open."

"If you think you're going to make up your losses on me, MacGregor," Shelby said mildly as she took her seat, "you're mistaken."

Daniel made a sound of appreciation. "Deal the cards, boy," he ordered Caine. "Deal the cards."

It took less than ten minutes for Shelby to discover that Justin Blade was the best she'd ever come across. And she'd sat at her share of tables—elegant and not so elegant. Daniel played defiantly, Caine with a combination of impulse and skill, but Justin simply played. And won. Because she knew she was up against a more clever gambler than she, Shelby fell back on what she considered her best asset. Blind luck.

Standing idly behind her, Alan watched her discard two hearts, choosing to draw for an inside straight. With a shake of his head, he walked over to the table in the corner to pour himself yet another cup of coffee.

He liked the way she looked, nearly elbow-to-elbow with his father, their fiery heads bent a bit as they studied their cards. It was strange how easily she had slipped into his life, making a quiet splash that promised endless, fascinating ripples. She fit here, in the odd tower room, playing poker with smoke clogging the air and coffee growing cold and bitter in the cups. And she would fit in an elegant Washington function in a room that shone with light and glitter, sipping champagne from a tulip glass.

She fit in his arms at night the way no woman ever had, or would, fit again. Alan needed her in his life as much as he needed food, water, and air.

"A pair of aces," Daniel said with a fierce look in his eye.

Justin set his cards down quietly and faceup. "Two pair. Jacks and sevens." He sat back as Caine swore in disgust.

"You son of—" In frustration, Daniel broke off, shifting his eyes from his daughter to Shelby. "The devil take you, Justin Blade."

"You're sending him off prematurely," Shelby commented, spreading her cards. "A straight, from the five to the nine."

Alan walked over to look at her cards. "I'll be damned, she drew the six and seven."

"No one but a bloody witch draws an inside straight," Daniel boomed, glaring at her.

"Or a bloody Campbell," Shelby said easily.

His eyes narrowed. "Deal the cards."

Justin grinned at her as Shelby scooped in chips. "Welcome aboard," he said quietly and began to shuffle.

They played for an hour, with Shelby sticking to a system of illogic that kept her head above water. Normally she wouldn't have labeled a twenty-five-dollar take impressive, but considering her competition, she was well pleased. Whether they would have played into the afternoon became academic the minute Daniel heard his wife's voice drifting up the stairs. Immediately he stubbed out the better part of a seven-dollar cigar, then shoved it and an ashtray under his desk.

"I'll raise you five," he said, leaning on his desk again.

"You haven't opened yet," Shelby reminded him sweetly. Plucking a peppermint from the bowl on his desk, she popped it into his mouth. "Gotta cover all your tracks, MacGregor."

Daniel grinned and tousled her hair. "A good lass, Campbell or not."

"We should have known they'd be busy losing their money to Justin," Anna stated as she stepped inside the room with Diana beside her.

"Lost a trick to the new kid on the block too." Caine held out a hand for his wife's.

"About time Justin had some competition." Hooking her arms around Caine's neck, Diana rested her chin on the top of his head. "Anna and I were thinking about a swim before lunch. Anyone interested?"

"Fine idea." Daniel eased the ashtray a bit further under his desk with his foot. "Do you swim, girl?"

"Yes." Shelby set down her cards. "But I didn't bring a suit."

"There's a closetful in the bathhouse," Serena told her. "You won't have any trouble finding one to fit."

"Really?" She shot Alan a look. "Isn't that handy? A closetful of suits."

He gave her an easy smile. "Didn't I mention it? A swim sounds good," he added as he dropped his hands to her shoulders. "I've never seen Shelby in a bathing suit.

Twenty minutes later Alan found himself in the relaxing heat of the sauna. Instead of Shelby, he was joined by his brother and Justin. Leaning back, letting his muscles relax, he remembered the damp, soft sheen on her skin and the flush of pink that had covered her when he'd held her.

"I like your taste," Caine commented and rested his shoulders against the side wall. "Even though it surprised me."

Alan opened his eyes enough to bring Caine into focus. "Did it?"

"Your Shelby isn't anything like the classy blonde with the, uh, interesting body you were dating a few months ago." Caine brought up one knee to settle more comfortably. "She wouldn't have lasted five minutes with Dad."

"Shelby isn't like anyone."

"I have to respect someone who draws to an inside straight." Justin added stretching out on his back on the bench above Alan. "Serena tells me she suits you."

"It's always nice to have family approval," Alan said dryly.

Justin only laughed and pillowed his head on his folded arms. "You MacGregors have a habit of interfering in this sort of thing."

"He speaks, of course, from personal experience." Caine pushed damp hair from his forehead. "At the moment, I'm rather enjoying the old man's preoccupation with Alan. It takes the heat off Diana and me."

"You'd think he'd be too involved with Rena and his expected grandchild to put energy into anything else." Alan rested his arms on the upper bench and let the sweat roll off him.

"Hell, he's not going to be satisfied until he's knee-deep in little MacGregors and/or Blades." Caine grinned. "Actually I've been giving it some thought myself."

"Thinking about it isn't going to produce another Comanche-Scotsman," Justin said lazily.

"Diana and I thought we'd test the waters with our niece or nephew first."

"How does it feel to have fatherhood looming before you, Justin?" Alan asked him.

Justin stared up at the wooden ceiling remembering what it was like to feel life move under his hand, inside the woman he loved. Thrilling. He could see how Serena looked, naked, swollen with his child. Beautiful. He knew how he felt sometimes in the early hours of dawn when she was warm and asleep beside him....

"Terrified," he murmured. "Scares the hell out of me. Babies add a multitude of 'What ifs' to your life. The more I want it, the closer it comes, the more scared I am." He managed to shrug from his prone position. "And the more I want to see just what that part of me and Serena is going to look like."

"Strong stock," Caine stated. "Good blood."

Justin gave a quiet chuckle and closed his eyes.

"Apparently Daniel's decided to feel the same way about Campbells. Are you going to marry her, Alan?"

"Here, in the fall."

"Dammit, why didn't you say so?" Caine demanded. "Dad would've had an excuse to dip into that vintage champagne he hoards."

"Shelby doesn't know it yet," Alan said easily. "I thought it wiser to tell her first."

"*Hmm.* She doesn't strike me as a woman who takes to being told."

"Very observant," Alan told Justin. "But then, I've tried asking. Sooner or later I might have to change my tactics."

Caine's brows drew together. "She said no?"

Alan opened his eyes again. "God, there're times you look just like him. She didn't say no—or yes. Shelby's father was Senator Robert Campbell."

"Robert Campbell," Caine repeated quietly. "Oh, I see. She'd have an understandably difficult time with your profession. Her father was campaigning in the presidential primaries when he was assassinated, wasn't he?"

"Yes." Alan read the unspoken question in his brother's eyes. "And yes, I intend to run when the time's right." It was the first time, he realized, that he'd said it out loud. Eight years wasn't so very long to prepare for such a long hard road. He let out a long quiet breath. "It's something else Shelby and I have to discuss."

"You were born for it, Alan," Justin said simply. "It isn't something you can turn your back on."

"No, but I need her. If it came down to making a choice—"

"You'd take Shelby," Caine finished, understanding perfectly what it meant to find one love, one woman. "But I wonder if either of you could live with it."

Alan remained silent a moment, then closed his eyes again. "I don't know." A choice, one way or the other, would split him neatly in two.

On the Wednesday following her weekend in Hyannis Port, Shelby received her first Daniel MacGregor phone call. Holding Auntie Em's water dish in one hand, she picked up the receiver with the other.

"Shelby Campbell?"

"Yes." Her lips curved. No one else boomed at you in quite that way. "Hello, Daniel."

"You've closed down shop for the day?"

"I toss clay on Wednesdays," she told him as she caught the receiver between her ear and shoulder and replaced the bird's water dish. "But yes, I've closed down. How are you?"

"Fine, fine, lass. I'm going to make it a point to take a look at that shop of yours the next time I'm in Washington."

"Good." She dropped to the arm of a chair. "And you'll buy something."

Daniel gave a wheezy chuckle. "That I might, if you're as clever with your hands as you are with your tongue. The family plans to spend the Fourth of July weekend at the Comanche in Atlantic City," Daniel stated abruptly. "I wanted to extend the invitation to you myself."

The Fourth of July, Shelby mused. Fireworks, hot

dogs, and beer. It was less than a month away—how had time gone so quickly? She wanted to picture herself standing on the beach with Alan, watching colors explode in the sky. And yet…her future, their future, was something she still couldn't see. "I appreciate it, Daniel. I'd love to come." That much was true, Shelby told herself. Whether she would or not was another matter.

"You're right for my son," Daniel told her, shrewd enough to have caught her brief hesitation. "Never thought I'd hear myself say that about a Campbell, but I'm saying it. You're strong and bright. And you know how to laugh. You've good Scottish blood in you, Shelby Campbell. I'll see it in my grandchildren."

She did laugh, because her eyes had filled too abruptly for her to stop the tears. "You're a pirate, Daniel MacGregor, and a schemer."

"Aye. I'll see you at the Comanche."

"Good-bye, Daniel."

When she hung up, Shelby pressed her fingers to her eyes. She wasn't going to fall apart over a few bluff words. She'd known from the first morning she'd woken in Alan's arms that she was only postponing the inevitable. Right for him? Daniel said she was right for him, but perhaps he only saw the surface. He didn't know what she was holding inside her. Not even Alan knew how deep-seated the fear was, how real and alive it had remained all these years.

If she allowed herself, she could still hear those three quick explosions that had been bullets. And she could see, if she let herself see, the surprised jerk of her father's body, the way he had fallen to the ground almost at her feet. People shouting, rushing, crying. Her father's blood on the skirt of her dress. Someone had pushed her aside to get to him. Shelby had sat on the floor, alone. It had been for perhaps no more than thirty seconds: it had been a lifetime.

She hadn't needed to be told her father was dead— she'd seen the life spill out of him. She'd felt it spill out of herself.

Never again, Shelby thought on a shaky breath. She would never—could never—die so painfully again.

The knock on the door had to be Alan. Shelby gave herself an extra minute to be certain the tears were under control. Taking a last deep breath, she went to answer the door. "Well, MacGregor. No food," she commented with an arched brow. "Too bad."

"I thought his might make up for it." He held out a single rose whose petals were the color of her hair. A traditional gift, she thought, trying to take it casually. But nothing he gave her would ever be taken casually. As her fingers closed around the stem she knew it was a token. A traditional, serious-minded man was offering her a very serious part of himself.

"One rose is supposed to be more romantic than dozens," she said easily enough. Then the tears backed up behind her eyes. It was. "Thank you." She threw her arms around him, pressing her mouth to his with force and a hint of desperation. It was the desperation that had Alan holding her gently, one hand stroking her wild tangle of hair as his lips soothed hers.

"I love you," she whispered, burying her face against his neck until she was certain her eyes were dry.

Alan slipped a hand under her chin to lift it, then studied her. "What's wrong, Shelby?"

"Nothing," she said too quickly. "I get sentimental when someone brings me a present." The quiet intensity in his eyes didn't change; the churning emotion inside her didn't ease. "Make love to me, Alan." She pressed her cheek against his. "Come to bed with me now."

He wanted her. She could make his desire springboard from easy to urgent with a look, but he knew it wasn't the answer either of them needed then. "Let's sit down. It's time we talked."

"No, I—"

"Shelby." He took her by the shoulders. "It's time."

Her breath came out in a jerk. He'd given her all the room he would give her. She'd known he'd draw the line sooner or later. With a nod, she walked to the couch, still clutching the rose. "Would you like a drink?"

"No." With a hand on her shoulder again, he eased her down, then sat beside her. "I love you," he said simply. "You know that and that I want you to marry me. We haven't known each other for long," he continued when Shelby remained silent. "If you were a different kind of woman, I might be persuaded that you needed time to be certain of your feelings for me. But you're not a different kind of woman."

"You know I love you, Alan," she interrupted. "You're going to be logical, and I—"

"Shelby." He could stop an impassioned speech with a whisper. "I know you have a problem with my profession. I understand it, maybe only in a limited way, but I do understand it. It's something you and I have to work out from this point on." He took her hands and felt the tension. "We'll deal with it, Shelby, in whatever way we have to."

She still didn't speak but stared at him as if she already knew what he would say. "I think I should tell you now that I've been approached by a few key members of the party and that I'm seriously considering running for president. It won't be for nearly a decade, but the nuts and bolts of it have already started."

She'd known it—of course she'd known it—but hearing it out loud had the muscles in her stomach contracting like a fist. Feeling the pressure building in her lungs, she let out a long slow breath. "If you're asking my opinion," she managed in a calm voice, "you shouldn't consider it, you should do it. It's something you were meant to do, Alan, something you were meant to be." The words, even as she said them, knew them for the truth, tore at her.

"I know with you, it's not simply a matter of power and ambition. You'd see the hardships as well, the strain, the impossible responsibility." Shelby rose, knowing if she sat still a moment longer, she'd explode. Quickly she set the rose down. Too quickly. The stem nearly snapped between her fingers. "There is such a thing as destiny," she murmured.

"Perhaps." He watched as she paced the room, running her hand over the back of a pillow she snatched from the couch. "You're aware that it's more than just putting my name on the ballot. When the time comes, it'll mean long hard campaigning. I need you with me, Shelby."

She stopped a moment, her back to him, to squeeze her eyes tight. Fighting for composure, she turned around. "I can't marry you, Alan."

Something flashed in his eyes—fury or pain, she couldn't be sure—but his voice was calm when he spoke. "Why?"

Her throat was so dry, she wasn't certain she could answer. With an effort, she swallowed. "You're fond of logic; be logical. I'm not a political hostess; I'm not a diplomat or an organizer. That's what you need."

"I want a wife," Alan returned evenly. "Not a staff."

"Dammit, Alan, I'd be useless. Worse than useless." With a sound of frustration, she began to pace again. "If I tried to fit the mold, I'd go mad. I haven't the patience for beauty shops and secretaries and being tactful twenty-four hours a day. How could I be First Lady when I'm not even a lady half the time?" she tossed out. "And damn you, you'll win. I'd find myself in the White House stifled by elegance and protocol."

He waited as her ragged breathing filled the room. "Are you saying you'd marry me if I chose not to run?"

She whirled around, eyes brilliant and tormented. "Don't do that to me. You'd hate me...I'd hate myself. It can't be a choice between what you are and me, Alan."

"But a choice between what you are and me," he countered. The anger he'd strapped in broke free. "You can make a choice." He sprang up from the couch to grab both of her arms. Fury poured out of

him, overwhelming her. She'd known it would be
deadly, she'd seen hints of it, but she had no defense.
"You can choose to push me out of your life with a
simple *no,* expect me to accept it knowing you love
me. What the hell do you think I'm made of?"

"It's not a choice," she said passionately. "I can't
do anything else. I'd be no good for you, Alan; you
have to see that."

He shook her with enough violence to snap her
head back. "Don't lie to me, and don't make excuses.
If you're going to turn your back on me, do it with
the truth."

She crumbled so quickly, she would have slid to
the floor if he hadn't been holding her. "I can't handle it." Tears streamed down her face, huge, fast,
painful. "I can't go through it all again, Alan, waiting, just waiting for someone to—" On a sob, she
covered her face with her hands. "Oh, God, please, I
can't stand it. I didn't want to love you like this; I
didn't want you to matter so much that everything
could be taken from me again. I can see it happening
all over again. All those people pressing close, all
those faces and the noise. I watched someone I love
die in front of my eyes once. I can't again; I can't!"

Alan held her close, wanting to soothe, needing to
reassure. What words could he use to penetrate this
kind of fear, this kind of grief? There was no place
for logic here, no place to be calm and rationalize. If
it was her love that made her so deadly afraid, how
could he ask her to change it?

"Shelby, don't. I won't—"

"No!" She cut him off, struggling out of his hold.
"Don't say it. *Don't!* Please, Alan, I can't bear it.

You have to be what you are, and so do I. If we tried to change, we wouldn't be the same people each of us fell in love with.''

"I'm not asking for you to change," he said evenly as his patience began to strain again. "I'm only asking for you to have faith in me."

"You're asking too much! Please, please just leave me alone." Before he could speak, she dashed into the bedroom and slammed the door.

Chapter Twelve

Maine was beautiful in June—green and wild. Shelby drove along the coast, keeping her mind a blank. Through the open windows of the car, she could hear the water hurl itself against rock. Passion, anger, grief—the sound expressed all three. She understood it.

From time to time there were wildflowers along the roadside, tough little blossoms that could stand up to the salt and the wind. For the most part there were rocks, worn smooth from the eternal beating of water, glistening near the shoreline, dry and brooding above it, until the tide would rise and claim them as well.

If she drew deep, Shelby could breathe again. Perhaps that's why she had come, and come quickly, before Washington could suffocate her. The air here was brisk and clean. The summer that had taken over spring so quickly had yet to reach this far north. She needed to hold on to spring for just a bit longer.

She saw the lighthouse on the narrow point of land that jutted arrogantly into the sea and forced her tense fingers to relax on the wheel. Peace of mind—perhaps she would find it here as her brother always sought to do.

It was barely dawn. When her plane had landed, it had still been dark. She could see the sun rising, streaming color into the sea while gulls dipped and floated over rock and sand and water. It was still too early for their shadows. They called out above the noise of the surf, an empty, lonely sound. Shelby shook that off. She wouldn't think of emptiness or loneliness now. She wouldn't think at all.

The beach was deserted, the air cool and breezy when she stepped from her car. The lighthouse was a wide sphere of white, solitary and strong against the elements. Perhaps it was worn and a bit weather-beaten in places, but it held a simple power that remained timeless and real. It seemed a good place to shelter from any storm.

Shelby took her bag from the back of the car and approached the door at the base. It would be locked, she knew. Grant never gave open invitations. She pounded on the wood with the side of her fist, wondering just how long he'd ignore it before answering. He'd hear it, because Grant heard everything, just as he saw everything. Isolating himself from the rest of humanity hadn't changed that.

Shelby pounded again and watched the sun rise. It took a bit more than five full minutes before the door creaked open.

He had the look of their father, Shelby thought—dark, intelligent good looks, a bit rough around the edges. The surprisingly deep green eyes were clouded with sleep, the thick just-a-bit-too-long hair, rumpled with it.

Grant scowled at her and rubbed a hand over his unshaven chin. "What the hell are you doing here?"

"A typical Grant Campbell welcome." She stood on her toes to brush his lips with hers.

"What time is it?"

"Early."

Swearing, he dragged a hand through his hair and stepped back to let her through. For a moment, he leaned against the door to get his bearings, one thumb hooked in his only concession to modesty—a pair of faded cutoffs. Then he followed her up the steep, creaky flights of stairs to his living quarters.

Straightening, he took his sister by the shoulders and studied her, quickly, and with an intensity she had never quite grown used to. She stood passively, a half-smile on her lips and shadows under her eyes.

"What's wrong?" he asked bluntly.

"Wrong?" She shrugged and tossed her bag on a chair that could have done with reupholstering. "Why does there have to be something wrong for me to pay a visit?" She glanced back at him, noting that he still hadn't put on any weight. His build teetered between lean and thin, and yet, like his home, there was a basic strength about him. She needed that too. "You gonna make the coffee?"

"Yeah." Grant moved through what served as a living room, despite the dust, and into a tidy, organized kitchen. "Want breakfast?"

"Always."

With what might have been a chuckle, he pulled out a slab of bacon. "You're skinny, kid."

"You're not exactly husky these days yourself."

His answer was a grunt. "How's Mom?"

"She's fine. I think she's going to marry the Frenchman."

"Dilleneau, with the big ears and the cagey brain."

"That's the one." Shelby dropped into a chair at the round oak table as bacon began to sizzle. "Are you going to immortalize him?"

"Depends." He shot Shelby a wicked grin. "I don't suppose Mom would be surprised to see her fiancé in Macintosh."

"Surprised, no—pleased..." She trailed off with a shrug. "She'd really like you to come down for a visit."

"Maybe." Grant plopped a plate of bacon on the table.

"Are we going to have eggs too?" She got up for plates and mugs while Grant broke a half-dozen into a pan. "Sure, scrambled's fine," Shelby said wryly to his back. "Getting many tourist these days?"

"No."

The word was so flat and final, Shelby nearly laughed. "You could always try land mines and barbed wire. It amazes me how anyone so in tune with people could dislike them so much."

"I don't dislike them." Grant heaped eggs on another plate. "I just don't want to be around them." Without standing on ceremony, he sat down and began to fill his plate. He ate; Shelby pretended to. "How're your roommates?"

"They've settled on peaceful coexistence," Shelby

told him as she nibbled on a slice of bacon. "Kyle's looking in on them until I get back."

Grant shot her a look over the rim of his mug. "How long are you staying?"

This time she did laugh. "Always gracious. A few days," she told him. "No more than a week. No, please." She held up her hand, palm up. "Don't beg me to extend my visit; I simply can't stay any longer." She knew he would scowl and swear and open his home to her for as long as she needed.

He finished off the last of his eggs. "Okay, you can drive into town for supplies while you're here."

"Always happy to be of service," Shelby muttered. "How do you manage to get every major newspaper in the country delivered out here?"

"I pay for it," he said simply. "They think I'm odd."

"You are odd."

"Just so. Now…" He pushed his plate aside and leaned his elbows on the table. "Why are you here, Shelby?"

"I just wanted to get away for a few days," she began, only to be cut off by a rude four-letter word. Instead of responding with a joke or an equally rude rejoinder, she dropped her gaze to her plate. "I had to get away," she whispered. "Grant, my life's a mess."

"Whose isn't?" he responded, but put one long slender finger under her chin to lift it. "Don't do that, Shelby," he murmured when he saw her eyes were brimming over. "Take a deep breath and tell me about it."

She took the breath, though it was a shaky one, and

struggled to control the tears. "I'm in love and I shouldn't be, and he wants me to marry him and I can't."

"Well, that sums things up. Alan MacGregor." When Shelby sent him a swift look, Grant shook his head. "No, no one told me. You've been linked with him in the papers half a dozen times in the last month. Well, he's one of that tidy little group I can honestly say I respect."

"He's a good man," Shelby stated, blinking back tears. "Maybe a great one."

"So what's the problem?"

"I don't want to love a great man," she said fiercely. "I can't marry one."

Grant rose, retrieved the coffeepot, and filled both mugs again. He sat, then pushed the cream at Shelby. "Why?"

"I won't go through it again, Grant."

"Through what?"

Her look sharpened; the tears dried up. "Damn you, don't pull that on me."

Calmly he sipped his coffee, pleased that she would snipe at him now rather than weep. "I've been hearing a rumor or two that the Senator might try for the top spot sooner or later. Maybe sooner than expected."

"You hear correctly, as usual."

He lingered over the coffee, black and strong. "Don't you fancy having one of your dresses in the Smithsonian, Shelby?"

"Your humor's always been on the odd side, Grant."

"Thanks."

Annoyed, she pushed her plate aside. "I don't want to be in love with a senator."

"Are you?" he countered. "Or are you in love with the man?"

"It's the same thing!"

"No, it's not." He set down the coffee and plucked a piece of untouched bacon from Shelby's plate. "You, better than most, know it."

"I can't risk it!" she said with sudden passion. "I just can't. He'll win, Grant, he will if he lives long enough. I can't deal with it—the possibilities..."

"You and your possibilities," he flung back. The memory hurt, but he pushed it aside. "Okay, let's take a few of them. First, do you love him?"

"Yes, yes, I love him. Dammit, I just told you I did."

"How much does he mean to you?"

Shelby dragged both hands through her hair. "Everything."

"Then, if he runs for president and something happens to him..." He paused as the color drained from her face. "Is it going to hurt any less whether you have his ring on your finger or not?"

"No." She covered her mouth with her hand. "Don't, Grant."

"You've got to live with it," he said harshly. "We've both had to live with it, carry it around with us. I was there, too, and I haven't forgotten. Are you going to shut yourself off from life because of something that happened fifteen years ago?"

"Haven't you?"

Direct hit, he thought ruefully, but didn't acknowledge it. "We're not talking about me. Let's take another of your possibilities, Shelby. Suppose he loves you enough to chuck it for you.''

"I'd despise myself.''

"Exactly. Now, the last one. Suppose…'' And for the first time he linked his hand with hers. "He runs and wins and lives to a ripe old age writing his memoirs and traveling as an ambassador of goodwill or playing Parcheesi on the sun porch. You're going to be damned mad he had fifty years without you.''

She let out a long breath. "Yeah. But—''

"We've already gone through the buts,'' he interrupted. "Of course, there're probably several million possibilities in between. He could get hit by a car crossing the street—or you could. He could lose the election and become a missionary or an anchor on the six o'clock news.''

"All right.'' Shelby dropped her forehead to their joined hands. "Nobody makes me see what a fool I am better than you.''

"One of my minor talents. Listen, walk out on the beach; clear your head. When you come back, eat something, then get about twelve-hours sleep, because you look like hell. Then…'' He waited until she lifted her head to smile at him. "Go home. I've got work to do.''

"I love you, you creep.''

"Yeah.'' He shot her one of his quick grins. "Me too.''

His house was too empty and too quiet, but there was nowhere Alan wanted to go. He'd forced himself to give Shelby a full day alone, then had gone half mad when he'd learned on Friday that she was nowhere to be found. Twenty-four hours later, he was still trying to reason with himself.

She had a right to go when and where she chose. He had no reason to expect her to answer or to explain to him. If she decided to go off for a few days, he had no right to be angry, certainly no reason to be worried.

He rose from the desk in his study to pace. Where the hell was she? How long was she going to stay away? Why hadn't she at least let him know?

Frustrated, he balled his hands into his pockets. He'd always been able to find the route out of a problem. If it didn't work one way, it worked another, but there was always a viable system. It was only a matter of time and patience. He had no more patience. He was hurting like he'd never been aware he could hurt—everywhere, all at once, and unrelentingly.

When he found her, he'd... What? Alan demanded of himself. Force her, bully her, plead, beg? What was left? He could give up pieces of himself for her and still be whole, but without her, he'd never be more than part of a man. She'd stolen something from him, then shut the door, he thought furiously. No... He'd given it to her freely, though she'd been reluctant to take the love he offered. He couldn't take it back now, even if she disappeared from his life.

She was capable of that, he realized with a sudden surge of panic. Shelby could pack her bags and take off without leaving a trace behind. Damn if she would! Alan frowned at the phone again. He'd find her. First he'd find her. Then he'd deal with her, one way or another.

He'd start by calling her mother, then work his way

through everyone she knew. With a brittle laugh, Alan picked up the receiver. With Shelby, it could take the better part of a week.

Before he could dial, the doorbell sounded. Alan let it ring three times before he remembered that McGee was in Scotland. Swearing, he slammed down the phone and went to answer.

The messenger grinned at him. "Delivery for you, Senator," he said brightly and handed Alan a clear plastic bag. "You guys are strange," he added before he sauntered away. While he stared at the bag in his hand, Alan closed the door. Swimming around a bit frantically in the trapped water was a bright-orange goldfish.

Slowly Alan moved into the parlor, studying his gift with wary eyes. What the hell was he supposed to do with this? he wondered. Impatient with the interruption, he pulled out a Waterford goblet and breaking the seal on the plastic, dumped fish and water inside. After setting the bag aside, Alan opened the little card that had been attached to it.

Senator,
    If you can take life in the goldfish bowl, so can I.

After reading the one sentence three times, Alan shut his eyes. She'd come back. The card dropped to the table as he turned to head for the door. Even as he opened it, the doorbell rang.

"Hi." Shelby smiled, though the greeting had been bright enough to reveal her nerves. "Can I come in?"

He wanted to grab her quickly, hold her to be sure

she stayed. It wasn't the way to keep Shelby. "Sure."
When he wanted to step forward, Alan stepped back
to let her come in on her own. "You've been away."

"Just a quick pilgrimage." She thrust her hands
into the wide pockets of a pair of baggy denim over-
alls. He looked tired, she noted, as if he hadn't slept.
Her hands itched to touch his face, but she kept them
both firmly tucked away.

"Come in and sit down." Alan gestured toward the
parlor before they walked, both cautious and conscious of the other. "McGee's away. I could fix coffee."

"No, not for me." Shelby wandered the room.
How was she going to start? What was she going to
say? All the careful speeches, the glib ones, the passionate ones, slipped quietly out of her head. He'd
placed the krater she'd made him near the window
where it caught the sun. She stared at it. "I suppose
I should begin by apologizing for falling apart on you
the other day.

"Why?"

"Why?" Shelby turned around to face him again.
"Why what?"

"Why would you apologize?"

She lifted her shoulders, then let them fall. "I hate
to cry. I'd rather swear, or kick something." Nerves
were jumping inside her—something she hadn't expected, and something his calm, steady gaze did nothing to soothe. "You're angry with me."

"No."

"You were." She moved restlessly around the
room. "You had a right to be, I…" Shelby trailed off
when she spotted the goldfish swimming in circles

inside the Waterford. "Well, he's come up in the world," she said with a jerky laugh. "I don't think he appreciates it. Alan." When she faced him this time, her eyes were huge and questioning and vulnerable. "Do you still want me? Have I ruined it?"

He would have gone to her then, taken her on any terms—hers or his. But he wanted more than the moment, much more.

"Why did you change your mind?"

Shelby went toward him, grabbing his hands. "Does it matter?"

"It matters." He released her hands only to frame her face with his own. His eyes held that brooding serious look that could still turn her knees to jelly. "I have to know you'll be happy; have what you want, what you can live with. I want forever from you."

"All right." Shelby lifted her hands to his wrists, holding them a moment before she backed away. "I considered the possibilities," she began. "I thought through all the ifs and the maybes. I didn't like all of them, but the one I hated the most was life without you. You're not going to play Parcheesi without me, MacGregor."

His brow lifted. "I'm not?"

"No." She brushed at her bangs with another unsteady laugh. "Marry me, Alan. I won't agree with all your policies, but I'll try to be tactful in print— some of the time. I won't head any committees, and I'll only go to luncheons if there's no way out, but my own career's an understandable excuse for that. I won't give conventional parties, but I'll give interesting ones. If you're willing to take the risk of setting me loose on world politics, who am I to argue?"

He hadn't thought he could love her any more than he already did. He'd been wrong. "Shelby, I could go back to law, open a practice right here in Georgetown."

"No!" She whirled away from him. "No, dammit, you're not going back to law, not for me, not for anyone! I was wrong. I loved my father, I adored him, but I can't let what happened to him control the rest of my life—or yours." She stopped, needed to control her voice to calmness again. "I'm not changing for you, Alan. I can't. But I can do what you asked and have faith in you." She shook her head before he could speak. "I won't pretend that I won't ever be frightened, or that there won't be parts of the way we live that I'll hate. But I'll be proud of what you do." Calmer, she turned back to him. "I'm proud of who you are. If I still have a few dragons to fight, Alan, I'll do it."

He came to her, looking into her eyes before he gathered her close. "With me?"

She let out a long relieved sigh. "Always." When she turned her head, her mouth found his as hungry and seeking as her own. She felt it had been years rather than days and urged him down, with a murmur of his name, on the carpet with her.

There was no patience in either of them, only needs. Alan swore, fighting with snaps until Shelby laughed and rolled atop him to drive him senseless with her lips on his naked chest. He wasn't content only to be touched. His hands sought her through the denim, causing her strength to sag and her brain to cloud.

When at last there were no more obstructions, he

added his mouth to his hands, devouring and molding. The house was silent except for breathless murmurs and quiet sighs. Once more he buried his face in her hair to absorb the fragrance, to let it absorb him, as Shelby drew him into her.

Then there was nothing but pleasure, the desperate, whirling pleasure of being together.

It was late afternoon with softening light when Shelby stirred against him. They lay together on the couch, tangled and naked and drowsy. A bottle of wine grew warm on the table beside them.

When she opened her eyes, she saw that he slept on, his face relaxed, his breathing even. Here was the contentment, the easy, solid contentment she felt each time she lay quiet in his arms. Tilting her head back, Shelby watched him until he, too, stirred and his eyes opened. With a smile, she leaned closer to touch her lips to his.

"I can't remember when I've spent a more... enjoyable Saturday." She sighed, then teased his tongue with hers.

"Since I don't intend to move for at least twenty-four hours, we'll see how you like Sunday as well."

"I think I'm going to love it." She slid a hand over his shoulder. "I don't like to be pushy, Senator, but when are you going to marry me?"

"I thought September in Hyannis Port."

"The MacGregor fortress." He saw by her eyes the idea appealed to her. "But September's two and a half months away."

"We'll make it August," he said as he nibbled at her ear. "In the meantime, you and your roommates can move in here, or we can start looking for another place. Would you like to honeymoon in Scotland?''

Shelby nestled into his throat. ''Yes.'' She tilted her head back. ''In the meantime,'' she said slowly as her hands wandered down to his waist. ''I've been wanting to tell you that there's one of your domestic policies I'm fully in favor of, Senator.''

''Really?'' His mouth lowered to hover just above hers.

''You have—'' she nipped at his bottom lip ''—my full support. I wonder if you could just…run through the procedure for me one more time.''

Alan slid a hand down her side. ''It's my civic duty to make myself available to all my constituents.''

Shelby's fingers ran up his chest to stop his jaw just before he captured her lips. ''As long as it's only me, Senator.'' She hooked her arm around his neck. ''This is the one-man one-vote system.''

*   *   *   *   *

One Man's Art

Chapter One

Gennie knew she'd found it the moment she passed the first faded clapboard building. The village, pragmatically and accurately called Windy Point, at last captured her personal expectations for a coastal Maine settlement. She'd found her other stops along the rugged, shifting coastline scenic, picturesque, at times postcard perfect. Perhaps the perfection had been the problem.

When she'd decided on this working vacation, she'd done so with the notion of exploring a different aspect of her talent. Where before, she'd always fancified, mystified, relying on her own bent toward illusions, she'd made a conscious decision to stick to realism, no matter how stark. Indeed, her trunk was laden with her impressions of rock and sea and earth on canvas and sketch pads, but...

There was something more about Windy Point. Or

perhaps it was something less. There was no lushness here or soft edges. This was hard country. There were no leafy shade trees, but a few stunted fir and spruce, gnarled and weather-beaten. The road had more than its fair share of bumps.

The village itself, though it wasn't precisely tumbledown, had the air of old age with all its aches and pains. Salt and wind had weathered the buildings, picking away at the paint, scarring the windows. The result wasn't a soft wash, but a toughness.

Gennie saw a functional beauty. There were no frivolous buildings here, no gingerbread. Each building served its purpose—dry goods, post office, pharmacy. The few houses along the main road held that implacable New England practicality in their sturdy shape and tidy size. There might be flowers, adding a surprisingly gay and smiling color against the stern clapboard, but she noted nearly every home had a well-tended vegetable patch at the rear or the side. The petunias might be permitted to grow a bit unruly, but the carrots were tidily weeded.

With her car window down she could smell the village. It smelled quite simply of fish.

She drove straight through first, wanting a complete impression of the main street. She stopped by a churchyard where the granite markers were rather stern and the grass was high and wild, then turned to drive back through again. It wasn't a large town and the road was rather narrow, but she had a sense of spaciousness. You wouldn't bump into your neighbor here unless you meant to. Pleased, Gennie pulled up in front of the dry goods store, guessing this would be the hub of Windy Point's communications network.

The man sitting in an old wooden rocker on the stoop didn't stare, though she knew he'd seen her drive through and backtrack. He continued to rock while he repaired a broken lobster trap. He had the tanned brown face of the coast, guarded eyes, thinning hair, and gnarled strong hands. Gennie promised herself she'd sketch him just like that. She stepped from the car, grabbing her purse as an afterthought, and approached him.

"Hello."

He nodded, his hands still busy with the wooden slats of the trap. "Need some help?"

"Yes." She smiled, enjoying the slow, thick drawl that somehow implied briskness. "Perhaps you can tell me where I can rent a room or a cottage for a few weeks."

The shopkeeper continued to rock while he summed her up with shrewd, faded eyes. City, he concluded, not altogether disdainfully. And South. Though he was a man who considered Boston South, he pegged her as someone who belonged in the humid regions below the Mason-Dixon line. She was neat and pretty enough, though he felt her dark complexion and light eyes had a substantially foreign look. Then again, if you went much farther south than Portland, you were talking foreign.

While he rocked and deliberated, Gennie waited patiently, her rich black hair lifting from her shoulders and blowing back in the salt-scented breeze. Her experience in New England during the past few months had taught her that while most people were fair-minded and friendly enough, they generally took their time about it.

Didn't look like a tourist, he thought—more like one of those fairy princesses his granddaughter read about in her picture books. The delicate face came to a subtle point at the chin and the sweep of cheekbones added hauteur. Yet she smiled, softening the look, and her eyes were the color of the sea.

"Don't get many summer people," he said at length. "All gone now anyhow."

He wouldn't ask, Gennie knew. But she could be expansive when it suited her purpose. "I don't think I qualify as summer people, Mr...."

"Fairfield—Joshua Fairfield."

"Genviève Grandeau." She offered a hand which he found satisfactorily firm in his work-roughened one. "I'm an artist. I'd like to spend some time here painting."

An artist, he mused. Not that he didn't like pictures, but he wasn't sure he completely trusted the people who produced them. Drawing was a nice hobby, but for a job...still, she had a good smile and she didn't slouch. "Might be there's a cottage 'bout two miles out. Widow Lawrence ain't sold it yet." The chair creaked as he moved back and forth. "Could be she'll rent it for a time."

"It sounds good. Where can I reach her?"

"'Cross the road, at the post office." He rocked for another few seconds. "Tell her I sent you over," he decided.

Gennie gave him a quick grin. "Thank you, Mr. Fairfield."

The post office was hardly more than a counter and

four walls. One of the walls was taken up with slots where a woman in a dark cotton dress deftly sorted mail. She even *looks* like a Widow Lawrence, Gennie thought with inner pleasure as she noted the neat circular braid at the back of the woman's head.

"Excuse me."

The woman turned, giving Gennie a quick, birdlike glance before she came over to the counter. "Help you?"

"I hope so. Mrs. Lawrence?"

"Ayah."

"Mr. Fairfield told me you might have a cottage to rent."

The small mouth pursed—the only sign of facial movement. "I've a cottage for sale."

"Yes, he explained that." Gennie tried her smile again. She wanted the town—and the two miles distance from it the cottage would give her. "I wonder if you'd consider renting it for a few weeks. I can give you references if you'd like."

Mrs. Lawrence studied Gennie with cool eyes. She made her own references. "For how long?"

"A month, six weeks."

She glanced down at Gennie's hands. There was an intricate gold twist of a ring, but it was on the wrong finger. "Are you alone?"

"Yes." Gennie smiled again. "I'm not married, Mrs. Lawrence. I've been traveling through New England for several months, painting. I'd like to spend some time here at Windy Point."

"Painting?" the widow finished with another long look.

"Yes."

Mrs. Lawrence decided she liked Gennie's looks—
and that she was a young woman who didn't run on
endlessly about herself. And fact was fact. An empty
cottage was a useless thing. "The place is clean and
the plumbing's good. Roof was fixed two years back,
but the stove's got a temperament of its own. There's
two bedrooms but one of 'em stands empty."

This is painful for her, Gennie realized, though the
widow's voice stayed even and her eyes were steady.
She's thinking about all the years she lived there.

"Got no close neighbors, and the phone's been
taken out. Could be you could have one put in if
you've a mind to."

"It sounds perfect, Mrs. Lawrence."

Something in Gennie's tone made the woman clear
her throat. It had been sympathy and understanding
quietly offered. After a moment she named a sum for
the month's rent far more reasonable than Gennie had
expected. Characteristically she didn't hesitate, but
went with her instincts.

"I'll take it."

The first faint flutter of surprise showed on the
widow's face. "Without seeing it?"

"I don't need to see it." With a brisk practicality
Mrs. Lawrence admired, Gennie pulled a checkbook
out of her purse and dashed off the amount. "Maybe
you can tell me what I'll need in the way of linen and
dishes."

Mrs. Lawrence took the check and studied it. "Ge-
nevieve," she murmured.

"Geneviève," Gennie corrected, flowing easily over
the French. "After my grandmother." She smiled

again, softening that rather ruthless fairy look. "Everyone calls me Gennie."

An hour later Gennie had the keys to the cottage in her purse, two boxes of provisions in the back seat of her car and directions to the cottage in her hand. She'd passed off the distant, wary stares of the villagers and had managed not to chuckle at the open ogling of a scrawny teenager who'd come into the dry goods store while she was mulling over a set of earthenware dishes.

It was dusk by the time she was ready to set out. The clouds were low and unfriendly now, and the wind had picked up. It only added to the sense of adventure. Gennie set out on the narrow, bumpy road that led to the sea with a restless inner excitement that meant something new was on the horizon.

She came by her love of adventure naturally. Her great-great-grandfather had been a pirate—an unapologetic rogue of the sea. His ship had been fast and fierce, and he had taken what he wanted without qualm. One of Gennie's treasures was his logbook. Philippe Grandeau had recorded his misdeeds with flair and a sense of irony she'd never been able to resist. She might have inherited a strong streak of practicality from the displaced aristocrats on her mother's side, but Gennie was honest enough to know she'd have sailed with the pirate Philippe and loved every minute of it.

As her car bounced along the ruts, she took in the scenery, so far removed from her native New Orleans it might have been another planet. This was no place for long lazy days and riotous nights. In this rocky, windswept world, you'd have to be on your toes every minute. Mistakes wouldn't be easily forgiven here.

But she saw more than hard land and rock. Integrity. She sensed it in the land that vied continually with the sea. It knew it would lose, inch by minute inch, century after endless century, but it wasn't giving in. Though the shadows lengthened with evening, she stopped, compelled to put some of her impressions on paper.

There was an inlet some yards from the road, restless now as the storm approached. As Gennie pulled out a sketchbook and pencil, she caught the smell of decaying fish and seaweed. It didn't make her wrinkle her nose; she understood that it was part of the strange lure that called men forever to the sea.

The soil was thin here, the rocks worn smooth. Near the road were clumps of wild blueberry bushes, pregnant with the last of the summer fruit. She could hear the wind—a distinctly feminine sound—sighing and moaning. She couldn't see the sea yet, but she could smell it and taste it in the air that swirled around her.

She had no one to answer to, no timetable to keep. Gennie had long since taken her freedom for granted, but solitude was something else. She felt it here, near the little windswept inlet, along the narrow, impossible road. And she held it to her.

When she was back in New Orleans, a city she loved, and she soaked up one of those steamy days that smelled of the river and humanity, she would remember passing an hour in a cool, lonely spot where she might have been the only living soul for miles.

Relaxed, but with that throb of excitement just buzzing along her skin, she sketched, going into much more detail than she had intended when she'd stopped. The lack of human noises appealed to her. Yes, she was going to enjoy Windy Point and the little cottage very much.

Finished, she tossed her sketchbook back in the car. It was nearly dark now or she might have stayed longer, wandered closer to the water's edge. Long days of painting stretched ahead of her...and who knew what else a month could bring? With a half smile, she turned the key in the ignition.

When she got only a bad-tempered rattle, she tried again. She was rewarded with a wheeze and a groan and a distinctly suspicious clunk. The car had given her a bit of trouble in Bath, but the mechanic there had tightened this and fiddled with that. It had been running like a top ever since. Thinking of the jolting road, Gennie decided that what could be tightened could just as easily be loosened again. With a mildly annoyed oath, she got out of the car to pop the hood.

Even if she had the proper tools, which she didn't think included the screwdriver and flashlight in her glove compartment, she would hardly know what to do with them. Closing the hood again, she glanced up and down the road. Deserted. The only sound was the wind. It was nearly dark, and by her calculations she was at the halfway point between town and the cottage. If she hiked back, someone was bound to give her a lift, but if she went on she could probably be in the cottage in fifteen minutes. With a shrug, she dug her flashlight out of the glove compartment and did what she usually did. She went forward.

She needed the light almost immediately. The road was no better to walk on than to drive on, but she'd have to take care to keep to it unless she wanted to end up lost or taking a dunking in an inlet. Ruts ran deeply here, rocks worked their way up there, so that she wondered how often anyone actually traveled this stretch.

Darkness fell swiftly, but not in silence. The wind whipped at her hair, keeping up its low, keening sound. There were wisps of fog at her feet now which she hoped would stay thin until she was indoors. Then she forgot the fog as the storm burst out, full of fury.

Under other circumstances, Gennie wouldn't have minded a soaking, but even her sense of adventure was strained in the howling darkness where her flashlight cut a pitiful beam through the slashing rain. Annoyance was her first reaction as she continued to trudge along the uneven road in thoroughly wet sneakers. Gradually annoyance became discomfort and discomfort, unease.

A flash of lightning would illuminate a cropping of rocks or stunted bush, throwing hard, unfriendly shadows. Even a woman possessing a pedestrian imagination might have had a qualm. Gennie had visions of nasty little elves grinning out of the cloaking darkness. Humming tunelessly to stave off panic, she concentrated on the beam of her flashlight.

So I'm wet, Gennie told herself as she dragged dripping hair out of her eyes. It's not going to kill me. She gave another uneasy glance at the side of the road. There was no dark, Gennie decided, like the dark of the countryside. And where was the cottage? Surely she'd walked more than a mile by now. Halfheartedly she swung the light in a circle. Thunder boiled over her head while the rain slapped at her face. It would take a minor miracle to find a dark, deserted cottage with only the beam of a household flashlight.

Stupid, she called herself while she wrapped her arms tightly around her chest and tried to think. It was always stupid to set out toward the unknown when you had a choice. And yet she would always do so. There seemed to be nothing left but find her way back to the car and wait out the storm there. The prospect of a long wet night in a compact wasn't pleasant, but it had it all over wandering around lost in a thunderstorm. And there was a bag of cookies in the car, she remembered while she continued to stroke the flashlight back and forth, just in case there was— something out there. With a sigh, she gave one last look down the road.

She saw it. Gennie blinked rain out of her eyes and looked again. A light. Surely that was a light up ahead. A light meant shelter, warmth, company. Without hesitation, Gennie headed toward it.

It turned out to be another mile at best, while the storm and the road worsened. Lightning slashed the sky with a wicked purple light, tossing out a brief eerie glow that made the darkness only deeper when it faded. To keep from stumbling, she was forced to move slowly and keep her eyes on the ground. She began to be certain she'd never be dry or warm again. The light up ahead stayed steady and true, helping her to resist glancing over her shoulder too often.

She could hear the sea now, beating violently on rocks and shale. Once in a flash of lightning, she thought she saw the crest of angry waves, white-capped and turbulent in the distance. Even the rain smelled of the sea now—an angry, vengeful one. She wouldn't—couldn't—allow herself to be frightened, though her heart was beating fast from more than the two-mile walk. If she admitted she was frightened, she would give in to the urge to run and would end up over a cliff, in a ditch, or in some soundless vacuum.

The sense of displacement was so great, she might have simply sat on the road and wept had it not been for the steady beam of light sending out the promise of security.

When Gennie saw the silhouette of the building behind the curtain of rain she nearly laughed aloud. A lighthouse—one of those sturdy structures that proved man had some sense of altruism. The guiding light hadn't come from the high revolving lens but from a window. Gennie didn't question, but quickened her pace as much as she dared. Someone was there—a gnarled old man perhaps, a former seaman. He'd have a bottle of rum and talk in brief salty sentences. As a new bolt of lightning slashed across the sky, Gennie decided she already adored him.

The structure seemed huge to her—a symbol of safety for anyone lost and storm-tossed. It looked stunningly white under the play of her flashlight as she searched the base for a door. The window that was lit was high up, the top of three on the side Gennie approached.

She found a door of thick rough wood and beat on it. The violence of the storm swallowed the sound and tossed it away. Nearer to panic than she wanted to admit, Gennie pounded again. Could she have come so far, got so close, and then not be heard? The old keeper was in there, she thought as she beat on the door, probably whistling and whittling, perhaps idling away the evening putting a ship into a bottle.

Desperate, Gennie leaned against the door, feeling the hard, wet wood against her cheek as well as the side of her fist as she continued to thud against it. When the door opened, she went with it, overbalancing. Her arms were gripped hard as she pitched forward.

"Thank God!" she managed. "I was afraid you wouldn't hear me." With one hand she dragged her sopping hair out of her face and looked up at the man she considered her savior.

The one thing he wasn't was old. Nor was he gnarled. Rather he was young and lean, but the narrow, tanned face of planes and angles might have been a seafaring one—in her great-great-grandfather's line. His hair was as dark as hers, and as thick, with that careless windblown effect a man might get if he stood on the point of a ship. His mouth was full and unashamedly sensual, the nose a bit aristocratic in the rugged face. His eyes were a deep, deep brown under dark brows. They weren't friendly, Gennie decided, not even curious. They were simply annoyed.

"How the hell did you get here?"

It wasn't the welcome she had expected, but her trek through the storm had left her a bit muddled. "I walked," she told him.

"Walked?" he repeated. "In this? From where?"

"A couple of miles back—my car stalled." She began to shiver, either with chill or with reaction.

He'd yet to release her, and she'd yet to recover enough to demand it.

"What were you doing driving around on a night like this?"

"I—I'm renting Mrs. Lawrence's cottage. My car stalled, then I must have missed the turnoff in the dark. I saw your light." She heaved a long breath and realized abruptly that her legs were shaking. "Can I sit down?"

He stared at her for another minute, then with something like a grunt nudged her toward a sofa. Gennie sank down on it, dropped her head back, and concentrated on pulling herself together.

And what the hell was he supposed to do with her? Grant asked himself. Brows lowered, he stared down at her. At the moment she looked like she'd keel over if he breathed too hard. Her hair was plastered to her head, curling just a bit and dark as the night itself. Her face wasn't fine or delicate, but beautiful in the way of medieval royalty—long bones, sharp features. A Celtic or Gallic princess with a compact athletic little body he could see clearly as her clothes clung to it.

He thought the face and body might be appealing enough, under certain circumstances, but what had thrown him for an instant when she'd looked up at him had been her eyes. Sea green, huge, and faintly slanted. Mermaid's eyes, he'd thought. For a heartbeat, or perhaps only half of that, Grant had wondered if she'd been some mythical creature who'd been tossed ashore in the storm.

Her voice was soft and flowing, and though he recognized it as Deep South, it seemed almost a foreign tongue after the coastal Maine cadence he'd grown used to. He wasn't a man to be pleased with having a magnolia blossom tossed on his doorstep. When she opened her eyes and smiled at him, Grant wished fervently he'd never opened the door.

"I'm sorry," Gennie began, "I was barely coherent, wasn't I? I suppose I wasn't out there for more than an hour, but it seemed like days. I'm Gennie."

Grant hooked his thumbs in the pockets of his jeans and frowned at her again. "Campbell, Grant Campbell."

Since he left it at that and continued to frown, Gennie did her best to pick things up again. "Mr. Campbell, I can't tell you how relieved I was when I saw your light."

He stared down at her another moment, thinking briefly that she looked familiar. "The turnoff for the Lawrence place's a good mile back."

Gennie lifted a brow at the tone. Did he actually expect her to go back outside and stumble around until she found it? She prided herself on being fairly even-tempered for an artist, but she was wet and cold, and Grant's unfriendly, scowling face tripped the last latch. "Look, I'll pay you for a cup of coffee and the use of this—" she thumped a hand on the sofa and a soft plume of dust rose up "—thing for the night."

"I don't take in lodgers."

"And you'd probably kick a sick dog if he got in your way," she added evenly. "But I'm not going back out there tonight, Mr. Campbell, and I wouldn't advise trying to toss me out, either."

That amused him, though the humor didn't show in his face. Nor did he correct her assumption that he had meant to shove her back into the storm. The statement had been simply meant to convey his displeasure and the fact that he wouldn't take her money. If he hadn't been annoyed, he might have appreciated the fact that soaking wet and slightly pale, she held her own.

Without a word he walked over to the far side of the room and crouched to rummage through a scarred oak cabinet. Gennie stared straight ahead, even as she heard the sound of liquid hitting glass.

"You need brandy more than coffee at the moment," Grant told her, and shoved the glass under her nose.

"Thank you," Gennie said in an icy tone southern women are the champions of. She didn't sip, but drank it down in one swallow, letting the warmth shock her system back to normal. Distantly polite, she handed the empty glass back to him.

Grant glanced down at it and very nearly smiled. "Want another?"

"No," she said, frigid and haughty, "thank you."

I have, he mused wryly, been put in my place. Princess to peasant. Considering his option, Grant rocked back on his heels. Through the thick walls of the lighthouse, the storm could be heard whipping and wailing. Even the mile ride to the Lawrence place would be wild and miserable, if not dangerous. It would be less trouble to bed her down where she was than to drive her to the cottage. With an oath that was more weary than pungent he turned away.

"Well, come on," he ordered without looking back, "you can't sit there shivering all night."

Gennie considered—seriously considered—heaving her purse at him.

The staircase charmed her. She nearly made a comment on it before she stopped herself. It was iron and circular, rising up and up the interior. Grant stepped off onto the second level which Gennie calculated was a good twenty feet above the first. He moved like a cat in the dark while she held on to the rail and waited for him to hit the light switch.

It cast a dim glow and many shadows over the bare wood floor. He passed through a door on the right into what she discovered were his sleeping quarters— small, not particularly neat, but with a curvy antique brass bed Gennie fell instantly in love with. Grant went to an old chifforobe that might have been beautiful with refinishing. Muttering to himself, he routed around and unearthed a faded terrycloth robe.

"Shower's across the hall," he said briefly, and dumped the robe in Gennie's arms before he left her alone.

"Thank you very much," she mumbled while his footsteps retreated back down the stairs. Chin high, eyes gleaming, she stalked across the hall and found herself charmed all over again.

The bath was white porcelain and footed with brass fixtures he obviously took the time to polish. The room was barely more than a closet, but somewhere in its history it had been paneled in cedar and lacquered. There was a pedestal sink and a narrow little mirror. The light was above her, operated by a pull string.

Stripping gratefully out of her cold, wet clothes, Gennie stepped into the tub and drew the thin circular curtain. In an instant, she had hot water spraying out of the tiny shower head and warming her body. Gennie was certain paradise could have felt no sweeter, even when it was guarded by the devil.

In the kitchen Grant made a fresh pot of coffee. Then, as an afterthought, he opened a can of soup. He supposed he'd have to feed her. Here, at the back of the tower, the sound of the sea was louder. It was a sound he was used to—not so he no longer heard it, but so he expected to. If it was vicious and threatening as it was tonight, Grant acknowledged it, then went about his business.

Or he would have gone about his business if he hadn't found a drenched woman outside his door. Now he calculated he'd have to put in an extra hour that night to make up for the time she was costing him. With his first annoyance over, Grant admitted it couldn't be helped. He'd give her the basic hospitality of a hot meal and a roof over her head, and that would be that.

A smile lightened his features briefly when he remembered how she had looked at him when she'd sat dripping on his sofa. The lady, he decided, was no pushover. Grant had little patience with pushovers. When he chose company, he chose the company of people who said what they thought and were willing to stand by it. In a way, that was why Grant was off his self-imposed schedule.

It had barely been a week since his return from Hyannis Port where he'd given away his sister, Shelby, in her marriage to Alan MacGregor. He'd discovered, uncomfortably, that the wedding had made him sentimental. It hadn't been difficult for the

MacGregors to persuade him to stay on for an extra couple of days. He'd liked them, blustery old Daniel in particular, and Grant wasn't a man who took to people quickly. Since childhood he'd been cautious, but the MacGregors as a group were irresistible. And he'd been weakened somewhat by the wedding itself.

Giving his sister away, something that would have been his father's place had he lived, had brought such a mix of pain and pleasure that Grant had been grateful to have the distraction of a few days among the MacGregors before he returned to Windy Point—even to the extent of being amused by Daniel's not so subtle probing into his personal life. He'd enjoyed himself enough to accept an open-ended invitation to return. An invitation even he was surprised that he intended to act on.

For now there was work to be done, but he resigned himself that a short interruption wouldn't damage his status quo beyond repair. As long as it remained short. She could bunk down in the spare room for the night, then he'd have her out and away in the morning. He was nearly in an amiable mood by the time the soup started to simmer.

Grant heard her come in, though the noise from outside was still fierce. He turned, prepared to make a moderately friendly comment, when the sight of her in his robe went straight to his gut.

Damn, she was beautiful. Too beautiful for his peace of mind. The robe dwarfed her, though she'd rolled the frayed sleeves nearly to the elbow. The faded blue accented the honey-rich tone of her skin. She'd brushed her damp hair back, leaving her face unframed but for a few wayward curls that sprung out near her temples. With her eyes pale green and the dark lashes wet, she looked to him more than ever like the mermaid he'd nearly taken her for.

"Sit down," he ordered, furiously annoyed by the flare of unwelcome desire. "You can have some soup."

Gennie paused a moment, her eyes skimming up and down his back before she sat at the rough wooden table. "Why, thank you." His response was an unintelligible mutter before he thumped a bowl in front of her. She picked up the spoon, not about to let pride get in the way of hunger. Though surprised, she said nothing when he sat opposite her with a bowl of his own.

The kitchen was small and brightly lit and very, very quiet. The only sound came from the wind and restless water outside the thick walls. At first Gennie ate with her eyes stubbornly on the bowl in front of her, but as the sharp hunger passed she began to glance around the room. Tiny certainly, but with no wasted space. Rough oak cabinets ringed the walls giving generous room for supplies. The counters were wood as well, but sanded and polished. She saw the modern conveniences of a percolator and a toaster.

He took better care of this room, she decided, than he did the rest of the house. No dishes in the sink, no crumbs or spills. And the only scents were the kitcheny aromas of soup and coffee. The appliances were old and a bit scarred, but they weren't grimy.

As her first hunger ebbed, so did her anger. She had, after all, invaded his privacy. Not everyone offered hospitality to a stranger with smiles and open arms. He had scowled, but he hadn't shut the door in her face. And he had given her something dry to wear and food, she added as she did her best to submerge pride.

With a slight frown she skimmed her gaze over the tabletop until it rested on his hands. Good God, she thought with a jolt, they were beautiful. The wrists were narrow, giving a sense not of weakness but of graceful strength and capability. The backs of his hands were deeply tanned and unmarred, long and lean, as were his fingers. The nails were short and straight. Masculine was her first thought, then delicate came quickly on the tail of it. Gennie could picture the hands holding a flute just as easily as she could see them wielding a saber.

For a moment she forgot the rest of him in her fascination with his hands, and her reaction to them. She felt the stir but didn't suppress it. She was certain any woman who saw those romantic, exquisite hands would automatically wonder just what they would feel like on her skin. Impatient hands, clever. They were the kind that could either rip the clothes off a woman or gently undress her before she had any idea what was happening.

When a thrill Gennie recognized as anticipation sprinted up her spine, she caught herself. What was she thinking of! Even her imagination had no business sneaking off in that direction. A little dazed by the feeling that wouldn't be dismissed, she lifted her gaze to his face.

He was watching her—coolly, like a scientist watching a specimen. When she'd stopped eating so suddenly, he'd seen her eyes go to his hands and remain there with her lashes lowered just enough to conceal their expression. Grant had waited, knowing sooner or later she'd look up. He'd been expecting that icy anger or frosty politeness. The numb shock on her face puzzled him, or more accurately intrigued him. But it was the vulnerability that made him want her almost painfully. Even when she had stumbled into the house, wet and lost, she hadn't looked defenseless. He wondered what she would do if he simply got up, hauled her to her feet and dragged her up into his bed. He wondered what in the hell was getting into him.

They stared at each other, each battered by feelings neither of them wanted while the rain and the wind beat against the walls, separating them from everything civilized. He thought again that she looked like some temptress from the sea. Gennie thought he'd have given her rogue of an ancestor a run for his money.

Grant's chair legs scraped against the floor as he pushed back from the table. Gennie froze.

"There's a room on the second level with a bunk." His eyes were hard and dark with suppressed anger— his stomach knotted with suppressed desire.

Gennie found that her palms were damp with nerves and was infuriated. Better to be infuriated with him. "The couch down here is fine," she said coldly.

He shrugged. "Suit yourself." Without another word, he walked out. Gennie waited until she heard his footsteps on the stairs before she pressed a hand to her stomach. The next time she saw a light in the dark, she told herself, she'd run like hell in the opposite direction.

Chapter Two

Grant hated to be interrupted. He'd tolerate being cursed, threatened or despised, but he never tolerated interruptions. It had never mattered to him particularly if he was liked, as long as he was left alone to do as he chose. He'd grown up watching his father pursue the goodwill of others—a necessary aspect in the career of a senator who had chosen to run for the highest office in the country.

Even as a child Grant knew his father was a man who demanded extreme feelings. He was loved by some, feared or hated by others, and on a campaign trail he could inspire a fierce loyalty. He had been a man who would go out of his way to do a favor— friend or stranger—it had never mattered. His ideals had been high, his memory keen, and his flair for words admirable. Senator Robert Campbell had been a man who had felt it his duty to make himself ac-

cessible to the public. Right up to the moment someone had put three bullets into him.

Grant hadn't only blamed the man who had held
the gun, or the profession of politics, as his sister had
done. In his own way Grant had blamed his father.
Robert Campbell had given himself to the world, and
it had killed him. Perhaps it was as a direct result that
Grant gave himself to no one.

He didn't consider the lighthouse a refuge. It was
simply his place. He appreciated the distance it gave
him from others, and enjoyed the harshness and the
harmony of the elements. If it gave him solitude, it
was as necessary to his work as it was to himself. He
required the hours, even the days, of aloneness. Un-
interrupted thought was something Grant considered
his right. No one, absolutely no one, was permitted
to tamper with it.

The night before he'd been midway through his
current project when Gennie's banging had forced
him to stop. Grant was perfectly capable of ignoring
a knock on the door, but since it had broken his train
of thought, he had gone down to answer—with the
idea of strangling the intruder. Gennie might consider
herself lucky he'd only resorted to rudeness. A hapless tourist had once found himself faced with an irate
Grant, who had threatened to toss him into the ocean.

Since it had taken Grant the better part of an hour
after he'd left Gennie in the kitchen to get his mind
back on his work, he'd been up most of the night.
Interruptions. Intrusions. Intolerable. He'd thought so
then, and now as the sun slanted in the window and
onto the foot of his bed, he thought so again.

Groggy after what amounted to almost four hours

sleep, Grant listened to the voice that drifted up the stairwell. She was singing some catchy little tune you'd hear every time you turned on the radio— something Grant did every day of his life, just as religiously as he turned on the TV and read a dozen newspapers. She sang well, in a low-pitched, drumming voice that turned the cute phrasing into something seductive. Bad enough she'd interrupted his work the night before, now she was interrupting his sleep.

With a pillow over his head, he could block it out. But, he discovered, he couldn't block out his reaction to it. It was much too easy in the dark, with the sheet warm under his chest, to imagine her. Swearing, Grant tossed the pillow aside and got out of bed to pull on a pair of cutoffs. Half asleep, half aroused, he went downstairs.

The afghan she'd used the night before was already neatly folded on the sofa. Grant scowled at it before he followed Gennie's voice into the kitchen.

She was still in his robe, barefoot, with her hair waving luxuriously down her back. He'd like to have touched it to see if those hints of red that seemed to shimmer through the black were really there or just a trick of the light.

Bacon sizzled in a pan on the stove, and the coffee smelled like heaven.

"What the hell are you doing?"

Gennie whirled around clutching a kitchen fork, one hand lifting to her heart in reflex reaction. Despite the discomfort of the sofa, she'd woken in the best of moods—and starving. The sun was shining, gulls were calling, and the refrigerator had been liberally stocked. Gennie had decided Grant Campbell deserved another chance. As she'd puttered in his kitchen, she'd made a vow to be friendly at all costs.

He stood before her now, half naked and obviously angry, his hair sleep-tumbled and a night's growth of beard shadowing his chin. Gennie gave him a determined smile. "I'm making breakfast. I thought it was the least I could do in return for a night's shelter."

Again he had the sensation of something familiar about her he couldn't quite catch. His frown only deepened. "I don't like anyone messing with my things."

Gennie opened her mouth, then shut it again before anything nasty could slip out. "The only thing I've broken is an egg," she said mildly as she indicated the bowl of eggs she intended to scramble. "Why don't you do us both a favor? Get a cup of coffee, sit down, and shut up." With an almost imperceptible toss of her head, she turned her back on him.

Grant's brows rose not so much in surprise as in appreciation. Not everyone could tell you to shut up in a butter-melting voice and make it work. He had the feeling he wasn't the first person she'd given the order to. With something perilously close to a grin, he got a mug and did exactly what she said.

She didn't sing anymore as she finished making the meal, but he had the feeling she would've muttered bad-temperedly if she hadn't wanted him to think she was unaffected by him. In fact, he was certain there was a good bit of muttering and cursing going on inside her head.

As he sipped coffee the grogginess gave way to alertness, and hunger. For the first time he sat in the

tiny kitchen while a woman fixed his breakfast. Not
something he'd want to make a habit of, Grant mused
while he watched her—but then again, it wasn't an
unpleasant experience.

Still clinging to silence, Gennie set plates on the
table, then followed them with a platter of bacon and
eggs. "Why were you going to the old Lawrence
place?" he asked as he served himself.

Gennie sent him a narrowed-eyed glare. So now
we're going to make polite conversation, she thought
and nearly ground her teeth. "I'm renting it," she
said briefly, and dashed salt on her eggs.

"Thought the Widow Lawrence had it up for sale."

"She does."

"You're a little late in the season for renting a
beach cottage," Grant commented over a mouthful of
eggs.

Gennie gave a quick shrug as she concentrated on
her breakfast. "I'm not a tourist."

"No?" He gave her a long steady look she found
both deft and intrusive. "Louisiana, isn't it? New Orleans, Baton Rouge?"

"New Orleans." Gennie forgot annoyance long
enough to study him in turn. "You're not local, either."

"No," he said simply, and left it at that.

Oh, no, she thought, he wasn't going to start a conversation, then switch it off when it suited him. "Why
a lighthouse?" she persisted. "It's not operational, is
it? It was the light from the window I followed last
night, not the beacon."

"Coast Guard takes care of this stretch with radar.
This station hasn't been used in ten years. Did you

run out of gas?'' he asked before she realized he'd never answered the why.

"No. I'd pulled off the side of the road for a few minutes, then when I tried to start the car again, it just made a few unproductive noises.'' She shrugged and bit into a slice of bacon. "I guess I'll have to get a tow truck in town.''

Grant made a sound that might have been a laugh. "You might get a tow truck up at Bayside, but you're not going to find one at Windy Point. I'll take a look at it,'' he told her as he finished off his breakfast. "If it's beyond me, you can get Buck Gates from town to come out and get it started.''

She studied him for nearly thirty seconds. "Thank you,'' Gennie said warily.

Grant rose and put his plate in the sink. "Go get dressed,'' he ordered. "I've got work to do.'' For the second time he left Gennie alone in the kitchen.

Just once, she thought as she stacked her plate on top of his, she'd like to get in the last word. Giving the belt of Grant's robe a quick tug, she started out of the room. Yes, she'd go get dressed, Gennie told herself. And she'd do it quickly before he changed his mind. Rude or not, she'd accept his offer of help. Then as far as she was concerned, Grant Campbell could go to the devil.

There wasn't any sign of him on the second floor when she slipped into the bathroom to change. Gennie stripped out of the robe and hung it on a hook on the back of the door. Her clothes were dry, and she thought she could ignore the fact that her tennis shoes were still a bit cold and damp. With luck she could be settled into the cottage within the hour. That should leave her the best of the afternoon for sketching. The idea kept Gennie's spirits high as she made her way back downstairs. Again there was no sign of Grant. After a brief fight with the heavy front door, Gennie went outside.

It was so clear she nearly caught her breath. Whatever fog or fury had visited that place the night before had been swept clean. The places on the earth where the air really sparkled were rare, she knew, and this was one of them. The sky was blue and cloudless, shot through with the yellow light of the sun. There was some grass on this side of the lighthouse, tough and as wild as the few hardy flowers that were scattered through it. Goldenrod swayed in the breeze announcing the end of summer, but the sun shone hotly.

She could see the narrow rut of a road she'd traveled on the night before, but was surprised by the three-story farmhouse only a few hundred yards away. That it was deserted was obvious by the film of dirt on the windows and the waist-high grass, but it wasn't dilapidated. It would have belonged to the keeper and his family, Gennie concluded, when the lighthouse was still functional. They would have had a garden and perhaps a few chickens. And there would have been nights when the wind howled and the waves crashed that the keeper would have stayed at his station while his family sat alone and listened.

The white paint was faded, but the shutters hung true. She thought it sat on its hill waiting to be filled again.

There was a sturdy little pickup near the base of the slope which she assumed was Grant's. Because he was nowhere in sight, Gennie wandered around the side of the lighthouse, answering the call of the sea.

This time Gennie did catch her breath. She could see for miles, down the irregular coastline, over to tiny islands, and out to the distant horizon. There were boats on the water, staunch, competent little boats of the lobstermen. She knew she would see no chrome and mahogany crafts here, nor should she. This was a place of purpose, not idle pleasure. Strength, durability. That's what she felt as she looked out into blue-green water that frothed white as it flung itself at the rocks.

Seaweed floated in the surf, gathering and spreading with the movement of the water. The sea had its way with everything here. The rocks were worn smooth by it, and the ledges rose showing colors from gray to green with a few muted streaks of orange. Shells littered the shoreline, flung out by the sea and yet to be trampled under a careless foot. The smell of salt and fish was strong. She could hear the toll of the bell buoys, the hollow hoot of the whistling markers, the distant putter of the lobster boats and the mournful cry of gulls. There was nothing, no sound, no sight, no smell, that came from anything other than that endless, timeless sea.

Gennie felt it—the pull, the tug that had called men and women to it from the dawn of time. If humanity had truly sprung from there, perhaps that was why they were so easily lured back to it. She stood on the ledge above the narrow, rocky beach and lost herself in it. Danger, challenge, peace; she felt them all and was content.

She didn't hear Grant come behind her. Gennie was

too caught up in the sea itself to sense him, though he watched her as a minute stretched to two and two into three. She looked right there, he thought and could have cursed her for it. The land was his, this small, secluded edge of land that hovered over the sea.

He wouldn't claim to own the sea, not even when it rose high at noon to lick at the verge of his land, but this slice of rock and wild grass belonged to him, exclusively. She had no right to look as though she belonged—to make him wonder if the cliff would ever be only his again.

The wind plastered her clothes against her, as the rain had done the night before, accenting her slim, athletic body with its woman's roundness. Her hair danced frantically and free while the sun teased out those touches of fire in the ebony that seemed to hint of things he was nearly ready to test. Before he realized what he was doing, Grant took her arm and swung her to face him.

There was no surprise in her face as she looked at him, but excitement—and an arousal he knew came from the sea. Her eyes mirrored it and tempted.

"I wondered last night why anyone would choose to live here." She tossed the hair from her eyes. "Now I wonder how anyone lives anywhere else." She pointed to a small fishing boat at the end of the pier. "Is that yours?"

Grant continued to stare at her, realizing abruptly he'd nearly hauled her against him and kissed her—so nearly he could all but taste her mouth against his. With an effort he turned his head in the direction she pointed. "Yes, it's mine."

"I'm keeping you from your work." For the first time, Gennie gave him the simple gift of a real smile. "I suppose you'd have been up at dawn if I hadn't gotten in the way."

With an unintelligible mutter as an answer, Grant began to propel her toward his pickup. Sighing, Gennie gave up her morning vow to be friendly as a bad bet. "Mr. Campbell, do you have to be so unpleasant?"

Grant stopped long enough to shoot her a look— one Gennie would have sworn was laced with amused irony. "Yes."

"You do it very well," she managed as he began to pull her along again.

"I've had years of practice." He released her when they reached the truck, then opened his door and got in. Without comment, Gennie skirted the hood and climbed in the passenger side.

The engine roared into life, a sound so closely associated with towns and traffic, Gennie thought it a sacrilege. She looked back once as he started down the bumpy road and knew instantly she would paint— had to paint—that scene. She nearly stated her intention out loud, then caught a glimpse of Grant's frowning profile.

The hell with him, Gennie decided. She'd paint while he was out catching lobsters or whatever he caught out there. What he didn't know wouldn't hurt her, in this case. She sat back in the seat, primly folded her hands, and kept quiet.

Grant drove a mile before he started to feel guilty. The road was hardly better than a ditch, and at night it would have been a dark series of ruts and rocks.

Anyone walking over that stretch in a storm had to have been exhausted, miserable. Anyone who hadn't known the way would have been half terrified as well. He hadn't exactly dripped sympathy and concern. Still frowning, he took another quick look at her as the truck bounced along. She didn't look fragile, but he never would have believed she'd walked so far in that weather along a dark, rutted road.

He started to form what Gennie would have been astonished to hear was an apology when she lifted her chin. ''There's my car.'' Her voice was distantly polite again—master to servant this time. Grant swallowed the apology.

He swung toward her car, jostling Gennie in her seat a bit more than was absolutely necessary. Neither of them commented as he switched off the engine and climbed out. Grant popped the hood of her car, while Gennie stood with her hands in the back pockets of her jeans.

He talked to himself, she noticed, softly, just under his breath, as he fiddled with whatever people fiddled with under hoods of cars. She supposed it was a natural enough thing for someone who lived alone at the edge of a cliff. Then again, she thought with a grin, there were times in the thickly populated *Vieux Carré* when she found herself the very best person to converse with.

Grant walked back to his truck, pulling a toolbox out of the back of the cab. He rummaged around, chose a couple of different-sized wrenches, and returned to dive under her hood again. Pursing her lips, Gennie moved behind him to peer over his shoulder. He seemed to know what he was about, she decided.

And a couple of wrenches didn't seem so complicated. If she could just... She leaned in closer, automatically resting her hand on his back to keep her
balance.

Grant didn't straighten, but turned, his arm brushing firmly across her breast with the movement. It
could easily happen to strangers in a crowded elevator
and hardly be noticed. Both of them felt the power
of contact, and the surge of need.

Gennie would have backed up if she hadn't so suddenly found herself staring into those dark, restless
eyes—feeling that warm, quick breath against her
lips. Another inch, she thought, just another inch and
it would be his mouth on hers instead of just the hint
of it. Her hand had slipped to his shoulder, and without her realizing it, her fingers had tightened there.

Grant felt the pressure, but it was nothing compared
to what had sprung up at the back of his neck, the
base of his spine, the pit of his stomach. To take what
was within his reach might relieve the pressure, or it
might combust it. At the moment Grant wasn't certain
what result he'd prefer.

"What are you doing?" he demanded, but this time
his voice wasn't edged with anger.

Dazed, Gennie continued to stare into his eyes. She
could see herself in there, she thought numbly. When
did she get lost in there? "What?"

They were still leaning into the car, Gennie with
her hand on his shoulder, Grant with one hand on a
bolt, the other on a wrench. He had only to shift his
weight to bring them together. He nearly did before
he remembered how uncomfortably right she had
looked standing on his land gazing out to sea.

Touch this one, Campbell, and you're in trouble, the kind of trouble a man doesn't walk away from whistling a tune.

"I asked what you were doing," he said in the same quiet tone, but his gaze slid down to her mouth.

"Doing?... What *had* she been doing? "I-ah-I wanted to see how you fixed it so..." His gaze swept up and locked on hers again, scattered every coherent thought.

"So?" Grant repeated, enjoying the fact that he could confuse her.

"So... His breath whispered over her lips. She caught herself running her tongue along them to taste it. "So if it happens again I could fix it."

Grant smiled—slowly, deliberately. Insolently? Gennie wasn't sure, but her heart rose to her throat and stuck there. However he smiled, whatever his intent, it added a wicked, irresistible charm to his face. She thought it was a smile a barbarian might have given his woman before he tossed her over his shoulder and took her into some dark cave. Just as slowly, he turned away to begin working with the wrench again.

Gennie backed up and let out a long, quiet breath. That had been close—too close. To what, she wasn't precisely sure, but to something no smart woman would consider safe. She cleared her throat. "Do you think you can fix it?"

"Hmmm."

Gennie took this for the affirmative, then stepped closer, this time keeping to the side of the hood. "A mechanic looked at it a couple weeks ago."

"Think you're going to need new plugs soon. I'd have Buck Gates take a look if I were you."

"Is he a mechanic? At the service station?"

Grant straightened. He wasn't smiling now, but there was amusement in his eyes. "There's no service station in Windy Point. You need gas, you go down to the docks and pump it. You got car trouble, you see Buck Gates. He repairs the lobster boats—a motor's a motor." The last was delivered in an easy Down East cadence, with a hint of a smile that had nothing to do with condescension. "Start her up."

Leaving her door open, Gennie slid behind the wheel. A turn of the key had her engine springing cheerfully to life. Even as she let out a relieved sigh, Grant slammed the hood into place. Gennie cut the engine again as he walked back to his truck to replace his tools.

"The Lawrence cottage's about three quarters of a mile up on the left. You can't miss the turnoff unless you're hiking through a storm in the middle of the night with only a flashlight."

Gennie swallowed a chuckle. Don't let him have any redeeming qualities, she pleaded. Let me remember him as a rude, nasty man who just happens to be fatally sexy. "I'll keep that in mind."

"And I wouldn't mention that you'd spent the night at Windy Point Station," he added easily as he slipped the toolbox back into place. "I have a reputation to protect."

This time she bit her lip to hold back a smile. "Oh?"

"Yeah." Grant turned back, leaning against the truck a moment as he looked at her again. "The villagers think I'm odd. I'd slip a couple notches if they found out I hadn't just shoved you back outside and locked the door.''

This time she did smile—but only a little. ''You have my word, no one will hear from me what a good samaritan you are. If anyone should happen to ask, I'll tell them you're rude, disagreeable, and generally nasty.''

''I'd appreciate it.''

When he started to climb back into the truck, Gennie reached for her wallet. ''Wait, I haven't paid you for—''

''Forget it.''

She hooked her hand on the door handle. ''I don't want to be obligated to you for—''

''Tough.'' Grant started the engine. ''Look, move your car, I can't turn around with you in my way.''

Eyes narrowed, she whirled away. So much for gratitude, she told herself. So the villagers thought he was odd, she mused as she slammed the car door. Perceptive people. Gennie started down the road at a cautious speed, making it a point not to look into the rearview mirror. When she came to the turnoff, she veered left. The only sign of Grant Campbell was the steady hum of his truck as he went on. Gennie told herself she wouldn't think of him again.

And she didn't as she drove down the straight little lane with black-eyed Susans springing up on either side. The sound of his truck was a distant echo, soon lost. Without any trees to block the view, Gennie saw the cottage almost immediately, and was charmed. Small certainly, but it didn't evoke images of seven dwarfs heigh-hoing. Gennie immediately had a picture of a tidy woman in a housedress hanging out the wash, then a rough-featured fisherman whittling on the tiny porch.

It had been painted blue but had weathered to a soft blue-gray. A one-story boxlike structure, it had a modest front porch facing the lane and, she was to discover, another screened porch looking out over the inlet. A pier that looked like it might be a bit shaky stretched out over the glassily calm water. Someone had planted a willow near the shore, but it wasn't flourishing.

Gennie turned off the engine and was struck with silence. Pleasant, peaceful—yes, she could live with this, work with this. Yet she discovered she preferred the thrash and boom of the sea that Grant had outside his front door.

Oh, no, she reminded herself firmly, she vowed not to think of him. And she wouldn't. After stepping from the car, Gennie hefted the first box of groceries and climbed the plank stairs to the front door. She had to fight with the lock a moment, then it gave a mighty groan and yielded.

The first thing Gennie noticed was tidiness. The Widow Lawrence had meant what she said when she had stated the cottage was clean. The furniture was draped in dustcovers but there was no dust. Obviously, she came in regularly and chased it away. Gennie found the idea touching and sad. The walls were painted a pale blue, and the lighter patches here and there indicated where pictures had hung for years. Carrying her box of supplies, Gennie wandered toward the back of the house and found the kitchen.

The sense of order prevailed here as well. Formica

counters were spotless, the porcelain sink gleamed. A flick of the tap proved the plumbing was indeed cooperative. Gennie set down the box and went through the back door onto the screened porch. The air was warm and moist, tasting of the sea. Someone had repaired a few holes in the screen and the paint on the floor was cracked but clean.

Too clean, Gennie realized. There was no sign of life in the cottage, and barely any echo of the life that had once been there. She would have preferred the dusty disorder she had found in Grant's lighthouse. Someone *lived* there. Someone vital. Shaking her head, she pushed him to the back of her mind. Someone lived here now—and in short order the house would know it. Quickly she went back to her car to unpack.

Because she traveled light and was inherently organized, it took less than two hours for Gennie to distribute her things throughout the house. Both bedrooms were tiny, and only one had a bed. When Gennie made it up with the linens she had bought, she discovered it was a feather bed. Delighted, she spent some time bouncing on it and sinking into it. In the second bedroom she stowed her painting gear. With the dustcovers removed and a few of her own paintings hung on the faded spots, she began to feel a sense of home.

Barefoot and pleased with herself, she went out to walk the length of the pier. A few boards creaked and others shook, but she decided the structure was safe enough. Perhaps she would buy a small boat and explore the inlet. She could do as she pleased now, go where she liked. Her ties in New Orleans would pull her back eventually, but the wanderlust which had driven her north six months before had yet to fade.

Wanderlust, she repeated as her eyes clouded. No, the word was guilt—or pain. It was still following her, perhaps it always would. It's been more than a year, Gennie thought as she closed her eyes. Seventeen months, two weeks, three days. And she could still see Angela. Perhaps she should be grateful for that— for the fact that her artist's memory could conjure up her sister's face exactly as it had been. Young, beautiful, vibrant. But on the other side of the coin, it was too easy to see Angela lifeless and broken—the way her sister had looked after she'd killed her.

Not your fault. How many times had she heard that?
It wasn't your fault, Gennie. You can't blame yourself.

Oh, yes, I can, she thought with a sigh. If I hadn't been driving…. If my reflexes had been quicker…. If I'd only seen that car running the red light.

There was no going back, and Gennie knew it. The times the helpless guilt and grief flooded her were fewer now, but no less painful. She had her art, and sometimes she thought that alone had saved her sanity after her sister's death. All in all this trip had been good for her—by taking her away from the memories that were still too close, and by letting her concentrate on painting for painting's sake.

Art had become too much like a business to her in the past few years. She'd nearly lost herself in the selling and showings. Now it was back to basics— she needed that. Oil, acrylic, watercolor, charcoal; and the canvases that waited to be filled.

Perhaps the hard realism of losing her sister had influenced her to seek the same hard realism in her work. It might have been her way of forcing herself to accept life, and death. Her abstracts, the misty quality of her painting had always given the world she created a gentle hue. Not quite real but so easy to believe in. Now she was drawn to the plain, the everyday. Reality wasn't always pretty, but there was a strength in it she was just beginning to understand.

Gennie drew in a deep breath. Yes, she would paint this—this quiet, settled little inlet. There'd be a time for it. But first, now, she needed the challenge and power of the ocean. A glance at her watch showed her it was noon. Surely he would be out on his boat now, making up the time she had cost him that morning. She could have three or four hours to sketch the lighthouse from different angles without him even knowing. And if he did, Gennie added with a shrug, what difference would it make? One woman with a sketch pad could hardly bother him. In any case, he could just bolt himself up inside and ignore her if he didn't like it. Just as she intended to ignore him.

Grant's studio was on the third level. More precisely, Grant's studio *was* the third level. What had been three cubbyhole rooms had been remodeled into one with good natural light, strongest from the north. Glass-topped cabinets, called taborets, held an assortment of tools, completely organized. Fountain pens, ballpoints, knives, sable brushes, a wide variety of pencils and erasers, bow compass, T square. An engineer or architect would have recognized several of the tools and approved the quality. Matte paper was already taped down to his drawing board.

On the whitewashed wall he faced hung a mirror and a framed reprint of *The Yellow Kid*, a cartoon strip nearly a hundred years old. On the other side of the room was a sophisticated radio and a small color TV. The stack of newspapers and magazines in the corner was waist-high. The room had the sense of practical order Grant bothered with in no other aspect of his life.

He worked without hurry this morning. There were times he worked frantically, not because of a deadline—he was always a month ahead of schedule—but because his own thoughts pushed at him. At times he would take a week or perhaps two to simply gather ideas and store them. Other times, he would work through the night as those same ideas fretted to be put down with pen and ink.

He'd finished the project he'd been working on in the early hours of the morning. Now a new angle had been pushing at him, one he didn't seem to be able to resist. Grant rarely resisted anything that applied to his art. Already he had scaled the paper, striking diagonal lines with the blue pencil that wouldn't photograph. He knew what he wanted, but the preparation came first, those finite, vital details no one would ever notice in the few seconds it took to view his work.

When the paper was set and scaled, divided into five sections double the size they would be when reproduced, he began to sketch lightly. Doodling really, he brought his main character to life with a few loops and lines. The man was quite ordinary. Grant had insisted he be when he had created what his sister called his alter ego ten years before. An ordinary man, perhaps a bit scruffy, with a few features—the nose, the puzzled eyes—a bit exaggerated. But Grant's Macintosh was easily recognizable as someone you might pass on the street. And barely notice.

He was always too thin so that his attempts at dressing sharply never quite came off. He carried the air of someone who knew he was going to be put upon. Grant had a certain fondness for his general ineptitude and occasional satirical remarks.

Grant knew all of his friends—he'd created them as well. Not precisely a motley crew, but very close. Well-meaning dreamers, smart alecks. They were the shades of the people Grant had known in college—friends and acquaintances. Ordinary people doing ordinary things in an unusual way. That was the theme of his craft.

He'd given birth to Macintosh in college, then had left him in a closet while he had pursued art in a more traditional manner for almost three years. Perhaps he would have been successful; the talent had been there. But Grant had discovered he was much happier sketching a caricature than painting a portrait. In the end Macintosh had won. Grant had hauled him back out of the closet, and at the end of seven years the slightly weary, bleary-eyed character appeared in every major newspaper in the country seven days a week.

People followed his life and times over coffee, on the subway, on buses, and in bed. Over a million Americans opened their newspapers and looked to see just what he was up to that day before they had to face their own.

As a cartoonist, Grant knew it was his responsibility to amuse, and to amuse quickly, with a few short sentences and simple drawings. The strip would be looked at for ten or twelve seconds, chuckled over, then tossed aside. Often to line a bird cage. Grant had few illusions. It was the chuckle that was important, the fact that for those few seconds, he had given people something to laugh at—something to relate to. In *Macintosh*, Grant looked for the common experience, then twisted it.

What he wanted, what he insisted on having, was the right to do so, and the right to be left alone to do it. He was known to the public only by his initials. His contract with United Syndicate specifically stated his name would never be used in conjunction with the strip, nor would he grant any interviews or do any guest spots. His anonymity was as much a part of his price as his annual income.

Still using only the pencil, he began on the second section—Macintosh mumbling as the thudding on the door interrupted his newest hobby. Stamp collecting. Grant had gotten two full weeks out of this particular angle—Macintosh's bumbling attempts, his friends' caustic comments about his terminal boredom. Macintosh had fussed with his stamps and wondered if he'd finally hit a gold mine as the television had droned on behind him on the latest increase in the first-class mail service.

Here, he would open his door to be faced with a wet, bad-tempered siren. Grant didn't have any trouble drawing Gennie. In fact, he felt making her a character would put her firmly in perspective. She'd be just as ridiculous, and as vulnerable, as the rest of the people in his world. He'd begin to think of her as a character instead of a woman—flesh, blood, soft, fragrant. He didn't have any room for a woman, but he always had room for a character. He could tell them when to come, when to go, what to say.

He named her Veronica, thinking the more sophisticated name suited her. Deliberately, he exaggerated the tilt of her eyes and the lush sensuality of her mouth. Since the setting was Washington, D.C., rather than coastal Maine, Grant gave her a flat tire on the way home from a White House function. Macintosh goggled at her. Grant captured this by giving himself several stunned stares in the mirror above the drawing board.

He worked for two hours, perfecting the storyline—the situation, the setup, the punchline. After changing her tire and practicing macho lines to impress her, Macintosh ended up with five dollars, a stutter, and soaked shoes as Veronica zoomed out of his life.

Grant felt better when the sketches were done. He'd put Gennie just where he wanted—driving away. Now he would detail his work with India ink and brush. Solid black would accent or focus, the Benday patterns—zones of dots or lines—would give the gray areas.

Detailing Macintosh's room was simple enough; Grant had been there a thousand times. But it still took time and precision. Balance was crucial, the angles and positioning in order to draw the reader's attention just where you wanted it for the few seconds they would look at the individual panel. His supply of patience was consumed by his work, giving him little for the other areas of his life. The strip was half finished and the afternoon waning before he stopped to rest his hand.

Coffee, he thought, stretching his back and shoulders as he noticed the ache. And food. Breakfast had been too long ago. He'd grab something and take a walk down on the beach. He still had two papers to read and a few hours of television. Too much could happen in a day for him to ignore either form of communication. But the walk came first, Grant decided as he moved idly to the window. He needed some fresh air....

The hand he had lifted to rub at the back of his neck dropped. Leaning closer, he narrowed his eyes and stared down. It was bad enough when he had to deal with the occasional stray tourist, he thought furiously. A few curt words sent them away and kept them away. But there was no mistaking, even at this height, that thick ebony hair.

Veronica had yet to drive out of his life.

Chapter Three

It was beautiful, no matter what angle you chose or how the light shifted. Gennie had a half dozen sketches in her pad and knew she could have a half dozen more without catching all the aspects of that one particular jut of land. Look at the colors in the rocks! Would she ever be able to capture them? And the way the lighthouse stood there, solid, indomitable. The whitewash was faded here and there, the concrete blocks pockmarked with time and salt spray. That only added to the humanity of it. Man's strike for safety against the mercurial sea.

There would have been times the sea would have won, Gennie mused. Because man was fallible. There would have been times the lighthouse would have won. Because man was tenacious. Pitted together they spoke of harmony, perseverance, sweat, and strength.

She lost track of the time she had sat there, undisturbed, disturbing no one. Yet she knew she could go on sitting as long as the sun gave enough light. There were so few places in New Orleans where she could go to paint without the distractions of curiosity seekers or art buffs. When she chose to paint in the city, she was invariably recognized, and once recognized, watched or questioned.

Even when she went out—into the bayou, along a country road, she was often followed. She'd grown used to working around that and to saving most of her serious work for her studio. Over the years she'd nearly forgotten the simple freedom of being able to work outdoors, having the advantage of smelling and tasting what you drew while you drew it.

The past six months had given her something she hadn't been aware she'd looked for—a reminder of what she had been before success had put its limitations on her.

Content, half dreaming, she sketched what she saw and felt, and needed nothing else.

"Damn it, what do you want now?"

To her credit, Gennie didn't jolt or drop her sketch pad. She'd known Grant was around somewhere as his boat hadn't been moved. And she'd already decided he wasn't going to spoil what she'd found here. She was arrogant enough to feel it her right to be there to paint what her art demanded she paint. Thinking he was rather casual about his trade as a fisherman, she turned to him.

He was furious, she thought mildly. But she'd hardly seen him any other way. She decided he was suited to the out-of-doors—the sun, the wind, and the sea. Perhaps she'd do a sketch or two of him before she was finished. Tilting her head back, Gennie studied him as she would any subject that interested her.

"Good afternoon," she said in her best plantation drawl.

Knowing he was being measured and insulted might have amused him under different circumstances. At the moment it made him yearn to give her a hefty shove off her rock. All he wanted was for her to go away, and stay away—before he gave in to the urge to touch her.

"I asked you what you wanted."

"No need for you to bother. I'm just taking some preliminary sketches." Gennie kept her seat on the contorted rock near the verge of the cliff and shifted back to sea. "You can just go on with whatever you were doing."

Grant's eyes narrowed to dark slits. Oh, she was good at this, he thought. Dismissing underlings. "You're on my land."

"Mmm-hmm."

The idea of helping her off the rock became more appealing. "You're trespassing."

Gennie sent him an indulgent glance over her left shoulder. "You should try barbed wire and land mines. Nothing like a land mine to make a statement. Not that I can blame you for wanting to keep this little slice of the world to yourself, Grant," she added as she began to sketch again. "But I'm going to leave it exactly as I found it—no pop cans, no paper plates, no cigarette butts."

Even lifted over the roar of the sea, her voice held a mild, deliberately placating tone designed to set nerve ends on edge. Grant came very close to grab-

bing her by the hair and dragging her to her feet when
he was distracted by her pencil moving over the paper. What he saw halted the oath on the tip of his
tongue.

It was more than good, too true to life for a mere
excellent. With dashes and shading, she was capturing
the swirl of the sea on rock, the low swoop of gulls
and the steady endurance of the lighthouse. In the
same way, she'd given the sketch no hint of quiet
beauty. It was all hard edges, chips, flaws, and simplicity. It wouldn't make a postcard, nor would it
make a soothing touch of art over a mantel. But anyone who'd ever stood on a point where sea battled
shore would understand it.

Frowning in concentration rather than anger, Grant
bent closer. Hers weren't the hands of a student; hers
wasn't the soul of an amateur. In silence Grant waited
until she had finished, then immediately took the
sketchbook from her.

"Hey!" Gennie was halfway off her rock.

"Shut up."

She did, only because she saw he wasn't going to
hurl her work into the sea. Settling back on her rock,
she watched Grant as he flipped through her pages.
Now and again he stopped to study one sketch a bit
longer than the others.

His eyes were very dark now, she noted, while the
wind blew his hair over his forehead and away again.
There was a line, not of temper but of intensity, between his brows. His mouth was unsmiling, set, Gennie thought, to judge. It should have amused her to
have her work critiqued by a reclusive fisherman.
Somehow it didn't. There was a faint ache behind her

temple she recognized as tension. She'd felt that often enough before every one of her showings.

Grant's eyes skimmed over the page and met hers. For a long moment there was only the crash of the surf and the distant bell of a buoy. Now he knew why he'd had that nagging sense of having seen her before. But her newspaper pictures didn't do her justice. "Grandeau," he said at length. "Genviève Grandeau."

At any other time she wouldn't have been surprised to have had her work or her name recognized. Not in New York, California, Atlanta. But it was intriguing to find a man at some forgotten land's end who could recognize her work from a rough sketch in a notepad.

"Yes." She stood then, combing her hair back from her forehead with her hand and holding it there. "How did you know?"

He tapped the sketchbook on his palm while his eyes stayed on hers. "Technique is technique whether it's sketches or oils. What's the toast of New Orleans doing in Windy Point?"

The dry tone of the question annoyed her enough that she forgot how easily he had recognized her work. "I'm taking a year's sabbatical." Rising, she held out her hand for her pad.

Grant ignored the gesture. "An odd place to find one of the country's most...social artists. Your work's in art papers almost as often as your name's in the society section. Weren't you engaged to an Italian count last year?"

"He was a baron," she corrected coolly, "and we weren't engaged. Do you fill your time between catches reading the tabloids?"

The flash of temper in her eyes made him grin. "I do quite a bit of reading. And you," he added before she could think of some retort, "manage to get yourself in the *New York Times* almost as often as you get yourself in the tabloids and the glossies."

Gennie tossed her head in a gesture so reminiscent of royal displeasure, his grin widened. "It seems some live and others only read about life."

"You do make good copy, Genviève." He couldn't resist, and hooked his thumbs in his pockets as new ideas for Veronica raced through his mind. It seemed inevitable that she would come back and drive Macintosh crazy for a while. "You're a favorite with the paparazzi."

Her voice remained cool and distant, but she began to tap her pencil against the rock. "I suppose they have to make their living like anyone else."

"I seem to recall something about a duel being fought in Brittany a couple of years ago."

A smile lit her face, full of fun, when he hadn't expected it. "If you believe that, I have a bridge in New York you might be interested in."

"Don't spoil my illusions," Grant said mildly. The smile wasn't easy to resist, he discovered, not when it was genuine and touched with self-deprecating humor.

"If you'd rather believe tripe," she said graciously, "who am I to argue?"

Better to keep digging at her than to dwell too long on that smile. "Some tripe's fascinating in its way. There was a film director before the count—"

"Baron," Gennie reminded him. "The count

you're thinking of was French, and one of my first patrons.''

"You've had quite a selection of...patrons.''

She continued to smile, obviously amused. "Yes. Are you an art buff or do you just like gossip?''

"Both,'' he told her easily. "Come to think of it, there hasn't been a great deal about your—adventures—in the press for the last few months. You're obviously keeping your sabbatical very low key. The last thing I recall reading was...

He remembered then and could have cut out his tongue. The car accident—her sister's death—a beautiful and intrusive wire-service photo of Genviève Grandeau at the funeral. Devastation, shock, grief; that much had been clear even through the veil she had worn.

She wasn't smiling now, but looking at him with a mask of placid blankness. "I'm sorry,'' he said.

The apology nearly buckled her knees. She'd heard those words so many times before, from so many different people, but they'd never struck her with such simple sincerity. From a stranger, Gennie thought as she turned toward the sea again. It shouldn't mean so much coming from a stranger.

"It's all right.'' The wind felt so cool, so vital. It wasn't the place to dwell on death. If she had to think of it, she would think of it when she was alone, when there was silence. Now she could breathe deep and drink in the sea, and the strength. "So you spend your leisure time reading all the gossip in this wicked world. For a man who's so interested in people, you chose a strange place to live.''

"Interested in them,'' Grant agreed, grateful that

she was stronger than she looked. "That doesn't mean I want to be around them."

"You don't care for people, then." When she turned back, the smile was there again, teasing. "The tough recluse. In a few years you might even make crusty."

"You can't be crusty until you're fifty," he countered. "It's an unwritten law."

"I don't know." Gennie stuck her pencil behind her ear and tilted her head. "I wouldn't think you'd bother with laws, unwritten or otherwise."

"Depends," he said simply, "on whether they're useful or not."

She laughed. "Tell me..." She glanced down to the sketchbook Grant still held. "Do you like the sketches?"

He gave a short laugh. "I don't think Genviève Grandeau needs an unsolicited critique."

"Genviève has a tremendous ego," Gennie corrected. "Besides, it's not unsolicited if I ask for it."

Grant gave her a long, steady look before answering. "Your work's always very moving, very personal. The publicity attached to it isn't necessary."

"I believe, from you, that's a compliment," Gennie considered. "Are you going to give me free rein to paint here, or am I going to have to fight you every step of the way?"

He frowned again, and his face settled into the lines so quickly, Gennie swallowed a laugh. "Why here, pre- cisely?"

"I was beginning to think you were perceptive," Gennie said with a sigh. She made a sweep with her hand, wide, graceful, encompassing. "Can't you see it? It's life and it's death. It's a war that never ends, one we'll never see the outcome of. I can put that on canvas—only a part of it, a small, small slice. But I can do it. I couldn't resist if I wanted to.''

''The last thing I want here is a bunch of eager reporters or a few displaced European noblemen.''

Gennie lifted a brow, at once haughty and amused. It was the casual superiority of the look, Grant told himself, that made him want to drag her to the ground and prove to them both she was only a woman. ''I think you take your reading too seriously,'' she told him in an infuriatingly soft drawl. ''But I could give my word, if you like, that I won't phone the press or any of the two dozen lovers you seem to think I have.''

''Don't you?'' His banked temper came out in sarcasm. Gennie met it coolly.

''That's none of your business. However,'' she continued, ''I could sign a contract in blood—yours preferably—and pay you a reasonable fee, since it's your lighthouse. I'm going to paint here, with your cooperation or without it.''

''You seem to have a disregard for property rights, Genviève.''

''You seem to have a disregard for the rights of art.''

He laughed at that, a sound that was appealing, masculine, and puzzling. ''No,'' he said after a moment, ''as it happens, I feel very strongly about the rights of the artist.''

''As long as it doesn't involve you.''

He sighed, a sound she recognized as frustrated. His feelings about art and censorship were too ingrained to allow him to bar her way. And he knew, even as he stood there, that she was going to give him a great deal of trouble. A pity she hadn't chosen Penobscot Bay. "Paint," he said briefly. "And stay out of my way."

"Agreed." Gennie stepped up on the rock and looked out to sea again. "It's your rocks I want, your house, your sea." The lazily feminine smile touched her lips as she turned to him again. "But you're quite safe, Grant. I haven't any designs on you."

It was bait, they both knew it. But he nibbled anyway. "You don't worry me, Genviève."

"Don't I?" *What are you doing?* her common sense demanded. She ignored it. He thought she was some kind of twentieth-century siren. Why not humor him? With the aid of the rock she was a few inches above him. His eyes were narrowed against the sun as he looked up at her, hers were wide and smiling. With a laugh, she rested her hands on his shoulders. "I could have sworn I did."

Grant considered simply yanking her from the rock and into his arms. He ignored the stab of desire that came so quickly then left a nagging ache. She was taunting him, damn her, and she would win if he wasn't careful. "It's your ego again," he told her. "You're not the type that appeals to me."

Anger flashed into her eyes again, making her nearly irresistible. "Does any?"

"I prefer a softer type," he said, knowing her skin would be soft enough to melt if he gave in and put his hands on her. "Quieter," he lied. "Someone a bit less aggressive."

Gennie struggled not to lose her temper completely

and slug him. "Ah, you prefer women who sit silently and don't think."

"Who don't flaunt their—attributes." This time his smile was taunting. "I don't have any trouble resisting you."

The bait was cast again, and this time Gennie swallowed it whole. "Really? Let's see about that."

She brought her mouth down to his before she had a chance to consider the consequences. Her hands were still on his shoulders, his still in his pockets, but the contact of lips brought on a full-scale explosion. Grant felt it rocket through him, fierce and fast, while his fingers balled into fists.

What in God's name was this? he demanded while he used every ounce of control not to bring her body against his. Instinctively he knew that would be the end for him. He had only to weather this one assault on his system, and it would be over.

Why didn't he back away? He wasn't chained. Grant told himself to, ordered himself to, then stood helpless while her mouth moved over his. Dozens, dozens of images and fantasies rained in his head until he nearly drowned in them. Witch, he thought as his mind hazed. He'd been right about her all along. He felt the ground tilt under his feet, the roar of the sea fill his brain. Her taste, warm, mysterious, spiced with woman, seeped into everything. And even that wasn't enough. For a moment he believed that there could be more than everything, a step just beyond what men knew. Perhaps women understood it. He felt his body tense as though he'd been shot. Perhaps this woman did.

In some part of his brain, he knew that for one brief moment he was completely vulnerable.

Gennie drew away quickly. Grant thought he felt the hands still on his shoulders tremble lightly. Her eyes were dazed, her lips parted not in temptation but in astonishment. Through his own shock, he realized she'd been just as moved as he, and just as weakened by it.

"I-I have to go," she began, then bit her lip as she realized she was stuttering again—a habit she seemed to have developed in the past twenty-four hours. Forgetting her sketch pad, she stepped off the rock and prepared to make an undignified dash for her car. In the next instant she was whirled around.

His face was set, his breathing unsteady. "I was wrong." His voice filled her head, emptying it of everything else. "I have a great deal of trouble resisting you."

What had she done, Gennie wondered frantically, to both of them? She was trembling—she never trembled. Frightened? Oh, God, yes. She could face the storm and the dark now with complete confidence. It was nothing compared to this. "I think we'd better—"

"So do I," he muttered as he hauled her against him. "But it's too late now."

In the next instant his mouth covered hers, hard, undeniable. But she would deny it, Gennie told herself. She had to or be swallowed up. How had she ever thought she understood emotions, sensations? Translating them with paints was nothing compared with an onslaught of experience. He poured through her until she wasn't certain she'd ever be free of him.

She lifted her hands to push him away. She drew him yet closer. His fingers gripped her hair, not gently. The savageness of the cliff, the sea, the wind, tore into both of them and ruled. He tugged her head back, perhaps to pretend he was still in command. Her lips parted, and her tongue raced to meet his.

Is this what she'd always ached to feel? Gennie wondered. This wild liberation, this burning, searing need? She'd never known what it was like to be so filled with another's taste that you could remember no others. She'd known he had this kind of strength in him, had sensed it from the first. But to feel it now, to know she was caught up in it was such a conflicting emotion—power and weakness—that she couldn't tell one from the other.

His skin was rough, scraping against hers as he slanted his mouth to a new angle. Feeling the small, intimate pain, she moaned from the sheer pleasure of it. His hands were still in her hair, roaming, gripping, tangling, while their mouths met in mutual assault.

Let yourself go. It was an order that came from somewhere deep inside of her. Let yourself feel. Helpless, she obeyed.

She heard the gulls, but the sound seemed romantic now, no longer mournful. The sea beat against the land. Power, power, power. She knew the full extent of it as her lips clung to Grant's. The edge of the cliff was close, she knew. One step, two, and she would be over, cartwheeling into space to be brought up short by the hard earth of reality. But those few seconds of giddy freedom would be worth the risk. Her sigh spoke of yielding and of triumph.

Grant swore, the sound muffled against her lips be-

fore he could force himself to break away from her.
This was exactly what he had sworn wouldn't happen.
He'd done enough fishing to know when he was being
reeled in. He didn't have time for this—that's what
he told himself as he looked down at Gennie. Her
face was soft, flushed with passion, her hair trailing
down to be tugged at by the wind as she kept her
head tilted back. His lips ached to press against that
slender, golden throat. It was her eyes, half closed and
gleaming with the ageless power of woman, that
helped him resist. It was a trap he wouldn't be caught
in no matter which of them baited it.

His voice was low when he spoke, and as furious
as his eyes. "I might want you. I might even take
you. But it'll be when I'm damn good and ready. You
want to call the tune, play the games, stick with your
counts and your barons." Grant whirled away, cursing both of them.

Too stunned to move, Gennie watched him disappear inside the lighthouse. Was that all it had meant
to him? she thought numbly. Just any man, any
woman, any passion? Hadn't he felt that quicksilver
pain that had meant unity, intimacy, destiny? Games?
How could he talk of games after they had... Closing
her eyes, she ran an unsteady hand through her hair.

No, it was her fault. She was making something
out of nothing. There was no unity between two people who didn't even know each other, and intimacy
was just a handy word to justify the needs of the
physical. She was being fanciful again, turning something ordinary into something special because it was
what she wanted.

Let him go. She reached down to pick up her

sketch pad and found the pencil Grant had dislodged from her hair. Let him go, and concentrate on your work, she ordered herself. It was the scene that carried you away, not the content. Careful not to look back, she walked to her car.

Her hands didn't stop trembling until she reached the lane to the cottage. This was better, she thought as she listened to the quiet lap of water and the gentle sounds of swallows coming back to nest for the evening. There was peace here, and the light was easy. This was what she should paint instead of the turbulence of the ocean and the ruggedness of rocks. This was where she should stay, soaking up the drifting solitude of still water and calm air. When you challenged the tempestuousness of nature, odds were you lost. Only a fool continued to press against the odds.

Suddenly weary, Gennie got out of the car and wandered down to the pier. At the end she sat down on the rough wood to let her feet dangle over the side. If she stayed here, she'd be safe.

She sat in silence while the sun lowered in the sky. It took no effort to feel the lingering pressure of Grant's lips on hers. She'd never known a man to kiss like that—forceful, consuming, yet with a trace of vulnerability. Then again, she wasn't as experienced as Grant assumed.

She dated, she socialized, she enjoyed men's company, but as her art had always come first, her more intimate relationships were limited. Classes, work, showings, traveling, parties: almost everything she'd ever done for almost as long as she could remember had been connected with her art, and the need to express it.

Certainly she enjoyed the social benefits, the touches of glitter and glamor that came her way after days and weeks of isolation. She didn't mind the image the press had created, because it seemed rather unique and bohemian. She didn't mind taking a bit of glitz here and there after working herself to near exhaustion in silence and solitude. At times the Genviève the papers tattled about amused or impressed her. Then it would be time for the next painting. She'd never had any trouble tucking the socialite away from the artist.

Wouldn't the press be shocked, Gennie mused, to learn that Genviève Grandeau of the New Orleans Grandeaus, successful artist, established socialite, and woman of the world had never had a lover?

With a half laugh, she leaned back on her elbows. She'd been wedded to her art for so long, a lover had seemed superfluous. Until… Gennie started to block out the thought, then calling herself a coward, finished it out. Until Grant Campbell.

Staring up at the sky, she let herself remember those sensations, those feelings and needs he'd unlocked in her. She would have made love with him without a thought, without a moment's hesitation. He'd rejected her.

No, it was more than that, Gennie remembered as anger began to rise again. Rejection was one thing, painful, humiliating, but that hadn't been all of it. Grant had dumped his arrogance on top of rejection— that was intolerable.

He'd said he'd *take* her when *he* was ready. As if she were a-a chocolate bar on a store counter. Her eyes narrowed, pale green with fury. We'll see about that, Gennie told herself. We'll just see about that!

Standing, she brushed off the seat of her pants with one clean swipe. No one rejected Genviève Grandeau. And no one took her. It was games he wanted, she thought as she stalked toward the cottage, it would be games he'd get.

Chapter Four

She wasn't going to be chased away. Gennie told
herself that with a grim satisfaction as she packed her
painting gear the next morning. *No one* chased her
away—especially a rude, arrogant idiot. Grant Campbell was going to find her perched on his doorstep—
in a manner of speaking—until she was good and
ready to move on.

The painting, Gennie mused as she checked her
brushes. Of course the painting was of first importance, but...while she was about it, she thought with
a tight smile, she would take a bit of time to teach
that man a lesson. Oh, he deserved one. Gennie tossed
the hair out of her eyes as she shut the lid on her
paint box. No one, in all of her experience, deserved
a good dig in the ribs as much as Grant Campbell.
And she was just the woman to give it to him.

So he thought she wanted to play games. Gennie

snapped the locks on the case a bit violently, so that the sound echoed like two shots through the empty cottage. She'd play games all right—her games, her rules.

Gennie had spent twenty-six years watching her grandmother beguile and enchant the male species. An amazing woman, Gennie thought now with an affectionate smile. Beautiful and vibrant in her seventies, she could still twist a man of any age around her finger. Well, she was a Genviève, too. She stuck her hands on her hips. And Grant Campbell was about to take a short walk off a high cliff.

Take me, will he? she thought, seething all over again with the memory. Of all the impossible gall. When *he's* ready? Making a low sound in her throat, she grabbed a paint smock. She'd have Grant Campbell crawling at her feet before she was through with him!

The anger and indignation Gennie had nursed all night made it easy to forget that sharp, sweet surge of response she'd felt when his mouth had been on hers. It made it easy to forget the fact that she'd wanted him—blindly, urgently—as she'd never wanted any man before. Temper was much more satisfying than depression, and Gennie rolled with it. She'd take her revenge coolly; it would taste better that way.

Satisfied that her gear was in order, Gennie walked through the cottage to her bedroom. Critically, she studied herself in the mirror over the old bureau. She was artist enough to recognize good bone structure and coloring. Perhaps suppressed anger suited her, she considered, as it added a faint rose flush to the honey tone of her skin.

As grimly as a warrior preparing for battle, she picked up a pot of muted green eyeshadow. When you had an unusual feature, she thought as she smudged it on her lids, you played it up. The result pleased her—a bit exotic, but not obvious. Lightly, she touched her lips with color—not too much, she reflected, just enough to tempt. With a lazy smile, she dabbed her scent behind her ears. Oh, she intended to tempt him all right. And when he was on his knees, she'd stroll blithely away.

A pity she couldn't wear something a bit sexier, she thought as she pursed her lips and turned sideways in the mirror. But the painting did come first, after all. One couldn't wear something slinky to sit on a rock. The jeans and narrow little top would have to do. Pleased with the day's prospects, Gennie started back for her gear when the sound of an approaching car distracted her.

Her first thought was Grant, her first reaction a flood of nerves. Annoyed, Gennie told herself it was simply the anticipation of the contest that had her heart pounding. When she went to the window, she saw it wasn't Grant's pickup, but a small, battered station wagon. The Widow Lawrence stepped out, neat and prim, carrying a covered plate. Surprised, and a bit uncomfortable, Gennie opened the door to her landlady.

"Good morning." She smiled, trying to ignore the oddness of inviting the woman inside a cottage where she had lived, slept, and worked for years.

"See you're up and about." The widow hovered

at the threshold with her tiny, dark eyes on Gennie's face.

"Yes." Gennie would have taken her hand instinctively if the widow hadn't been gripping the plate with both of them. "Please, come in, Mrs. Lawrence."

"Don't want to bother you. Thought maybe you'd like some muffins."

"I would." Gennie forgot her plans for an early start and opened the door wider. "Especially if you'd have some coffee with me."

"Wouldn't mind." The widow hesitated almost imperceptibly, then stepped inside. "Can't stay long, I'm needed at the post office." But her gaze skimmed over the room as she stood in front of the door.

"They smell wonderful." Gennie took the plate and headed back toward the kitchen, hoping to dispel some of the awkwardness. "You know, I can never drum up much energy for cooking when it's only for me."

"Ayah. There's more pleasure when you've a family to feed."

Gennie felt another well of sympathy, but didn't offer it. She faced the stove as she measured out coffee in the little pot she'd bought in town. The widow would be looking at her kitchen, Gennie thought, and remembering.

"You settled in all right, then."

"Yes." Gennie took two plates and set them on the narrow drop-leaf table. "The cottage is just what I needed. It's beautiful, Mrs. Lawrence." She hesitated as she took down cups and saucers, then turned to face the woman again. "You must have hated to leave here."

Mrs. Lawrence shifted her shoulders in what might have been a shrug. "Things change. Roof hold up all right in the storm the other night?"

Gennie gave her a blank look, but caught herself before she said she hadn't been there to notice. "I didn't have any trouble," she said instead. Gennie saw the gaze wander around the room. Perhaps it would be best if she talked about it. Everyone had told Gennie that about Angela, but she hadn't believed them then. Now she began to wonder if it would help to talk about a loss instead of submerging it.

"Did you live here long, Mrs. Lawrence?" She brought the cups to the table as she asked, then went for the cream.

"Twenty-six years," the woman said after a moment. "Moved in after my second boy was born. A doctor he is, a resident in Bangor." Stiff New England pride showed in the jut of her chin. "His brother's got himself a job on an oil rig—couldn't keep away from the sea."

Gennie came to join her at the table. "You must be very proud of them."

"Ayah."

"Was your husband a fisherman?"

"Lobsterman." She didn't smile, but Gennie heard it in her voice. "A good one. Died on his boat. Stroke they tell me." She added a dab of cream to her coffee, hardly enough to change the color. "He'd've wanted to die on his boat."

She wanted to ask how long ago, but couldn't. Perhaps the time would come when she would be able to speak of the loss of her sister in such simple terms of acceptance. "Do you like living in town?"

"Used to it now. There be friends there, and this road…" For the first time, Gennie saw the wisp of a smile that made the hard, lined face almost pretty. "My Matthew could curse this road six ways to Sunday."

"I believe it." Tempted by the aroma, Gennie removed the checkered dishcloth from the plate. "Blueberry!" She grinned, pleased. "I saw wild blueberry bushes along the road from town."

"Ayah, they'll be around a little while more." She watched, satisfied as Gennie bit into one. "Young girl like you might get lonely away out here."

Gennie shook her head as she swallowed. "No, I like the solitude for painting."

"You do the pictures hanging in the front room?"

"Yes, I hope you don't mind that I hung them."

"Always had a partiality for pictures. You do good work."

Gennie grinned, as pleased with the simple statement as she would have been with a rave review. "Thank you. I plan to do quite a bit of painting around Windy Point—more than I had expected at first," she added, thinking of Grant. "If I decided to stay an extra few weeks—"

"You just let me know."

"Good." Gennie watched as the widow broke off a small piece of muffin. "You must know the lighthouse…" Still nibbling, Gennie toyed with exactly what information she wanted and how to get it.

"Charlie Dees used to keep that station," Mrs.

Lawrence told her. "Him and his missus had it since I was a girl. Use radar now, but my father and his father had that light to keep them off the rocks."

There were stories here, Gennie thought. Ones she'd like to hear, but for now it was the present keeper who interested her.

"I met the man who lives there now," she said casually over the rim of her coffee cup. "I'm going to do some painting out there. It's a wonderful spot."

The widow's stiff straight brows rose. "You tell him?"

So they knew him in town, Gennie thought with a mental sniff. "We came to an…agreement of sorts."

"Young Campbell's been there near on to five years." The widow speculated on the gleam in Gennie's eyes, but didn't comment on it. "Keeps to himself. Sent a few out-of-towners on their way quick enough."

"No doubt," Gennie murmured. "He's not a friendly sort."

"Stays out of trouble." The widow gave Gennie a quick, shrewd look. "Nice-looking boy. Hear he's been out with the men on the boats a time or two, but does more watching than talking."

Confused, Gennie swallowed the last of the muffin. "Doesn't he fish for a living?"

"Don't know what he does, but he pays his bills right enough."

Gennie frowned, more intrigued than she wanted to be. "That's odd, I got the impression…" Of what? she asked herself. "I don't suppose he gets a lot of mail," she hazarded.

The widow gave her wispy smile again. "Gets his

due,'' she said simply. ''I thank you for the coffee, Miss Grandeau,'' she added, rising. ''And I'm happy to have you stay here as you please.''

''Thank you.'' Knowing she had to be satisfied with the bare snips of information, Gennie rose with her. ''I hope you'll come back again, Mrs. Lawrence.''

Nodding, the widow made her way back to the front door. ''You let me know if you have any problems. When the weather turns, you'll be needing the furnace. It's sound enough mind, but noisier than some.''

''I'll remember. Thanks.''

Gennie watched her walk to her car and thought about Grant. He wasn't one of them, she mused, but she had sensed a certain reserved affection for him in Mrs. Lawrence's tone. He kept to himself, and that was something the people of Windy Point would respect. Five years, she thought as she wandered back for her paints. A long time to seclude yourself in a lighthouse...doing what?

With a shrug, she gathered her gear. What he did wasn't her concern. Making him crawl a bit was.

The only meal Grant ate with regularity was breakfast. After that, he grabbed what he wanted when he wanted—or when his work permitted. He'd eaten at dawn only because he couldn't sleep, then had gone out on his boat only because he couldn't work. Gennie, tucked into bed two miles away, had managed to interfere with his two most basic activities.

Normally, he would have enjoyed the early run at sea, catching the rosy light with the fishermen and facing the chill dawn air. He would try his luck, and if it was good, have his catch for dinner. If it was bad, he'd broil a steak or open a can.

He hadn't enjoyed his outing this morning, because he had wanted to sleep—then he'd wanted to work. His mood hadn't been tuned to fishing, and the diversion hadn't been a success. The sun had still been low in the sky when he'd returned.

It was high now, but Grant's mood was little better than it had been. Only the discipline he'd imposed on himself over the years kept him at his drawing board, perfecting and refining the strip he'd started the day before.

She'd thrown him off schedule, he thought grimly. And she was running around inside his head. Grant often let people do just that, but they were *his* people, and he controlled them. Gennie refused to stay in character.

Genviève, he thought, as he meticulously inked in Veronica's long, lush hair. He'd admired her work, its lack of gimmickry, its basic class. She painted with style, and the hint, always the hint of a raging passion underneath a misty overlay of fancy. Her paintings asked you to pretend, to imagine, to believe in something lovely. Grant had never found any fault with that.

He remembered seeing one of her landscapes, one of the bayou scenes that often figured prominently in her showings. The shadows had promised secrets, the dusky blue light a night full of possibilities. There'd been a fog over the water that had made him think of muffled whispers. The tiny house hanging over the river hadn't seemed ramshackle, but lovely in a faded, yesterday way. The serenity of the painting had appealed to him, the clever lighting she'd used had amused him. He could remember being disappointed that the work had already been sold. He wouldn't have even asked the price.

The passion that often lurked around the edges of her works was a subtle contrast to the serenity of her subjects. The fancy had always been uppermost.

She got enough passion in her personal life, he remembered as his mouth tightened. If he hadn't met her, hadn't touched her, he would have kept to the opinion that ninety percent of the things printed about her were just what she had said. Tripe.

But now all he could think was that any man who could get close to Geneviève Grandeau would want her. And that the passion that simmered in her paintings, simmered in her equally. She knew she could make a slave out of a man, he thought, and forced himself to complete his drawing of Veronica. She knew it and enjoyed it.

Grant set down his brush a moment and flexed his fingers. Still, he had the satisfaction of knowing he'd turned her aside.

Turned her aside, hell, he thought with a mirthless laugh. If he'd done that he wouldn't be sitting here remembering how she'd been like a fire in his arms—hot, restless, dangerous. He wouldn't be remembering how his mind had gone blank one instant and then had been filled—with only her.

A siren? By God, yes, he thought savagely. It was easy to imagine her smiling and singing and luring a man toward some rocky coast. But not him. He wasn't a man to be bewitched by a seductive voice and a pair of alluring eyes. After his parting shot, he doubted she'd be back in any case. Though he glanced toward the window, Grant refused to go to it. He picked up his brush and worked for another hour, with Gennie teasing the back of his mind.

Satisfied that he had finished the strip on schedule after all, Grant cleaned his brushes. Because the next one was already formed in his mind, his mood was better. With a meticulousness that carried over into no other area of his life, he set his studio to rights. Tools were replaced in a precise manner in and on the glass-topped cabinet beside him. Bottles and jars were wiped clean, tightly capped, and stored. His copy would remain on the drawing board until well dried.

Taking his time, Grant went down to rummage in the kitchen for some food while he kept the portable radio on, filling him in on whatever was going on in the outside world.

A mention of the Ethics Committee, and a senator Grant could never resist satirizing, gave him an angle for another strip. It was true that his use of recognizable names and faces, often in politics, caused some papers to place his work on the editorial page. Grant didn't care where they put it, as long as his point got across. Caricaturing politicians had become a habit when he'd been a child—one he'd never had the least inclination to break.

Leaning against the counter, idly depleting a bag of peanut butter cookies, Grant listened to the rest of the report. An awareness of trends, of moods, of events was as essential to his art as pen and ink. He'd remember what he'd need when the time came to use it. For now it was filed and stored in the back of his mind and he wanted air and sunshine.

He'd go out, Grant told himself, not because he expected to see Gennie—but because he expected not to.

Of course, she was there, but he wanted to believe the surge he felt was annoyance. It was always annoyance—never pleasure—that he felt when he found someone infringing on his solitude.

It wouldn't be much trouble to ignore her.... The wind had her hair caught in its dragging fingers, lifting it from her neck. He could simply go the other way and walk north on the beach.... The sun slanted over the skin of her bare arms and face and had it gleaming. If he turned his back and moved down the other side of the cliff, he'd forget she was even there.

Swearing under his breath, Grant went toward her.

Gennie had seen him, of course, the moment he stepped out. Her brush had only hesitated for a moment before she'd continued to paint. If her pulse had scrambled a bit, she told herself it was only the anticipation of the battle she was looking forward to engaging in—and winning. Because she knew she couldn't afford to keep going now that her concentration was broken, she tapped the handle of her brush to her lips and viewed what she'd done that morning.

The sketch on the canvas gave her precisely what she wanted. The colors she'd already mixed satisfied her. She began to hum, lightly, as she heard Grant draw closer.

"So..." Gennie tilted her head, as if to study the canvas from a different angle. "You decided to come out of your cave."

Grant stuck his hands in his pockets and deliberately stood where he couldn't see her work. "You didn't strike me as the kind of woman who asked for trouble."

Barely moving the angle of her head, Gennie slid her eyes up to his. Her smile was very faint, and very taunting. "I suppose that makes you a poor judge of character, doesn't it?"

The look was calculated to arouse, but knowing it didn't make any difference. He felt the first kindling of desire spread low in his stomach. "Or you a fool," he murmured.

"I told you I'd be back, Grant." She allowed her gaze to drift briefly to his mouth. "Generally I try to—follow through. Would you like to see what I've done?"

He told himself he didn't give a hang about the painting or about her. "No."

Gennie moved her mouth into a pout. "Oh, and I thought you were such an art connoisseur." She set down her brush and ran a hand leisurely through her hair. "What are you, Grant Campbell?" Her eyes were mocking and alluring.

"What I choose to be."

"Fortunate for you." She rose. Taking her time, she drew off the short-sleeved smock and dropped it on the rock beside her. She watched his face as his eyes traveled over her, then ran a lazy finger down his shirtfront. "Shall I tell you what I see?" He didn't answer, but his eyes stayed on hers. Gennie wondered if she pressed her hand to his heart if the beat would be fast and unsteady. "A loner," she continued, "with the face of a buccaneer and the hands of a poet.

And the manners," she added with a soft laugh, "of a lout. It seems to me that the manners are all you've had the choice about."

It was difficult to resist the gleam of challenge in her eyes or the promise in those soft, full lips that smiled with calculated feminine insolence. "If you like," Grant said mildly while he kept the hands that itched to touch her firmly in his pockets.

"I can't say I do." Gennie walked a few steps away, close enough to the cliff edge so that the spray nearly reached her. "Then again, your manners add a rather rough-and-ready appeal." She glanced over her shoulder. "I don't suppose a woman always wants a gentleman. You wouldn't be a man who looks for a lady."

With the sea behind her, reflecting the color of her eyes, she looked more a part of it than ever. "Is that what you are, Geneviève?"

She laughed, pleased with the frustration and fury she read in his eyes. "It depends," she said, deliberately mimicking him, "on whether it's useful or not."

Grant came to her then but resisted the desire to shake her until her teeth rattled. Their bodies were close, so that little more than the wind could pass between them. "What the hell are you trying to do?"

She gave him an innocent stare. "Why, have a conversation. I suppose you're out of practice."

He glared, narrowed-eyed, then turned away. "I'm going for a walk," he muttered.

"Lovely." Gennie slipped her arm through his. "I'll go with you."

"I didn't ask you," Grant said flatly, stopping again.

"Oh." Gennie batted her eyes. "You're trying to charm me by being rude again. It's so difficult to resist."

A grin tugged at his mouth before he controlled it. There was no one he laughed at more easily than himself. "All right, then." There was a gleam in his eyes she didn't quite trust. "Come on."

Grant walked swiftly, without deference to the difference in their strides. Determined to make him suffer before the afternoon was over, Gennie trotted to keep up. After they'd circled the lighthouse, Grant started down the cliff with the confidence of long experience. Gennie took a long look at the steep drop, at the rock ledges Grant walked down with no more care than if they'd been steps. Below, the surf churned and battered at the shoreline. She wasn't about to be intimidated, Gennie reminded herself. He'd just love that. Taking a deep breath, she started after him.

For the first few feet her heart was in her throat. She'd really make him suffer if she fell and broke her neck. Then she began to enjoy it. The sea grew louder with the descent. Salt spray tingled along her skin. Doubtless there was a simpler way down, but at the moment she wouldn't have looked for it.

Grant reached the bottom in time to turn and see Gennie scrambling down the last few feet. He'd wanted to believe she'd still be up on the cliff, yet somehow he'd known better. She was no hot-house magnolia no matter how much he'd like to have tossed her in that category. She was much too vital to be admired from a distance.

Instinctively, he reached for her hand to help her down. Gennie brushed against him on the landing, then stood, head tilted back, daring him to do something about it. Her scent rushed to his senses. Before, she'd only smelled of the rain. This was just as subtle, but infinitely more sensuous. She smelled of night in the full light of the afternoon, and of all those whispering, murmuring promises that bloomed after sundown.

Infuriated that he could be lured by such an obvious tactic, Grant released her. Without a word he started down the narrow, rocky beach where the sea boomed and echoed and the gulls screamed. Smug and confident with her early success, Gennie moved with him.

Oh, I'm getting to you, Grant Campbell. And I haven't even started.

"Is this what you do with your time when you're not locked in your secret tower?"

"Is this what you do with your time when you're not hitting the hot spots on Bourbon Street?"

Tossing back her hair, Gennie deliberately slipped her arm through his again. "Oh, we talked enough about me yesterday. Tell me about Grant Campbell. Are you a mad scientist conducting terrifying experiments under secret government contract?"

He turned his head, then gave her an odd smile. "At the moment I'm stamp collecting."

That puzzled her enough that she forgot the game and frowned. "Why do I feel there's some grain of truth in that?"

With a shrug, Grant continued to walk, wondering why he didn't shake her off and go on his way alone.

When he came here, he always came alone. Walks along this desolate, rocky beach were the only time other than sleep that he allowed his mind to empty. There where the waves crashed like thunder and the ground was hard and unforgiving was his haven against his own thoughts and self-imposed pressure. He'd never allowed anyone to join him there, not even his own creations. He wanted to feel the sense of intrusion he'd expected with Gennie at his side; instead he felt something very close to contentment.

"A secret place," Gennie murmured.

Distracted, Grant glanced down at her. "What?"

"This." Gennie gestured with her free hand. "This is a secret place." Bending she picked up a shell, pitted by the ocean, dried like a bone in the sun. "My grandmother has a beautiful old plantation house filled with antiques and silk pillows. There's a room off the attic upstairs. It's gloomy and dusty. There's a broken rocker in there and a box full of perfectly useless things. I could sit up there for hours." Bringing her gaze back to his, she smiled. "I've never been able to resist a secret place."

Grant remembered, suddenly and vividly, a tiny storeroom in his parents' home in Georgetown. He'd closeted himself in there for hours at a stretch with stacks of comic books and a sketch pad. "It's only a secret if nobody knows about it."

She laughed, slipping her hand into his without any thought. "Oh, no, it can still be a secret with two—sometimes a better secret." She stopped to watch a gull swoop low over the water. "What are those islands out there?"

Disturbed, because her hand felt as though it belonged in his, Grant scowled out to sea. "Hunks of rock mostly."

"Oh." Gennie sent him a desolate look. "No bleached bones or pieces of eight?"

The grin snuck up on him. "There be talk of a skull that moans when a storm's brewing," he told her, slipping into a thick Down East cadence.

"Whose?" Gennie demanded, ready for whatever story he could conjure.

"A seaman's," Grant improvised. "He lusted after his captain's woman. She had the eyes of a sea-witch and hair like midnight." Despite himself Grant took a handful of Gennie's while the rest tossed in the wind. "She tempted him, made him soft, wicked promises if he'd steal the gold and the longboat. When he did, because she was a woman who could drive a man to murder with a look, she went with him." Grant felt her hair tangle around his fingers as though it had a life of its own.

"So he rowed for two days and two nights, knowing when they came to land he'd have her. But when they spotted the coast, she drew out a saber and lopped off his head. Now his skull sits on the rocks and moans in frustrated desire."

Amused, Gennie tilted her head. "And the woman?"

"Invested her gold, doubled her profits, and became a pillar of the community."

Laughing, Gennie began to walk with him again. "The moral seems to be never trust a woman who makes you promises."

"Certainly not a beautiful one."

"Have you had your head lopped off, Grant?"

He gave a short, appreciative laugh. "No."

"A pity." She sighed. "I suppose that means you make a habit of resisting temptation."

"It's not necessary to resist it," he countered. "As long as you keep one eye open."

"There's no romance in that," Gennie complained.

"I've other uses for my head, thanks."

She shot him a thoughtful look. "Stamp collecting?"

"For one."

They walked in silence again while the sea crashed close beside them. On the other side the rocks rose like a wall. Far out on the water there were dots of boats. That one sign of humanity only added to the sense of space and aloneness.

"Where did you come from?" she asked impulsively.

"The same place you did."

It took her a minute, then she chuckled. "I don't mean biologically. Geographically."

He shrugged, trying not to be pleased she had caught on so quickly. "South of here."

"Oh, well that's specific," she muttered, then tried again. "What about family? Do you have family?"

He stopped to study her. "Why?"

With an exaggerated sigh, Gennie shook her head. "This is called making friendly conversation. It's a new trend that's catching on everywhere."

"I'm a noncomformist."

"No! Really?"

"You do that wide-eyed, guileless look very well, Genviève."

"Thank you." She turned the shell over in her hand, then looked up at him with a slow smile. "I'll tell you something about my family, just to give you a running start." She thought for a moment, then hit on something she thought he'd relate to. "I have a cousin, a few times removed. I've always thought he was the most fascinating member of the family tree, though you couldn't call him a Grandeau."

"What would you call him?"

"The black sheep," she said with relish. "He did things his own way, never giving a damn about what anyone thought. I heard stories about him from time to time—though I wasn't meant to—and it wasn't until I was a grown woman that I met him. I'm happy to say we took to each other within minutes and have kept in touch over the last couple of years. He'd lived his life by his wits, and done quite well—which didn't sit well with some of the more staid members of the family. Then he confounded everyone by getting married."

"To an exotic dancer."

"No." She laughed, pleased that he was interested enough to joke. "To someone absolutely suitable—intelligent, well bred, wealthy—" She rolled her eyes. "The black sheep, who'd spent some time in jail, gambled his way into a fortune, had outdone them all." With a laugh, Gennie thought of the Comanche Blade. Cousin Justin had indeed outdone them all. And he didn't even bother to thumb his nose.

"I love a happy ending," Grant said dryly.

With her eyes narrowed, Gennie turned to him. "Don't you know that the less you tell someone, the more they want to know? You're better off to make something up than to say nothing at all.''

"I'm the youngest of twelve children of two South African missionaries,'' he said with such ease, she very nearly believed him. ''When I was six, I wandered into the jungle and was taken in by a pride of lions. I still have a penchant for zebra meat. Then when I was eighteen, I was captured by hunters and sold to a circus. For five years I was the star of the sideshow.''

"The Lion Boy,'' Gennie put it.

"Naturally. One night during a storm the tent caught fire. In the confusion I escaped. Living off the land, I wandered the country—stealing a few chickens now and again. Eventually an old hermit took me in after I'd saved him from a grizzly.''

"With your bare hands,'' Gennie added.

"I'm telling the story,'' he reminded her. ''He taught me to read and write. On his deathbed he told me where he'd buried his life savings—a quarter million in gold bullion. After giving him the Viking funeral he'd requested, I had to decide whether to be a stockbroker or go back to the wilderness.''

"So you decided against Wall Street, came here, and began to collect stamps.''

"That's about it.''

"Well,'' Gennie said after a moment. ''With a boring story like that, I can see why you keep it to yourself.''

"You asked,'' Grant pointed out.

"You might have made something up.''

"No imagination.''

She laughed then and leaned her head on his shoulder. "No, I can see you have a very literal mind."

Her laugh rippled along his skin, and the casual intimacy of her head against his shoulder shot straight down to the soles of his feet. He should shake her off, Grant told himself. He had no business walking here with her and enjoying it. "I've got things to do," he said abruptly. "We can go up this way."

It was the change in his tone that reminded Gennie she'd come there for a purpose, and the purpose was not to wind up liking him.

The way up was easier than the way down, she noted as he turned toward what was now a slope rather than a cliff. Though his fingers loosened on hers, she held on, shooting him a smile that had him muttering under his breath as he helped her climb. Thinking quickly, she stuck the shell in her back pocket. When they neared the top, Gennie held her other hand out to him. With her eyes narrowed a bit against the sun, her hair flowing down her back, she looked up at him. Swearing, Grant grabbed her other hand and hauled her up the last few feet.

On level ground she stayed close, her body just brushing his as their hands remained linked. His breath had stayed even during the climb, but now it came unsteadily. Feeling a surge of satisfaction, Gennie gave him a slow, lazy smile.

"Going back to your stamps?" she murmured. Deliberately, she leaned closer to brush her lips over his chin. "Enjoy yourself." Drawing her hands from his, Gennie turned. She'd taken three steps before he grabbed her arm. Though her heart began to thud, she

looked over her shoulder at him. ''Want something?''
she asked in a low, amused voice.

She could see it on his face—the struggle for control. And in his eyes she could see a flare of desire
that had her throat going dry. No, she wasn't going
to back down now, she insisted. She'd finish out the
game. When he yanked her against him, she told herself it wasn't fear she felt, it wasn't passion. It was
self-gratification.

''It seems you do,'' she said with a laugh, and slid
her hands up his back.

When his mouth crushed down on hers, her mind
spun. All thoughts of purpose, all thoughts of revenge
vanished. It was as it had been the first time—the
passion, and over the passion a rightness, and with
the rightness a storm of confused needs and longings
and wishes. Opening to him was so natural she did
so without thought, and with a simplicity that made
him groan as he drew her closer.

His tongue skimmed over her lips then tangled with
hers as his hands roamed to mold her hips. Strong
hands—she'd known they'd be strong. Her skin tingled with the image of being touched without barriers
even as her mouth sought to take all he could give
her through a kiss alone. She strained against him,
offering, demanding, and it seemed he couldn't give
or take fast enough to satisfy either of them. His
mouth ravaged, but hers wouldn't surrender. What
she drew out of him excited them both.

It wasn't until she began to feel the weakness that
Gennie remembered to fear. This wasn't what she'd
come for... Was it? No, she wouldn't believe she'd
come to feel this terrifying pleasure, this aching,

gnawing need to give what she'd never given before. Panic rose and she struggled against it in a way she knew she'd never be able to struggle against desire. She had to stop him, and herself. If he held her much longer, she would melt, and melting, lose.

Drawing on what was left of her strength she pulled back, determined not to show either the passion or the fear that raced through her. "Very nice," she murmured, praying he wouldn't notice how breathless her voice was. "Though your technique's a bit—rough for my taste."

His breath came quick and fast. Grant didn't speak, knowing if he did madness would pour out. For the second time she'd emptied him out then filled him again with herself. Need for her, raw, exclusive, penetrating, ripped through him as he stared into her eyes and waited for it to abate. It didn't.

He was stronger than she was, he told himself as he gathered her shirtfront in his hand. Her heart thudded against his knuckles. There was nothing to stop him from... He dropped his hand as though she'd scalded him. No one pushed him to that, he thought furiously while she continued to stare up at him. No one.

"You're walking on dangerous ground, Genviève," he said softly.

She tossed back her head. "I'm very sure-footed." With a parting smile, she turned, counting each step as she went back to her canvas. Perhaps her hands weren't steady as she packed up her gear. Perhaps her blood roared in her ears. But she'd won the first round. She let out a deep breath as she heard the door to the lighthouse slam shut.

The first round, she repeated, wishing she wasn't looking forward quite so much to the next one.

Chapter Five

Grant managed to avoid Gennie for three days. She came back to paint every morning, and though she worked for hours, she never saw a sign of him. The lighthouse was silent, its windows winking blankly in the sun.

Once his boat was gone when she arrived and hadn't returned when she lost the light she wanted. She was tempted to go down the cliff and walk along the beach where he had taken her. She found she could have more easily strolled into his house uninvited than gone to that one particular spot without his knowledge. Even had she wanted to paint there, the sense of trespassing would have forbidden it

She painted in peace, assured that since she had gotten her own back with Grant she wouldn't think of him. But the painting itself kept him lodged in her mind. She would never be able to see that spot, on canvas or in reality, and not see him. It was his, as surely as if he'd been hewed from the rocks or tossed up by the sea. She could feel the force of his personality as she guided her brush, and the challenge of it as she struggled to put what should have only been nature's mood onto canvas.

But it wouldn't only be nature's, she discovered as she painted sea and surf. Though his form wouldn't be on the canvas, his substance would. Gennie had always felt a particle of her own soul went into each one of her canvases. In this one she would capture a part of Grant's as well. Neither of them had a choice.

Somehow knowing it drove her to create something with force and muscle. The painting excited her. She knew she'd been meant to paint that view, and to paint it well. And she knew when it was done, she would give it to Grant. Because it could never belong to anyone else.

It wouldn't be a token of affection, she told herself, or an offer of friendship. It was simply something that had to be done. She'd never be able, in good conscience, to sell that canvas. And if she kept it herself, he'd haunt her. So before she left Windy Point, she would make him a gift of it. Perhaps, in her way, she would then haunt him.

Her mornings were filled with an urgency to finish it, an urgency she had to block again and again unless she miss something vital in the process. Gennie knew it was imperative to move slowly, to absorb everything around her and give it to the painting. In the afternoons she forced herself to pack up so that she wouldn't work longer than she should and ignore the changing light.

She sketched her inlet and planned a watercolor. She fretted for morning so that she could go back to the sea.

Her restlessness drove her to town. It was time to make some sketches there, to decide what she would paint and in what medium. She told herself she needed to see people again to keep her mind from focusing so continually on Grant.

In the midafternoon, Windy Point was sleepy and quiet. Boats were out to sea, and a hazy summer heat shimmered in the air. She saw a woman sitting on her porch stringing the last of the season's beans while a toddler plucked at the clover in the yard.

Gennie parked her car at the end of the road and began to walk. She could sketch the buildings, the gardens. She could gather impressions that would bring them to life again when she began to paint. This was a different world from the force at Windy Point Station, different yet from the quiet inlet behind her cottage, but they were all connected. The sea touched all of them in different ways.

She wandered, glad she had come though the voices she heard were voices of strangers. It was a town she'd remember more clearly than any of the others she'd visited on her tour of New England. But it was the sea that continued to tug at her underneath it all—and the man who lived there.

When would she see him again? Gennie wondered, forced to admit that she missed him. She missed the scowl and the curt words, the quick grin and surprising humor, the light of amused cynicism she caught in his eyes from time to time. And though it was the hardest to admit, she missed that furious passion he'd brought to her so suddenly.

Leaning against the side of a building, she wondered if there would be another man somewhere who would touch her that way. She couldn't imagine one. She'd never looked for a knight in armor—they were simply too much trouble, expecting a helpless damsel in return. Helpless she would never be, and chivalry, for the most part, got in the way of an intelligent relationship. Grant Campbell, Gennie mused, would never be chivalrous, and a helpless female would infuriate him.

Remembering their first meeting, she chuckled. No, he didn't care to be put out by a lady in distress anymore than she cared to be one. She supposed, on both parts, it went back to a fierce need for independence.

No, he wasn't looking for a lady, and while she hadn't been looking for a knight, she hadn't been searching out ogres, either. Gennie thought Grant came very close to fitting into that category. While she enjoyed men's company, she didn't want one tangling up her life—at least not until she was ready. And she certainly didn't want to be involved with an ogre—they were entirely too unpredictable. Who knew when they'd just swallow you whole?

Shaking her head, she glanced down, surprised to see that she'd not only been thinking of Grant, but had been sketching him. Lips pursed, Gennie lifted the pad for a critical study. A good likeness, she decided. His eyes were narrowed a bit, dark and intense on the point of anger. His brows were lowered, forming that faint vertical line of temper between them. She'd captured that lean face with its planes and shadows, the aristocratic nose and unruly hair. And his mouth…

The little jolt of response wasn't surprising, but it was unwelcomed. She'd drawn his mouth as she'd seen it before it came down on hers—the sensuousness, the ruthlessness. Yes, she could taste that stormy flavor even now, standing in the quiet town with the scent of fish and aging flowers around her.

Carefully closing the book, Gennie reminded herself she'd be much better off sticking to the buildings she'd come to draw. With the pencil stuck behind her ear, Gennie crossed the road to go into the post office. The skinny teenager she remembered from her first trip through the town turned to goggle at her when she entered. As she walked up to the counter, she smiled at him, then watched his Adam's apple bob up and down.

"Will." Mrs. Lawrence plunked letters down on the counter. "You'd best be getting Mr. Fairfield his mail before you lose your job."

"Yes, ma'am." He scooped at the letters while he continued to stare at Gennie. When he dropped the lot of them on the floor, Gennie bent to help him and sent him into a blushing attack of stutters.

"Will Turner," Mrs. Lawrence repeated with the pitch of an impatient schoolteacher. "Gather up those letters and be on your way."

"You missed one, Will," Gennie said kindly, then handed the envelope to him as his jaw went slack. Face pink, eyes glued to hers, Will stumbled to the door and out.

Mrs. Lawrence gave a dry chuckle. "Be lucky he doesn't fall off the curb."

"I suppose I should be flattered," Gennie considered. "I don't remember having that effect on anyone before."

"Awkward age for a boy when he starts noticing females is shaped a bit different."

With a laugh, Gennie leaned on the counter. "I wanted to thank you again for coming by the other day. I've been painting out at the lighthouse and haven't been into town."

Mrs. Lawrence glanced down at the sketchbook Gennie had set on the counter. "Doing some drawing here?"

"Yes." On impulse, Gennie opened the book and flipped through. "It was the town that interested me right away—the sense of permanence and purpose."

Cool-eyed, the widow paged through the book while Gennie nibbled on her lip and waited for the verdict. "Ayah," she said at length. "You know what you're about." With one finger, she pushed back a sheet, then studied Gennie's sketch of Grant. "Looks a bit fierce," she decided as the wispy smile touched her mouth.

"*Is* a bit for my thinking," Gennie countered.

"Ayah, well there be a woman who like a touch of vinegar in a man." She gave another dry chuckle and for once her eyes were more friendly than shrewd. "I be one of them." With a glance over Gennie's shoulder, the widow closed the book. "Afternoon, Mr. Campbell."

For a moment Gennie goggled at the widow much as Will had goggled at her. Recovering, she laid a hand on the now closed book.

"Afternoon, Mrs. Lawrence." When he came to

stand at the counter beside her, Gennie caught the scent of the sea on him. "Genviève," he said, giving her a long, enigmatic look.

He'd wondered how long he could stand it before he saw her up close again. There'd been too many times in the past three days that he hadn't been able to resist the urge to go to his studio window and watch her paint. All that had stopped him from going down to her was the knowledge that if he touched her again, he'd be heading down a road he'd never turn back from. As yet he was uncertain what was at the end of it.

A picture of the blushing, stuttering teenager ran through her mind and straightened Gennie's spine. "Hello, Grant." When she smiled, she was careful to bank down the warmth and make up for it with mockery. "I thought you were hibernating."

"Been busy," he said easily. "Didn't know you were still around." That gave him the satisfaction of seeing annoyance dart into her eyes before she controlled it.

"I'll be around for some time yet."

Mrs. Lawrence slid a thick bundle of mail on the counter, then followed it with a stack of newspapers. Gennie caught the Chicago return address of the top letter and the banner of the *Washington Post* before Grant scooped everything up. "Thanks."

With a frown between her brows, Gennie watched him walk out. There must have been a dozen letters *and* a dozen newspapers. Letters from Chicago, a Washington paper for a man who lived on a deserted cliff outside a town that didn't even boast a stoplight. What in the hell...

"Fine-looking young man," Mrs. Lawrence commented behind Gennie's back.

With a mumbled answer, Gennie started for the door. "Bye, Mrs. Lawrence."

Mrs. Lawrence tapped a finger on the counter thinking there hadn't been such tugging and pulling in the air since the last storm. Maybe another one was brewing.

Puzzled, Gennie began to walk again. It wasn't any of her business why some odd recluse received so much mail. For all she knew, he might only come into town to pick it up once a month…but that had been yesterday's paper. With a brisk shake of her head, she struggled against curiosity. The real point was that she'd been able to get a couple shots in— even if he'd had a bull's-eye for her.

She loitered at the corner, doing another quick sketch while she reminded herself that instead of thinking of him, she should be thinking what provisions she needed before she headed back to the cottage.

But she was restless again. The sense of order and peace she'd found after an hour in town had vanished the moment he'd walked into the post office. She wanted to find that feeling again before she went back to spend the night alone.

Aimlessly, she wandered down the road, pausing now and then at a store window. She was nearly to the edge of town when she remembered the churchyard. She'd sketch there until she was tired enough to go home.

A truck rattled by, perhaps the third vehicle Gennie had seen in an hour. After waiting for it, she crossed the road. She passed the small, uneven plot of the cemetery, listening to the quiet. The grass was high enough to bend in the breeze. Overhead a flock of gulls flew by, calling out on their way to the sea.

The paint on the high fence was rusted and peeling. Queen Anne's lace grew stubbornly between the posts. The church itself was small and white with a single stained-glass panel at the V of the roof. Other windows were clear glass and paned, and the door itself was sturdy and scarred with time. Gennie walked to the side and sat where the grass had been recently tended. She could smell it.

Fleetingly she wondered how it was possible one tiny scrap on the map could have so much that demanded to be painted. She could easily spend six months there rather than six weeks and never capture all she wanted to.

The restlessness evaporated as she began to sketch. Perhaps she wouldn't be able to transfer everything into oils or watercolor before she left, but she'd have the sketches. In months to come, she could use them to go back to Windy Point when she felt the need for it.

She'd turned over the page to start a second sketch when a shadow fell over her. A quick fluctuation of her pulse, a swift warmth on her skin. She knew who stood behind her. Shading her eyes, she looked up at Grant. "Well," she said lightly, "twice in one day."

"Small town." He gestured toward her pad. "You finished out at the station?"

"No, the light's wrong this time of day for what I want there."

It was annoyance he was supposed to feel, not relief. Casually, he dropped to the grass beside her. "So now you're going to immortalize Windy Point."

"In my own small way," she said dryly, and started to sketch again. Was she glad he had come? Hadn't she known, somehow, he would? "Still playing with stamps?"

"No, I've taken up classical music." He only smiled when she turned to study him. "You'd have been reared on that, I imagine. A little Brahms after dinner."

"I favored Chopin." She tapped her pencil on her chin. "What did you do with your mail?"

"I stowed it."

"I didn't notice your truck."

"I brought the boat." Taking the sketchbook, he flipped through to the front.

"For someone who's so keen on privacy," she began heatedly, "you have little respect when it belongs to someone else."

"Yeah." Unceremoniously, he shoved her hand away when she reached for the pad. While she simmered, Grant went through the book, pausing, then going on until he came to the sketch of himself. He studied it a moment, wordlessly, then surprised Gennie by grinning. "Not bad," he decided.

"I'm overwhelmed by your flattery."

He considered her a moment, then acted on impulse. "One deserves another."

Plucking the pencil out of her fingers, he turned the pages over until he came to a blank one. To her astonishment, he began to draw with the easy confidence of long practice. Mouth open, she stared at him while he whistled between his teeth and looped lines and curves onto the paper. His eyes narrowed a moment as he added some shading, then he tossed the book back into her lap. Gennie gave him a long, last stare before she looked down.

It was definitely her—in clever, merciless carica-ture. Her eyes were slanted—exaggerated, almost predatory, her cheekbones an aristocratic slash, her chin a stubborn point. With her mouth just parted and her head tilted back, he'd given her the expression of royalty mildly displeased. Gennie studied it for a full ten seconds before she burst into delighted laughter.

"You pig!" she said and laughed again. "I look like I'm about to have a minion beheaded."

He might have been saved if she'd gotten angry, been insulted. Then he could have written her off as vain and humorless and not worth his notice—at least he could have tried. Now with her laughter bouncing on the air and her eyes alive with it, Grant stepped off the cliff.

"Gennie." He murmured her name as his hand reached up to touch her face. Her laughter died.

What she would have said if her throat hadn't closed, she didn't know. She thought the air went very still very suddenly. The only movement seemed to be the fingers that brushed the hair back from her face, the only sound her own uneven breath. When he lowered his face toward hers, she didn't move but waited.

He hesitated, though the pause was too short to measure, before he touched his mouth to hers. Gentle, questioning, it sent a line of fire down her spine. For him, too, she realized, as his fingers tightened, briefly, convulsively, on her neck before they relaxed again.

He must be feeling, as she did, that sudden urgent thrust of power that was followed by a dazed kind of weakness.

Floating…were people meant to float like this? Limitless, mindless. How could she have known one man's lips could bring such an endless variety of sensations when touched to hers? Perhaps she'd never been kissed before and only thought she had. Perhaps she had only imagined another man casually brushing her mouth with his. Because this was real.

She could taste—warm breath. She could feel—lips soft, yet firm and knowing. She could smell—that subtle scent on him that meant wind and sea. She could see—his face, blurred and close when her lashes drifted up to assure her. And when he moaned her name, she heard him.

Her answer was to melt, slowly, luxuriously against him. With the melting came a pain, unexpected and sharp enough to make her tremble. How could there be pain, she wondered dazedly, when her body was so truly at peace? Yet it came again on a wave that rocked her. Some lucid part of her mind reminded her that love hurt.

But no. She tried to shake off the pain, and the knowledge it brought her even as her lips clung to his. She wasn't falling in love, not now, not with him. That wasn't what she wanted…. What did she want? *Him.*

The answer came so clearly, so simply. It drove her into panic.

"Grant, no." She drew away, but the hand on her face slid to the back of her neck and held her still.

"No, what?" His voice was very quiet, with rough edges.

"I didn't intend—we shouldn't be—I didn't... Oh!" She shut her eyes, frustrated that she could be reduced to stammering confusion.

"Why don't you run that by me again?"

The trace of humor in his voice had her springing to her feet. She wasn't lightheaded, she told herself. She'd simply sat too long and rose too quickly. "Look, this is hardly the place for this kind of thing."

"What kind of thing?" he countered, rising, too, but with a lazy ease that moved muscle by muscle. "We were only kissing. That's more popular than making friendly conversation. Kissing you's become a habit." He reached out for her hair, then let it drift through his spread fingers. "I don't break them easily."

"In this case—" she paused to even her breathing "—I think you should make an exception."

He studied her, trying to make light of something that had struck him down to the bone. "You're quite a mix, Geneviève. The practiced seductress one minute, the confused virgin the next. You know how to fascinate a man."

Pride moved automatically to shield her. "Some men are more easily fascinated than others."

"True enough." Grant wasn't sure just what emotion was working through him, but he knew it wasn't comfortable. "Damn if I won't be glad to see the last of you," he muttered.

Listening to the sound of his retreating footsteps, Gennie bent to pick up her sketchbook. By some malicious coincidence, it had fallen open to Grant's face.

Gennie scowled at it. "And I'll be glad to see the last of you." She closed the book, made a business of brushing off her jeans, and started to leave the church-yard with quiet dignity.

The hell with it!

"Grant!" She raced down the steps to the sidewalk and tore after him. "Grant, wait!"

With every sign of impatience, he turned and did so. "What?"

A little breathless, she stopped in front of him and wondered what it was she wanted to say. No, she didn't want to see the last of him. If she didn't un-derstand why yet, she felt she was at least entitled to a little time to find out.

"Truce," she decided and held out a hand. When he only stared at her, she gave a quick huff and swal-lowed another morsel of pride. "Please."

Trapped by the single word, he took the offered hand. "All right." When she would have drawn her hand away, he tightened his grip. "Why?"

"I don't know," Gennie told him with fresh im-patience. "Just a wild urge to see if I can get along with an ogre." At the ironic lift of his brow, she sighed. "All right, that was just a quick slip. I take it back."

Idly, he twisted the thin gold chain she wore around his finger. "So, what now?"

What now indeed? Gennie thought as even the brush of his knuckles had her skin humming. She wasn't going to give in to it—but she wasn't going to jump like a scared rabbit either. "Listen, I owe you a meal," she said impulsively. "I'll pay you back, that way we'll have a clean slate."

"How?"

"I'll cook you dinner."

"You've already cooked me breakfast."

"That was your food," Gennie pointed out. Already planning things out, she looked past him into town. "I'll need to pick up a few things."

Grant studied her, considering. "You going to bring them to the lighthouse?"

Oh, no, she thought immediately. She knew better than to trust herself with him there, that close to the sea and the power. "To my cottage. There's a little brick barbecue out back if you like steaks."

What's going on in her mind? he wondered as he watched secret thoughts flicker in her eyes. He knew he'd never be able to resist finding out. "I've been known to choke down a bite or two in my time."

"Okay." She gave a decisive nod and took his hand. "Let's go shopping."

"Wait a minute," Grant began as she pulled him down the sidewalk.

"Oh, don't start complaining already. Where do I buy the steaks?"

"Bayside," Grant said dryly, and brought her up short.

"Oh."

Grinning at her expression, he draped an arm around her shoulder. "Once in a while Leeman's Market gets in a few good cuts of meat."

Gennie shot him a suspicious look. "From where?"

Still grinning, Grant pushed open the market door. "I love a mystery."

Gennie wasn't certain she was amused until she

found there was indeed a steak—only one, but sizable enough for two people—and that it was from a nearby farm, authorized and licensed. Satisfied with this, and a bag of fresh salad greens, Gennie drew Grant outside again.

"Okay, now where can I buy a bottle of wine?"

"Fairfield's," he suggested. "He carries the only spirits in town. If you're not too particular about the label."

As they started across the road, a boy biked by, shooting Grant a quick look before he ducked his chin on his chest and pedaled away.

"One of your admirers?" Gennie asked dryly.

"I chased him and three of his friends off the cliffs a few weeks back."

"You're a real sport."

Grant only grinned, remembering his first reaction had been fury at having his peace interrupted, then fear that the four careless boys would break their necks on the rocks. "Ayah," he said, recalling with pleasure the acid tongue-lashing he'd doled out.

"Do you really kick sick dogs?" she asked as she caught the gleam in his eye.

"Only on my own land."

Heaving a hefty sigh, Gennie pushed open the door of Fairfield's store. Across the room, Will immediately dropped the large pot he'd been about to stock on a shelf. Red to the tips of his ears, he left it where it was. "Help you?" His voice cracked painfully on the last word.

"I need a bag of charcoal," Gennie told him as she crossed the room. "And a bottle of wine."

"Charcoal's in the back," he managed, then took

a step in retreat as Gennie came closer. His elbow
caught a stack of cans and sent them crashing.
"What—what size?"

Torn between laughter and sympathy, Gennie swallowed. "Five pounds'll be fine."

"I'll get it." The boy disappeared, and Gennie
caught Fairfield's voice demanding what the devil
ailed him before she was forced to press a hand to
her mouth to hold back the laughter.

Thinking of Macintosh's reaction to Veronica,
Grant felt a wave of empathy. "Poor kid's going to
be mooning like a puppy for a month. Did you have
to smile at him?"

"Really, Grant. He can't be more than fifteen."

"Old enough to break out in a sweat," he commented.

"Hormones," she murmured as she found Fairfield's sparse selection of wine. "They just need time
to balance."

Grant's gaze drifted down and focused as she bent
over. "It should only take thirty or forty years," he
muttered.

Gennie found a domestic burgundy and plucked it
from the bottom shelf. "Looks like we feast after
all."

Will came back with a bag of charcoal and almost
managed not to trip over his own feet. "Brought you
some starter, too, in case..." He broke off as his
tongue tied itself into knots.

"Oh, thanks." Gennie set the wine on the counter
and reached for her wallet.

"You gotta be of age to buy the wine," Will began. Gennie's smile widened and his blush deepened. "Guess you are, huh?"

Unable to resist, Gennie gestured to Grant. "He is."

Enraptured, Will stared at Gennie until she gently asked what the total was. He came to long enough to punch out numbers on the little adding machine, send it into clanking convulsions, and begin again.

"It be five-oh-seven, with—" a long sigh escaped "—tax."

Gennie resisted the urge to pat his cheek and counted out the change into his damp palm. "Thank you, Will."

Will's fingers closed over the nickel and two pennies. "Yes, ma'am."

For the first time the boy's eyes left Gennie's. Grant was struck with a look of such awe and envy, he wasn't sure whether to preen or apologize. In a rare gesture of casual affection, he reached over and squeezed Will's shoulder. "Makes a man want to sit up and beg, doesn't she?" he murmured when Gennie reached the door.

Will sighed. "Ayah." Before Grant could turn, Will plucked at his sleeve. "You gonna have dinner with her and everything?"

Grant lifted a brow but managed to keep his composure. *Everything,* he reminded himself, meant different things to different people. At the moment it conjured up rather provocative images in his brain. "Things are presently unsettled," he murmured, using one of Macintosh's stock phrases. Catching himself, he grinned. "Yeah, we're going to have dinner."

And something, he added as he strolled out after Gennie.

"What was all that about?" she demanded.

"Man talk."

"Oh, I beg your pardon."

The way she said it—very antebellum and disdainful—made him laugh and pull her into his arms to kiss her in full view of all of Windy Point. As the embrace lingered on, Grant caught the muffled crash from inside Fairfield's. "Poor Will," he murmured. "I know just how he feels." Humor flashed into his eyes again. "I better start around in the boat if we're going to have dinner...and everything."

Confused by his uncharacteristic lightheartedness, Gennie gave him a long stare. "All right," she said after a moment. "I'll meet you there."

Chapter Six

It was foolish to feel like a girl getting ready for a date. Gennie told herself that as she unlocked the door to the cottage. She'd told herself the same thing as she'd driven away from town...and as she'd turned down the quiet lane.

It was a spur of the moment cookout—two adults, a steak, and a bottle of burgundy that may or may not have been worth the price. A person would have to look hard to find any romance in charcoal, lighter fluid, and some freshly picked greens from a patch in the backyard. Not for the first time, Gennie thought it a pity her imagination was so expansive.

It had undoubtedly been imagination that had brought on that rush of feeling in the churchyard. A little unexpected tenderness, a soft breeze, and she heard bells. Silly.

Gennie set the bags on the kitchen counter and

wished she'd bought candles. Candlelight would make even that tidy, practical little kitchen seem romantic. And if she had a radio, there could be music…

Catching herself, Gennie rolled her eyes to the ceiling. What was she thinking of? She'd never had any patience with such obvious, conventional trappings in the first place, and in the second place she didn't *want* a romance with Grant. She'd go halfway toward making a friendship—a very careful friendship—with him, but that was it.

She'd cook dinner for him because she owed him that much. They'd have conversation because she found him interesting despite the thorns. And she'd make very, very certain she didn't end up in his arms again. Whatever part of her longed for a repeat of what had happened between them in the churchyard would have to be overruled by common sense. Grant Campbell was not only basically unpleasant, he was just too complicated. Gennie considered herself too complex a person to be involved with anyone who had so many layers to him.

Gennie grabbed the bag of charcoal and the starter and went into the side yard to set the grill. It was so quiet, she mused, looking around as she ripped the bag open. She'd hear Grant coming long before she saw him.

It was the perfect time for a ride on the water, with the late afternoon shadows lengthening and the heat draining from the day. The light was bland as milk now, and as soothing. She could hear the light lap-slap of water against the pier and the rustle of insects in the high grass on the bank. Then, barely, she heard the faint putt of a distant motor.

Her nerves gathered together so quickly, Gennie nearly dropped the five pounds of briquettes on the ground. When she'd finished being exasperated with herself, she laughed and poured a neat pile of charcoal into the barbecue pit. So this was the coolly sophisticated Genviève Grandeau, she thought wryly; established member of the art world and genteel New Orleans society, about to drop five pounds of charcoal on her toes because a rude man was going to have dinner with her. How the mighty have fallen.

With a grin, she rolled the bag up and dropped it on the ground. So what? she asked herself before she strolled down to the pier to wait for him.

Grant took the turn into the inlet at a speed that sent water spraying high. Laughing, Gennie stretched on her toes and waved, wishing he were already there. She hadn't realized, not until just that moment, how much she'd dreaded spending the evening alone. And yet, there was no one she wanted to spend it with but him. He'd infuriate her before it was over, she was certain. She was looking forward to it.

He cut back the motor so that it was a grumble instead of a roar, then guided the boat alongside the pier. When the engine shut off completely, silence snapped back—water lapping and wind in high grass.

"When are you going to take me for a ride?" Gennie demanded when he tossed her a line.

Grant stepped lightly onto the pier and watched as she deftly secured the boat. "Was I going to?"

"Maybe you weren't, but you are now." Straightening, she brushed her hands on the back of her jeans.

"I was thinking about renting a little rowboat for the inlet, but I'd much rather go out to sea."

"A rowboat?" He grinned, trying to imagine her manning oars.

"I grew up on a river," she reminded him. "Sailing's in my blood."

"Is that so?" Idly, Grant took her hand, turning it over to examine the palm. It was smooth and soft and strong. "This doesn't look as if it's hoisted too many mainsails."

"I've done my share." For no reason other than she wanted to, Gennie locked her fingers with his. "There've always been seamen in my family. My great-great-grandfather was a…freelancer."

"A pirate." Intrigued, Grant caught the tip of her hair in his hand then twirled a lock around his finger. "I get the feeling you think more of that than the counts and dukes scattered through your family tree."

"Naturally. Almost anyone can find an aristocrat somewhere if they look hard enough. And he was a very good pirate."

"Good-hearted?"

"Successful," she corrected with a wicked smile. "He was almost sixty when he retired in New Orleans. My grandmother lives in the house he built there."

"With money plucked from hapless merchants," Grant finished, grinning again.

"The sea's a lawless place," Gennie said with a shrug. "You take your chances. You might get what you want—" now she grinned as well "—or you could get your head lopped off."

"It might be smarter to keep you land-locked,"

Grant murmured, then tugging on the hair he held, brought her closer.

Gennie put a hand to his chest for balance, but found her fingers straying up. His mouth was tempting, very tempting as it lowered toward hers. It would be smarter to resist, she knew, but she rose on her toes to meet it with her own.

With barely any pressure, he kept his lips on hers, as if unsure of his moves, unsure just how deeply he dared plunge this time. He could have swept her against him; she could have drawn him closer with no more than a sigh. Yet both of them kept that slight, tangible distance between them, as a barrier—or a safety hatch. It was still early enough for them to fight the current that was drawing them closer and closer to the point of no return.

They moved apart at the same moment and took a small, perceptible step back.

"I'd better light the charcoal," Gennie said after a moment.

"I didn't ask before," Grant began as they started down the pier. "But do you know how to cook one of those things?"

"My dear Mr. Campbell," Gennie said in a fluid drawl, "you appear to have several misconceptions about southern women. I can cook on a hot rock."

"And wash shirts in a fast stream."

"Every bit as well as you could," Gennie tossed back. "You might have some advantage on me in mechanical areas, but I'd say we're about even otherwise."

"A strike for the woman's movement?"

Gennie narrowed her eyes. "Are you about to say something snide and unintelligent?"

"No." Picking up the can of starter fluid, he handed it to her. "As a sex, you've had a legitimate gripe for several hundred years which has been handled one way as a group and another individually. Unfortunately there's still a number of doors that have to be battered down by women as a whole while the individual woman occasionally unlocks one with hardly a sound. Ever hear of Winnie Winkle?"

Fascinated despite herself, Gennie simply stared at him. "As in Wee Willie?"

Grant laughed and leaned against the side of the barbecue. "No. *Winnie Winkle, the Breadwinner*, a cartoon strip from the twenties. It touched on women's liberation several decades before it became a household word. Got a match?"

"Hmmm." Gennie dug in her pocket. "Wasn't that a bit before your time?"

"I did some research on social commentary in college."

"Really?" Again, she sensed a grain of truth that only hinted at the whole. Gennie lit the soaked charcoal, then stepped back as the fire caught and flames rose. "Where did you go?"

Grant caught the first whiff, a summer smell he associated with his childhood. "Georgetown."

"They've an excellent art department there," Gennie said thoughtfully.

"Yeah."

"You did study art there?" Gennie persisted.

Grant watched the smoke rise and the haze of heat that rippled the air. "Why?"

"Because it's obvious from that wicked little caricature you drew of me that you have talent, and that you've had training. What are you doing with it?"

"With what?"

Gennie drew her brows together in frustration. "The talent and the training. I'd have heard of you if you were painting."

"I'm not," he said simply.

"Then what are you doing?"

"What I want. Weren't you going to make a salad?"

"Damn it, Grant—"

"All right, don't get testy. I'll make it."

As he started toward the back door, Gennie swore again and grabbed his arm. "I don't understand you."

He lifted a brow. "I didn't ask you to." He saw the frustration again, but more, he saw hurt, quickly concealed. Why should he suddenly feel the urge to apologize for his need for privacy? "Gennie, let me tell you something." In an uncharacteristic gesture, he stroked his knuckles gently over her cheek. "I wouldn't be here right now if I could stay away from you. Is that enough for you?"

She wanted to say yes—and no. If she hadn't been afraid of what the words might trigger, she would have told him she was already over her head and sinking fast. Love, or perhaps the first stirrings of love that she had felt only a short time before, was growing swiftly. Instead, she smiled and slipped her hands into his.

"I'll make the salad."

It was as simple as she'd told herself it could be. In the kitchen they tossed together the dewy fresh greens and argued over the science of salad making. Meat smoked and sizzled on the grill while they sat on the grass and enjoyed the last light of the afternoon of one of the last days of summer.

Lazy smells...wet weeds, cook smoke. A few words, an easy silence. Gennie bound them up and held them close, knowing they'd be important to her on some rainy day when she was crowded by pressures and responsibilities. For now, she felt as she had when she'd been a girl and August had a few precious days left and school was light-years away. Summer always seemed to have more magic near its end.

Enough magic, Gennie mused, to make her fall in love where there was no rhyme or reason.

"What're you thinking?" Grant asked her.

She smiled and stretched her head back to the sky one last time. "That I'd better tend to that steak."

He grabbed her arm, toppling her onto her back before she could rise. "Uh-uh."

"You like it burnt?"

"Uh-uh, that's not what you were thinking," he corrected. He traced a finger over her lips, and though the gesture was absent, Gennie felt the touch in every pore.

"I was thinking about summer," she said softly. "And that it always seems to end before you're finished with it."

When she lifted her hand to his cheek, he took her wrist and held it there. "The best things always do."

As he stared down at her she smiled in that slow, easy way she had that sent ripples of need, flurries of emotion through him. All thought fled as he lowered his mouth to hers. Soft, warm, ripe, her lips answered his, then drew and drew until everything he was, felt, wished for, was focused there. Bewitched, beguiled, bedazed, he went deeper, no longer sure what path he was on, only that she was with him.

He could smell the grass beneath them, sweet and dry; a scent of summer like the smoke that curled above their heads. He wanted to touch her, every inch of that slimly rounded body that had tormented his dreams since the first moment he'd seen her. If he did once, Grant knew his dreams would never be peaceful again. If her taste alone—wild fruit, warm honey— could so easily take over his mind, what would the feel of her do to him?

His need for her was like summer—or so he told himself. It had to end before he was finished.

Lifting his head he looked down to see her eyes, faintly slanted, barely open. Without guards, she'd bring him to his knees with a look. Cautiously, he drew away then pulled her to her feet.

"We'd better get that steak off before we have to make do with salad."

Her knees were weak. Gennie would have sworn such things happened only in fiction, yet here she was throbbingly alive with joints that felt like water. Turning, she stabbed the steak with a kitchen fork to lift it to the platter.

"The fat's in the fire," she murmured.

"I was thinking the same thing myself," Grant said quietly before they walked back into the house.

By unspoken agreement, they kept the conversation light as they ate. Whatever each had felt during that short, enervating kiss was carefully stored away.

I'm not looking for a relationship, their minds rationalized separately.

We're not suited to each other in the first place....There isn't time for this.

Good God, I'm not *falling in love.*

Shaken, Gennie lifted her wine and drank deeply while Grant scowled down at his plate.

"How's your steak?" she asked him for lack of anything else.

"What? Oh, it's good." Pushing away the uncomfortable feeling, Grant began to eat with more enthusiasm. "You cook almost as well as you paint," he decided. "Where'd you learn?"

Gennie lifted a brow. "Why, at my mammy's knee."

He grinned at the exaggerated drawl. "You've got a smart mouth, Genviève." Lifting the bottle, he poured more wine into the sturdy water glasses she'd bought in town. "I was thinking it odd that a woman who grew up with a house full of servants could grill a steak." He grinned, thinking of Shelby, who'd considered cooking a last resort.

"In the first place," she told him, "cookouts were always considered a family affair. And in the second, when you live alone you learn, or you live in restaurants."

He couldn't resist poking at her a bit as he sat back with his wine. "You've been photographed in or around every restaurant in the free world."

Not to be baited, Gennie mirrored his pose, watching him over the rim as she drank. "Is that why you get a dozen newspapers? So you can read how people live while you hibernate?"

Grant thought about it a moment. "Yeah." He didn't suppose he could have put it better himself.

"Don't you consider that an arrogant sort of attitude?"

Again he pondered on it, studying the dark red wine in his water glass. "Yeah."

Gennie laughed despite herself. "Grant, why don't you like people?"

Surprised, he looked back at her. "I do, individually in some cases, and as a whole. I just don't want them crowding me."

He meant it, she realized as she rose to stack the plates. There was just no understanding him. "Don't you ever have the need to rub elbows? Listen to a babble of voices?"

He'd had his share of elbows and voices before he'd been seventeen, Grant thought ruefully. But... No, he supposed it wasn't quite true. There were times he needed a heavy dose of humanity with all its flaws and complications; for his work and for himself. He thought of his week with the MacGregors. He'd needed that, and them, though he hadn't fully realized it until he'd settled back into his own routine.

"I have my moments," he murmured. He automatically began to clear the table as Gennie ran hot water in the sink. "No dessert?"

She looked over her shoulder to see that he was perfectly serious. He packed away food like a truck driver, yet there wasn't an ounce of spare flesh on him. Nervous energy? Metabolism? With a shake of her head, Gennie wondered why she persisted in trying to understand him. "I have a couple of fudge bars in the freezer."

Grant grinned and took her at her word. "Want one?" he asked as he ripped the thin white paper from the ice cream stick.

"No. Are you eating that because you want it or because it gets you out of drying these?" She stacked a plate into the drainer.

"Works both ways."

Leaning on the counter, he nibbled on the bar. "I could eat a carton of these when I was a kid."

Gennie rinsed another plate. "And now?"

Grant took a generous bite. "You only have two."

"A polite man would share."

"Yeah." He took another bite.

With a laugh, Gennie flicked some water into his face. "Come on, be a sport."

He held out the bar, pausing a half inch in front of her lips. Up to her elbows in soapy water, Gennie opened her mouth. Grant drew the bar away, just out of reach. "Don't get greedy," he warned.

Sending him an offended look, Gennie leaned forward enough to nibble delicately on the chocolate, then still watching him took a bite large enough to chill her mouth.

"Nasty," Grant decided, frowning at what was left of his fudge bar as Gennie laughed.

"You can have the other one," she said kindly after she'd swallowed and then dried her hands. "I just don't have any willpower when someone puts chocolate under my nose."

Deliberately, Grant ran his tongue over the bar. "Any other...weaknesses?"

As the heat expanded in her stomach, she wandered toward the porch door. "A few." She sighed as the call of swallows announced dusk. "The days are getting shorter," she murmured.

Already the lowering sun had the white clouds edged with pink and gold. The smoke from the grill struggled skyward, thinning. Near the bank of the inlet was a scrawny bush, its sparse leaves hinting of autumn red.

When Grant's hands came to her shoulders, she leaned back toward him instinctively. Together, in silence, they watched the approach of evening.

He couldn't remember the last time he'd shared a sunset with anyone, when he'd felt the desire to. Now it seemed so simple, so frighteningly simple. Would he think of her now whenever he watched the approach of evening?

"Tell me about your favorite summer," he asked abruptly.

She remembered a summer spent in the south of France and another on her father's yacht in the Aegean. Smiling, she watched the clouds deepen to rose. "I stayed with my grandmother for two weeks once while my parents had a second honeymoon in Venice. Long, lazy days with bees humming around honeysuckle blossoms. There was a big old oak outside my bedroom window just dripping with moss. Some nights I'd climb out the window to sit on a branch and look at the stars. I must have been twelve," she remembered. "There was a boy down at the stables." She laughed suddenly with her back comfortably nestled against Grant's chest. "Oh, Lord, he was a bit like Will, all sharp, awkward edges."

"You were crazy about him."

"I'd spend hours mucking out stalls and grooming

horses just to get a glimpse of him. I wrote pages and pages about him in my diary and one very mushy poem.''

"And kept it under your pillow."

"Apparently you've had a nodding acquaintance with twelve-year-old girls."

He thought of Shelby and grinned, resting his chin on the top of her head. Her hair smelled as though she'd washed it with rain-drenched wildflowers. "How long did it take you to get him to kiss you?"

She laughed. "Ten days. I thought I'd discovered the answer to the mysteries of the universe. I was a woman."

"No female's more sure of that than a twelve-year-old."

She smiled into the dimming sky. "More than a nodding acquaintance it appears," she commented. "One afternoon I found Angela giggling over my diary and chased her all over the house. She was..." Gennie stiffened as the grief washed over her, wave after tumultuous wave. Before Grant could tighten his hold, she had moved away from him to stare through the patched screen into twilight. "She was ten," Gennie continued in a whisper. "I threatened to shave her head if she breathed a word about what was in that diary."

"Gennie."

She shook her head as she felt his hand brush through her hair. "It'll be dark soon. You can already hear the crickets. You should start back."

He couldn't bear to hear the tears in her voice. It would be easier to leave her now, just back away. He told himself he had no skill when it came to comforting. His hands massaged gently on her shoulders. "There's a light on the boat. Let's sit down." Ignoring her resistance, Grant drew her to the porch glider. "My grandmother had one of these," he said conversationally as he slipped an arm around her and set it into creaking motion. "She had a little place on Maryland's Eastern Shore. A quiet little spot with land so flat it looked like it'd been laid out with a ruler. Ever been to the Chesapeake?"

"No." Deliberately, Gennie relaxed and closed her eyes. The motion was easy, his voice curiously soothing. She hadn't known he could speak in such quiet, gentle tones.

"Soft-shell crabs and fields of tobacco." Already he could feel the tautness in her shoulders easing. "We had to take a ferry to get to her house. It wasn't much different than this cottage except it was two stories. My father and I could go across the street and fish. I caught a trout once using a piece of Longhorn cheese as bait."

Grant continued to talk, ramble really, recounting things he'd forgotten, things he'd never spoken of aloud before. Unimportant things that droned quietly on the air while the light softened. For the moment it seemed to be the right thing, the thing she needed. He wasn't certain he had anything else to give.

He kept the motion of the glider going while her head rested against his shoulder and wondered how he'd never noticed just how peaceful dusk could be when you shared it with someone.

Gennie sighed, listening more to his tone than his words. She let herself drift as the chirp of crickets grew more insistent.... Dreams are often no more than memories.

"Oh, Gennie, you should have been there!" Angela, golden and vibrant, turned in her seat to laugh while Gennie maneuvered through the traffic of downtown New Orleans. The streets were damp with a chilly February rain, but nothing could dampen Angela. She was sunlight and spring flowers.

"I'd rather have been there than freezing in New York," Gennie returned.

"You can't freeze when you're basking in the limelight," Angela countered, twisting a bit closer to her sister.

"Wanna bet?"

"You wouldn't have missed that showing for a dozen parties."

No, she wouldn't have, Gennie thought with a smile. But Angela... "Tell me about it."

"It was so much fun! All that noise and music. It was so crowded, you couldn't take a step without bumping into someone. The next time Cousin Frank throws a bash on his houseboat you have to come."

Gennie sent Angela a quick grin. "It doesn't sound like I was missed."

Angela laughed, the quick bubble that was irresistible. "Well, I got a little tired of answering questions about my talented sister."

Gennie gave a snort as she stopped at a light. She could see the hazy red glow as the windshield wipers moved briskly back and forth. "They just use that as a line to get to you."

"Well, there was someone..." When Angela

trailed off, Gennie turned to look at her. So beautiful, she thought. Gold and cream with eyes almost painfully alive and vivid.

"Someone?"

"Oh, Gennie." Excitement brought a soft pink to her cheeks. "He's gorgeous. I could hardly make a coherent sentence when he started to talk to me."

"You?"

"Me," Angela agreed, laughing again. "It felt like someone had drained off half my brain. And now... Well, I've been seeing him all week. I think—ta-da— this is it."

"After a week?" Gennie countered.

"After five seconds. Oh, Gennie, don't be practical. I'm in love. You have to meet him."

Gennie shifted into first as she waited for the light to change. "Do I get to size him up?"

Angela shook back her rich gold hair and laughed as the light turned green. "Oh, I feel wonderful, Gennie. Absolutely wonderful!"

The laugh was the last thing Gennie heard before the squeal of brakes. She saw the car skidding toward them through the intersection. In the dream it was always so slow, second by terrifying second, closer and closer. Water spewed out from the tires and seemed to hang in the air.

There wasn't time to breathe, there wasn't time to react or prevent before there was the sound of metal striking metal, the explosion of blinding lights. Terror. Pain. And darkness.

"No!" She jerked upright, rigid with fear and shock. There were arms around her, holding her

close…safe. Crickets? Where had they come from? The light, the car. Angela.

Gasping for breath, Gennie stared out at the darkened inlet while Grant's voice murmured something comforting in her ear.

"I'm sorry." Pushing away, she rose, lifting nervous hands to her hair. "I must have dozed off. Poor company," she continued in a jerky voice. "You should have given me a jab, and—"

"Gennie." He stood, grabbing her arm. "Stop it."

She crumbled. He hadn't expected such complete submission and had no defense against it. "Don't," he murmured, stroking her hair as she clung to him. "Gennie, don't cry. It's all right now."

"Oh, God, it hasn't happened in weeks." She buried her face against his chest as the grief washed over her as fresh as the first hour. "At first, right after the accident, I'd go through it every time I closed my eyes."

"Come on." He kissed the top of her head. "Sit down."

"No, I can't—I need to walk." She held him tight another moment, as if gathering her strength. "Can we walk?"

"Sure." Bringing her to his side, Grant opened the screen door. For a time he was silent, his arm around her shoulders as they skirted the inlet and walked aimlessly. But he knew he needed to hear as much as she needed to tell. "Gennie, talk to me."

"I was remembering the accident," she said slowly, but her voice was calmer now. "Sometimes when I'd dream of it, I'd be quick enough, swerve out of the way of that car and everything was so different. Then I'd wake up and nothing was different at all.''

"It's a natural reaction," he told her, though the thought of her being plagued by nightmares began to gnaw at his gut. He'd lived through a few of his own. "They'll fade after a while."

"I know. It hardly ever happens anymore." She let out a long breath and seemed steadier for it. "When it does, it's so clear. I can see the rain splattering on the windshield right before the wipers whisk it away. There're puddles near the curbs, and Angela's voice is so—vital. She was so beautiful, Grant, not just her face, but her. She never outgrew sweetness. She was telling me about a party she'd been to where she'd met someone. She was in love, bubbling over with it. The last thing she said was that she felt wonderful, absolutely wonderful. Then I killed her.''

Grant took her shoulders, shaking her hard. "What the hell kind of craziness is that?"

"It was my fault," Gennie returned with deadly calm. "If I'd seen that car, if I'd seen it just seconds earlier. Or if I'd *done* something, hit the brakes, the gas, anything. The impact was all on her side. I had a mild concussion, a few bruises, and she…''

"Would you feel better if you'd been seriously injured?" he demanded roughly. "You can mourn for her, cry for her, but you can't take the blame."

"I was driving, Grant. How do I forget that?"

"You don't forget it," he snapped back, unnerved by the dull pain in her voice. "But you put it in perspective. There was nothing you could have done, you know that."

"You don't understand." She swallowed because

the tears were coming and she'd thought she was through with them. "I loved her so much. She was part of me—a part of me I needed very badly. When you lose someone who was vital to your life, it takes a chunk out of you."

He did understand—the pain, the need to place blame. Gennie blamed herself for exposing her sister to death. Grant blamed his father for exposing himself. Neither way changed the loss. "Then you have to live without that chunk."

"You can't know what it's like," she began.

"My father was killed when I was seventeen," he said, saying the words he would rather have avoided. "I needed him."

Gennie let her head fall against his chest. She didn't offer sympathy, knowing he wanted none. "What did you do?"

"Hated—for a long time. That was easy." Without realizing it, he was holding her against him again, gaining comfort as well as giving it. "Accepting's tougher. Everyone does it in different ways."

"How did you?"

"By realizing there was nothing I could have done to stop it." Drawing her away a little, he lifted her chin with his hand. "Just as there was nothing you could have done."

"It's easier, isn't it, to tell yourself you could have done something than to admit you were helpless?"

He'd never thought about it—perhaps refused to think about it. "Yeah."

"Thank you. I know you didn't want to tell me that even more than I didn't want to tell you. We can get very selfish with our grief—and our guilt."

He brushed the hair away from her temples. He kissed her cheeks where tears were still drying and felt a surge of tenderness that left him shaken. Defenseless, she made him vulnerable. If he kissed her now, really kissed her, she'd have complete power over him. With more effort than he'd realized it would take, Grant drew away from her.

"I have to get back," he said, deliberately putting his hands in his pockets. "Will you be all right?"

"Yes, but—I'd like you to stay." The words were out before she realized she'd thought them. But she wouldn't take them back. Something flared in his eyes. Even in the dim light she saw it. Desire, need, and something quickly banked and shuttered.

"Not tonight."

The tone had her brows drawing together in puzzlement. "Grant," she began, and reached for him.

"Not tonight," he repeated, stopping the motion of her outstretched hand.

Gennie put it behind her back as if he'd slapped it. "All right." Her pride surged forward to cover the hurt of fresh rejection. "I appreciated the company." Turning, she started back to the house.

Grant watched her go, then swore, taking a step after her. "Gennie."

"Good night, Grant." The screen door swung shut behind her.

Chapter Seven

She was going to lose it. Gennie cast a furious look at the clouds whipping in from the north, and swore. Damn, she was going to lose the light and she wasn't ready. The energy was pouring through her, flowing from her mind and heart to her hand in one of the rare moments an artist recognizes as *right*. Everything, everything told her that something lasting, something important would spring onto the canvas that morning; she had only to let herself go with it. But to go with it now, she had to race against the storm.

Gennie knew she had perhaps thirty minutes before the clouds would spoil her light, an hour before the rain closed out everything. Already a distant thunder rumbled over the sound of crashing waves. She cast a defiant look at the sky. By God, she would beat it yet!

The impetus was with her, an urgency that said today—it's going to happen today. Whatever she'd done before—the sketches, the preliminary work, the spread of paint on canvas—was just a preparation for what she would create today.

Excitement rippled across her skin with the wind. And a frustration. She seemed to need them both to draw from. Maybe a storm was brewing in her as well. It had seemed so since the night before when her mood had fluctuated and twisted, with Grant, without him. The last rejection had left her numb, ominously calm. Now her emotions were raging free again—fury, passion, pride, and torment. Gennie could pour them into her art, liberating them so that they wouldn't fester inside her.

Need him? No, she needed neither him nor anyone, she told herself as she streaked her brush over the canvas. Her work was enough to fill her life, cleanse her wounds. It was always fresh, always constant. As long as her eyes could see and her fingers could lift pencil or brush, it would be with her.

It had been her friend during her childhood, a solace during the pangs of adolescence. It was as demanding as a lover, and as greedy for her passion. And it was passion she felt now, a vibrant, physical passion that drove her forward. The moment was ripe, and the electricity in the air only added to the sense of urgency that shimmered inside her.

Now! it shouted at her. The time for merging, soul and heart and mind was now. If not now, it would be never. The clouds raced closer. She vowed to beat them.

Skin cool with anticipation, blood hot, Grant came

outside. Like a wolf, he'd scented something in the air and had come in search of it. He'd been too restless to work, to tense too relax. Something had been driving at him all morning, urging him to move, to look, to find. He'd told himself it was the approach of the storm, the lack of sleep. But he'd known, without understanding, that each of those things was only a part of the whole. Something was brewing, brewing in more than that cauldron of a sky.

He was hungry without wanting to eat, dissatisfied without knowing what he would change. Restless, reckless, he'd fretted against the confines of his studio, all walls and glass. Instinct had led him out to seek the wind and the sea. And Gennie.

He'd known she'd be there, though he'd been convinced that he'd closed his mind to even the thought of her. But now, seeing her, he was struck, just as surely as the north sky was struck with the first silver thread of lightning.

He'd never seen her like this, but he'd known. She stood with her head thrown back in abandon to her work, her eyes glowing green with power. There was a wildness about her only partially due to the wind that swept up her hair and billowed the thin smock she wore. There was strength in the hand that guided the brush so fluidly and yet with such purpose. She might have been a queen overlooking her dominion. She might have been a woman waiting for a lover. As his blood quickened with need, Grant thought she was both.

Where was the woman who'd wept in his arms only hours before? Where was the fragility, the defenselessness that had terrified him? He'd given her what comfort he could, though he knew little of soothing tearful women. He'd spoken of things he hadn't said aloud in fifteen years—because she'd needed to hear them and he, for some indefinable reason, had needed to say them. And he'd left her because he'd felt himself being sucked into something unknown, and inevitable.

Now, she looked invulnerable, magnificent. This was a woman no man would ever resist, a woman who could choose and discard lovers with a single gesture. It wasn't fear he felt now, but challenge, and with the challenge a desire so huge it threatened to swallow him.

She stopped painting on a roll of thunder then looked up to the sky in a kind of exaltation. He heard her laugh, once, with an arousing defiance that had him struggling with a fresh slap of desire.

Who in God's name was she? he demanded. And why, in heaven and hell, couldn't he stay away?

The excitement that had driven her to finish the painting lingered. It was done, Gennie thought with a breathless triumph. And yet...there was something more. Her passion hadn't been diffused by the consummation of woman and art, but spun in her still; restless, waiting.

Then she saw him, with the sea and the storm at his back. The wind blew wilder. Her blood pounded with it. For a long moment they only stared at each other while thunder and lightning inched closer.

Ignoring him, and the flash of heat that demanded she close the distance between them, Gennie turned back to the canvas. This and only this was what called to her, she told herself. This and only this was what she needed.

Grant watched her pack her paints and brushes. There was something both regal and defiant about the way she had turned her back on him and gone about her business. Yet there was no denying that jolt of recognition he had felt when their gazes had locked. Under his feet the ground shook with the next roll of thunder. He went to her.

The light shifted, dimming as clouds rolled over the sun. The air was so charged, sparks could be felt along the skin. Gennie packed up her gear with deft, steady hands. She'd beaten the storm that morning. She could beat anything.

"Geneviève." She wasn't Gennie now. He'd seen Gennie in the churchyard, laughing with young, fresh delight. It had been Gennie who had clung to him, weeping. This woman's laugh would be low and seductive, and she would shed no tears at all. Whichever, whoever she was, Grant was drawn to her, irrevocably.

"Grant." Gennie closed the lid on her paint case before she turned. "You're out early."

"You've finished."

"Yes." The wind blew his hair wildly around his face, and while the face was set, his eyes were dark and restless. Gennie knew her own emotions matched his like two halves of the same coin. "I've finished."

"You'll go now." He could see the flush of triumph on her face and the moody, unpredictable green of her eyes.

"From here?" She tossed her head as her gaze shifted to the sea. The waves were swelling higher, and no boat dared test them now. "Yes. I have other things I want to paint."

It was what he wanted. Hadn't he wanted to be rid of her from the very first? But Grant said nothing as the grumbling thunder rolled closer.

"You'll have your solitude back." Gennie's smile was light and mocking. "That's what's most important to you, isn't it? And I've gotten what I needed here."

His eyes narrowed, but he wasn't certain of the origin of his temper. "Have you?"

"Have a look," she invited with a gesture of her hand.

He hadn't wanted to see the painting, had deliberately avoided even a glance at it. Now her eyes dared him and the flick of her wrist was too insolent to deny. Hooking his thumbs in his pockets, Grant turned toward the canvas.

She saw too much of what he needed there, what he felt. The power of limitless sea, the glory of space and unending challenge. She'd scorned muted colors and had chosen bold. She'd forsaken delicacy for muscle. What had been a blank canvas was now as full of force as the turbulent Atlantic, and as full of secrets. The secrets there were nature's, as the strength and solidity of the lighthouse were man's. She'd captured both, pitting them against each other even while showing their timeless harmony.

The painting moved him, disturbed him, pulled at him, as much as its creator.

Gennie felt the tension build up at the base of her neck as Grant only frowned at the painting. She knew it was everything she'd wanted it to be, felt it was perhaps the best work she'd ever done. But it was his—his world, his force, his secrets that had dominated the emotions she'd felt when she'd painted it. Even as she'd finished, the painting had stopped being hers and had become his.

Grant took a step away from the painting and looked out to sea. The lightning was closer; he saw it shimmer dangerously behind the dark, angry clouds. He seemed to have lost the words, the phrases that had always come so easily to him. He couldn't think of anything but her, and the need that had risen up to work knots in his stomach. "It's fine," he said flatly.

He could have struck her and hurt her no less. Her small gasp was covered by the moan of the wind. For a moment Gennie stared at his back while pain rocketed through her. Rejection...would she never stop setting herself up for his rejection?

Pain altered to anger in the space of seconds. She didn't need his approval, his pleasure, his understanding. She had everything she needed within herself. In raging silence she slipped the canvas into its carrying case, then folded her easel. Gathering her things together, she turned toward him slowly.

"Before I go, I'd like to tell you something." Her voice was cool over flowing vowels. "It isn't often one finds one's first impression was so killingly accurate. The first night I met you, I thought you were a rude, arrogant man with no redeeming qualities." The wind blew her hair across her eyes and with a toss of her head she sent it flying back so that she could keep her icy gaze on his. "It's very gratifying to learn just how right I was...and to be able to dislike you so intensely." Chin high, Gennie turned and walked to her car.

She jerked up the trunk of her car and put her equipment and canvas in, perversely glad to flow with the fury that consumed her. When Grant's hand closed over her arm, she slammed the trunk closed and whirled around, ready to battle on any terms, any grounds. Blind with her own emotions, she didn't notice the heat in his eyes or the raggedness of his breathing.

"Do you think I'm just going to let you walk away?" he demanded. "Do you think you can walk into my life and take and not leave anything behind?"

Her chest was heaving, her eyes brilliant. With calculated disdain, she looked down at the fingers that circled her arm. "Take your hand off me," she told him, spacing her words with insolent precision.

Lightning shot across the sky as they stared at each other, cold white heat against boiling gray and angry purple. The deafening roar of thunder drowned out Grant's oath. The moment stood poised, crackling, then swirled like the wind that screamed in triumph.

"You should have taken my advice," he said between his teeth, "and stuck with your counts and barons." Then he was pulling her across the tough grass, against the wind.

"What the hell do you think you're doing?"

"What I should have done the minute you barged into my life."

Murder? Gennie stared at the cliffs and the raging sea below. God knew he looked ready for it at that moment—and perhaps he would have liked her to believe he was capable of tossing her over the edge. But she knew what the violence in him meant, where it would lead them both. She fought him wildly as he pulled her toward the lighthouse.

"You must be mad! Let me go!"

"I must be," he agreed tightly. Lightning forked again, opening the sky. Rain spewed out.

"I said take your hands off me!"

He whirled to her then, his face sculptured and shadowed in the crazed light of the storm. "It's too late for that!" he shouted at her. "Damn it, you know it as well as I do. It was too late from the first minute." Rain poured over them, pounding and warm.

"I won't be dragged into your bed, do you hear me!" She grabbed his soaking shirt with her free hand while her body vibrated with fury and with wanting. "I won't be dragged anywhere. Do you think you can just suddenly decide you need a lover and haul me off?"

His breath was raging in and out of his lungs. The rain pouring down his face only accented the passionate darkness of his eyes. She was sleek and wet. A siren? Maybe she was, but he'd already wrecked on the reef. "Not any lover." He swung her against him so that their wet clothes fused then seemed to melt away. "You. Damn it, Gennie, you know it's you."

Their faces were close, their eyes locked. Each had forgotten the storm around them as the tempest within took over. Heart pounded against heart. Need pounded against need. Full of fear and triumph, she threw her head back.

"Show me."

Grant crushed her closer so that not even the wind

could have forced its way between. "Here," he said roughly. "By God, here and now."

His mouth took hers madly, and she answered. Unleashed, the passion drove them far past sanity, beyond the civilized and into the dark tunnel of chaotic desire. His lips sped across her face, seeking to devour all that could be consumed and more. When his teeth scraped over the cord of her neck, Gennie moaned and drew him with her to the ground.

Raw, keening wind, hard, driving rain, the pound and crash of the stormy sea. They were nothing in the face of this tempest. Grant forgot them as he pressed against her, feeling every line and curve as though he'd already torn the clothes from her. Her heart pounded. It seemed as if it had worked its way inside his chest to merge with his.

Her body felt like a furnace. He hadn't known there could be such heat from a living thing. But alive she was, moving under him, hands seeking, mouth greedy. The rain sluicing over them should have cooled the fire, yet it stoked it higher so that the water might have sizzled on contact.

He knew only greed, only ageless need and primitive urges. She'd bewitched him from the first instant, and now, at last, he succumbed. Her hands were in his hair, bringing his mouth back to hers again and again so that her lips could leave him breathless, arouse more hunger.

They rolled on the wet grass until she was on top of him, her mouth ravaging his with a strength and power only he could match. In a frenzy, she dragged at his shirt, yanking and tugging until it was over his head and discarded. With a long, low moan she ran her hands over him. Grant's reason shattered.

Roughly, he pushed her on her back, cutting off her breath as lightning burst overhead. Ignoring buttons, he pulled the blouse from her, desperate to touch what he had denied himself for days. His hands slid over her wet skin, kneading, possessing, hurrying in his greed for more. And when she arched against him, agile and demanding, he buried his mouth at her breast and lost himself.

He tasted the rain on her, laced with summer thunder and her own night scent. Like a drowning man he clung to her as he sank beneath the depths. He knew what it was to want a woman, but not like this. Desire could be controlled, channeled, guided. So what was it that pounded in him? His fingers bruised her, but he was unaware in his desperation to take all and take it quickly.

When he dragged the jeans down her hips, he felt both arousal and frustration as they clung to her skin and those smooth, narrow curves. Struggling with the wet denim, he followed its inching progress with his mouth, thrilling as Gennie arched and moaned. His teeth scraped over her hip, down her thigh to the inside of her knee as he pulled the jeans down her, then left them in a heap.

Mindlessly, he plunged his tongue into her and heard her cry out with the wind. Heat suffused him. Rain fell on his back unfelt, ran from his hair onto her skin but did nothing to wash away the passion that drove them both closer and closer to the peak.

Then they were both fighting with his jeans, hands tangling together while their lips fused again. The sounds coming low from her throat might have been his name or some new spell she was weaving over him. He no longer cared.

Lightning illuminated her face once, brilliantly— the slash of cheekbone, the eyes slanted and nearly closed, the soft full lips parted and trembling with her breathing. At that moment she was witch, and he, willingly bewitched.

With his mouth against the hammering pulse in her throat, he plunged into her, taking her with a violent kind of worship he didn't understand. When she stiffened and cried out, Grant struggled to find both his sanity and the reason. Then she was wrapped around him drawing him into the satin-coated darkness.

Breathless, dazed, empty, Grant lay with his face buried in Gennie's hair. The rain still fell, but until that moment he didn't realize that it had lost its force. The storm was passed, consumed by itself like all things of passion. He felt the hammer-trip beat of her heart beneath him, and her trembles. Shutting his eyes, he tried to gather his strength and the control that meant lucidity.

"Oh, God." His voice was rough and raw. The apology wouldn't come; he thought it less than useless. "Why didn't you tell me?" he murmured as he rolled from her to lie on his back against the wet grass. "Damn it, Gennie, why didn't you tell me?"

She kept her eyes closed so that the rain fell on her lids, over her face and throbbing body. Was this how it was supposed to be? she wondered. Should she feel so spent, so enervated while her skin hummed everywhere, everywhere his hand had touched it? Should she feel as though every lock she had, had been broken? By whom, him or her, it didn't matter. But her privacy was gone, and the need for it. Yet now, hearing the harsh question—accusation?—she felt a ripple of pain sharper than the loss of innocence. She said nothing.

"Gennie, you let me think you were—"

"What?" she demanded, opening her eyes. The clouds were still dark, she saw, but the lightning was gone.

Cursing himself, Grant dragged a hand through his hair. "Gennie, you should have told me you hadn't been with a man before." And how was it possible, he wondered, that she'd let no man touch her before? That he was the first...the only.

"Why?" she said flatly, wishing he would go, wishing she had the strength to leave. "It was my business."

Swearing, he shifted, leaning over her. His eyes were dark and angry, but when she tried to pull away, he pinned her. "I don't have much gentleness," he told her, and the words were unsteady with feeling. "But I would have used all I had, I would have tried to find more, for you." When she only stared at him, Grant lowered his forehead to hers. "Gennie..."

Her doubts, her fears, melted at that one softly murmured word. "I wasn't looking for gentleness then," she whispered. Framing his face with her hands, she lifted it. "But now..." She smiled, and watched the frown fade from his eyes.

He dropped a kiss on her lips, soft, more like a whisper, then rising, lifted her into his arms. Gennie laughed at the feeling of weightlessness and ease. "What're you doing now?"

"Taking you inside so you can warm up, dry off, and make love with me again—maybe not in that order."

Gennie curled her arms around his neck. "I'm beginning to like your ideas. What about our clothes?"

"We can salvage what's left of them later." He pushed open the door of the lighthouse. "We won't be needing them for quite a while."

"Definitely liking your ideas." She pressed her mouth against his throat. "Are you really going to carry me up those stairs?"

"Yeah."

Gennie cast a look at the winding staircase and tightened her hold. "I'd just like to mention it wouldn't be terribly romantic if you were to trip and drop me."

"The woman casts aspersions on my machismo."

"On your balance," she corrected as he started up. She shivered as her wet skin began to chill, then abruptly laughed. "Grant, did it occur to you what those assorted piles of clothes would look like if someone happened by?"

"They'd probably look a great deal like what they are," he considered. "And it should discourage anyone from trespassing. I should have thought of it before—much better than a killer-dog sign."

She sighed, partially from relief as they reached the landing. "You're hopeless. Anyone would think you were Clark Kent."

Grant stopped in the doorway to the bathroom to stare at her. "Come again?"

"You know, concealing a secret identity. Though you're anything but mild-mannered," she added as she toyed with a damp curl that hung over his ear. "You've set up this lighthouse as some kind of Fortress of Solitude."

The long intense look continued. "What was Clark Kent's Earth mother's name?"

"Is this a quiz?"

"Do you know?"

She arched a brow because his eyes were so suddenly serious. "Martha."

"I'll be damned," he murmured. He laughed, then gave her a quick kiss that was puzzlingly friendly considering they were naked and pressed together. "You continue to surprise me, Genviève. I think I'm crazy about you."

The light words went straight to her heart and turned it over. "Because I know Superman's adoptive mother's first name?"

Grant nuzzled his cheek against her, the first wholly sweet gesture she'd ever seen in him. In that one instant she was lost, as she'd never been lost before. "For one thing." Feeling her tremble, Grant drew her closer. "Come on, into the shower; you're freezing."

He stepped into the tub before he set her down, then still holding her close, pressed his mouth to hers in a long, lingering kiss. With the storm, with the passion, she'd felt invulnerable. Now, no longer innocent, no longer unaware, the nerves returned. Only a short time before she had given herself to him, perhaps demanded that he take her, but now she could only cling while her mind reeled with the wonder of it.

When the water came on full and hot, she jolted,

gasping. With a low laugh, Grant stroked a hand intimately over her hip. "Feel good?"

It did, after the initial shock, but Gennie tilted back her head and eyed him narrowly. "You might have warned me."

"Life's full of surprises."

Like falling in love, she thought, when you hadn't the least intention of doing so. Gennie smiled, finding her arms had wound around his neck.

"You know..." He traced his tongue lightly over her mouth. "I'm getting used to the taste—and the feel of you wet. It's tempting just to stay right here for the next couple of hours."

She nuzzled against him when he ran his hands down her back. Strong hands, toughened in contrast to the elegance of their shape. There were no others she could ever imagine touching her.

With the steam rising around him, and Gennie soft and giving in his arms, Grant felt that rushing, heady desire building again. His muscles contracted with it—tightening, preparing.

"No, not this time," he murmured, pressing his mouth to her throat. This time he would remember her fragility and the wonder of being the only man to ever possess her. Whatever tenderness he had, or could find in himself, would be for her.

"You should dry off." He nibbled lightly at her lips before he drew her away. She was smiling, but her eyes were uncertain. As he turned off the water he tried to ignore the very real fear her vulnerability brought to him. Taking a towel from the rack, he stroked it over her face. "Here, lift your arms."

She did, laying her hands on his shoulders as he

wrapped the towel around her. Slowly, running soft, undemanding kisses over her face, he drew the towel together to knot it loosely at her breasts. Gennie closed her eyes, the better to soak up the sensation of being pampered.

Using a fresh towel, Grant began to dry her hair. Gently, lazily, while her heart began to race, he rubbed the towel over it. "Warm?" he murmured, dipping his head to nibble at her ear. "You're trembling."

How could she answer when her heart was hammering in her throat? Heat was creeping into her, yet her body shivered with anticipation, uncertainties, longings. He had only to touch his mouth to hers to know that for that moment, for always, she was his.

"I want you," he said softly. "I wanted you right from the start." He skimmed his tongue over her ear. "You knew that."

"Yes." The word came out breathlessly, like a sigh.

"Do you know how much more I want you now than I did even an hour ago?" His mouth covered hers before she could answer. "Come to bed, Gennie."

He didn't carry her, but took her hand so that they could walk together into the thin gray light of his room. Her pulses pounded. The first time there had been no thought, no doubts. Desire had ruled her and the power had flowed. Now her mind was clear and her nerves jumping. She knew now where he could take her with a touch, with a taste. The journey was as much feared as it was craved.

"Grant—"

But he barely touched her, only cupping her face as they stood beside the bed. "You're beautiful." His eyes were on hers, intense, searching. "The first time I saw you, you took my breath away. You still do."

As moved by the long look and soft words as she had been by the tempestuous kisses, she reached up to take his wrists. "I don't need the words unless you want to give them. I just want to be with you."

"Whatever I tell you will be the truth, or I won't tell you at all." He leaned toward her, touching his mouth to hers, but nibbling only, testing the softness, lingering over that honey-steeped taste. As he took her deep with tenderness, his fingers moved over her face, skimming, stroking. Gennie's head went light while her body grew heavy. She barely felt the movement when they lowered to the bed.

Then it seemed she felt everything—the tiny nubs in the bedspread, the not quite smooth, not quite rough texture of Grant's palms, the thin mat of hair on his chest. All, she felt them all, as if her skin had suddenly become as soft and sensitive as a newborn's. And he treated her as though she were that precious with the slow, whisper-light kisses he brushed over her face and the hands that touched her—arousing, but stopping just short of demand.

The floating weightlessness she had experienced in the churchyard drifted back over her, but now, with the shivering excitement of knowledge. Aware of where they could lead each other, Gennie sighed. This time the journey would be luxurious, lazy and loving.

The light through the window was thin, misty gray from the clouds that still hid the sun. It cast shadows and mysteries. She could hear the sea—not the deafening, titanic roar, but the echo and the promise of power. And when he murmured to her, it was like the sea, with its passionate pull and thrust. The urgency she had felt before had become a quiet enjoyment. Though the needs were no less, there was a comfort here, an unquestioning trust she'd never expected to feel. He would protect if she needed him, cherish in his own fashion. Beneath the demands and impatience was a man who would give unselfishly where he cared. Discovering that was discovering everything.

Touch me—don't ever stop touching me. And he seemed to hear her silent request as he caressed, lingered, explored. The pleasure was liquid and light, like a lazy river, like rain misting. Her mind was so clouded with him, only him, she no longer thought of her body as separate, but a part of the two that made one whole.

Soft murmurs and quiet sighs, the warmth that only flesh can bring to flesh. Gennie learned of him—the man he showed so rarely to anyone. Sensitivity, because it was not his way, was all the sweeter. Gentleness, so deeply submerged, was all the more arousing.

She hardly knew when her pliancy began to kindle to excitement. But he did. The subtle change in her movements, her breathing, had a shiver of pleasure darting down his spine. And he drew yet more pleasure in the mere watching of her face in the gloomy light. A flicker of passion reminded him that no one had ever touched her as he did. And no one would. For so long he'd taken such care not to allow anyone to get too close, to block off any feelings of possession, to avoid being possessed. Though the proprietary sensation disturbed him, he couldn't fight it. She was his. Grant told himself it didn't yet mean he was hers. Yet he could think of no one else.

He ran kisses over her slowly, until his mouth brushed then loitered at her shoulder. And when he felt her yield, completely, unquestioningly, he took her once, gasping, to the edge. On her moan, he pressed his lips to hers, wanting to feel the sound as well as hear it.

Mindless, boneless, burning, Gennie moved with him, responding to the agonizingly slow pace by instinct alone. She wanted to rush, she wanted to stay in that cloudy world of dreams forever. Now, and only now, did she fully understand why the coming together of two separate beings was called making love.

She opened to him, offering everything. When he slipped inside her she felt his shudder, heard the groan that was muffled against her throat. His breath rasped against her ear but he kept the pace exquisitely slow. There couldn't be so much—she'd never known there could be—but he showed her.

She drifted down a tunnel with soft melting edges. Deeper and lusher it grew until her whole existence was bound there in the velvet heat that promised forever. Reason peeled away layer by layer so that her body was guided by senses alone. He was trembling—was she? As her hands glided over his shoulders she could feel the hard, tense muscles there while his movements were gentle and easy. Through the mists of pleasure she knew he was blocking off his own needs for hers. A wave of emotion struck her that was a hundred times greater than passion.

''Grant.'' His name was only a whisper as her arms tightened around him. ''Now. Take me now.''

''Gennie.'' He lifted his face so that she had a glimpse of dark, dark eyes before his mouth met hers. His control seemed to snap at the contact and he swallowed her gasps as he rushed with her to the peak.

There were no more thoughts nor the need for any.

Chapter Eight

With a slow stretch and a long sigh, Gennie woke. Ingrained habit woke her early and quickly. Her first feeling of disorientation faded almost at once. No, the sun-washed window wasn't hers, but she knew whose it was. She knew where she was and why.

The morning warmth had a new texture—body to body, man to woman, lover to lover. Simultaneous surges of contentment and excitement swam through her to chase away any sense of drowsiness. Turning her head, Gennie watched Grant sleep.

He sprawled, taking up, Gennie discovered to her amusement, about three-fourths of the bed. During the night, he had nudged her to within four inches of the edge. His arm was tossed carelessly across her body—not loverlike, she thought wryly, but because she just happened to be in his space. He had most of her pillow. Against the plain white, his face was deeply tanned, shadowed by the stubble that grew on his jaw. Looking at him, Gennie realized he was completely relaxed as she had seen him only once before—on their walk along the beach.

What drives you, Grant? she wondered as she gave in to the desire to toy with the tips of his rumpled hair. What makes you so intense, so solitary? And why do I want so badly to understand and share whatever secrets you keep?

With a fingertip, carefully, delicately, Gennie traced down the line of his jaw. A strong face, she thought, almost hard, and yet occasionally, unexpectedly the humor and sensitivity would come into his eyes. Then the hardness would vanish and only the strength would remain.

Rude, remote, arrogant; he was all of those things. And she loved him—despite it, perhaps because of it. It had been the gentleness he had shown her that had allowed her to admit it, accept it, but it had been true all along.

She longed to tell him, to say those simple, exquisite words. She'd shared her body with him, given her innocence and her trust. Now she wanted to share her emotions. Love, she believed, was meant to be given freely, without conditions. Yet she knew him well enough to understand that step would have to be taken by him first. His nature demanded it. Another man might be flattered, pleased, even relieved to have a woman state her feelings so easily. Grant, Gennie reflected, would feel cornered.

Lying still, watching him, she wondered if it had been a woman who had caused him to isolate himself. Gennie felt certain it had been pain or disillusionment that had made him so determined to be unapproachable. There was a basic kindness in him which he hid, a talent he apparently wasn't using and a warmth he hoarded. Why? With a sigh, she brushed the hair from his forehead. They were his mysteries; she only hoped she had the patience to wait until he was ready to share them.

Warm, content, Gennie snuggled against him, murmuring his name. Grant's answer was an unintelligible mutter as he shifted onto his stomach and buried his face in the pillow. The movement cost Gennie a few more precious inches of mattress.

"Hey!" Laughing, she shoved against his shoulder. "Move over."

No response.

You're a romantic devil, Gennie thought wryly, then pressing her lips to that unbudgeable shoulder, slipped out of the bed. Grant immediately took advantage of all the available space.

A loner, Gennie thought, studying him as he lay crosswise over the twisted sheets. He wasn't a man used to making room for anyone. With a last thoughtful glance, Gennie walked across the hall to shower.

Gradually the sound of running water woke him. Hazy, Grant lay still, sleepily debating how much effort it would take to open his eyes. It was his ingrained habit to put off the moment of waking until it could no longer be avoided.

With his face buried in the pillow, he could smell Gennie. It brought dreamy images to him, images sultry but not quite formed. There were soft, fuzzy-edged pictures that both aroused and soothed.

Barely half awake, Grant shifted enough to discover he was alone in bed. Her warmth was still there—on the sheets, on his skin. He lay steeped in it a moment, not certain why it felt so right, not trying to reason out the answers.

He remembered the feel of her, the taste, the way her pulse would leap under the touch of his finger. Had there ever been a woman who had made him want so badly? Who could make him comfortable one moment and wild the next? How close was he to the border between want and need, or had he already crossed it?

They were more questions he couldn't deal with—not now while his mind was still clouded with sleep and with Gennie. He needed to shake off the first and distance himself from the second before he could find any answers.

Groggy, Grant sat up, running a hand over his face as Gennie came back in.

"Morning." With her hair wrapped in a towel and Grant's robe belted loosely at her waist, Gennie dropped onto the edge of the bed. Linking her hands behind his neck, she leaned over and kissed him. She smelled of his soap and shampoo—something that made the easy kiss devastatingly intimate. Even as this began to soak into him, she drew away to give him a friendly smile. "Awake yet?"

"Nearly." Because he wanted to see her hair, Grant pulled the towel from her head and let it drop to the floor. "Have you been up long?"

"Only since you pushed me out of bed." She laughed when his brows drew together. "That's not much of an exaggeration. Want some coffee?"

"Yeah." As she rose, Grant took her hand, holding

it until her smile became puzzled. What did he want to say to her? Grant wondered. What did he want to tell her—or himself? He wasn't certain of anything except the knowledge that whatever was happening inside him was already too far advanced to stop.

"Grant?"

"I'll be down in a minute," he mumbled, feeling foolish. "I'll fix breakfast this time."

"All right." Gennie hesitated, wondering if he would say whatever he'd really meant to say, then she left him alone.

Grant remained in bed a moment, listening to the sound of her footsteps on his stairs. Her footsteps—his stairs. Somehow, the line of demarcation was smearing. He wasn't certain he'd be able to lie in his bed again without thinking of her curled beside him.

But he'd had other women, Grant reminded himself. He'd enjoyed them, appreciated them. Forgotten them. Why was it he was so certain there was nothing about Gennie he'd forget? Nothing, down to that small, faint birthmark he'd found on her hip—a half moon he could cover with his pinkie. Foolishly it had pleased him to discover it—something he knew no other man had seen or touched.

He was acting like an idiot, he told himself—enchanted by the fact that he was her first lover, obsessed with the idea of being her last, her only. He needed to be alone for a while, that was all, to put his feelings back in perspective. The last thing he wanted was to start tying strings on her, and in turn, on himself.

Rising, he rummaged in his drawers until he found

a pair of cutoffs. He'd fix breakfast, send her on her way, then get back to work.

But when he reached the bottom of the stairs, he smelled the coffee, heard her singing. Grant was struck with a powerful wave of *déjà vu*. He could explain it, he told himself he could explain it because it had been just like this the first morning after he'd met her. But it wasn't that—that was much, much too logical for the strength of the feeling that swamped him. It was more than an already seen—it was a sensation of rightness, of always, of pleasure so simple it stung. If he walked into that kitchen a hundred times, year after year, it would never seem balanced, never seem whole, unless she was waiting for him.

Grant paused in the doorway to watch her. The coffee was hot and ready as she stretched up for the mugs that he could reach easily. The sun shot light into her hair, teasing out those deep red hints until they shimmered, flame on velvet. She turned, catching her breath in surprise when she saw him, then smiling.

"I didn't hear you come down." She swung her hair behind her shoulder as she began to pour coffee. "It's gorgeous out. The rain's got everything gleaming and the ocean's more blue than green. You wouldn't know there'd ever been a storm." Taking a mug in each hand, she turned back to him. Though she'd intended to cross to him, the look in his eyes stopped her. Puzzlement quickly became tension. Was he angry? she wondered. Why? Perhaps he was already regretting what had happened. Why had she been so foolish as to think what had been between them had been as special, as unique for him as it had been for her?

Her fingers tightened on the handles. She wouldn't let him apologize, make excuses. She wouldn't cause a scene. The pain was real, physically real, but she told herself to ignore it. Later, when she was alone, she would deal with it. But now she would face him without tears, without pleas.

"Is something wrong?" Was that her voice, so calm, so controlled?

"Yeah, something's wrong."

Her fingers held the mugs so tightly she wondered that the handles didn't snap off. Still, it kept her hands from shaking. "Maybe we should sit down."

"I don't want to sit down." His voice was sharp as a slap but she didn't flinch. She watched as he paced to the sink and leaned against it, muttering and swearing. Another time the Grantlike gesture would have amused her, but now she only stood and waited. If he was going to hurt her, let him do it quickly, at once, before she fell apart. He whirled, almost violently, and stared at her accusingly. "Damn it, Gennie, I've had my head lopped off."

It was her turn to stare. Her fingers went numb against the stoneware. Her pulse seemed to stop long enough to make her head swim before it began to race. The color drained from her face until it was like porcelain against the glowing green of her eyes. On another oath, Grant dragged a hand through his hair.

"You're spilling the coffee," he muttered, then stuck his hands in his pockets.

"Oh." Gennie looked down foolishly at the tiny twin puddles that were forming on the floor, then set down the mugs. "I'll—I'll wipe it up."

"Leave it." Grant grabbed her arm before she

could reach for a towel. "Listen, I feel like someone's just given me a solid right straight to the gut—the kind that doubles you over and makes your head ring at the same time. I feel that way too often when I look at you." When she said nothing, he took her other arm and shook. "In the first place I never asked to have you walk into my life and mess up my head. The last thing I wanted was for you to get in my way, but you did. So now I'm in love with you, and I can tell you, I'm not crazy about the idea."

Gennie found her voice, though she wasn't quite certain what to do with it. "Well," she managed after a moment, "that certainly puts me in my place."

"Oh, she wants to make jokes." Disgusted, Grant released her to storm over to the coffee. Lifting a mug, he drained half the contents, perversely pleased that it scalded his throat. "Well, laugh this off," he suggested as he slammed the mug down again and glared. "You're not going anywhere until I figure out what the hell I'm going to do about you."

Struggling against conflicting emotions of amusement, annoyance, and simple wonder, she put her hands on her hips. The movement shifted the too-big robe so that it threatened to slip off of one shoulder. "Oh, really? So you're going to figure out what to do about me, like I was an inconvenient head cold."

"Damned inconvenient," he muttered.

"You may not have noticed, but I'm a grown woman with a mind of my own, accustomed to making my own decisions. You're not going to *do* anything about me," she told him as her temper began to overtake everything else. She jabbed a finger at him, and the gap in the robe widened. "If you're in love with me, that's your problem. I have one of my own because I'm in love with you.''

''Terrific!'' he shouted at her. ''That's just terrific. We'd both have been better off if you'd waited out that storm in a ditch instead of coming here.''

''You're not telling me anything I don't already know,'' Gennie retorted, then spun around to leave the room.

''Just a minute.'' Grant had her arm again and backed her into the wall. ''You're not going anywhere until this is settled.''

''It's settled!'' Tossing her hair out of her face, she glared at him. ''We're in love with each other and I wish you'd go jump off that cliff. If you had any finesse—''

''I don't.''

''Any sensitivity,'' she continued, ''you wouldn't announce that you were in love with someone in the same tone you'd use to frighten small children.''

''I'm not in love with someone!'' he shouted at her, infuriated because she was right and he couldn't do a thing about it. ''I'm in love with you, and damn it, I don't like it.''

''You've made that abundantly clear.'' She straightened her shoulders and lifted her chin.

''Don't pull that regal routine on me,'' Grant began. Her eyes sharpened to dagger points. Her skin flushed majestically. Abruptly he began to laugh. When she tossed her head back in fury, he simply collapsed against her. ''Oh, God, Gennie, I can't take it when you look at me as though you were about to have me tossed in the dungeon.''

''Get off of me, you ass!'' Incensed, insulted, she

shoved against him, but he only held her tighter. Only quick reflexes saved him from a well-aimed knee at a strategic point.

"Hold on." Still chuckling, he pressed his mouth to hers. Then as abruptly as his laughter had begun, it stilled. With the gentleness he so rarely showed, his hands came up to frame her face, and she was lost. "Gennie." With his lips still on hers he murmured her name so that the sound of it shivered through her. "I love you." He combed his fingers through her hair, drawing her head back so that their eyes met. "I don't like it, I may never get used to it, but I love you." With a sigh, he brought her close again. "You make my head swim."

With her cheek against his chest, Gennie closed her eyes. "You can take time to get used to it," she murmured. "Just promise you won't ever be sorry it happened."

"Not sorry," he agreed on a long breath. "A little crazed, but not sorry." As he ran a hand down her hair, Grant felt a fresh need for her, softer, calmer than before but no less vibrant. He nuzzled into her neck because he seemed to belong there. "Are you really in love with me, or did you say that because I made you mad?"

"Both. I decided this morning I'd have to bend to your ego and let you tell me first."

"Is that so?" With his brows drawn together, he tilted her head back again. "My ego."

"It tends to get in the way because it's rather over-sized." She smiled, sweetly. In retaliation, he crushed his mouth to hers.

"You know," he managed after a moment. "I've lost my appetite for breakfast."

Smiling again, she tilted her face back to his. "Have you really?"

"Mmmm. And I don't like to mention it..." He took his fingertips to the lapel of the robe, toying with it before he slid them down to the belt. "But I didn't say you could use my robe."

"Oh, that was rude of me." The smile became saucy. "Would you like it back now?"

"No hurry." He slipped his hand into hers and started toward the steps. "You can wait until we get upstairs."

From his bedroom window, Grant watched her drive away. It was early afternoon now, and the sun was brilliant. He needed some distance from her—perhaps she needed some from him as well. That's what he told himself even while he wondered how long he could stay away.

There was work waiting for him in the studio above his head, a routine he knew was directly connected to the quality and quantity of his output. He needed that one strict discipline in his life, the hours out of the day and night that were guided by his creativity and his drive. Yet how could he work when his mind was so full of her, when his body was still warm from hers?

Love. He'd managed to avoid it for so many years, then he had thoughtlessly opened the door. It had barged in on him, Grant reflected, uninvited, unwelcomed. Now he was vulnerable, dependent—all the things he'd once promised himself he'd never be again. If he could change it, he was sure he would. He had lived by his own rules, his own judgment, his own needs for so long he wasn't certain he was willing or able to make the compromises love entailed.

He would end up hurting her, Grant thought grimly, and the pain would ricochet back on him. That was the inevitable fate of all lovers. What did they want from each other? Shaking his head, Grant turned from the window. For now, time and affection were enough, but that would change. What would happen when the demands crept in, the strings? Would he bolt? He had no business falling in love with someone like Gennie, whose life-style was light-years away from the one he had chosen, whose very innocence made her that much more susceptible to hurt.

She'd never be content to live with him there on his isolated finger of land, and he'd never ask her to. He couldn't give up his peace for the parties, the cameras, the social whirl. If he'd been more like Shelby…

Grant thought of his sister and her love for crowds, people, noise. Each of them had compensated in their own way for the trauma of losing their father in such a hideous, public fashion. But after fifteen years, the scars were still there. Perhaps Shelby had healed more cleanly, or perhaps her love for Alan MacGregor was strong enough to overcome that nagging fear. The fear of exposure, of losing, of depending.

He remembered Shelby's visit to him before she made her decision to marry Alan. She'd been miserable, afraid. He'd been rough on her because he'd wanted to hold her, to let her weep out the memories that haunted them both. He'd spoken the truth because the truth was what she'd needed to hear, but Grant wasn't certain he could live by it.

"Are you going to shut yourself off from life because of something that happened fifteen years ago?"

He'd asked her that, scathingly, when she'd sat in his kitchen with her eyes brimming over. And he remembered her angry, intuitive, *"Haven't you?"*

In his own way he had, though his work and the love of it kept him permanently connected with the world. He drew for people, for their pleasure and entertainment, because in a fashion perhaps only he himself understood, he liked them—their flaws and strengths, their foolishness and sanity. He simply wouldn't be crowded by them. And he'd refused, successfully until Gennie, to be too deeply involved with anyone on a one to one level. It was so simple to deal with humanity on a general scope. The pitfalls occurred when you narrowed it down.

Pitfalls, he thought with a snort. He'd fallen into a big one. He was already impatient to have her back with him, to hear her voice, to see her smile at him.

She'd be setting up now for the watercolor she'd told him she was going to begin. Maybe she'd still be wearing the shirt Grant had lent her. Her own had been torn beyond repair. Without effort, he could picture her setting up her easel near the inlet. Her hair would be brushed away from her face to fall behind her. His shirt would be hanging past her hips....

And while she was getting her work done, he was standing around mooning like a teenager. On a sound of frustration, Grant strode into the hall just as the phone began to ring. He started to ignore it, something he did easily, then changed his mind and loped down the stairs. He kept only one phone, in the kitchen, because he refused to be disturbed by anything while he was in his studio or in his bed. Grant snatched the receiver from the wall and leaned against the doorway.

"Yeah?"

"Grant Campbell?"

Though he'd only met the man once, Grant had no trouble identifying the voice. It was distinctive, even without the slight slur it cast on the *Campbell*. "Hello, Daniel."

"You're a hard man to reach. Been out of town?"

"No." Grant grinned. "I don't always answer the phone."

The snort Daniel gave caused Grant's grin to widen. He could imagine the big MacGregor sitting in his private tower room, smoking one of his forbidden cigars behind his massive desk. Grant had caricatured him just that way, then had slipped the sketch to Shelby during her wedding reception. Absently he reached for a bag of corn chips on the counter and ripped them open.

"How are you?"

"Fine. More than fine." Daniel's booming voice took on hints of pride and arrogance. "I'm a grandfather—two weeks ago."

"Congratulations."

"A boy," Daniel informed him, taking a satisfied puff on his thick, Cuban cigar. "Seven pounds, four ounces, strong as a bull. Robert MacGregor Blade. They'll be calling him Mac. Good stock." He took a deep breath that strained the buttons on his shirt. "The boy has my ears."

Grant listened to the rundown on the newest MacGregor with a mixture of amusement and affection. His sister had married into a family that he personally found irresistible. He knew pieces of them would be popping up in his strip for years to come. "How's Rena?"

"Came through like a champ." Daniel bit down on his cigar. "Of course, I knew she would. Her mother was worried. Females."

He didn't mention it was he who had insisted on chartering a plane the minute he'd learned Serena had gone into labor. Or that he had paced the waiting room like a madman while his wife, Anna, had calmly finished the embroidery on a baby blanket.

"Justin stayed with her the whole time." There was just a touch of resentment in the words—enough to tell Grant the hospital staff had barred the MacGregor's way into the delivery room. And probably hadn't had an easy time of it.

"Has Shelby seen her nephew yet?"

"Off on their honeymoon during the birthing," Daniel told him with a wheezy sigh. It was difficult for him to understand why his son and daughter-in-law hadn't canceled their plans to be on hand for such a momentous occasion. "But then, she and Alan are making up for it this weekend. That's why I called. We want you to come down, boy. The whole family's coming, the new babe, too. Anna's fretting to have all the children around again. You know how women are."

He knew how Daniel was, and grinned again. "Mothers need to fuss, I imagine."

"Aye, that's it. And with a new generation started,

she'll be worse than ever.'' Daniel cast a wary eye at his closed door. You never knew when someone might be listening. ''Now, then, you'll come, Friday night.''

Grant thought of his schedule and did some quick mental figuring. He had an urge to see his sister again, and the MacGregors. More, he felt the need to take Gennie to the people whom, without knowing why, he considered family. ''I could come down for a couple of days, Daniel, but I'd like to bring someone.''

''Someone?'' Daniel's senses sharpened. He leaned forward with the cigar smoldering in his hand. ''Who might this someone be?''

Recognizing the tone, Grant crunched on a corn chip. ''An artist I know who's doing some painting in New England, in Windy Point at the moment. I think she'd be interested in your house.''

She, Daniel thought with an irrepressible grin. Just because he'd managed to comfortably establish his children didn't mean he had to give up the satisfying hobby of matchmaking. Young people needed to be guided in such matters—or shoved along. And Grant—though he was a Campbell—was by way of being family....

''An artist...aye, that's interesting. Always room for one more, son. Bring her along. An artist,'' he repeated, tapping out his cigar. ''Young and pretty, too, I'm sure.''

''She's nearly seventy,'' Grant countered easily, crossing his ankles as he leaned against the wall. ''A little dumpy, has a face like a frog. Her paintings are timeless, tremendous emotional content and physicality. I'm crazy about her.'' He paused, imagining Daniel's wide face turning a deep puce. "Genuine emotion transcends age and physical beauty, don't you agree?"

Daniel choked, then found his voice. The boy needed help, a great deal of help. "You come early Friday, son. We'll need some time to talk." He stared hard at the bookshelf across the room. "Seventy, you say?"

"Close. But then true sensuality is ageless. Why just last night she and I—"

"No, don't tell me," Daniel interrupted hastily. "We'll have a long talk when you get here. A long talk," he added after a deep breath. "Has Shelby met— No, never mind," he decided. "Friday," Daniel said in a firmer tone. "We'll see about all this on Friday."

"We'll be there." Grant hung up, then leaning against the doorjamb, laughed until he hurt. That should keep the old boy on his toes until Friday, Grant thought. Still grinning, he headed for the stairs. He'd work until dark—until Gennie.

Chapter Nine

Gennie had never known herself to be talked into anything so quickly. Before she knew what was happening, she was agreeing to pack her painting gear and a suitcase and fly off to spend a weekend with people she didn't know.

Part of the reason, she realized when she had a moment to sort it out, was that Grant was enthusiastic about the MacGregors. She learned enough about him in little more than a week to know that he rarely felt genuine affection for anyone—enough affection at any rate to give up his precious privacy and his time. She had agreed primarily because she simply wanted to be where he was, next because she was caught up in his pleasure. And finally because she wanted to see him under a different set of circumstances, interacting with people, away from his isolated spot on the globe.

She would meet his sister. The fact that he had one

had come as a surprise. Though she admitted it was foolish, Gennie had had a picture of Grant simply popping into the world as an adult, by himself, already prepared to fight for the right to his place and his privacy.

Now she began to wonder about his childhood—what had formed him? What had made him into the Grant Campbell she knew? Had he been rich or poor, outgoing or introverted? Had he been happy, loved, ignored? He rarely talked about his family, his past...for that matter, of his present.

Oddly, because the answers were so important, she couldn't ask the questions. Gennie found she needed that step to come from him, as proof of the love he said he felt. No, perhaps proof was the wrong word, she mused. She believed he loved her, in his way, but she wanted the seal. To her, there was no separating trust from love, because one without the other was just an empty word. She didn't believe in secrets.

From childhood until her sister's death, Gennie had had that one special person to share everything with—all her doubts, insecurities, wishes, dreams. Losing Angela had been like losing part of herself, a part she was only beginning to feel again. It was the most natural thing in the world for her to give that trust and affection to Grant. Where she loved, she loved without boundaries.

Beneath the joy she felt was a quiet ache that came from knowing he had yet to open to her. Until he did, Gennie felt their future extended no further than the moment. She forced herself to accept that, because the thought of the moment without him was unbearable.

Grant glanced over as he turned onto the narrow cliff road that led to the MacGregor estate. He glimpsed Gennie's profile, the quiet expression, the eyes dreamy and not quite happy. "What're you thinking?"

She turned her head, and with her smile the wisp of sadness vanished. "That I love you."

It was so simple. It made his knees weak. Needing to touch her, Grant pulled onto the shoulder of the road and stopped. She was still smiling when he cupped her face in his hands, and her lashes lowered in anticipation of the kiss.

Softly, with a reverence he never expected to feel, he brushed his lips over her cheeks, first one, then the other. Her breath caught in her throat to lodge with her heart. His rare spurts of gentleness never failed to undo her. Anything, everything he might have asked of her at that moment, she would have given without hesitation. The whisper of his lashes against her skin bound her to him more firmly than any chain.

Her name was only a sigh as he trailed kisses over her closed lids. With her tremble, his thoughts began to swirl. What was this magic she cast over him? It glittered one instant, then pulsed the next. Was it only his imagination, or had she always been there, waiting to spring into his life and make him a slave? Was it her softness or her strength that made him want to kill or to die for her? Did it matter?

He knew it should. When a man got pulled in too deeply—by a woman, an ideal, a goal—he became vulnerable. Then the instinct for survival would take second place. Grant had always understood this was what had happened to his father.

But now all he could grasp was that she was so soft, so giving. His.

Lightly, Grant touched his lips to hers. Gennie tilted back her head and opened to him. His fingers tightened on her, his breath quickened, rushing into her mouth just before his tongue. The transition from gentle to desperate was too swift to be measured. Her fingers tangled in his hair to drag him closer while he ravished a mouth more demanding than willing. Caught in the haze, Gennie thought her passion rose higher and faster each time he touched her until one day she would simply explode from a mere look.

"I want you." She felt the words wrench from her. As they slipped from her mouth into his, he crushed her against him in a grip that left all gentleness behind. His lips savaged, warred, absorbed, until they were both speechless. With an inarticulate murmur, Grant buried his face in her hair and fought to find reason.

"Good God, in another minute I'll forget it's still daylight and this is a public road."

Gennie ran her fingers down the nape of his neck. "I already have."

Grant forced the breath in and out of his lungs three times, then lifted his head. "Be careful," he warned quietly. "I have a more difficult time remembering to be civilized than doing what comes naturally. At this moment I'd feel very natural dragging you into the back seat, tearing off your clothes, and loving you until you were senseless."

A thrill rushed up and down her spine, daring her, urging her. She leaned closer until her lips were nearly against his. "One should never go against one's nature."

"Gennie..." His control was so thinly balanced, he could already feel the way her body would heat and soften beneath his. Her scent contradicted the lowering sun and whispered of midnight. When she slid her hands up his chest, he could hear his own heartbeat vibrate against her palm. Her eyes were clouded, yet somehow they held more power. Grant couldn't look away from them. He saw himself a prisoner, exulting in the weight of the chains.

Just as the scales tipped away from reason, the sound of an approaching engine had him swearing and turning his head. Gennie looked over her shoulder as a Mercedes pulled to a halt beside them. The driver was in shadows, so that she had only the impression of dark, masculine looks while the passenger rolled down her window.

A cap of wild red hair surrounding an angular face poked out the opening. The woman leaned her arms on the base of the window and grinned appealingly. "You people lost?"

Grant sent her a narrow-eyed glare, then astonished Gennie by reaching out and twisting her nose between his first two fingers. "Scram."

"Some people just aren't worth helping," the woman stated before she gave a haughty toss of her head and disappeared back inside. The Mercedes purred discreetly, then disappeared around the first curve.

"Grant!" Torn between amusement and disbelief, Gennie stared at him. "Even for you that was unbelievably rude."

"Can't stand busybodies," he said easily as he started the car again.

She let out a gusty sigh as she flopped back against the cushions. "You certainly made that clear enough. I'm beginning to think it was a miracle you didn't just slam the door in my face that first night."

"It was a weak moment."

She slanted a look at him, then gave up. "How close are we? You might want to run off the cast of characters for me so I'll have an idea who…" She trailed off. "Oh, God."

It was incredible, impossible. Wonderful. Stark gray in the last lights of the sun, it was the fairy castle every little girl imagined herself trapped in. It would take a valiant knight to free her from the high stone walls of the tower. That it was here, in this century of rockets and rushing was a miracle in itself.

The structure jutted and spread, and quite simply dominated the cliff on which it stood. No ivy clung to its walls. What ivy would dare encroach? But there were flowers—wild roses, blooms in brambles, haunting colors that stubbornly shouted of summer while the nearby trees were edged with the first breath of fall.

Gennie didn't simply want to paint it. She had to paint it in essentially the same way she had to breathe.

"I thought so," Grant commented.

Dazed, Gennie continued to stare. "What?"

"You might as well have a brush in your hand already."

"I only wish I did."

"If you paint this with half the insight and the

power you used in your study of the cliffs and light-house, you'll have a magnificent piece of work.''

Gennie turned to him then, confused. "But I—you didn't seem to think too much of the painting.''

He snorted as he negotiated the last curve. "Don't be an idiot.''

It never occurred to him that she would need re-assurance. Grant knew his own skills, and accepted with a shrug the fact that he was considered one of the top in his field. What others thought mattered lit-tle, because he knew his own capabilities. He as-sumed Gennie would feel precisely the same about herself.

If he had known the agony she went through before each of her showings, he would have been flabber-gasted. If he had known just how much he had hurt her by his casual comment the day she had finished the painting, he would have been speechless.

Gennie frowned at him, concentrating. "You did like it, then?''

"Like what?''

"The painting,'' she snapped impatiently. "The painting I did in your front yard.''

With their minds working at cross purposes, Grant didn't hear the insecurity in the demand. "Just be-cause I don't paint,'' he began curtly, "doesn't mean I have to be slugged over the head with genius to recognize it.''

They lapsed into silence, neither one certain of the other's mood, or their own.

If he liked the painting, Gennie fumed, why didn't he just say so instead of making her drag it out of him?

Grant wondered if she thought *serious* art was the only worthwhile medium. What the hell would she have to say if he told her he made his living by depicting people as he saw them through cartoons? Funny papers. Would she laugh or throw a fit if she caught a glimpse of his Veronica in the New York *Daily* in a couple of weeks?

They pulled up in front of the house with a jerk of brakes that brought them both back to the moment. "Wait until we get inside," he began, picking up the threads of their earlier conversation. "I only believed half of what I saw myself."

"Apparently everything I've ever read or heard about Daniel MacGregor's true." Gennie stepped out of the car with her eyes trained on the house again. "Forceful, eccentric, a man who makes his own deals his own way. But I'm vague on personal details. His wife's a doctor?"

"Surgeon. There're three children, and as you'll be hearing innumerable times over the weekend, one grandson. My sister married the eldest son, Alan."

"Alan MacGregor.... He's—"

"Senator MacGregor, and in a few years..." With a shrug, he trailed off.

"Ah, yes, you'd have a direct line into the White House if the murmurs about Alan MacGregor's aspirations become fact." She grinned at the man in khakis leaning against the hood of the rented car while the wind played games with his hair. "How would you feel about that?"

Grant gave her an odd smile, thinking of Macintosh. "Things are presently unsettled," he murmured. "But I've always had a rather—wry affection for politics in general.'' Grabbing her hand, he began to walk toward the rough stone steps. ''Then there's Caine, son number two, a lawyer who recently married another lawyer who as it happens, is the sister of Daniel's youngest offspring's husband.''

''I'm not sure I'm keeping up.'' Gennie studied the brass-crowned lion's head that served as a door knocker.

''You have to be a quick study.'' Grant lifted the knocker and let it fall resoundingly. ''Rena married a gambler. She and her husband own a number of casinos and live in Atlantic City.''

Gennie gave him a thoughtful glance. ''For someone who keeps to himself so much, you're well informed.''

''Yeah.'' He grinned at her as the door opened.

The redhead that Gennie recognized from the Mercedes leaned against the thick panel and looked Grant up and down. ''Still lost?''

This time Grant tugged her against him and gave her a hard kiss. ''Apparently you've survived a month of matrimony, but you're still skinny.''

''And compliments still roll trippingly off your tongue,'' she retorted, drawing back. After a moment she laughed and hugged him fiercely. ''Damn, I hate to say it out loud, but it's good to see you.'' Grinning over Grant's shoulder, she pinned Gennie with a curious, not unfriendly glance. ''Hi, I'm Shelby.''

Grant's sister, Gennie realized, thrown off by the total lack of any familial resemblance. She had the impression of hordes of energy inside a long lean body, unruly fiery curls, and smoky eyes. While Grant had a rugged, unkempt attractiveness, his sister was a combination of porcelain and flame.

"I'm Gennie." She responded instinctively to the smile Shelby shot her before she untangled herself from her brother. "I'm glad to meet you."

"Pushing seventy, hmmm?" Shelby said cryptically to Grant before she clasped Gennie's hand. "We'll have to get to know each other so you can tell me how you tolerate this jerk's company for more than five minutes at a time. Alan's in the throne room with the MacGregor," she continued before Grant could retort. "Has Grant given you a rundown on the inmates?"

"An abbreviated version," Gennie replied, instantly charmed.

"Typical." She hooked her arm through Gennie's. "Well, sometimes it's best to jump in feet first. The most important thing to remember is not to let Daniel intimidate you. What extraction are you?"

"French mostly. Why?"

"It'll come up."

"How was the honeymoon?" Grant demanded, wanting to veer away from the subject that would, indeed, come up.

Shelby beamed at him. "I'll let you know when it's over. How's your cliff?"

"Still standing." He glanced to his left as Justin started down the main stairs. Justin's expression of mild curiosity changed to surprise—something rarely seen on his face—then pleasure.

"Gennie!" He took the rest of the stairs in quick, long strides then whirled her into his arms.

"Justin." Laughing, she hooked her arms around his neck while Grant's eyes narrowed to slits.

"What're you doing here?" they asked together.

Chuckling, he took both of her hands, drawing back for a long, thorough study. "You're beautiful," he told her. "Always."

Grant watched her flush with pleasure and experienced the first genuine jealousy of his life. He found it a very unpleasant sensation. "It seems," he said in a dangerously mild voice that had Shelby's brows lifting, "you two have met."

"Yes, of course," Gennie began before realization dawned. "The gambler!" she exclaimed. "Oh, I never put it together. Rena—Serena. Hearing you were getting married was a shock in itself, I hated to miss the wedding...and a father!" She threw her arms around him again, laughing. "Good God, I'm surrounded by cousins."

"Cousins?" Grant echoed.

"On my French side," Justin said wryly. "A dis tant connection, carefully overlooked by all but a—" he tilted Gennie's face to his "—select few."

"Aunt Adelaide's a stuffy old bore," Gennie said precisely.

"Are you following this?" Shelby asked Grant.

"Barely," he muttered.

With another laugh, Gennie held out her hand to him. "To keep it simple, Justin and I are cousins, third, I think. We happened to meet about five years ago at one of my shows in New York."

"I wasn't—ah—close to that particular end of my family," Justin continued. "Some chance comment led to another until we ferreted out the connection."

When Justin smiled down at Gennie, Grant saw it. The eyes, the green eyes. Man, woman, they were almost identical to the shade. For some obscure reason that, more than the explanations, had him relaxing the muscles that had gone taut the moment Justin had scooped her up. The black sheep, he realized, who'd outdone them all.

"Fascinating," Shelby decided. "All those clichés about small worlds are amazingly apt. Gennie's here with Grant."

"Oh?" Justin glanced over, meeting Grant's dark, appraising eyes. As a gambler he habitually sized up the people he met and stored them into compartments. At Shelby's wedding the month before, Justin had found him a man with wit and secrets who refused to be stored anywhere. They'd gotten along easily, perhaps because the need for privacy was inherent in both of them. Now, remembering Daniel's blustering description of Grant's weekend companion, Justin controlled a grin. "Daniel mentioned you were bringing—an artist."

Grant recognized, as few would have, the gleam of humor in Justin's eyes. "I'm sure he did," he returned in the same conversational tone. "I haven't congratulated you yet on ensuring the continuity of the line."

"And saving the rest of us from the pressure to do so immediately," Shelby finished.

"Don't count on it," a smooth voice warned.

Gennie looked up to see a blond woman descending the steps, carrying a bundle in a blue blanket.

"Hello, Grant. It's nice to see you again." Serena cradled her son in one arm as she leaned over to kiss

Grant's cheek. "It was sweet of you to answer the royal summons."

"My pleasure." Unable to resist, he nudged the blanket aside with a finger.

So little. Babies had always held a fascination for him—their perfection in miniature. This one was smooth-cheeked and wide awake, staring back at him with dark blue eyes he thought already hinted of the violet of his mother's. Perhaps Mac had Daniel's ears and Serena's eyes, but the rest of him was pure Blade. He had the bones of a warrior, Grant thought, and the striking black hair of his Comanche blood.

Looking beyond her son, Serena studied the woman who was watching Grant with a quiet thoughtfulness. It surprised her to see her husband's eyes in a feminine face. Waiting until those eyes shifted to hers, she smiled. "I'm Rena."

"Gennie's a friend of Grant's," Justin announced, easily slipping an arm around his wife's shoulders, "She also happens to be my cousin." Before Serena could react to the first surprise, he hit her with the second. "Genviève Grandeau."

"Oh, those marvelous paintings!" she exclaimed while Shelby's eyes widened.

"Damn it, Grant." After giving him a disgusted look, Shelby turned to Gennie. "Our mother had two of your landscapes. I badgered her into giving me one as a wedding present. *Evening*," she elaborated. "I want to build a house around it."

Pleased, Gennie smiled at her. "Then maybe you'll help me convince Mr. MacGregor that I should paint his house."

"Just watch how you have to twist his arm," Serena said dryly.

"What is this, a summit meeting?" Alan demanded as he strode down the hall. "It's one thing to be the advance man," he continued as he cupped a hand around the back of his wife's neck, "and another to be the sacrificial lamb. Dad's doing a lot of moaning and groaning about this family scattering off in all directions."

"With Caine getting the worst of it," Serena put in.

"Yeah." Alan grinned once, appealingly. "Too bad he's late." His gaze shifted to Gennie then— dark, intense eyes, a slow, serious smile. "We've met...." He hesitated briefly as he flipped through his mental file of names and faces. "Geneviève Grandeau."

A little surprised, Gennie smiled back at him. "A very quick meeting at a very crowded charity function about two years ago, Senator."

"Alan," he corrected. "So you're Grant's artist." He sent Grant a look that had lights of humor softening his eyes. "I must say you outshine even Grant's description of you. Shall we all go in and join the MacGregor before he starts to bellow?"

"Here." Justin took the baby from Serena in an expert move. "Mac'll soften him up."

"What description?" Gennie murmured to Grant as they started down the wide hall.

She saw the grin tug at his mouth before he slipped an arm around her shoulders. "Later."

Gennie immediately saw why Shelby had referred to it as the throne room. The expansive floor space was covered with a scarlet rug. All the woodwork was lushly carved while magnificent paintings hung in ornate frames. There was the faint smell of candlewax, though no candles were lit. Lamps glowed to aid the soft light of dusk that trailed in the many mullioned windows.

She saw at a glance that the furniture was ancient and wonderful, all large-scaled and perfect in the enormous room. Logs were laid and ready in the huge fireplace in anticipation of the chill that could come during the evenings when summer warred with autumn.

But the room, superb in its unique fashion, was nothing compared to the man holding court from his high-backed Gothic chair. Massive, with red hair thick and flaming, he watched the procession file into the room with narrowed, sharp blue eyes in a wide, lined face.

To Gennie, he looked like a general or a king—both, perhaps, in the way of centuries past where the monarch led his people into battle. One huge hand tapped the wooden arm of his chair while the other held a glass half-filled with liquid. He looked fierce enough to order executions arbitrarily. Her fingers itched for a pad and a pencil.

"Well," he said in a deep, rumbling voice that made the syllable an accusation.

Shelby was the first to go to him, bravely, Gennie thought, to give him a smacking kiss on the mouth. "Hi, Grandpa."

He reddened at that and struggled with the pleasure the title gave him. "So you decided to give me a moment of your time."

"I felt duty bound to pay my respects to the newest MacGregor first."

As if on cue, Justin strode over to arrange Mac in the crook of Daniel's arm. Gennie watched the fierce giant turn into a marshmallow. "There's a laddie," he crooned, holding out his glass to Shelby, then chucking the baby under the chin. When the baby grabbed his thick finger, he preened like a rooster. "Strong as an ox." He grinned foolishly at the room in general, then zeroed in on Grant. "Well, Campbell, so you've come. You see here," he began, jiggling the baby, "why the MacGregors could never be conquered. Strong stock."

"Good blood," Serena murmured, taking the baby from the proud grandfather.

"Get a drink for the Campbell," he ordered. "Now, where's this artist?" His eyes darted around the room, landed on Gennie and clung. She thought she saw surprise, quickly veiled, then amusement as quickly suppressed, tug at the corners of his mouth.

"Daniel MacGregor," Grant said with wry formality, "Genviève Grandeau."

A flicker of recognition ran across Daniel's face before he rose to his rather amazing height and held out his hand. "Welcome."

Gennie's hand was clasped, then enveloped. She had simultaneous impressions of strength, compassion, and stubbornness.

"You have a magnificent home, Mr. MacGregor," she said, studying him candidly. "It suits you."

He gave a great bellow of a laugh that might have shook the windows. "Aye. And three of your paintings hang in the west wing." His eyes slid briefly to

Grant's before they came back to hers. "You carry your age well, lass."

She gave him a puzzled look as Grant choked over his Scotch. "Thank you."

"Get the artist a drink," he ordered, then gestured for her to sit in the chair next to his. "Now, tell me why you're wasting your time with a Campbell."

"Gennie happens to be a cousin of mine," Justin said mildly as he sat on the sofa beside his son. "On the aristocratic French side."

"A cousin." Daniel's eyes sharpened, then an expression that could only be described as cunning pleasure spread over his face. "Aye, we like to keep things in the family. Grandeau—a good strong name. You've the look of a queen, with a bit of sorceress thrown in."

"That was meant as a compliment," Serena told her as she handed Gennie a vermouth in crystal.

"So I've been told." Gennie sent Grant an easy look over the rim of her glass. "One of my ancestors had an—encounter with a gypsy resulting in twins."

"Gennie has a pirate in her family tree as well," Justin put in.

Daniel nodded in approval. "Strong blood. The Campbells need all the help they can get."

"Watch it, MacGregor," Shelby warned as Grant gave him a brief, fulminating look.

There were undercurrents here to confuse a newcomer, but not so subtle Gennie didn't catch the drift. He's trying to arrange a betrothal, she thought, and struggled with a chuckle. Seeing Grant's dark, annoyed look only made it more difficult to maintain her composure. The game was irresistible. "The

Grandeaus can trace their ancestry back to a favored courtesan of Philip IV le Bel.'' She caught Shelby's look of amused respect. In the time it took for eyes to meet, a bond was formed.

Though he was enjoying the signals being flashed around the room, Alan remembered all too well being in the position Grant was currently…enjoying. ''I wonder what's keeping Caine,'' he said casually, aware how the comment would shift his father's focus.

''Hah!'' Daniel downed half his drink in one swallow. ''The boy's too bound up in his law to give his mother a moment's thought.''

At Gennie's lifted brows, Serena curled her legs under her. ''My mother's still at the hospital,'' she explained, a smile lurking around her mouth. ''I'm sure she'll be devastated if she arrives before Caine does.''

''She worries about her children,'' Daniel put in with a sniff. ''I try to tell her that they have lives of their own to lead, but a mother's a mother.''

Serena rolled her eyes and said something inarticulate into her glass. It was enough, however, to make Daniel's face flush. Before he could retort, the sound of the knocker thudding against wood vibrated against the walls.

''I'll get it,'' Alan said, feeling that would give him a moment to warn Caine of their father's barometer.

Because he felt a certain kinship with Caine at that moment, Grant turned to Daniel in an attempt to shift his mood. ''Gennie was fascinated by the house,'' he began. ''She's hoping to persuade you into letting her paint it.''

Daniel's reaction was immediate. Not unlike his reaction to his grandson, he preened. "Well, now, we should be able to arrange something that suits us both."

A Grandeau of the MacGregor fortress. He knew the financial value of such a painting, not to mention the value to his pride. The legacy for his grandchildren.

"We'll talk," he said with a decisive nod just as the latest MacGregors came into the room. Daniel cast a look in their direction. "Hah!"

Gennie saw a tall, lean man with the air of an intelligent wolf stroll in. Were all the MacGregors such superb examples of the human species? she wondered. There was power there, the same as she had sensed in Alan and Serena. Because it wasn't wholly the same as Daniel's, Gennie speculated on their mother. Just what sort of woman was she?

Then her attention was caught by the woman who entered with Caine, Justin's sister. Gennie glanced at her cousin to see him eyeing his sister with a slight frown. And she understood why. The tension Caine and Diana had brought into the room was palpable.

"We got held up in Boston," Caine said easily, shrugging off his father's scowl before he walked over to look at his nephew. The rather hard lines of his face softened when he glanced up at his sister. "Good job, Rena."

"You might call when you're going to be late," Daniel stated. "So your mother wouldn't worry."

Caine took in the room with a sweeping glance, noticing his mother's absence, then lifted an ironic brow. "Of course."

"It's my fault," Diana said in a low voice. "An appointment ran over."

"You remember Grant," Serena began, hoping to smooth over what looked like very rough edges.

"Yes, of course." Diana managed a smile that didn't reach her large, dark eyes.

"And Grant's guest," Serena continued with the wish that she could have a few moments alone with Diana. "Who turns out to be a cousin of yours, Genviève Grandeau."

Diana stiffened instantly, her face cool and expressionless when she turned to Gennie.

"Cousin?" Caine said curiously as he moved to stand beside his wife.

"Yes." Gennie spoke up, wanting to ease something she didn't understand. "We met once," she went on, offering a smile, "when we were children, at a birthday party, I think. My family was in Boston, visiting."

"I remember," Diana murmured.

Though she tried, Gennie could remember nothing she had done at the silly little party to warrant the cool, remote look Diana gave her. Her reaction was instinctive. Her chin angled slightly, her brows arched. With the regal look settling over her, she sipped her vermouth. "As Shelby pointed out, it's a small world."

Caine recognized Diana's expression, and though it exasperated him, he laid a reassuring hand on her shoulder. "Welcome, cousin," he said to Gennie, giving her an unexpectedly charming smile. He turned to Grant then, and the smile tilted mischievously. "I'd really like to talk to you—about frogs."

Grant responded with a lightning fast grin. "Anytime."

Before Gennie could even begin to sort this out, or the laughter that followed it, a small, dark woman came into the room. Here was the other end of the power. Gennie sensed it immediately as the woman became the center of attention. There was a strength about her, and the serious, attractive looks that she had passed on to her eldest son. She carried a strange dignity, though her hair was slightly mussed and her suit just a bit wrinkled.

"I'm so glad you could come," she said to Gennie when they were introduced. Her hands were small and capable, and Gennie discovered, chilled. "I'm sorry I wasn't here when you arrived. I was—detained at the hospital."

She's lost a patient. Without knowing how she understood it, Gennie was certain. Instinctively, she covered their joined hands with her free one. "You have a wonderful family, Mrs. MacGregor. A beautiful grandson."

Anna let out a tiny sigh that was hardly audible. "Thank you." She moved to brush a kiss over her husband's cheek. "Let's go in to dinner," she said when he patted her hair. "You all must be starving by now."

The cast of characters was complete, Gennie mused as she rose to take Grant's hand. It was going to be a very interesting weekend.

Chapter Ten

It was late when Gennie lounged in an oversized tub filled with hot, fragrant water. The MacGregors, from Daniel down to Mac, were not an early-to-bed group. She liked them—their boisterousness, their contrasts, their obvious and unapologetic unity. And, with the exception of Diana, they had given her a sense of welcome into their family boundaries.

Thinking of Diana now, Gennie frowned and soaped her leg. Perhaps Diana Blade MacGregor was withdrawn by nature. It hadn't taken any insight to see that there was tension between Caine and his wife, and that Diana drew closer into herself because of it, but Gennie felt there had been something more personal in Diana's attitude toward her.

Leave me alone. The signal had been clear as crystal and Gennie had obliged. Not everyone was inherently friendly—not everyone *had* to like her on

sight. Still, it disturbed her that Diana had been neither friendly nor particularly hostile, but simply remote.

Shaking off the mood, she pulled on the old-
fashioned chain to let the water drain. Tomorrow,
she'd spend some time with her new cousins by marriage, and do as many sketches as she could of the
MacGregor home. Perhaps she and Grant would
walk along the cliffs, or take a dip in the pool she'd
heard was at one of the endless, echoing corridors.

She'd never seen Grant so relaxed for such a long
period of time. Oddly, though he was still the remote, arrogant man she'd reluctantly fallen in love
with, he'd been comfortable with the numerous, loud
MacGregors. In one evening she'd discovered yet
something more about him: He enjoyed people, being with them, talking with them—as long as it remained on his terms.

Gennie had caught the tail end of a conversation
Grant had been having with Alan after dinner. It had
been political, and obviously in depth, which had
surprised her. That had surprised her no more, however, than watching him jiggle Serena's baby on his
knee while he carried on a debate with Caine in-
volving a controversial trial waging in the Boston
courts. Then he had badgered Shelby into a heated
argument over the social significance of the afternoon soap opera.

With a shake of her head, Gennie patted her skin
dry. Why did a man with such eclectic tastes and
opinions live like a recluse? Why did a man obviously at ease in a social situation scare off stray tourists? An enigma.

Gennie slipped into a short silk robe. Yes, he was that, but knowing it and accepting it were entirely different things. The more she learned about him, the more quick peeks she had into the inner man, the more she longed to know.

Patience, just a little more patience, Gennie warned herself as she walked into the adjoining bedroom. The room was huge, the wallpaper old and exquisite. There was an ornate daybed upholstered in rich rose satin and a vanity carved with cupids. It had all the ostentatious charm of the eighteenth century down to the fussy framed embroidery that must have been Anna's work.

Pleasantly tired, Gennie sat on the skirted stool in front of the triple-mirrored vanity and began to brush her hair.

When Grant opened the door, he thought she looked like some fairy princess—part ingenue, part seductress. Her eyes met his in the glass, and she smiled while following through with the last stroke of the brush.

"Take the wrong turn?"

"I took the right one." He closed the door behind him, then flicked the lock.

"Is that so?" Tapping the brush against her palm, Gennie arched a brow. "I thought you had the room down the hall."

"The MacGregors forgot to put something in there." He stood where he was for a moment, pleased just to look at her.

"Oh? What?"

"You." Crossing to her, Grant took the brush from her hand. The scent of her bath drifted through the room. With his eyes on hers in the glass, he began to draw the brush through her hair. "Soft," he murmured. "Everything about you is just too soft to resist."

He could always make her blood heat with his passion, with his demands, but when he was gentle, when his touch was tender, she was defenseless. Her eyes grew wide and cloudy, and remained fixed on his. "Do you want to?" she managed.

There was a slight smile on his face as he continued to sweep the brush through her hair in long, slow strokes. "It wouldn't make any difference, but no, I don't want to resist you, Geneviève. What I want to do..." He followed the path of the brush with his fingers. "Is touch you, taste you, to the absence of everything else. You're not my first obsession," he murmured, with an odd expression in his eyes, "but you're the only one I've been able to touch with my hands, taste with my mouth. You're not the only woman I've loved." He let the brush fall so that his hands were free to dive into her hair. "But you're the only woman I've been in love with."

She knew he spoke no more, no less than the truth. The words filled her with a soaring power. She wanted to share it with him, give back some of the wonder he'd brought to her life. Rising, she turned to face him. "Let me make love to you," she whispered. "Let me try."

The sweetness of the request moved him more than he would have thought possible. But when he reached for her, she put her hands to his chest.

"No." She slid her hands up to his neck, fingers spread. "Let me."

Carefully, watching his face, she began to unbutton his shirt. Her eyes reflected confidence, her fingers were steady, yet she knew she would have to rely on instinct and what he had only begun to teach her. Did you make love to a man as you wanted him to make love to you? She would see.

His wants could be no less than hers, she thought as her fingers skimmed over his skin. Would they be so much different? With a sound that was both of pleasure and approval, she ran her hands down his rib cage, then back up again before she pushed the loosened shirt from his shoulders.

He was lean, almost too lean, but his skin was smooth and tight over his bones. Already it was warming under the passage of her hands. Leaning closer, Gennie pressed her mouth to his heart and felt the quick, unsteady beat. Experimentally, she used the tip of her tongue to moisten. She heard him suck in his breath before the arms around her tightened.

"Gennie..."

"No, I just want to touch you for a little while." She traced the breathless kisses over his chest and listened to the sound of his racing heartbeat.

Grant closed his eyes while the damp, light kisses heated his skin. He fought the urge to drag her to the bed, or to the floor, and tried to find the control she seemed to be asking him for. Her curious fingers roamed, with the uncanny ability to find and exploit weaknesses he'd been unaware he had. All the while she murmured, sighed, promised. Grant wondered if this was the way people quietly lost their sanity.

When she trailed her fingers down slowly to the

snap of his jeans, the muscles in his stomach trembled, then contracted. She heard him groan as he lowered his face to the top of her head. Her throat was dry, her palms damp as she loosened the snap. It was as much from uncertainty as the wish to seduce that she loitered over the process.

His briefs ran low at his hips, snug, and to Gennie, fascinatingly soft. In her quest to learn, she touched him and felt the swift convulsive shudder that wracked his body. So much power, she thought, so much strength. Yet she could make him tremble.

"Lie down with me," she whispered, then tilted back her head to look into eyes dark and opaque with need for her. His mouth rushed down to hers, taking as though he were starving. Even as her senses began to swim, the knowledge of her hold over him expanded. She knew what he wanted from her, and she would give it willingly. But she wanted to give much, much more. And she would.

With her hands on either side of his face, she drew him away. His quick, labored breaths fluttered over her face. "Lie down with me," she repeated, and moved to the bed. She waited until he came to her, then urged him down. The old mattress sighed as she knelt beside him. "I love to look at you." Combing the hair back from his temples, she replaced it with her lips.

And so she began, roaming, wandering with a laziness that made him ache. He felt the satin smoothness of her lips, the rustling silkiness of her robe as she slowly seduced him into helplessness. His skin grew damp from the flick and circle of her tongue and his own need. Around him, seeping into the very air he breathed, was the scent she had bathed in. She sighed, then laid her lips on his, nipping and sucking until he heard nothing but the roaring in his own head.

Her body merged with his as she lay down on him and began to do torturous things to his neck with her teeth and tongue. He tried to say her name, but could manage only a groan as his hands—always so sure—fumbled for her.

Her skin was as damp as his and drove him mad as it slid over him, lower and lower so that her lips could taste and her hands enjoy. She'd never known anything so heady as the freedom power and passion gave when joined together. It had a scent—musky, secret—she drew it in. Its flavor was the same, and she devoured it. As her tongue dipped lower, she had the dizzying pleasure of knowing her man was absorbed in her.

He seemed no longer to be breathing, but moaning only. She was unaware that her own sighs of pleasure joined his. How beautifully formed he was, was all she could think. How incredible it was that he belonged to her. She was naked now without having felt him tug off her robe. Gennie knew only that his hands stroked over her shoulders, warm, rough, desperate, then dipped to her breasts in a kind of crazed worship.

How much time passed was unknown. Neither of them heard a clock chime the hour from somewhere deep in the house. Boards settled. Outside a bird—perhaps a nightingale—set up a long, pleading call for a lover. A few harmless clouds blew away from the moon. Neither of them was aware of any sound, any movement outside of that wide, soft bed.

Her mouth found his again, greedy and urgent. Warm breath merged, tongues tangled. Minds clouded. He murmured into her mouth; a husky plea. His hands gripped her hips as if he were falling.

Gennie slid down and took him inside her, then gasped at the rocketing, terrifying thrill. She shuddered, her body flinging back as she peaked instantly then clung, clung desperately to delirium.

He tried to hold on to that last light of reason as she melted against him, spent. But it was too late. She'd stolen his sanity. All that was animal in him clawed to get out. With more of a growl than a groan, he tossed her onto her back and took her like a madman. When she had thought herself drained, she revitalized, filled with him. Her body went wild, matching the power and speed of his. Higher and higher, faster and faster, hot and heady and dark. They rushed from one summit to a steeper one, until sated, they collapsed into each other.

Still joined, with the light still shining beside the bed, they fell asleep.

It was one of those rare, perfect days. The air was mild, just a bit breezy, while the sun was warm and bright. Gennie had nibbled over the casual, come-when-you-want breakfast while Grant had eaten enough for both of them. He'd wandered away, talking vaguely of a poker game, leaving Gennie free to take her sketch pad outdoors alone. Though, as it happened, she had little solitary time.

She wanted a straight-on view of the house first,

the same view that could be seen first when traveling up the road. Whether Daniel had planned it that way or not—and she felt he had—it was awesome.

She moved past the thorny rose bushes to sit on the grass near a chestnut tree. For a time it was quiet, with only the sound of gulls, land birds, and waves against rock. The sketch began with rough lines boldly drawn, then, unable to resist, Gennie began to refine it—shading, perfecting. Nearly a half hour had passed before a movement caught her eye. Shelby had come out of a side door while Gennie was concentrating on the tower and was already halfway across the uneven yard.

"Hi. Am I going to bother you?"

"No." Gennie smiled as she let the sketchbook drop into her lap. "I'll spend days sketching here if someone doesn't stop me."

"Fabulous, isn't it?" With a limber kind of grace that made Gennie think of Grant, Shelby sat beside her. She studied the sketch in Gennie's lap. "So's that," she murmured, and she, too, thought of Grant. As a child it had infuriated her that she couldn't match his skill with a pencil or crayon. As they had grown older, envy had turned to pride—almost exclusively. "You and Grant have a lot in common."

Pleased at the idea, Gennie glanced down at her own work. "He has quite a bit of talent, doesn't he? Of course I've only seen one impromptu caricature, but it's so obvious. I wonder…why he's not doing anything with it."

It was a direct probe; they both knew it. The statement also told Shelby that Grant hadn't yet confided in the woman beside her. The woman, Shelby was certain, he was in love with. Impatience warred with loyalty. Why the hell was he being such a stubborn idiot? But the loyalty won. "Grant does pretty much as he pleases. Have you known him long?"

"No, not really. Just a couple of weeks." Idly, she plucked a blade of grass and twirled it between her fingers. "My car broke down during a storm on the road leading to the lighthouse." She chuckled as a perfectly clear image of his scowling face flashed through her mind. "Grant wasn't too pleased to find me on his doorstep."

"You mean he was rude, surly, and impossible," Shelby countered, answering Gennie's grin.

"At the very least."

"Thank God some things are consistent. He's crazy about you."

"I don't know who that shocked more, him or me. Shelby..." She shouldn't pry, Gennie thought, but found she had to know something, anything that might give her a key to the inner man. "What was he like, as a boy?"

Shelby stared up at the clouds that drifted harmlessly overhead. "Grant always liked to go off by himself. Occasionally, when I hounded him, he'd tolerate me. He always liked people, though he looks at them in a rather tilted way. His way," she said with a shrug.

Shelby thought of the security they'd lived with as children, the campaigns, the press. And she thought briefly that with Alan, she had stepped right back into the whirlpool. With a little sigh Gennie didn't understand, Shelby leaned back on her elbows.

"He had a monstrous temper, a firm opinion on what was right and what was wrong—for himself and society in general. They weren't always the same things. Still, for the most part he was easygoing and kind, I suppose, for an older brother."

She was frowning up at the sky still, and remaining silent, Gennie watched her. "Grant has a large capacity for love and kindness," Shelby continued, "but he doles it out sparingly and in his own way. He doesn't like to depend on anyone." She hesitated, then looking at Gennie's calm face and expressive eyes, felt she had to give her something. "We lost our father. Grant was seventeen, between being a boy and being a man. It devastated me, and it wasn't until a long time after that I realized it had done the same to him. We were both there when he was killed."

Gennie closed her eyes, thinking of Grant, remembering Angela. This was something she could understand all too well. The guilt, the grief, the shock that never quite went away. "How was he killed?"

"Grant should tell you about that," Shelby said quietly.

"Yes." Gennie opened her eyes. "He should."

Wanting to dispel the mood, and her own memories, Shelby touched her hand. "You're good for him. I could see that right away. Are you a patient person, Gennie?"

"I'm not sure anymore."

"Don't be too patient," she advised with a smile. "Grant needs someone to give him a good swift punch once in a while. You know, when I first met

Alan, I was absolutely determined not to have anything to do with him.''

"Sounds familiar.''

She chuckled. "And he was absolutely determined
I would. He was patient, but—'' she grinned at the
memory "—not too patient. And I'm not half as
nasty as Grant.''

Gennie laughed, then flipped over a page and began to sketch Shelby. "How did you meet Alan?''

"Oh, at a party in Washington.''

"Is that where you're from?''

"I live in Georgetown—we live in Georgetown,''
she corrected. "My shop's there, too.''

Gennie's brow lifted as she drew the subtle line
of Shelby's nose. "What kind of a shop?''

"I'm a potter.''

"Really?'' Interested, Gennie stopped sketching.
"You throw your own clay? Grant never mentioned
it.''

"He never does,'' Shelby said dryly

"There's a bowl in his bedroom,'' Gennie remembered. "In a henna shade with etched wildflowers.
Is that your work?''

"I gave it to him for Christmas a couple of years
ago. I didn't know what he'd done with it.''

"It catches the light beautifully,'' Gennie told her,
noting that Shelby was both surprised and pleased.
"There isn't much else in that lighthouse he even
bothers to dust.''

"He's a slob,'' Shelby said fondly. "Do you want
to reform him?''

"Not particularly.''

"I'm glad. Though I'd hate to have him hear me

say it, I like him the way he is.'' She stretched her arms to the sky. ''I'm going to go in and lose a few dollars to Justin. Ever played cards with him?''

''Only once.'' Gennie grinned. ''It was enough.''

''I know what you mean,'' she murmured as she rose. ''But I can usually bluff Daniel out of enough to make it worthwhile.''

With a last lightning smile, she was off. Thoughtfully, Gennie glanced down at the sketch and sorted through the snatches of information Shelby had given her.

''Frog-faced?'' Caine asked when he met Grant in the hall.

''Beauty's in the eye of the beholder,'' Grant said easily.

With an appreciative grin, Caine leaned against one of the many archways. ''You had Dad going. We all got one of his phone calls, telling us the Campbell was in a bad way and it was our duty—he being by way of family—to help him.'' The grin became wolfish. ''You seem to be getting along all right on your own.''

Grant acknowledged this with a nod. ''The last time I was here, he was trying to match me up with some Judson girl. I didn't want to take any chances.''

''Dad's a firm believer in marriage and procreation.'' Caine's grin faded a bit when he thought of his wife. ''It's funny about your Gennie being Diana's cousin.''

''A coincidence,'' Grant murmured, noting the

troubled expression. "I haven't seen Diana this morning."

"Neither have I," Caine said wryly, then shrugged. "We disagree on a case she's decided to take." The cloud of trouble crossed his face again. "It's difficult being married and in the same profession, particularly when you look at that profession from different angles."

Grant thought of himself and Gennie. Could two people look at art from more opposing views? "I imagine it is. It seemed to me that Gennie made her uncomfortable."

"Diana had it rough as a kid." Dipping his hands in his pockets, Caine brooded into space. "She's still adjusting to it. I'm sorry."

"You don't have to apologize to me. And Gennie's well able to take care of herself."

"I think I'll take a look for Diana." He pulled himself back, then grinning, jerked his head toward the tower steps. "Justin's on a streak, as usual, if you want to risk it."

Outside, Diana moved around the side of the house and into the front garden before she spotted Gennie. Her first instinct was simply to turn away, but Gennie glanced up. Their eyes met. Stiffly, Diana moved across the grass, but unlike Shelby, she didn't sit. "Good morning."

Gennie gave her an equally cool look. "Good morning. The roses are lovely, aren't they?"

"Yes. They won't last much longer." Diana slipped her hands into the deep pockets of her jade-green slacks. "You're going to paint the house."

"I plan to." On impulse, she held the sketch pad up to her cousin. "What do you think?"

Diana studied it and saw all the things that had first impressed her about the structure—the strength, the fairy-tale aura, the superb charm. It moved her. It made her uncomfortable. Somehow the drawing made a bond between them she wanted to avoid. "You're very talented," she murmured. "Aunt Adelaide always sang your praises."

Gennie laughed despite herself. "Aunt Adelaide wouldn't know a Rubens from a Rembrandt, she only thinks she does." She could have bitten her tongue. This woman, she reminded herself, had been raised by Adelaide, and she had no right denigrating her to someone who might be fond of her. "Have you seen her recently?"

"No," Diana said flatly, and handed Gennie back the sketch.

Annoyed, Gennie shaded her eyes and gave Diana a long, thorough study. Casually, Gennie turned over a page, and as she had done with Shelby, began to sketch her. "You don't like me."

"I don't know you," Diana returned coolly.

"True, which makes your behavior all the more confusing. I thought you would be more like Justin."

Infuriated because the easily spoken words stung, Diana glared down at her. "Justin and I have different ways because we led different lives." Whirling, she took three quick strides away before she stopped herself. Why was she acting like a shrew? she demanded, then placed a hand to her stomach. Diana straightened her shoulders, and turned back.

"I'll apologize for being rude, because Justin's fond of you."

"Oh, thank you very much," Gennie said dryly, though she began to feel a slight stir of compassion at the struggle going on in Diana's eyes. "Why don't you tell me why you feel you have to be rude in the first place?"

"I'm simply not comfortable with the Grandeau end of the family."

"That's a narrow view for an attorney," Gennie mused. "And for a woman who only met me once before when we were what—eight, ten years old?"

"You fit in so perfectly," Diana said before she could think. "Adelaide must have told me a dozen times that I was to watch you and behave as you behaved."

"Adelaide has always been a foolish, self-important woman," Gennie returned.

Diana stared at her. Yes, she knew that—now—she simply hadn't thought anyone else in that part of the family did. "You knew everyone there," she continued, though she was beginning to feel like a fool. "And had your hair tied back in a ribbon that matched your dress. It was mint-green organdy. I didn't even know what organdy was."

Because her sympathies were instantly and fully aroused, Gennie rose. She didn't reach out yet, it wouldn't be welcomed. "I'd heard you were Comanche. I waited through that whole silly party for you to do a war dance. I was terribly disappointed when you didn't."

Diana stared at her again for a full thirty seconds. She felt the desperate urge to weep that was coming over her too often lately. Instead, she found herself laughing. "I wish I'd known how—and had had the courage to do it. Aunt Adelaide would have swooned." She stopped, hesitated, then held out her hand. "I'm glad to meet you again—cousin."

Gennie accepted the hand, then took it one step further and pressed her lips to Diana's cheek. "Perhaps, if you give us a chance, you'll find there are some of the Grandeaus who are almost as human as the MacGregors."

Diana smiled. The feeling of family always overwhelmed her just a little. "Yes, perhaps."

When Diana's smile faded, Gennie followed the direction of her gaze and saw Caine standing among the roses. The tension returned swiftly, but had nothing to do with her. "I need to get a new angle for my sketches," she said easily.

Caine waited until Gennie was some distance away before he went to his wife. "You were up early," he said while his eyes roamed over her face. "You look tired, Diana."

"I'm fine," she said too quickly. "Stop worrying about me," she told him as she turned away.

Frustrated, Caine grabbed her arm. "Damn it, you're tying yourself in knots over that case, and—"

"Will you drop that!" she shouted at him. "I know what I'm doing."

"Maybe," Caine said evenly, too evenly. "The point is, you've never taken on murder one before, and the prosecution has a textbook case built up."

"It's a pity you don't have any more confidence in my capabilities."

"It's not that." Furious, he grabbed her arms and

shook. "You know it's not. That's not what this is all about."

His voice grew more frustrated than angry now, while his eyes searched her face for the secrets she was keeping from him. "I thought we'd come farther than this, but you've shut me out. I want to know what it's all about, Diana. I want to know what the hell is wrong with you!"

"I'm pregnant!" she shouted at him, then pressed her hand to her mouth.

Stunned, he released her arms and stared at her. "Pregnant?" Over the wave of shock came a wave of pleasure, so steep, so dizzying, for a moment he couldn't move. "Diana." When he reached for her, she backed away so that pleasure was sliced away by pain. Very deliberately, he put his hands in his pockets. "How long have you known?"

She swallowed and struggled to keep her voice from shaking. "Two weeks."

This time he turned away to stare at the wild roses without seeing them. "Two weeks," he repeated. "You didn't think it necessary to tell me?"

"I didn't know what to do!" The words came out in a rush of nerves and feelings. "We hadn't planned—not yet—and I thought it must be a mistake, but..." She trailed off helplessly as he kept his back to her.

"You've seen a doctor?"

"Yes, of course."

"Of course," he repeated on a humorless laugh. "How far along are you?"

She moistened her lips. "Nearly two months."

Two months, Caine thought. Two months their

child had been growing and he hadn't known. "Have you made any plans?"

Plans? she thought wildly. What plans could she make? "I don't know!" She threw her hands up to her face. This wasn't like her, where was her control, her logic? "What kind of a mother would I make?" she demanded as her thoughts poured out into words. "I don't know anything about children, I hardly had a chance to be one."

The pain shimmered through him, very sharp, and very real. He made himself turn to face her. "Diana, are you telling me you don't want the baby?"

Not want? she thought frantically. What did he mean *not want*? It was already real—she could almost feel it in her arms. It scared her to death. "It's part of us," she said jerkily. "How could I not want part of us? It's your baby. I'm carrying your baby and I love it so much already it terrifies me."

"Oh, Diana." He touched her then, gently, his hands on her face. "You've let two weeks go by when we could have been terrified together."

She let out a shuddering sigh. Caine afraid? He was never afraid. "Are you?"

"Yeah." He kissed a teardrop from her cheek. "Yeah, I am. A couple months before Mac was born, Justin told Alan and me how he felt about becoming a father." Smiling, he lifted both her hands and pressed his lips to the palms. "Now I know."

"I've felt so—tied up." Her fingers tightened on his. "I wanted to tell you, but I wasn't sure how you'd feel. It happened so fast—we haven't even finished the house yet, and I thought... I just wasn't sure how you'd feel."

With their hands still joined, he laid them on her stomach. "I love you," he murmured, "both."

"Caine." And his name was muffled against his mouth. "I have so much to learn in only seven months."

"*We* have a lot to learn in seven months," he corrected. "Why don't we go upstairs." He buried his face in her hair and drew in the scent. "Expectant mothers should lie down—" he lifted his head to grin at her "—often."

"With expectant fathers," Diana agreed, laughing when he swept her into his arms. It was going to be all right, she thought. Her family was going to be just perfect.

Gennie watched them disappear into the house. Whatever was between them, she thought with a smile, was apparently resolved.

"What a relief."

Surprised, Gennie turned to see Serena and Justin behind her. Serena carried the baby in a sling that strapped across her breasts. Intrigued by it, Gennie peeped down to see Mac cradled snugly against his mother, sleeping soundly.

"Serena hasn't been able to get close enough to Diana to pry out what was troubling her," Justin put in.

"I don't pry," Serena retorted, then grinned. "Very much. You're sketching the house. May I see?"

Obligingly, Gennie handed over the sketchbook. As Serena studied, Justin took Gennie's hand. "How are you?"

She knew his meaning. The last time she had seen

him had been at Angela's funeral. The visit had been brief, unintrusive, and very important to her. In the relatively short time they'd known each other, Justin had become a vital part of her family. "Better," she told him. "Really. I had to get away from the family for a while—and their quiet, continuous concern. It's helped." She thought of Grant and smiled. "A lot of things have helped."

"You're in love with him," Justin stated.

"Now who's prying?" Serena demanded.

"I was making an observation," he countered. "That's entirely different. Does he make you happy?" he asked, then tugged on his wife's hair. "That was prying," he pointed out.

Gennie laughed and stuck her pencil behind her ear. "Yes, he makes me happy—and he makes me unhappy. That's all part of it, isn't it?"

"Oh, yes." Serena leaned her head against her husband's shoulder. She spotted Grant as he came out the front door. "Gennie," she said, laying a hand on her arm. "If he's too slow, as some men are," she added with a meaningful glance at Justin, "I have a coin I'll lend you." At Gennie's baffled look, she chuckled. "Ask me about it sometime."

She hooked her arm through Justin's and wandered away, making the suggestion that they see if anyone was using the pool. Gennie heard him murmur something that had Serena giving a low, delicious laugh.

Family, she thought. It was wonderful to have stumbled on family this way. Her family, and Grant's. There was a bond here that might inch him closer to her. Happy, she ran across the grass to meet him.

He caught her when she breathlessly launched herself into his arms. "What's all this?"

"I love you!" she said on a laugh. "Is there anything else?"

His arms tightened around her. "No."

Chapter Eleven

Gennie's life had always been full of people, a variety of people from all walks of life. But she'd never met anyone quite like the Clan MacGregor. Before the end of the weekend drew near, she felt she'd known them forever. Daniel was loud and blustering and shrewd—and so soft when it came to his family that he threatened to melt. Quite clearly they adored him enough to let him think he tugged their strings.

Anna was as warm and calm as a summer shower. And, Gennie knew intuitively, strong enough to hold her family together in any crisis. She, with the gentlest of touches, led her husband by the nose. And he, with all his shouts and wheezes, knew it.

Of the second generation, she thought Caine and Serena the most alike. Volatile, outspoken, emotional; they had their sire's temperament. Yet when she speculated on Alan, she thought that the serious, calm exterior he'd inherited from Anna covered a tremendous power...and a temper that might be wicked when loosed. He'd found a good match in Shelby Campbell.

The MacGregors had chosen contrasting partners—Justin with his gambler's stillness and secrets, Diana, reserved and emotional, Shelby, free-wheeling and clever; they made a fascinating group with interesting eddies and currents.

It didn't take much effort for Gennie to persuade them to sit for a family sketch.

Though they agreed quickly and unanimously, it was another matter to settle them. Gennie wanted them in the throne room, some seated, some standing, and this entailed a great deal of discussion on who did what.

"I'll hold the baby," Daniel announced, then narrowed his eyes in case anyone wanted to argue the point. "You can do another next year, lass," he added to Gennie when there was no opposition, "and I'll be holding two." He beamed at Diana before he shifted his look to Shelby. "Or three."

"You should have Dad sitting in his throne—chair," Alan amended quickly, giving Gennie one of his rare grins. "That'd make the clearest statement."

"Exactly." Her eyes danced as she kept her features sober. "And Anna, you'll sit beside him. Perhaps you'd hold your embroidery because it looks so natural."

"The wives should sit at their husbands' feet," Caine said smoothly. "That's natural."

There was general agreement among the men and definite scorn among the women.

"I think we'll mix that up just a bit—for esthetic purposes," Gennie said dryly over the din that ensued. With the organization and brevity of a drill sergeant, she began arranging them to her liking.

"Alan here...." She took him by the arm and stood him between his parents' chairs. "And Shelby." She nudged Shelby beside him. "Caine, *you* sit on the floor." She tugged on his hand, until grinning, he obliged her. "And Diana—" Caine pulled his wife down on his lap before Gennie could finish. "Yes, that'll do. Justin over here with Rena. And Grant—"

"I'm not—" he began.

"Do as you're told, boy," Daniel bellowed at him, then spoke directly to his grandson. "Leave it to a Campbell to make trouble."

Grumbling, Grant strolled over behind Daniel's chair and scowled down at him. "A fine thing when a Campbell's in a MacGregor family portrait."

"Two Campbells," Shelby reminded her brother with alacrity. "And how is Gennie going to manage to sketch and sit at the same time?"

Even as Gennie glanced at her in surprise, Daniel's voice boomed out. "She'll draw herself in. She's a clever lass."

"All right," she agreed, pleased with the challenge and her inclusion into the family scene. "Now, relax, it won't take terribly long—and it's not like a photo where you have to sit perfectly still." She perched herself on the end of the sofa and began, using the small, portable easel she'd brought with her. "Quite a colorful group," she decided as she chose a pastel charcoal from her box. "We'll have to do this in oils sometime."

"Aye, we'll want one for the gallery, won't we, Anna? A big one." Daniel grinned at the thought, then settled back with the baby in the crook of his arm. "Then Alan'll need his portrait done once he's settled in the White House," he added complacently.

As Gennie sketched, Alan sent his father a mild glance. "It's a little premature to commission that just yet." His arm went around Shelby, and stayed there.

"Hah!" Daniel tickled his grandson's chin.

"Did you always want to paint, Gennie?" Anna asked while she absently pushed the needle through her embroi- dery.

"Yes, I suppose I did. At least, I can never re-member wanting to do anything else."

"Caine wanted to be a doctor," Serena recalled with an innocent smile. "At least, that's what he told all the little girls."

"It was a natural aspiration," Caine defended himself, lifting his hand to his mother's knee while his arm held Diana firmly against him.

"Grant used a different approach," Shelby re-called. "I think he was fourteen when he talked Dee-Dee O'Brian into modeling for him—in the nude."

"That was strictly for the purpose of art," he countered when Gennie lifted a brow at him. "And I was fifteen."

"Life studies are an essential part of any art course," Gennie said as she started to draw again. "I remember one male model in particular—" She broke off as Grant's eyes narrowed. "Ah, that scowl's very natural, Grant, try not to lose it."

"So you draw, do you, boy?" Daniel sent him a speculative look. It interested him particularly because he had yet to wheedle out of either Grant or Shelby how Grant made his living.

"I've been known to."

"An artist, eh?"

"I don't—paint," Grant said as he leaned against Daniel's chair.

"It's a fine thing for a man and a woman to have a common interest," Daniel began in a pontificating voice. "Makes a strong marriage."

"I can't tell you how many times Daniel's assisted me in surgery," Anna put in mildly.

He huffed. "I've washed a few bloody knees in my time with these three."

"And there was the time Rena broke Alan's nose," Caine put in.

"It was supposed to be yours," his sister reminded him.

"That didn't make it hurt any less." Alan shifted his eyes to his sister while his wife snorted unsympathetically.

"Why did Rena break Alan's nose instead of yours?" Diana wanted to know.

"I ducked," Caine told her.

Gennie let them talk around her while she sketched them. Quite a group, she thought again as they argued—and drew almost imperceptibly closer together. Grant said something to Shelby that had her fuming, then laughing. He evaded another probe of Daniel's with a non-answer, then made a particularly apt comment on the press secretary that had Alan roaring with laughter.

All in all, Gennie thought as she chose yet another pastel, he fit in with them as though he'd sprung from the same carton. Witty, social, amenable—yet she could still see him alone on his cliff, snarling at anyone who happened to make a wrong turn. He'd changed to suit the situation, but he hadn't lost any of himself in the process. He was amenable because he chose to be, and that was that.

With a last glance at what she had done, she looped her signature into the corner. "Done," she stated, and turned her work to face the group. "The MacGregors—and Company."

They surrounded her, laughing, each having a definite opinion on the others' likenesses. Gennie felt a hand on her shoulder and knew without looking that it was Grant's. "It's beautiful," he murmured, studying the way she had drawn herself at his side. He bent over and kissed her ear. "So are you."

Gennie laughed, and the precious feeling of belonging stayed with her for days.

September hung poised in Indian summer—a glorious, golden time, when wildflowers still bloomed and the blueberry bushes flamed red. Gennie painted hour after hour, discovering all the nooks and crannies of Windy Point. Grant's routine had altered so subtly he never noticed. He worked shorter hours, but more intensely. For the first time in years he was greedy for company. Gennie's company.

She painted, he drew. And then they would come together. Some nights they spent in the big feather bed in her cottage, sunk together in the center. Other mornings they would wake in his lighthouse to the call of gulls and the crash of waves. Occasionally he would surprise her by popping up unexpectedly where she was working, sometimes with a bottle of wine—sometimes with a bag of potato chips.

Once he'd brought her a handful of wildflowers. She'd been so touched, she'd wept on them until in frustration he had pulled her into the cottage and made love to her.

It was a peaceful time for both of them. Warm days, cool nights, cloudless skies added to the sense of serenity—or perhaps of waiting.

"This is perfect!" Gennie shouted over the motor as Grant's boat cut through the sea. "It feels like we could go all the way to Europe."

He laughed and ruffled her wind-tossed hair. "If you'd mentioned it before, I'd have put in a full tank of gas."

"Oh, don't be practical—imagine it," she insisted. "We could be at sea for days and days."

"And nights." He bent over to catch the lobe of her ear between his teeth. "Full-mooned, shark-infested nights."

She gave a low laugh and slid her hands up his chest. "Who'll protect whom?"

"We Scots are too tough. Sharks probably prefer more tender—" his tongue dipped into her ear "—French delicacies."

With a shiver of pleasure she rested against him and watched the boat plow through the waves.

The sun was sinking low; the wind whipped by, full of salt and sea. But the warmth remained. They

skirted around one of the rocky, deserted little islands and watched the gulls flow into the sky. In the
distance Gennie could see some of the lobster boats
chug their way back to the harbor at Windy Point.
The bell buoys clanged with sturdy precision.

Perhaps summer would never really end, she
thought, though the days were getting shorter and
that morning there'd been a hint of frost. Perhaps
they could ride forever, without any responsibilities
calling them back, with no vocation nagging. She
thought of the showing she'd committed herself to
in November. New York was too far away, the gray
skies and naked trees of November too distant. For
some reason Gennie felt it was of vital importance
to think of now, that moment. So much could happen
in two months. Hadn't she fallen in love in a fraction
of that time?

She'd planned to be back in New Orleans by now.
It would be hot and humid there. The streets would
be crowded, the traffic thick. The sun would stream
through the lacework of her balcony and shoot patterns onto the ground. There was a pang of home-
sickness. She loved the city—its rich smells, its old-
world charm and new-world bustle. Yet she loved it
here as well—the stark spaciousness, the jagged
cliffs and endless sea.

Grant was here, and that made all the difference.
She could give up New Orleans for him, if that was
what he wanted. A life here, with him, would be so
easy to build. And children...

She thought of the old farmhouse, empty yet waiting within sight of the lighthouse. There would be
room for children in the big, airy rooms. She could

have a studio on the top floor, and Grant would have his lighthouse when he needed his solitude. When it was time to give a showing, she'd have his hand to hold and maybe those nerves would finally ease. She'd plant flowers—high, bushy geraniums, soft-petaled pansies, and daffodils that would come back and multiply every spring. At night she could listen to the sea and Grant's steady breathing beside her.

"What're you doing, falling asleep?" He bent to kiss the top of her head.

"Just dreaming," she murmured. They were still just dreams. "I don't want the summer to end."

He felt a chill and drew her closer. "It has to sometime. I like the sea in winter."

Would she still be here with him then? he wondered. He wanted her, and yet—he didn't feel he could hold her. He didn't feel he could go with her. His life was so bound up in his need for solitude, he knew he'd lose part of himself if he opened too far. She lived her life in the spotlight. How much would she lose if he asked her to shut it off? How could he ask? And yet the thought of living without her was impossible to contemplate.

Grant told himself he should never have let it come so far. He told himself he wouldn't give back a minute of the time he'd had with her. The tug-of-war went on within him. He'd let her go, he'd lock her in. He'd settle back into his own life. He'd beg her to stay.

As he turned the boat back toward shore, he saw the sun spear into the water. No, summer should never end. But it would.

"You're quiet," Gennie murmured as he cut the engine and let the boat drift against the dock.

"I was thinking." He jumped out to secure the line, then reached for her. "That I can't imagine this place without you."

Gennie started, nearly losing her balance as she stepped onto the pier. "It's—it's nearly become home to me."

He looked down at the hand he held—that beautiful, capable artist's hand. "Tell me about your place in New Orleans," he asked abruptly as they began walking over the shaky wooden boards.

"It's in the French Quarter. I can see Jackson Square from the balcony with the artists' stalls all around and the tourists and students roaming. It's loud." She laughed, remembering. "I've had my studio soundproofed, but sometimes I'll go downstairs so I can just listen to all the people and the music."

They climbed up the rough rocks, and there was no sound but the sea and the gulls. "Sometimes at night, I like to go out and walk, just listen to the music coming out of the doorways." She took a deep breath of the tangy, salty air. "It smells of whiskey and the Mississippi and spice."

"You miss it," he murmured.

"I've been away a long time." They walked toward the lighthouse together. "I went away—maybe ran away—nearly seven months ago. There was too much of Angela there, and I couldn't face it. Strange, I'd gotten through a year, though I'd made certain I was swamped with work. Then I woke up one morning and couldn't bear being there knowing she wasn't—would never be." She sighed. Perhaps it had taken that long for the shock to completely wear off. "When it got to the point where I had to force myself to drive around that city, I knew I needed some distance."

"You'll have to go back," Grant said flatly, "and face it."

"I already have." She waited while he pushed open the door. "Faced it—yes, though I still miss her dreadfully. New Orleans will only be that much more special because I had so much of her there. Places can hold us, I suppose." As they stepped inside she smiled at him. "This one holds you."

"Yes." He thought he could feel winter creeping closer, and drew her against him. "It gives me what I need."

Her lashes lowered so that her eyes were only slits with the green light and glowing. "Do I?"

He crushed his mouth to hers so desperately she was shaken—not by the force, but by the emotion that seemed to explode from him without warning. She yielded because it seemed to be the way for both of them. And when she did, he drew back, struggling for control. She was so small—it was difficult to remember that when she was in his arms. He was cold. And God, he needed her.

"Come upstairs," he murmured.

She went silently, aware that while his touch and his voice were gentle, his mood was volatile. It both intrigued and excited her. The tension in him seemed to grow by leaps and bounds as they climbed toward the bedroom. It's like the first time, she thought, trembling once in anticipation. Or the last.

"Grant..."

"Don't talk." He nudged her onto the bed, then slipped off her shoes. When his hands wanted to rush, to take, he forced them to be slow and easy. Sitting beside her, Grant put them on her shoulders, then ran them down her arms as he touched his mouth to hers.

The kiss was light, almost teasing, but Gennie could feel the rushing, pulsing passion beneath it. His body was tense even as he nibbled, drawing her bottom lip into his mouth, stroking his thumb over her wrists. He wasn't in a gentle mood, yet he strove to be gentle. She could smell the sea on him, and it brought back memories of that first, tumultuous lovemaking on the grass with lightning and thunder. That's what he needed now. And she discovered, as her pulse began to thud under his thumbs, it was what she needed.

Her body didn't melt, but coiled. The sound wasn't a sigh but a moan as she dragged him against her and pressed her open mouth aggressively against his.

Then he was like the lightning, white heat, cold fury as he crushed her beneath him on the bed. His hands went wild, seeking, finding, tugging at her clothes as though he couldn't touch her quickly enough. His control snapped, and in a chain reaction hers followed, until they were tangled together in an embrace that spoke of love's violence.

Demand after unrelenting demand they placed on each other. Fingers pressed, mouths ravaged. Clothes were yanked away in a fury of impatience to possess hot, damp skin. It wasn't enough to touch, they hurried to taste what was smooth and moist and salty from the sea and their mutual passion.

Dark, driving needs, an inferno of wanting; they gave over to both and took from each other. And what was taken was replenished, over and over as they loved with the boundless energy that springs from desperation. Urgent fingers possessed her. An avid mouth conquered him. The command belonged to neither, but to the primitive urges that pounded through them.

Shallow, gasping breaths, skin that trembled to the touch, flavors dark and heated, the scent of the sea and desire—these clouded their minds to leave them victims as well as conquerers. Their eyes met once, and each saw themselves trapped in the other's mind. Then they were moving together, racing toward delirium.

It was barely dawn when she woke. The light was rosy and warm, but there was a faint skim of frost on the window. Gennie knew immediately she was alone; touching the sheets beside her, she found them cold. Her body was sated from a long night of loving but she sat up and called his name. The simple fact that he was up before her worried her—she always woke first.

Thinking of his mood the night before, she wasn't certain whether to frown or smile. His urgency had never depleted. Time and time again he had turned to her, and their loving had retained that wild, desperate flavor. Once, when his hands and mouth had raced over her—everywhere—she thought he seemed bent on implanting all that she was onto his mind, as if he were going away and taking only the memory of her with him.

Shaking her head, Gennie got out of bed. She was being foolish; Grant wasn't going anywhere. If he had gotten up early, it was because he couldn't sleep and hadn't wanted to disturb her. How she wished he had.

He's only downstairs, she told herself as she stepped into the hall. He's sitting at the kitchen table having coffee and waiting for me. But when she reached the stairwell, she heard the radio, low and indistinct. Puzzled, she glanced up. The sound was coming from above her, not below.

Odd, she thought, she hadn't imagined he used the third floor. He'd never mentioned it. Drawn by her curiosity, Gennie began the circular climb. The radio grew louder as she approached, though the news broadcast was muted and sounded eerily out of place in the silent lighthouse. Until that moment, she hadn't realized how completely she had forgotten the outside world. But for that one weekend at the MacGregors, her summer had been insular, and bound up in Grant alone.

She stopped in the doorway of a sun-washed room. It was a studio. He'd cultivated the north light and space. Fleetingly, her gaze skimmed over the racks of newspapers and magazines, the television, and the one sagging couch. No easels, no canvases, but it was the den of an artist.

Grant's back was to her as he sat at his drawing board. She smelled—ink, she realized, and perhaps a trace of glue. The glass-topped cabinet beside him held a variety of organized tools.

An architect? she wondered, confused. No, that didn't fit and surely no architect would resist using his skills on that farmhouse so close at hand. He muttered to himself, hunched over his work. She might have smiled at that if she hadn't been so puzzled. When he moved his hand she saw he held an artist's brush—sable and expensive. And he held it with the ease of long practice.

But he'd said he didn't paint, Gennie remembered, baffled. He didn't appear to be—and what would a painter need with a compass and a T square? One wouldn't paint facing a wall in any case, but...what *was* he doing?

Before she could speak, Grant lifted his head. In the mirror in front of him their eyes met.

He hadn't been able to sleep. He hadn't been able to lie beside her and not want her. Somehow during the night, he'd convinced himself that they had to go their separate ways. And that he could cope with it. She lived in another world, more than in another part of the country. Glamor was part of her life—glamor and crowds and recognition. Simplicity was part of his—simplicity and solitude and anonymity. There was no mixing them.

He'd gotten up in the dark, deluding himself that he could work. After nearly two hours of frustration, he was beginning to succeed. Now she was here, a part of that last portion of himself he'd been determined to keep separate. When she went away, he'd wanted to have at least one sanctuary.

Too intrigued to notice his annoyance, Gennie crossed the room. "What're you doing?" He didn't answer as she came beside him and frowned down

at the paper attached to his board. It was crisscrossed
with light-blue lines and sectioned. Even when she
saw the pen and ink drawings taking shape in the
first section, she wasn't certain what she was looking
at.

Not a blueprint, surely, she mused. A mechanical…some kind of commercial art perhaps? Fascinated, she bent a bit closer to the first section. Then
she recognised the figure.

"Oh! Cartoons." Pleased with the discovery, she
inched closer. "Why, I've seen this strip hundreds
of times. I love it!" She laughed and pushed the hair
back over her shoulder. "You're a cartoonist."

"That's right." He didn't want her to be pleased
or impressed. It was simply what he did, and no
more. And he knew, if he didn't push her away then,
today, he'd never be able to do it again. Deliberately,
he set down his brush.

"So this is how you set one of these up," she
continued, caught up in the idea, enchanted with it.
"These blue lines you've struck on the paper, are
they for perspective? How do you come up with
something like this seven days a week?"

He didn't want her to understand. If she understood, it would be nearly impossible to push her
away. "It's my job," he said flatly. "I'm busy, Gen-
nic. I work on deadline."

"I'm sorry," she began automatically, then
caught the cool, remote look in his eye. It struck her
suddenly that he'd kept this from her, this essential
part of his life. He hadn't told her—more, had made
a point in not telling her. It hurt, she discovered as

her initial pleasure faded. It hurt like hell. "Why didn't you tell me?"

He'd known she would ask, but was no longer certain he had the real answer. Instead, he shrugged. "It didn't come up."

"Didn't come up," she repeated quietly, staring at him. "No, I suppose you made certain it didn't. Why?"

Could he explain that it was ingrained habit? Could he tell her the essential truth was that he'd grown so used to keeping it, and nearly everything else, to himself, he had done it without thinking? Then he had continued to do so in automatic defense. If he kept this to himself, he wouldn't have given her everything—because to give her everything terrified him. No, it was too late for explanations. It was time he remembered his policy of not giving them to anyone.

"Why should I have told you?" he countered. "This is my job, it doesn't have anything to do with you."

The color drained dramatically from her face, but as he turned to get off the stool, Grant didn't see. "Nothing to do with me," Gennie echoed in a whisper. "Your work's important to you, isn't it?"

"Of course it is," Grant snapped. "It's what I do. What I am."

"Yes, it would be." She felt the cold flow over her until she was numb from it. "I shared your bed, but not this."

Stung, he whirled back to her. The wounded look in her eyes was the hardest thing he'd ever faced. "What the hell does one have to do with the other?

What difference does it make what I do for a living?''

"I wouldn't have cared what you do. I wouldn't have cared if you did nothing at all. You lied to me."

"I never lied to you!" he shouted.

"Perhaps I don't understand the fine line between deception and dishonesty."

"Listen, my work is private. That's the way I want it." The explanation came tumbling out despite him, angry and hot. "I do this because I love to do it, not because I have to, not because I need recognition. Recognition's the last thing I want," he added while his eyes grew darker with temper. "I don't do lectures or workshops or press interviews because I don't want people breathing down my neck. I choose anonymity just as you choose exposure, because it's what works for me. This is my art, this is my life. And I intend to keep it just that way."

"I see." She was stiff from the pain, shattered by the cold. Gennie understood grief well enough to know what she was feeling. "And telling me, sharing this with me, would've equaled exposure. The truth is you didn't trust me. You didn't trust me to keep your precious secret or to respect your precious life-style."

"The truth is our life-styles are completely opposite." The hurt tore at him. He was pushing her away, he could feel it. And even as he pushed he ached to pull her back. "There's no mixing what you need and what I need and coming out whole. It has nothing to do with trust."

"It always has to do with trust," she countered. He was looking at her now as he had that first time—

the angry, remote stranger who wanted nothing more than to be left alone. She was the intruder here as she had been a lifetime ago in a storm. Then, at least, she hadn't loved him.

"You should have understood the word love before you used it, Grant. Or perhaps we should have understood each other's conception of the word." Her voice was steady again, rock steady as it only was when she held herself under rigid control. "To me it means trust and compromise and need. Those things don't apply for you."

"Damn it, don't tell me how I think. Compromise?" he tossed back, pacing the room. "What kind of compromise could we have made? Would you have married me and buried yourself here? Hell, we both know the press would have sniffed you out even if you could've stood it. Would you expect me to live in New Orleans until my work fell apart and I was half mad to get out?"

He whirled back to her, his back to the east window so that the rising sun shot in and shimmered all around him. "How long would it take before someone got curious enough to dig into my life? I have reasons for keeping to myself, damn it, and I don't have to justify them."

"No, you don't." She wouldn't cry, she told herself, because once she began she'd never stop. "But you'll never know the answer to any of those questions, will you? Because you never bothered to share them with me. You didn't share them, and you didn't share the reasons. I suppose that's answer enough."

She turned and walked from the room and down the long, winding stairs. She didn't start to run until she was outside in the chill of the morning.

Chapter Twelve

Gennie looked at her cards and considered. A nine and an eight. She should play it safe with seventeen; another card would be a foolish risk. Life was full of them, she decided, and signaled the dealer. The four she drew made her smile ironically. Lucky at cards...

What was she doing sitting at a blackjack table at seven-fifteen on a Sunday morning? Well, she thought, it was certainly a convenient way to pass the time. More productive then pacing the floor or beating on a pillow. She'd already tried both of those. Yet somehow, the streak of luck she'd been enjoying for the past hour hadn't lightened her mood. Perversely, she would have preferred it if she'd lost resoundingly. That way, she would have had some new hook to hang her depression on.

Restless, she cashed in her chips and stuffed the

winnings in her bag. Maybe she could lose them at the dice table later.

There was only a handful of people in the casino now. A very small elderly lady sat on a stool at a slot machine and systematically fed in quarters. Occasionally Gennie would hear the jingle of coins spill into the tray. Later, the huge, rather elegant room would fill, then Gennie could lose herself in the smoke and noise. But for now, she wandered out to the wide glass wall and looked out at the sea.

Was this why she had come here instead of going home as she had intended? When she had tossed her suitcase and painting gear into the car, her only thought had been to get back to New Orleans and pick up her life again. She'd made the detour almost before she'd been aware of it. Yet now that she was here, had been here for over two weeks, she couldn't bring herself to walk out on that beach. She could look at it, yes, and she could listen. But she couldn't go to it.

Why was she tormenting herself like this? she wondered miserably. Why was she keeping herself within reach of what would always remind her of Grant? Because, she admitted, no matter how many times she'd told herself she had, she had yet to accept the final break. It was just as impossible for her to go back to him as it was for her to walk down to that blue-green water. He'd rejected her, and the hurt of it left her hollow.

I love you, but...

No, she couldn't understand that. Love meant anything was possible. Love meant *making* anything possible. If his love had been real, he'd have understood that, too.

She'd have been better off resisting the urge to look up *Macintosh* in the paper. She wouldn't have seen that ridiculous and poignant strip where Veronica had walked into his life. It had made her laugh, then remembering had made her cry. What right did he have to use her in his work when he wouldn't share himself with her? And he'd used her again and again, in dozens of papers across the country where readers were following Macintosh's growing romance—his over-his-head, dazed-eyed involvement—with the sexy, alluring Veronica.

It was funny, and the touches of satire and cynicism made it funnier. It was human. He'd taken the foolishness and the pitfalls of falling in love and had given them the touch every man or woman who'd ever been there would understand. Each time she read the strip, Gennie could recognize something they'd done or something she'd said, though he had a way of tilting it to an odd angle. With his penchant for privacy, Grant still, vicariously, shared his own emotional roller coaster with the public.

It made her ache to read it day after day. Day after day, she read it.

"Up early, Gennie?"

As a hand touched her shoulder, she turned to Justin. "I've always been a morning person," she evaded, then smiled at him. "I cleaned up at your tables."

He returned the smile, while behind guarded eyes he assessed her. She was pale—still as pale as she had been when she'd so suddenly checked into the

Comanche. The pallor only accented the smudges of sleeplessness under her eyes. She had a wounded look that he recognized because he, too, was deeply in love. Whatever had come between her and Grant had left its mark on her.

"How about some breakfast?" He slipped an arm over her shoulders before she could answer, and began leading her toward his office.

"I'm not really hungry, Justin," she began.

"You haven't really been hungry for two weeks." He guided her through the outer office into his private one, then pushed the button on his elevator. "You're the only cousin I have whom I care about, Genviève. I'm tired of watching you waste away in front of my eyes."

"I'm not!" she said indignantly, then leaned her head against his arm. "There's nothing worse than having someone moping around feeling sorry for themselves, is there?"

"A damned nuisance," he agreed lightly as he drew her into the private car. "How much did you take me for in there?"

It took her a minute to realize he'd changed the subject. "Oh, I don't know—five, six hundred."

"I'll put breakfast on your tab," he said as the doors opened to his and Serena's suite. Her laugh pleased him as much as the hug she gave him.

"Just like a man," Serena stated as she came into the room. "Waltzing in with a beautiful woman at the crack of dawn while the wife stays home and changes the baby." She held a gurgling Mac over her shoulder.

Justin grinned at her. "Nothing worse than a jealous woman."

Lifting her elegant brows, Serena walked over and shifted the baby into his arms. "Your turn," she said, smiling, then collapsed into an armchair. "Mac's teething," she told Gennie. "And not being a terribly good sport about it."

"You are," Justin told her as his son began to soothe sore gums on his shoulder.

Serena grinned, tucked up her feet, and yawned hugely. "I'm assured this, too, shall pass. Have you two eaten?"

"I've just invited Gennie to have some breakfast."

Serena caught her husband's dry look and understood it. Railroaded would have been a more apt word, she imagined. "Good," she said simply, and picked up the phone. "One of the nicest things about living in a hotel is room service."

While Serena ordered breakfast for three, Gennie wandered. She liked this suite of rooms—so full of warmth and color and personality. If it had ever held the aura of a hotel room, it had long since lost it. The baby cooed as Justin sat on the couch to play with him. Serena's low, melodious voice spoke to the kitchen far below.

If you love enough, Gennie thought as she roamed to the window overlooking the beach, if you want enough, you can make a home anywhere. Rena and Justin had. Wherever they decided to live, and in whatever fashion, they were family. It was just that basic.

She knew they worked together to care for their

child, to run the casino and hotel. They were a unit. There were rough spots, she was sure. There had to be in any relationship—particularly between two strong-willed personalities. But they got through them because each was willing to bend when it was necessary to bend.

Hadn't she been? New Orleans would have become a place to visit—to see her family, to stir old memories if the need arose. She could have made her home on that rough coast of Maine—for him, with him. She'd have been willing to give so much if only he'd been willing to give in return. Perhaps it wasn't a matter of his being willing. Perhaps Grant had simply not been able to give. That's what she should accept. Once she did, she could finally close the door.

"The ocean's beautiful, isn't it?" Serena said from behind her.

"Yes." Gennie turned her head. "I've gotten used to seeing it. Of course, I've always lived with the river."

"Is that what you're going back to?"

Gennie turned back to the window. "In the end I suppose."

"It's the wrong choice, Gennie."

"Serena," Justin said warningly, but she turned on him with her eyes flashing and her voice low with exasperation.

"Damn it, Justin, she's miserable! There's nothing like a stubborn, pig-headed man to make a woman miserable, is there, Gennie?"

With a half laugh, she dragged a hand through her hair. "No, I don't guess there is."

"That works both ways," Justin reminded her.

"And if the man's pig-headed enough," Serena went on precisely, "it's up to the woman to give him a push."

"He didn't want me," Gennie said in a rush, then stopped. The words hurt, but she could say them. Maybe it was time she did. "Not really, or at any rate not enough. He simply wasn't willing to believe that there were ways we could have worked out whatever problems we had. He won't share—it's as though he's determined not to. It seemed we got close for that short amount of time in spite of him. He didn't want to be in love with me, he doesn't want to depend on anyone."

While she spoke, Justin rose and took Mac into another room. The tinkling music of his mobile drifted out. "Gennie," Justin began when he came back in, "do you know about Grant and Shelby's father?"

She let out a long sigh before she sank into a chair. "I know he died when Grant was about seventeen."

"Was assassinated," Justin corrected, and watched the horror cloud in her eyes. "Senator Robert Campbell. You'd have been a child, but you might remember."

She did, vaguely. The talk, the television coverage, the trial...and Grant had been there. Hadn't Shelby said both she and Grant had been there when their father was killed? Murdered right in front of their eyes. "Oh, God, Justin, it must've been horrible for them."

"Scars don't always heal cleanly," he murmured, touching an absent hand to his own side in a gesture his wife understood. "From what Alan's told me, Shelby carried around that fear and that pain for a long time. I can't imagine it would be any different for Grant. Sometimes…" His gaze drifted to Serena. "You're afraid to get too close, because then you can lose."

Serena went to him to slip her hand into his.

"Don't you see, he kept that from me, too." Gennie grabbed the back of the armchair and squeezed. She hurt for him—for the boy and the man. "He wouldn't confide in me, he wouldn't let me understand. As long as there're secrets, there's distance."

"Don't you believe he loves you?" Serena asked gently.

"Not enough," Gennie said with a violent shake of her head. "I'd starve needing more."

"Shelby called last night," Serena said as the knock on the door announced breakfast. As Justin went to answer she gestured Gennie toward the small dining area in front of the window. "Grant surprised her and Alan with a visit a few days ago."

"Is he—"

"No," Serena interrupted, sitting. "He's back in Maine now. She did say he badgered her with questions. Of course, she didn't have the answer until she spoke to me and found out you were here." Gennie frowned at the sea and said nothing. "She wondered if you were following *Macintosh* in the papers. It took me over two hours to figure why she would have asked that."

Gennie turned back with a speculative look which Serena met blandly. "Perhaps I'm not following you," she said, automatically guarding Grant's secret.

Serena took the pot the waiter placed on the table. "Coffee, Veronica?"

Gennie let out an admiring laugh and nodded her head. "You're very quick, Rena."

"I love puzzles," she corrected, "and the pieces were all there."

"That was the last thing we argued about." Gennie glanced at Justin as he took his seat. After adding cream to her coffee, she simply toyed with the handle of the cup. "All the time we were together, he never told me what he did. Then, when I stumbled across it, he was so angry—as if I had invaded his privacy. I was so pleased. When I thought he simply wasn't doing anything with his talent, I couldn't understand. Then to learn what he was doing—something so clever and demanding..." She trailed off, shaking her head. "He just never let me in."

"Maybe you didn't ask loud enough," Serena suggested.

"If he rejected me again, Rena, I'd fall apart. It's not a matter of pride, really. It's more a matter of strength."

"I've seen you making yourself sick with nerves before a showing," Justin reminded her. "But you always go through with it."

"It's one thing to expose yourself, your feelings to the public, and another to risk them with one person knowing there wouldn't be anything left if he didn't want them. I have a showing coming up in November," she said as she toyed with the eggs on her plate. "That's what I have to concentrate on now."

"Maybe you'd like to glance at this while you eat." Justin slipped the comics section out of the paper the waiter had brought up.

Gennie stared at it, not wanting to see, unable to resist. After a moment she took it from his hand.

The Sunday edition was large and brightly colored. This *Macintosh* was rather drab, however, and lost-looking. In one glance she could see the hues were meant to indicate depression and loneliness. She mused that Grant knew how to immediately engage the readers' attention and guide their mood.

In the first section Macintosh himself was sitting alone, his elbows on his knees, his chin sunk in his hands. No words or captions were needed to project the misery. The readers' sympathies were instantly aroused. Who'd dumped on the poor guy this time?

At a knock on the door he mumbled—it had to be mumbled—"Come in." But he didn't alter his position as Ivan, the Russian emigré, strolled in wearing his usual fanatically American attire—Western, this time, cowboy hat and boots included.

"Hey, Macintosh, I got two tickets for the basketball game. Let's go check out the cheerleaders."

No response.

Ivan pulled up a chair and tipped back his hat. "You can buy the beer, it's an American way of life. We'll take your car."

No response.

"But I'll drive," Ivan said cheeringly, nudging Macintosh with the toe of his pointed boot.

"Oh, hello, Ivan." Macintosh settled back into his gloom again.

"Hey, man, got a problem?"

"Veronica left me."

Ivan crossed one leg over the other and was obviously jiggling his foot. "Oh, yeah? For some other guy, huh?"

"No."

"How come?"

Macintosh never altered positions, and the very absence of action made the point. "Because I was selfish, rude, arrogant, dishonest, stupid, and generally nasty."

Ivan considered the toe of his boot. "Is that all?"

"Yeah."

"Women," Ivan said with a shrug. "Never satisfied."

Gennie read the strip twice, then looked up helplessly. Without a word, Serena took the paper from her hand and read it herself. She chuckled once, then set it back down.

"Want me to help you pack?"

Where the hell was she? Grant knew he'd go mad if he asked himself the question one more time.

Where the hell was she?

From the lookout deck of his lighthouse he could see for miles. But he couldn't see Gennie. The wind slapped at his face as he stared out to sea and wondered what in God's name he was going to do.

Forget her? He might occasionally forget to eat or to sleep, but he couldn't forget Gennie. Unfortunately, his memory was just as clear on the last ten minutes they had been together. How could he have been such a fool! Oh, it was easy, Grant thought in disgust. He'd had lots of practice.

If he hadn't spent those two days cursing her, and himself, stalking the beach one minute, shut up in his studio the next, he might not have been too late. By the time he'd realized he'd cut out his own heart, she'd been gone. The cottage had been closed up, and the Widow Lawrence knew nothing and was saying less.

He'd flown to New Orleans and searched for her like a madman. Her apartment had been empty—her neighbors hadn't heard a word. Even when he'd located her grandmother by calling every Grandeau in the phone book, he'd learned nothing more than that Gennie was traveling.

Traveling, he thought. Yes, she was traveling—away from him just as fast as she could. Oh, you deserve it, Campbell, he berated himself. You deserve to have her skip out of your life without a backward glance.

He'd called the MacGregors—thank God he'd gotten Anna on the phone instead of Daniel. They hadn't heard from her. Not a sound. She might have been anywhere. Nowhere. If it hadn't been for the painting she'd left behind, he might have believed she'd been a mirage after all.

She'd left the painting for him, he remembered, the one she'd finished the afternoon they'd become lovers. But there'd been no note. He'd wanted to fling it off the cliff. He'd hung it in his bedroom. Perhaps it was his sackcloth and ashes, for every time he looked at it, he suffered.

Sooner or later, he promised himself, he'd find her. Her name, her picture would be in the paper. He'd track her down and bring her back.

Bring her back, hell, Grant thought, dragging a hand through his hair. He'd beg, plead, grovel, whatever it took to make her give him another chance. It was her fault, he decided with a quick switch back to fury. *Her* fault, that he was acting like a maniac. He hadn't had a decent night's sleep in over two weeks. And the solitude he'd always prized was threatening to smother him. If he didn't find her soon, he'd lose what was left of his mind.

Infuriated, he swung away from the rail. If he couldn't work, he could go down to the beach. Maybe he'd find some peace there.

Everything looked the same, Gennie thought as she came to the end of the narrow, bumpy road. Though summer had finally surrendered to fall, nothing had really changed. The sea still crashed and roared, eating slowly at the rock. The lighthouse still stood, solitary and strong. It had been foolish for her to have worried that she would find that something important, perhaps essential, had altered since she'd left.

Grant wouldn't have changed, either. On a deep breath she stepped from the car. More than anything, she didn't want him to change what made him uniquely Grant Campbell. She'd fallen in love with the rough exterior, the reluctant sensitivity—yes, even the rudeness. Perhaps she was a fool. She didn't want to change him; all she wanted was his trust.

If she'd misinterpreted that strip—if he turned her

away... No, she wasn't going to think about that. She was going to concentrate on putting one foot in front of the other until she faced him again. It was time she stopped being a coward about the things most vital to her life.

As soon as she touched the door handle, Gennie stopped. He wasn't in there. Without knowing how or why, she was absolutely certain of it. The lighthouse was empty. Glancing back, she saw his truck parked in its spot near the farmhouse. Was he out in his boat? she wondered as she started around the side. It was at the dock, swaying gently at low tide.

Then she knew, and wondered she hadn't known from the first. Without hesitation, she started for the cliff.

With his hands in his pockets and the wind tugging at his jacket, Grant walked along the shoreline. So this was loneliness, he thought. He'd lived alone for years without feeling it. It was one more thing to lay at Gennie's feet. How was it possible that one lone female could have changed the essence of his life?

With a calculated effort, he worked himself into a temper. Anger didn't hurt. When he found her—and by God, he would—she'd have a lot to answer for. His life had been moving along exactly as he'd wanted it before she'd barged in on it. Love? Oh, she could talk about love, then disappear just because he'd been an idiot.

He hadn't asked to need her. *She'd* hammered at him until he'd weakened, then she'd taken off the minute he hurt her. Grant turned to the sea, but shut his eyes. God, he had hurt her. He'd seen it on her face, heard it in her voice. How could he ever make up for that? He'd rather have seen anger or tears than that stricken look he'd put in her eyes.

If he went back to New Orleans…she might be there now. He could go back, and if he couldn't find her, he could wait. She had to go back sooner or later; the city meant too much to her. Damn it, what was he doing standing there when he should be on a plane going south?

Grant turned, and stared. Now he was seeing things.

Gennie watched him with a calmness that didn't reveal the thudding of her heart. He'd looked so alone—not in that chosen solitary way he had, but simply lonely. Perhaps she'd imagined it because she wanted to believe he'd been thinking of her. Gathering all her courage, Gennie crossed to him.

"I want to know what you meant by this." She reached in her pocket and pulled out the clipping of his Sunday strip.

He stared at her. He might see things—he might even hear things, but…slowly, he reached out and touched her face. "Gennie?"

Her knees went weak. Resolutely, Gennie stiffened them. She wasn't going to fall into his arms. It would be so easy, and it would solve nothing. "I want to know what this means." She shoved the clipping into his hand.

Off balance, Grant looked down at his work. It hadn't been easy to get that into the papers so quickly. He'd had to pull all the strings at his disposal and work like a maniac himself. If that was what brought her, it had all been worth it.

"It means what it says," he managed, staring at her again. "There's not a lot of subtlety in this particular strip."

She took the paper back from him and stuck it in her pocket. It was something she intended to keep forever. "You've used me rather lavishly in your work recently." She had to tilt back her head in order to keep her eyes level with his. Grant thought she looked more regal than ever. If she turned her thumb down, she could throw him to the lions. "Didn't it occur to you to ask permission first?"

"Artist's privilege." He felt the light spray hit his back, saw it dampen her hair. "Where the hell did you go?" he heard himself demand. "Where the hell have you been?"

Her eyes narrowed. "That's my business, isn't it?"

"Oh, no." He grabbed her arms and shook. "Oh, no, it's not. You're not going to walk out on me."

Gennie set her teeth and waited until he'd stopped shaking her. "If memory serves, you did the walking figuratively before I did it literally."

"All right! I acted like an idiot. You want an apology?" he shouted at her. "I'll give you any kind you want. I'll—" He broke off, his breath heaving. "Oh God, first."

And his mouth crushed down on hers, his fingers digging into her shoulders. The groan that was wrenched from him was only one more sign of a desperate need. She was here, she was his. He'd never let her go again.

His mind started to clear so that his own thoughts jabbed at him. This wasn't how he wanted to do it.

This wasn't the way to make up for what he'd done—or hadn't done. And it wasn't the way to show her how badly he wanted to make her happy.

With an effort, Grant drew her away and dropped his hands to his sides. "I'm sorry," he began stiffly. "I didn't intend to hurt you—not now, not before. If you'd come inside, we could talk."

What was this? she wondered. *Who* was this? She understood the man who had shaken her, shouted at her, the man who had dragged her into his arms full of need and fury. But she had no idea who this man was who was standing in front of her offering a stilted apology. Gennie's brows drew together. She hadn't come all this way to talk to a stranger.

"What the hell's the matter with you?" she demanded. "I'll let you know when you hurt me." She shoved a finger into his chest. "*And* when I want an apology. We'll talk, all right," she added, flinging back her head. "And we'll talk right here."

"What do you want!" In exasperation, Grant threw up his hands. How was a man supposed to crawl properly when someone was kicking at him?

"I'll tell you what I want!" Gennie shouted right back. "I want to know if you want to work this out or sneak back into your hole. You're good at hiding out; if that's what you want to keep doing, just say so."

"I am not hiding out," he said evenly and between his teeth. "I live here because I like it here, because I can work here without having someone knocking on the door or ringing the phone every five minutes."

She gave him a long, level look edged with fury.

"That's not what I'm talking about, and you know it."

Yes, he knew it. Frustrated, he stuck his hands in his pockets to keep from shaking her again. "Okay, I kept things from you. I'm used to keeping things to myself, it's habit. And then... And then I kept things from you because the harder I fell in love with you, the more terrified I was. Look, damn it, I didn't want to depend on anyone for—" He broke off to drag a hand through his hair.

"For what?"

"For being there when I needed them," he said on a long breath. Where had that been hiding? he wondered, a great deal more surprised by his words than Gennie was. "I should tell you about my father."

She touched him then, her eyes softening for the first time. "Justin told me."

Grant stiffened instantly and turned away.

"Were you going to keep that from me, too, Grant?"

"I wanted to tell you myself," he managed after a moment. "Explain—make you understand."

"I do understand," she told him. "Enough, at least. We've both lost people we loved very much and depended on in our own ways. It seems to me we've compensated for the loss in our own ways as well. I do understand what it's like to have someone you love die, suddenly, right in front of your eyes."

Grant heard her voice thicken, and turned. He couldn't handle tears now, not when he was so tightly strung himself. "Don't. It's something you have to put aside, never away, but aside. I thought I

had, but it crept back up on me when I got involved
with you.''

She nodded and swallowed. This wasn't the time
for tears or a time to dwell on the past. ''You wanted
me to go that day.''

''Maybe—yes.'' He looked past her to the top of
the cliff. ''I thought it was the only way for both of
us. Maybe it still is; I just can't live with it.''

Confused, she put a hand on his arm. ''Why do
you think being apart might be the best thing?''

''We've chosen to live in two totally different
worlds, Gennie, and both of us were content before
we met. Now—''

''Now,'' she said, firing up again. ''Now what?
Are you still so stubborn you won't consider compromise?''

He looked at her blankly. Why was she talking
about compromises when he was about to fold up
everything and go with her anywhere. ''Compromise?''

''You don't even know the meaning of the word!
For someone as clever and astute as you are, you're
a closed-minded fool!'' Furious, she turned to stalk
away.

''Wait.'' Grant grabbed her arm so quickly, she
stumbled back against him. ''You're not listening to
me. I'll sell the land, give it away if you want. We'll
live in New Orleans. Damn it, I'll take out a front
page ad declaring myself as *Macintosh*'s artist if it'll
make you happy. We can have our picture plastered
on every magazine in the country.''

''Is that what you think I want?'' She'd thought
he'd already made her as angry as she was capable

of getting a dozen times during their relationship. Nothing had ever compared to this. "You simple, egotistical ass! I don't care whether you write your strip in blood under the cover of darkness. I don't care if you pose for a hundred magazines or snarl at the paparazzi. Sell the land?" she continued while he tried to keep up. "Why in God's name would you do that? Everything's black and white to you. *Compromise!*" Gennie raged at him. "It means give and take. Do you think I care where I live?"

"I don't know!" What little patience he had snapped. "I only know you've lived a certain way— you were happy. You've got roots in New Orleans, family."

"I'll always have roots and family in New Orleans, it doesn't mean I have to be there twelve months out of the year." She dragged both hands through her hair, holding it back from her face a moment as she wondered how such an intelligent man could be so dense. "And yes, I've lived a certain way, and I can live a different way to a point. I couldn't stop being an artist for you because I'd stop being me. I have a show to deal with in November— I need the shows and I need you to be with me. But there are other things I can give back, if you'd only meet me halfway. If I made the ridiculous move of falling in love with you, why would I want you to give up everything you are now?"

He stared at her, willing himself to be calm. Why was she making so much sense and he so little? "What do you want?" he began, then held up a hand before she could shout at him. "Compromise," he finished.

"More." She lifted her chin, but her eyes were more uncertain than arrogant. "I need you to trust me."

"Gennie." He took her hand and linked fingers. "I do. That's what I've been trying to tell you."

"You haven't been doing a good job of it."

"No." He drew her closer. "Let me try again." He kissed her, telling himself to be gentle and easy with her. But his arms locked and tightened, his mouth hungered. The spray shimmered over both of them as they stood entangled. "You're the whole focus of my world," he murmured. "After you left, I went crazy. I flew down to New Orleans, and—"

"You did?" Stunned, she drew back to look at him. "You went after me?"

"With various purposes in mind," he muttered. "First, I was going to strangle you, then I was going to crawl, then I was going to just drag you back and lock you upstairs."

Smiling, she rested her head on his chest. "And now?"

"Now." He kissed her hair. "We compromise. I'll let you live."

"Good start." With a sigh, she closed her eyes. "I want to watch the sea in winter."

He tilted her face to his. "We will."

"There is something else...."

"Before or after I make love to you?"

Laughing, she pulled away from him. "It better be before. Since you haven't mentioned marriage yet, it falls to me."

"Gennie—"

"No, this is one time we'll do it all my way."

She drew out the coin Serena had given her before she'd left the Comanche. "And, in a way, it's a kind of compromise. Heads, we get married. Tails we don't."

Grant grabbed her wrist before she could toss. "You're not going to play games with something like that, Genviève, unless that's a two-headed coin."

She smiled. "It certainly is."

Surprise came first, then his grin. "Toss it. I like the odds."

* * * * *

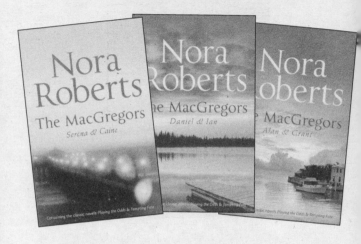

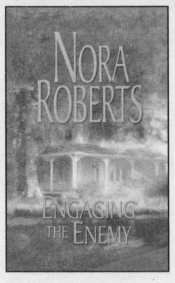

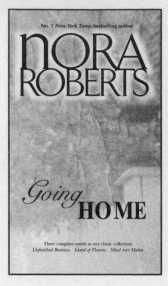

From No. 1 *New York Times* bestselling author Nora Roberts

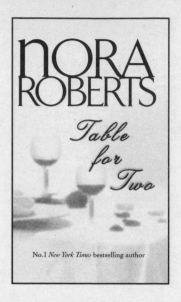

*Two world class chefs discover an
irresistible recipe for romance*

Features

Summer Desserts

and

Lessons Learned

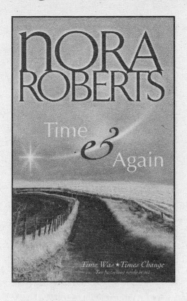

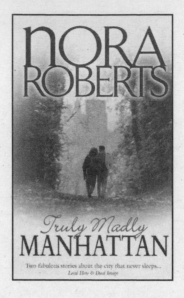

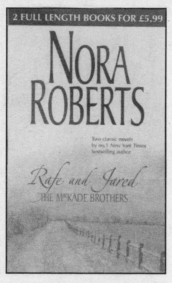

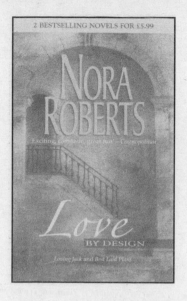

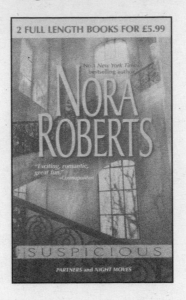

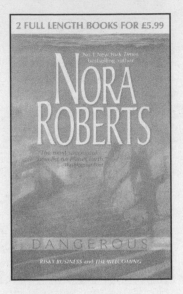